To Joanne
who helped with
so kindly
this is my first novel
Thank you

Dolores Cline Brown

# *Why Wait for Heaven*

## Dolores Cline Brown

### Edited by Lt./Col. William A. Wooten

Published by
Hara Publishing
P.O. Box 19732
Seattle, WA 98109

Copyright © 2001 by Dolores Cline Brown

All rights reserved

ISBN: 1-883697-85-9

Library of Congress Catalog Card Number:
00-110419

Manufactured in the United States
10 9 8 7 6 5 4 3 2

No part of this book may be reproduced, stored in or introduced into a retrieval system, or transmitted, in any form or by any means (electronic, mechanical, photocopying, recording or otherwise) without the prior written permission of the publisher.

Cover Design: Scott Fisher
Supervising Editor: Victoria McCown
Book Design & Production: Scott and Shirley Fisher

# Table of Contents

| | |
|---|---|
| Introduction | i |
| Chapter 1 - Doc's Darling Daughters | 1 |
| Chapter 2 - Show-Stopper in Dayton | 12 |
| Chapter 3 - Oh, Charlie | 24 |
| Chapter 4 - Doc Objects to the Caprice of Fashion | 36 |
| Chapter 5 - All in the Family | 51 |
| Chapter 6 - Cupid Strikes | 65 |
| Chapter 7 - Miracles by the Minute | 78 |
| Chapter 8 - Surprise Encounter | 90 |
| Chapter 9 - Preparation for Trouble | 103 |
| Chapter 10 - Rotgut for the Gullible | 116 |
| Chapter 11 - Fish Folly | 128 |
| Chapter 12 - Battle for the Baskets | 141 |
| Chapter 13 - Challenging the AMA | 154 |
| Chapter 14 - Mrs. Aims on the Attack | 165 |
| Chapter 15 - Soiled Wedding Day | 178 |
| Chapter 16 - Redskin Savior | 191 |
| Chapter 17 - Fulfillment of Dreams | 209 |
| Chapter 18 - Heartbeat of the Tom-Toms | 224 |
| Chapter 19 - Surprising Encounters | 240 |
| Chapter 20 - Sky Spirits of Salmon River | 251 |
| Chapter 21 - Changes in Destiny | 267 |
| Chapter 22 - Spectacular Spectacle | 284 |
| Chapter 23 - Fulfilled Destiny | 297 |
| Bibliogrraphy | 315 |
| Order Form | 317 |

# Table of Contents

# Introduction

Although this is a book of fiction, I have incorporated my Grandfather's belief in Hippocrates's doctrine of alternative medicine and his demonstrations of Cosmic energy.

I have retained the names of his descendants as a memorial to my uncle and aunts.

Also, I have drawn much of their lives from oral family history.

This book is meant to resurrect some of the sterling qualities of ancestral times and to remind the readers that civilizations travel in cycles, so we may look forward to less complex times and be more in harmony with our Creator.

*Dolores Cline Brown*

## Chapter 1

# Doc's Darling Daughters

The fiery glow of the setting sun highlighted the distant range of lofty peaks in Eastern Washington, home of the felicitous mule deer and, later, herds of elk on the high plateaus. On lower ridges prowled the wary cougar.

The foothills, heavily veined with swift glacier streams, lured fishermen to cast for the elusive Dolly Vardens and the more alluring and colorful rainbows. During summer spawning season the creeks were glutted with rosy-hued Chinook salmon.

The smoky haze hovering over the lower slopes of the Blue Mountains lent a lulling, sleepy atmosphere to the surrounding country but not to the small town they sheltered.

It was Saturday evening, the time the farming community of Dayton came alive. The one and only main street swarmed with swarthy farmers with their crisp-gingham-clad wives bringing the yields of their industrious labor to sell. They had willow baskets of fresh brown eggs, jars of thick jersey cream, savory sugar-cured hams, homemade sausages spiced to delight the palate, and always the spring fryers for Sunday dinners. Transactions of fresh, farm products were traded for shiny silver dollars or burnished gold coins with much chattering and laughter as the latest news was exchanged.

In Dayton, Saturday nights were also for people-watching. Passengers of deserted buggies joined the strolling throng to be viewed, assessed, and commented upon. It was a gay and happy crowd, excited over meeting old friends and catching up on who was engaged to whom, who had married, who had died, and who was going to win the next election. Politics were lightly eased over, since tempers could flare over the qualifications of certain candidates and Saturday nights were for fun, not fights.

These people were the pioneers of the great Western frontier. They were unaware that by their hard work, their strong belief in the Golden Rule, their pride in their word being as good as gold, their staunch family ties and their loyalty to their country, they were helping to build a great nation. They were the backbone of freedom, the kind of freedom the Founding Fathers of America could never have achieved but for the salt-of-the-earth kind of people who lived in Dayton.

The pride of Dayton was Lord Nelson Andrus, better known as and lovingly called Doc. Without him, half the town would be dead. He could sew them up and hang them up, for the law was the law to Doc, and anyone who thought he could outsmart the law could reconsider his misconception while hanging from a tree.

By day Doc was kept busy administering to the aches and pains of the town's ailing. No one knew whether Doc had a formal medical education; but who cared when Doc was a whiz at setting bones and giving relief for all sorts of ailments that plagued the human anatomy.

By night Doc was employed in upholding the law. The frontier town attracted many unsavory characters thinking a fast buck could be made by preying on the unsuspecting citizens of Dayton. But the lawless didn't count on Doc, who could ride with the best of the vigilantes. It was well known that Doc had saved the lives of men he had shot. Needless to say, they were reformed. In spite of the town's respect for Doc, the people also had a tinge of fear, for Lord Nelson Andrus had some very mysterious ways.

Dayton was the envy of Columbia County, for here, with the Blue Mountains as sentinels to all his activities, a man could raise his children in security, peace, and safety—that is, when a man like Doc was in charge.

On a street corner opposite the old, gray-stone courthouse stood a grizzled, beetle-browed farmer ringing a bell. He was taking his turn at manning a large black pot hanging from a wooden tripod. Last winter the town had suffered a tremendous loss when their one-room schoolhouse burned to the ground. Now the whole town was cooperating to raise funds for a new school and the money pot was one of their efforts. If anyone forgetfully passed without contributing, they were quickly reminded of their neglect by old Cryder's loudest hog-calling-contest-winning voice. The guilty culprit would sneak back to the money pot and grudgingly plunk in a coin, and if it were not of sufficient amount to please the old man, they again would receive some strong advice.

Back of the money pot in the large window of Harrison's General Delivery Store, a beautiful log-cabin quilt was displayed, hand-sewn by the women of the Baptist Missionary Society. Down the street in the window of the hardware store was a brightly colored quilt made in the Texas Star pattern and quilted by the Rebeccas, a women's auxiliary of the Odd Fellows Lodge. Yet another, known as the Crazy Quilt, was pieced and quilted by the Daughters of the Pioneers. All three quilts were to be auctioned off to raise funds to erect another academic structure for learning the three R's.

Not to be outdone, the ladies of the new Methodist church were having a baked-food sale. Their mouth-watering displays of rhubarb chiffon pies, sugared potato doughnuts, feathery angel food cake, whipped cream strawberry cakes, spicy nutmeg applesauce cakes, sourdough breads, and cookies of delightful flavors and unique shapes were hopefully expected to bring in enough for desks, blackboards, and school books.

The town's most popular meeting place was Neville's Ice Cream Parlor. Like a magnet, it attracted Saturday night's crowds. It was easily located by following the flocks of children with their nickels clutched tightly in their fists to buy the long-looked-forward-to ice cream cone.

Neville's Parlor was also a favorite trysting place for young lovers. The place breathed romance and balsam fir, for the whole ceiling had been wire-netted to hold fir branches, giving intimacy and fragrance to the sheltered booths.

Tonight excitement ran high for the chatauqua was in town. It came only once a year and was a great event for the small town. Rumors were that a famous magician would perform by making a horse disappear. It must be true for old man Cryder was furnishing the horse. That wasn't all. There was to be real black-face minstrels telling funny jokes and singing silly songs. Of course, there would be the usual juggling act, but the main interest was how anyone could make old Cryder's big Clydesdale stallion disappear.

A small group of women were gathered under the newly lit, gas street lamp, for twilight was descending, heralding the closeness of show time. The women, deciding their tickets entitled them to admission, were about to head for the red-and-green-striped chatauqua tent when a double-seated fringed surrey, pulled by a pair of high-spirited bays, pranced around the corner. The occupants were a very distinguished-looking gentleman and six stylishly dressed girls. All waved merrily to the crowd. Abigale Grey, now an unemployed schoolteacher, and Miss Cynthia Lynn, visiting her from Boston, waved their tickets in reply. Miss Lynn exclaimed, "For gracious sakes, who are they?"

"Oh, that's our doctor, Lord Nelson Andrus. How he loves strutting around, showing off his daughters," Abigale laughingly replied.

"Well, he has reason to be proud. They are very pretty and so stylishly dressed."

Abigale nodded in agreement. "Fannie, that's the eldest, is an excellent seamstress and makes most of all their clothes."

"I would love to have a closer look, as I do so much of my own sewing."

Abigale clutched her friend's arm. "Come. I feel sure the doctor is taking his daughters to the ice cream parlor and if we hurry, we can arrive before they do, so you will be able to have a close look as they enter."

In haste, the two women threaded their way through the crowd and seated themselves on the parlor's counter stools near the door just as the carriage pulled up to the hitching rack.

A small, black-and-white fox terrier bounded in, followed by a stalwart man of medium height. His heavy head of hair was snowy white, as was his beard. But it was his piercing eyes that riveted attention. His ramrod posture spoke of authority and his dignity demanded respect.

Neville, the proprietor of the parlor, greeted him. "Good evening, Dr. Andrus. I see you have brought your charming daughters."

"Charming?" blustered the old man. "They are downright flirts."

"Papa!" wailed all six girls.

"What's more, they are spoiled rotten," Doc lovingly teased.

"Papa, it's Charlie you spoil," his youngest reminded him.

The two women sitting at the counter looked at each other.

"He has a son?" the friend asked Abigale in surprise.

Abigale nodded, whispering, "Yes, he's in college."

"Oh, really! I shudder to think what life must be like for him with six sisters."

Abigale tried to smother her laughter. "Oh, he manages all six quite nicely."

Teddy's barking turned all eyes to the little dog frantically dancing around his master. The doctor heartily laughed, "Teddy, you know you have to ask Neville for your ice cream."

Teddy promptly trotted over to the counter, stood on his small hind legs, giving a little yip. Neville grinned, "Well, Teddy, what will it be today? Vanilla, chocolate, or strawberry?" Teddy gave a joyful bark and Neville laughed. "Okay, Teddy, strawberry it is." He placed a bowl with a scoop of pink ice cream on the floor. To the amusement of the customers, Teddy excitedly circled the dish, his little pink tongue furiously licking at the luscious mound as his tail wagged his pleasure.

The doctor, noticing the two women, strode over to them. "Abigale, how are you today? Did the herbal medicine help your cold?"

"Indeed it did. It cleared my head at once and even my rheumatism is better. See, I can now raise my arm."

"Splendid. Keep taking the Devil's Claw root tea and you'll be fine."

"Dr. Andrus, may I present my friend, Cynthia Lynn, visiting me from Boston."

Doc shook her hand. "You must find Dayton a very small place after Boston."

"Yes, but I love it and only wish I were able to stay."

"We have some very fine young men here. Maybe one of them can convince you to stay."

"I'm afraid not," Cynthia shook her head regretfully.

"I hope you will find time to visit us. My wife is home most afternoons."

"Thank you. I will look forward to meeting your wife."

"Good. And Abigale, don't forget to show your friend our park and new bandstand, and take her to one of the concerts." Doc tipped his hat and left to retrieve Teddy, who was sniffing for more ice cream behind the counter.

The doctor's daughters casually sauntered over to a glassed-in showcase, featuring rows of square-cut glass dishes heaped with a variety of tempting candies. Neville was famous for his hand-dipped chocolates.

Peering into the candy case together, they looked like a radiant bouquet of spring flowers. Fannie had tried to reproduce the fashions shown in *Harper's Bazaar* magazine, which was selling for ten cents a copy at the newsstand. She had succeeded in making her sisters a repository of the latest fashions. The result was pure confection, like mounds of spun-sugar candy in their dresses of soft, cool colors of lavender, azure blue, ice green, misty pink, pale gold, and lustrous white. Made from the same pattern, the skirts were draped in a polonaise, forming a large bustle in the back. The cuirass basque was lavishly trimmed with artificial flowers held with voluminous loops of satin ribbons.

Maybelle, the youngest and still a child, wore an eyelet-embroidered dress over ruffled pantalets.

Abigale, seeing her friend's fascination, whispered, "Nancy, their mother, is a close friend of mine. Tomorrow, I could take you to meet them. Fanny might even loan you some of her patterns."

"Yes, oh yes, I'd love that."

"Nels, you've made a new candy. I've never seen one cherry-topped before," one of the daughters exclaimed, using the young man's more informal name.

"Yes, Miss Mae. It's a new recipe. Will you girls try one and let me know if you think it's worth making again?"

Neville passed a plate of cherry-centered chocolates. The girls squealed their delight and assured him he was to keep on making the delicious candy forever.

Nels cautiously managed to maneuver himself between Mae and her sisters, creating more privacy for his hasty request while keeping a watchful eye on the retreating back of her father as he made his way to the rear of the parlor section. Nels nervously stuttered, "M…Miss Mae, may I…I have the honor of escorting you to the basket social at the Baptist church?"

"Why, Nels, I…I," blushed the sixteen-year-old girl. "I would love…"

"Mae," boomed Doc's voice. "None of that foolishness, Neville. You know my orders. No dating until my daughters are eighteen."

Neville, mustering his courage, blurted, "Girls now are married and have children before they're eighteen."

"Mine won't," snapped Doc.

Doc and Teddy walked on into the parlor section where dogs were banned, but everyone knew Teddy was special. Teddy was most always with the doctor when he made house calls. When the doctor was in his office counseling patients, Teddy sat on his knee looking interested and concerned.

The narrow booths were inadequate to accommodate bustles and twenty yards of petticoats, so the party chose one of the large round center tables of wrought iron and commodious chairs of artistic twisted-metal design.

Once seated, Mae voiced her fury. "Papa, you let Charlie date."

"My dear," Doc was fumbling for an answer when the shrill clanging of the fire bell interrupted him. Everyone rushed outside searching for a plume of smoke. The fire wagon, pulled by a sturdy team of white horses at full gallop, clanged past. Excited kids ran after the fire brigade.

Dayton people were proud of their fire department. The fire wagon was housed underneath the fire hall. At all times it was kept well-greased for quick action. Harnesses were suspended from the ceiling over the shafts so they could be quickly dropped onto the backs of the eager, stomping horses, impatient to be off to the fire. When not racing to fires, the horses were kept in a field adjacent to the hall. Whenever the fire bell rang, the horses raced around their enclosure ready to answer the call of duty with speed and reliability. The fire chief vowed they knew as well as any human what the fire bell meant. It was a volunteer fire department and depended on the speed of the volunteers for its efficiency to reach the fire hall within minutes. Whenever the fire bell rang, the store's general manager left his customer on the run, the blacksmith dropped his shoeing hammer, and the banker had been known to forget to lock the bank doors. Even Neville neglected to remove a bubbling pot of chocolate from the stove to answer the call.

"Jake's shack's on fire!" a boy yelled.

"Not again," someone groaned.

Jake was forever setting his mattress on fire by going to bed smoking his corncob pipe. Every time he snored, the hot ashes spewed out and ignited the straw mattress. This was the fifth time the fire department had been called to save Jake's humble abode.

Neville's customers headed for the fire, but Abigale's friend remonstrated, "Why, in heaven's name, should we go to the fire?"

Dragging her friend by the hand to follow the others, Abigale explained, "The last fire, the pump broke down and everyone was needed to man the water brigade."

"They should have good fire equipment like Boston."

"Can't afford it."

"They could borrow and..."

The girls rounded the corner and the brightly burning cabin hove into view.

"Oh dear, oh dear," wailed Abigale seeing a sheet of flames leap skywards.

Black billowing smoke was so thick no building could be seen. Dr. Andrus, just arriving, shook his head. "I'm afraid this time Jake's place is a goner."

"Where's Jake?" someone yelled.

"Nobody's seen him. Must be still in there," another replied.

Although two men were frenziedly pumping, only a small stream of water spurted from the hose. The fire chief disappeared in the smoke but was driven back by the heat. He came out yelling, "Man the water brigade."

People hurriedly got in line, passing buckets of water from a nearby creek. "We gotter save Jake," someone mumbled.

Although Jake was a contemptible old cuss, the town needed him. He was the only one who could keep the street gasolier lights going all night.

In spite of all their efforts, the old, dry, scrap-lumber shack was soon only a smoking pile of ashes. They were mourning the loss of their fellow citizen when old Cryder yelled, "Damn his hide, there he is!"

They looked up to see Jake stumbling and weaving towards them. Someone assessed the situation. "Dead drunk."

Jake later explained that he had been attending the streetlight when a pal had given him a bottle to help him deal with a malfunctioning street lamp. He was not so drunk that he didn't realize he no longer had a home and the old fellow was taking it pretty hard. A neighbor offered to bed him for the night, and everyone knew the citizens of Dayton would band together to build him a new home. The men would put up the building and the womenfolk would make him a couple of warm quilts.

Walking back to the ice cream parlor, Miss Lynn expressed her admiration. "The people of Boston would never show such cooperation nor such generosity. Dayton has such wonderful people."

Abigale cast a sly glance at her friend. "And such bravery shown by the fire chief."

"Yes, I noticed."

"He's so handsome and unmarried and..."

"Stop or you'll have me proposing to him!" The two friends laughed embarrassedly.

The proudly prancing horses passed them pulling an ash-covered fire wagon. A fireman straddling the hose called to them, "Fire's out."

Neville returned from his fireman's duty with an idea to surmount his vanquishment. He was smitten with the doctor's shiest daughter. Retying his apron string, he stopped at the counter holding a rack of Komikal Konversation cards published by the McLoughlin brothers. These conversation cards were a blessing to bashful lovers who were too timid to express their devotion in person. Neville hurriedly shuffled through the stack, quickly discarding "Do you desire a lover tall, or do you wish for one at all?" Another he flung down: "Would you rather be bitten by a dog than to go to a concert with me?" In desperation he grabbed a pencil and hurriedly scribbled on a card. Entering the parlor to take the interrupted orders, he had no idea how he was going to give the card to the girl he adored.

The six daughters had just finished their chocolate and strawberry sundaes, which Neville had recently invented, when a distinguished couple entered and Dr. Andrus quickly rose to greet them. "Judge Frankland, it's good to see you again. Have you come down from Walla Walla to try my son's case?"

"No, nothing like that. Your son is merely mischievous and doesn't rate a hearing, only a reprimand."

"I fear college isn't teaching him to be responsible for his actions."

"Don't worry too much. Boys will be boys."

"Thank you. And now may I present my daughters."

"It's lucky for you they are your daughters, for when I saw you with this bevy of beautiful ladies, I marked you down as a philanderer."

Flattered, the girls blushed, and they all laughed. Doc proudly patted each daughter as he introduced her. "Fannie is the eldest and a wonderful seamstress. Amy is our major domo and keeps us all in order. Mae is our financier and woe to the patient who fails to pay his doctor bill. Nettie is training to be my nurse. Anna is a splendid cook, and Maybelle is the flirt of the family."

"Papa, how can you say that?" remonstrated Maybelle, pouting.

"And girls, this is the best judge in Columbia County," Doc spoke with sincerity.

The judge acknowledged the compliment with a chuckle. "My dears, your father is shamelessly buttering me up in case he has to face me in the courtroom."

"Heaven forbid if I ever have to, for knowing you favor no one, you'd have me behind bars as quickly as the town's barfly."

"Never fear, Doctor, for if anything ever goes wrong with my anatomy, you are the first one I'd call on to fix me up."

A small, excited boy stuck his head in yelling, "Five minutes to show time."

"If we are going to make it for the first act, we better get going," advised the judge.

When they all crowded to the door, Mae hung back, making Nels' heart leap, for he knew she was waiting for a sign from him. Unnoticed, he slyly slipped the card into her hand.

# Chapter 2

# Show-Stopper in Dayton

The zealous crowd flowed into the big top, bumping into hawkers shouting, "Peanuts, popcorn, candy."

Neville had been awarded the concession and everyone knew his taffies were the best. For a special treat, to the delight of the children, he made pink spun-sugar-candy cones. The excitement grew to almost unbearable proportions. The crowd became intolerant waiting for the show to commence, the younger of the audience started stomping their feet, catcalling, and shrilly whistling. Not until the master of ceremonies was satisfied that the crowd had purchased most of the homemade root beer did he part the curtains to step into the glare of the footlights, wearing an elegant black suit, the first tuxedo seen in Dayton.

Holding both arms high over his head, he loudly intoned, "Ladies and gentlemen. You are about to witness the world's most famous high-wire trapeze performance! You will also see show-stopping minstrels, singing hilarious songs and doing incredible tap dancing! And the amazing tricks of man's best friend will delight you! Then, ladies and gentlemen, you will see the world's greatest magician, who will use his incredible power of magic to make one of the largest horses disappear and…"

"Stop your babbling and get on with the show!" some smart aleck yelled from the back row.

"Patience, my good fellow," replied the unruffled master of ceremonies.

Previous chatauquas had been of a cultural nature. Quiet dignity had announced the Italian tenor; a reverent introduction had been given the poetess who soulfully rendered her ethereal poetry; the chamber music orchestra rendered a polished presentation of Beethoven's piano concerto. Tonight, the master of ceremonies was more like a bombastic barker in a carnival and the crowd loved it.

Stepping back and holding his hand towards the wings, he loudly proclaimed, "Ladies and gentlemen! I now introduce to you the greatest trapeze artists, the flying Frandandos from Spain!" Out from the wings ran three performers, swirling dazzling orange-and-red toreador cloaks. Making their bows in front of the footlights, they flung their cloaks aside.

"Ma, she ain't got no clothes on!" a kid screeched. The third member of the troupe was indeed a woman wearing the scantiest and briefest costume Daytonites had ever seen. Her bloomers were above her knees, a shocker in an era when showing a dainty ankle was considered scandalous.

The embarrassed mother shushed her offspring. "How you expect her to walk a wire with skirts on?"

The brevity of her costume was soon forgotten as they watched her hurling through the air sixty feet above their heads.

The man's-best-friend act needed no introduction. Barking and yelping, the dogs hurled their furry bodies across the stage, balancing on balls, bouncing down slides, leaping through hoops of fire. A small poodle hopped onto one end of a teeter-totter, but before a little Maltese could climb the other end, Teddy dodged Doc's restraining hand, dashed past the Maltese, jumped onto the teeter-totter, and sent the toy poodle flying through the air.

The children screamed their delight but the crashing of their act by a stranger was strongly disputed by the performing dogs. The ringmaster had to wade into a whirling mass of bared teeth before he could extricate Teddy and return him, slightly chewed, to his master. Thereafter, Doc kept a tight grip on Teddy's collar while he barked insults at those who had rejected his extemporaneous performance.

A loud crash of drums whirled the audience around in their seats. The minstrel band was entering through the back of the tent blowing trumpets, saxophones, and bass horns and clashing cymbals, while the drummer whirled his sticks into the air before beating his drums.

The darkies wore garishly loud purple-and-orange suits with huge, black, polka-dot bow ties. They marched around the audience playing "There'll Be a Hot Time in the Old Town Tonight." Marching down the center aisle, they strutted onto the stage, sitting down with puckish grins.

Two of the darkies stood up. One slapped the other on the shoulder saying, "Mr. Bones, I ain't flyin' to heaven."

"Mr. Ames, why ain't you flyin' to heaven?"

"'Cause I'z ice skatin' to heaven."

"You can't ice skate to heaven."

"Why can't I ice skate to heaven?"

"'Cause where you're goin', it's too hot for ice!"

Both of the darkies howled with glee and the amused audience vigorously clapped.

Six of the minstrels jumped up to tap dance back and forth across the stage with such enthusiasm the kids spilled out into the aisle trying to imitate them. They finished their act by flip-flopping and cartwheeling off the stage.

Again the two previous minstrels stood up slapping each other on the back.

"You know some'n, Mr. Ames?"

"What some'n should I know, Mr. Bones?"

"A preacher went out huntin'."

"When he go huntin'?"

"'Twas on one Sunday morn."

"Dat's agin' his religion."

"But he took his gun along."

"What dat he shoot?"

"He shoot a little ole cottontail."

Two gunshots were heard off-stage and an outlandishly dressed preacher, with his clerical collar up to his eyes and wearing huge floppy shoes, came out holding up a bedraggled bunny. He walked off the stage, dragging a gun.

The two darkies resumed their conversation.

"Den what happ'n, Mr. Ames?"

"On his way home he met a great big grizzly bear."

There was a loud growl from the wings and out dashed the preacher throwing his gun in the air, yelling, "Oh Lord, if you can't help me, for heaven's sake, don't you help that bear."

The audience howled with laughter, wildly clapping their hands and yelling, "More! More!"

Picking up their instruments, the minstrels marched out of the tent playing the rollicking tune of "Dixie."

With their feet pounding the floor, the audience kept yelling for more and only the crash of drums silenced them enough for the master of ceremonies to announce, "I now present to you the only magician in the world who can make anything from a flea to an elephant disappear! Tonight he will make one of the largest breeds of horses vanish out of your sight! Please welcome the one and only Harris!"

A thunderous applause by the audience, a loud roll of drums, and a man of great austerity stepped from the wings. He was dressed in a flashy silver suit highlighted by a gruesome, glaring skeleton on his chest. The audience shuddered and shifted to the edge of their seats. From the opposite side of the stage came a beautiful young lady glittering in gold sequins, leading Cryder's big stallion under a sparkling blanket. The crowd murmured.

Rising about a foot above the stage was a large, square, four-poster platform with curtains at each corner. Led by the girl, the horse stomped up onto the platform. The magician and his assistant closed the curtains around the stallion. The audience sat breathless with expectancy. Weird music played as the magician briskly strode around the raised platform uttering eerie incantations. With a loud command and a crash of drums, he jerked back the curtains and the audience gasped in astonishment. There was no horse. Unbelievably the huge animal had disappeared. The crowd was stunned.

"He better bring back my horse or there's trouble," old man Cryder yelled.

A scream came from back of the tent and a woman came running up the aisle, stopping at Doc's side and grabbing his arm. "Come quickly, my sister is dying," she sobbed.

"What seems to be the matter?" Doc calmly asked.

The distraught woman pulled at his arm begging, "Oh hurry, please hurry."

Reluctant to leave the show, the doctor nevertheless agreed to follow the woman to her home. As the two reached her porch, they heard loud rasping gasps. Hastening in, the doctor made a hurried examination and demanded, "Bring me a piece of red flannel cloth."

"We don't have any red flannel," the woman said, wringing her hands.

Dr. Andrus bowed his head in deep concentration. Suddenly he jerked up his head and snapped, "Yes you have. Go to the attic and look in a bow-top trunk"

In a daze, the woman climbed the narrow, steep stairs up to the attic. She looked around the musty room, certain there was no bow-top trunk and certainly no red flannel. She was about to leave the attic, dreading to tell the doctor he was wrong, when she spotted what looked like a trunk under a pile of boxes. Swiftly she unloaded the boxes and stared in disbelief. She flung open the bow-top and almost fainted at the sight of a whole bolt of red flannel. Clutching her trembling hands together, she fearfully wondered how their doctor knew about the bow-top trunk and about the red flannel when he had never been in her house before. She returned to her sister's bedroom in awe and fright. Was Doc of the Lord or of the Devil?

She found the doctor rubbing ointment onto her sister's chest. The whole town knew about Doc's homemade unguent. Half the town had been greased with it. Many had used it to take out the kinks of muscle cramps; others had used it to relieve backaches. Even ailing horses, cows, and dogs had been treated with Doc's soothing remedy. As one old-timer testified, "It has a God-awful stink, but it sure made the rheumatism get the hell out of my bones."

The town knew when Doc was cooking up his healing brew. The doors and windows of the Andrus house were wide open and anyone passing by began to have smarting eyes.

After rubbing on more of the salve, Doc tore off a square of red flannel, placed it over the greased area, and drew up the covers. Already the woman was breathing easier. "She will be much better in the morning," he assured the worried sister. "Don't let her eat anything but chicken soup for the next few days. I'll be around again tomorrow."

Doc was a great help in boosting the economy of the farming community. He kept the farmers busy raising chickens to fill his prescription for all of his ailing patients: chicken soup.

Most of Doc's herbal medicine was so bitter it gagged one to swallow, but he had one that was a pleasure to take. In fact it caused an epidemic of coughs when it was discovered that people could get drunk on Doc's cough syrup, made of high-grade brandy and buds of the balm of Gilead trees. But Doc caught on and added bitters to the brew, stopping the epidemic and spoiling the fun.

When Dr. Andrus left the house and returned to his buggy, Teddy was still holding Molly's reins between his teeth. Doc had been in such a hurry he hadn't taken time to tie Molly to the hitching post and had tossed the reins to Teddy, saying, "Hold her until I get back."

Faithfully, Teddy had sat for two hours, growling a warning if Molly made a move. If she took a step seeking freedom, Teddy leaped, biting her nose. Not liking the nip, she stayed put.

After Doc left his patient, she had recovered enough to be enjoying a cup of chamomile tea. Her perplexed sister was vehemently declaring, "I would have staked my life there was no red flannel in the house."

Her sister exclaimed, "Why Minnie, don't you remember when mother died, we stored her things in the attic?"

"I was away visiting Ed at the time."

"But I told you about it."

"I'd forgotten."

"All the children have quilts mother made for us, all, that is, but brother Tom. She was piecing one for him when she passed away. The the red flannel was for the lining."

"But how did Dr. Andrus know it was there?"

"He didn't. Mother told him."

"She told him?" Minnie exclaimed incredulously. "How could she do that? She's been gone for all of six years."

"She once said, no matter where she was, she'd look after us and she did. She came back and told him where the red flannel was."

Minnie sniffed, glaring at her sister. "That's the most ridiculous thing I've ever heard. You're out of your head."

"Let's not question. Let's just be grateful."

"Well, I don't believe a word you're saying. We will all stay dead until the trumpet blows and that's what the Good Book says."

Doc was enjoying the drive back home. Teddy had put his head on his master's knee and fallen into sound asleep. It was the kind of night that made life worth living and restored one's faith in the Almighty. The full moon was lighting up the countryside, making it as bright as day. He was passing Miller's field when he stopped Molly with a jerk of the reins. He had seen a two-foot-tall plant, with leaves interspersed with numerous pale green drooping flowers. He needed this plant, which was a favorite herb of the Indians. It was known to be rich in iron and had other valuable properties for conditions of the blood and the glandular system. It also checked the bleeding in the lungs.

Reaching behind his seat, he picked up the trowel and bucket he always carried for gathering his herbs. Crawling through the barbwire fence, he knelt beside the plant and started digging it up. There are four varieties of yellow dock and Doc knew he was gathering rumex rumieis, the most potent of the four with the strongest healing properties.

The doctor had just returned to his buggy when old Cryder, leading his stallion, passed, heading for home. Doc called, "Well, Cryder, I see you got your old nag back."

"Damn good thing too. But I don't know how in hell he made him disappear."

"I heard it's done with mirrors."

"I don't give a damn how it's done. It sure made the hair on the back of my head stand up."

Doc laughed. "Well, Cryder, next time…"

"There ain't goin' to be a next time."

"Say, Cryder, I'd appreciate it, when you pass Miller's house, if you would step in and tell him not to plough his field until I dig up my plants."

"You mean them weeds? Sure I'll tell the old cuss. He borrowed my good rake and never returned it."

Dayton was laced with dusty dirt roads, but pioneers in earlier days had planted slender saplings of locust trees along each side of the streets, softening the harshness of the landscape. They had grown to enormous height, their branches arching over the streets as if in benediction. Tonight they were in full bloom, white waxy blossoms cascading over the trees in fragrant floral clusters. The moonlight peeping through the branches, turned the blooms into jumbled strands of pearls, sending an intoxicating fragrance through the town. Doc loved the old locust trees, thinking surely that Heaven could be no more beautiful. Driving slowly under the trees made him feel engulfed in some supernatural enchantment.

Doc was glad to see a light filtering through the lace curtains covering the bubbly glass windows in the living room. It meant his family was waiting up for him to read the day's lesson from the large Bible prominently displayed on a small marble-top table.

In its yellowed pages were written the dates of births and marriages of the family. One name was shrouded in mystery and his name was always whispered. He must remember to ask his wife about her relative who was connected with the French court. It might explain why his son had such a penchant for mischief.

The girls greeted their father with kisses and took his hat and coat. When he sank deep into his leather chair, Nancy handed him a cup of peppermint and comfrey tea. It felt good to have a family who loved him. Amy handed him the worn Bible. It was still beautiful, even if the red roses were fading on the worn leather cover from many reverent hands seeking comfort. The gold leaf on the edging of the pages remained untarnished.

The daily reading of the Bible was to please his wife, a devout Baptist. For himself, he didn't believe a man needed a Bible or a preacher. Mother Nature and the Great Spirit could teach him all he needed to know and one certainly didn't need the impassioned thunderings of any preacher to save him from hell fire.

Anna handed him his glasses. The Bible fell open to a silk-embroidered page marker, which noted the end of yesterday's lesson. Doc adjusted his glasses, cleared his throat, and started to read Colossians I, "For by him all things were created that…"

"Papa, I can't understand how God could make the whole big world with all the animals and birds in just six days," Maybelle asked looking very puzzled.

"You mustn't interrupt your father," her mother admonished.

"But I want to know."

"Six days!" Doc exploded. "Who's teaching you such trash?"

"Mrs. Aims, she's our Sunday school teacher."

Knowing her husband's views on religion, Nancy hurriedly explained, "The Bible clearly tells us that one day is with the Lord as a thousand years, and a thousand years as one day."

Anna piped up, "Even six thousand years seems a very short time to make all the big oceans, millions of rivers, and billions of stars and…"

"All the mountains too," Maybelle added.

Doc shook his head. "Of all the misinformation wreaking havoc on the intelligence of our children."

"Nelson, you promised you wouldn't argue about the Bible in front of the children," Nancy reminded him.

"My dear, how can you let that doltish fanatic turn our children into stupid ignoramuses? Children, this earth is four billion years old as proved by geological records."

"Papa, Mrs. Aims says the earth is flat as a pancake. Is that true?" Maybelle asked.

Anna shivered fearfully. "Some day we could fall off."

Nancy, glancing at her husband's reddening face, warned, "Nelson, you promised."

"Let me say this. Over two thousand years ago, Eratosthenes of Egypt scientifically proved the earth is round."

Maybelle, seeking assurance as to the validity of her Sunday school teachings, said, "Mrs. Aims says if I'm good, I can go to heaven when I die."

"Why wait for heaven?" her father asked. "Your Creator has put everything here on earth for you to make it a heaven here."

"How can I do that?"

Nancy, fearful things might be getting out of hand, said, "By practicing good works."

"What's that?" Maybelle earnestly asked her mother.

"By doing good deeds, words, thoughts, and actions."

Doc slammed the Bible shut. "And that's the highest religion there is."

With the frankness of a child, Maybelle said, "I don't think Mrs. Aims likes you. Do you think she will go to Heaven?"

"I hope she goes to a hotter place."

Nancy quickly grew alarmed. "Nelson, will you please continue reading."

Doc opened the Bible. "In the later days…"

A banging on the front door interrupted the Bible reading. Mae flew to the door intending to send the visitor on his way. Instead a young man pushed past her, hurriedly striding into the parlor. Stopping in front of the doctor, he jerked off his cap. "Dr.

Andrus, I'm sure sorry to be bothering you so late. I started out early but the hind wheel of my wagon came off and it took some time to fix it."

Doc laid down the Bible. "I understand, Sam, but couldn't you have waited until tomorrow?"

"No, I couldn't. You see, I brought some things to pay your doctor bill."

"You don't owe me any money."

"No, but Uncle Zak does."

"What was wrong with your uncle?" Nancy asked.

"He jumped from the hay loft and ran a pitch fork through his back. He was dying of gangrene. Ah Doc, you don't remember Uncle Zak, do you?"

"Of course I remember him. I slapped a balsam pitch poultice on his back and…"

"You saved his life. You cured him. He wants to pay the bill but he hasn't any money so he thought a ham, a couple dozen eggs, and six chickens could help you along until he can sell his heifer."

Nancy smiled. "How thoughtful. I was going to have to buy eggs tomorrow."

Blushing and stammering, Sam turned to Mae. "Your brother told me you were going to the basket social."

Mae shrank back behind her father's chair, thinking Charlie was not going to promote any dates for her.

Sam grinned, showing his buckteeth. "I made something pretty for you. It's to tie on the handle of your basket." Sam pulled from his pocket a small, carved wooden pig with a bright red ribbon tied around its neck. Again blushing, he added, "I made it just for you."

Mae hesitated. She saw her mother nod her head and she gingerly took the pig. "Thank you."

Slamming his cap back on his head, Sam said, "I gotter go. It's a long ways home and I gotter milk the cow. Miss Mae, be sure and tie my pig onto your basket." Making for the door, he turned. "Don't forget."

And that was exactly what she was going to do. Forget. Because she was going to tie a purple ribbon on her basket just as Neville had written on the card.

## Chapter 3

# Oh, Charlie

The next morning at breakfast, the Andrus family was discussing the basket social being held at the Baptist church when the door burst open. The girls shouted "Charlie!" and rushed to engulf their brother with hugs and kisses.

Charlie, a bit embarrassed, grinned. "Hi, Sisses."

Dr. Andrus sternly looked at this son, a boy of medium height, sandy hair, and snappy gray eyes. Charlie hurriedly explained, "Papa, it's not what you think. I'm not expelled. The college faculty has gone to Frisco for a couple of weeks to attend a convention."

Doctor affectionately gave his son's shoulder a pat. "In that case, I'll turn my duty of escorting my daughters to the basket social over to you."

"My pleasure," Charlie said and gave a mock bow. Winking wickedly at his sisters, he smirked, "I'll outbid all your lovelorn swain and eat with my darling sisters."

"Don't you dare," squealed his sisters. "Who wants to eat with their brother!"

"Since you object to having the pleasure of my company, I'll make a deal. Tip me off as to which basket belongs to the amenable Hanable Logans and I'll..."

"No deal," Anna snapped. "She's horrid and you'd have a life of misery with her."

"Good Lord, I don't want to wed her. I only want to eat with her. She makes swell rhubarb cream pie for her baskets."

Amy reminded her brother, "You know very well how many times winning a bid on a basket and eating with the girl leads to matrimony, and Hanable's chance of getting into this family is definitely OUT."

Charlie's chin stiffened. "I suppose you have my wife all picked out for me."

"Of course I have. Mary Ann is a wonderful girl."

Charlie exploded, "I'd rather be dead than to be hitched to that bitch. Stop being a stupid matchmaker."

"Charlie, be careful of your language," admonished his mother.

Dr. Andrus pushed back his chair, saying to Charlie, "I must check to see how Minnie's sister is getting along. I haven't the time to deliver Mr. Arnold's medicine and would appreciate it if you would take care of it."

"Of course. I'll go this morning. May I use the buggy?"

"Take the carriage, I'll be using the buggy."

"Take me!" Amy and Nettie both pleaded.

"Can't I go anywhere without a sister tagging along?"

"Oh Charlie, you know you love us."

"Hurry up, then. I haven't all day waiting while you primp."

The Arnolds lived on a logging road, well out of town. Charlie felt pretty dapper in his new fraternity jacket and cap, the latter rakishly cocked on the side of his head. In fact, he was having difficulty appearing modest under the adoring gaze of his proud sisters, reveling in their brother's swankish airs. After all, he was the only boy in Dayton going to college.

Charlie drove recklessly fast, making the girls squeal in protest while hanging onto their hats. After a few miles of choking dust, the road narrowed and anyone wanting to pass had to pull over into the roadside brush or into a fast-flowing mountain stream bordering the road.

Amy said, "I hope we don't meet anyone on this narrow place."

Just then a team of horses plodded around the bend. "Oh, no!" wailed Nettie, grabbing Charlie's arm as a wagon with a large load of logs bumped into view.

Charlie spat, "That hick better give us the road."

The oncoming team wasn't swerving but kept heading straight for them. Charlie stood up shaking his fist and yelling, "Pull off the road!"

"Get off yourself!" boomed a deep husky voice.

Infuriated this hick was going to force him off the road, Charlie bellowed, "Pull over or I'll..."

The bare-chested lumberjack with rippling muscles jumped from the high wagon seat, and leisurely strode over to the carriage. Stopping to firmly plant a boot on one of the carriage wheels, he stuck out his chin, "Come on, you dude, you're asking for it."

The brawny bulk of belligerence frightened Nettie and she begged, "Charlie, do give him the road."

Charlie, with a freshman's medal for boxing, was anxious to display his prowess as a fierce fighter to his idolizing sisters. He leaped over the wheel and lunged with what was suppose to be a knock-out punch to the logger's jaw, but the lumberjack nimbly ducked and Charlie bounced on the ground.

The girls screamed instructions, which Charlie failed to heed. Had he taken their warning that a left hook was on the way, Charlie wouldn't have made another contact with the ground. In the first place, Charlie had underestimated his opponent, whose weight gave him a sixty-pound advantage over Charlie. To his credit Charlie's rage brought him stumbling to his feet, jabbing his fist into hard chest muscles, which the logger seemed not to notice. Charlie had two cheerleaders encouraging, "Sock him harder, Charlie! Kill him, Charlie!"

Charlie was having a hard time staying on his feet. Seeing their brother getting the worst of it, the girls jumped over the dashboard with vengeance. Amy grabbed the buggy whip and brandishing it over her head yelled for Charlie to duck; instead he tripped over the logger's boot and, as he fell, Amy furiously lashed at the lumberjack. Nettie managed to lift the heavy iron horse anchor and dropped it on his foot. Howling with rage, the lumberjack grabbed Nettie and dumped her into the creek. He turned to do the same with Amy but her onslaught with the buggy whip forced him to protect his face with his hands. He backed up to his wagon yelling, "I ain't fightin' no women."

In fury, the man leaped to the wagon seat, and lashing his team, careened around the carriage, taking off one of its back wheels as he rambled away.

Charlie, humiliated and enraged that his sisters had finished the fight for him, scornfully blazed at them, "I would have licked that bastard if you hadn't butted in."

It was a subdued Charlie who limped back to town with his two bedraggled sisters, all showing signs of their skirmish.

Hot, dirty, and exhausted, they dragged themselves up to the kitchen door just as Fannie opened it. She stared at them in amazement.

"Shhh," they cautioned. "We have to get upstairs before Mama sees us. Where is she?"

"Mama should know about this. You look as if you'd been in a fight."

"We were. We have to get cleaned up before Mama sees us. No one and we mean NO ONE must know."

"I'd like to know what this is all about," Fannie said.

"We haven't time to tell you. Where is she?"

"Lucky for you, she is out in the front yard watering her peonies."

"Fannie, please keep watch while we sneak up stairs."

Nancy loved her luscious-hued peonies. She took meticulous care of them. She had shoe-horned them between the lilac bushes for protection. Their ruffled petals made her think of a picture she once saw of a ballerina, her tutu projecting in buffeted frills as she pirouetted.

Their full-bloomed beauty took away the pain when decorating the family graves, and she raised tubs of them to express her love on Decoration Day for those dear ones who had passed into memory.

The spray from the nozzle was making her feel chilly. Dropping the hose she went into the house for a sweater. Nettie, Amy, and Charlie were tiptoeing down the hall, heading for the stairs when they heard her footsteps on the porch. They dove back into the cloak closet under the stairs, hunched themselves on the floor behind the coats, holding their breath when Nancy rummaged for her sweater only inches from them.

Fannie heard a scream and came running. Nancy's face was white with fright as she told her daughter, "Fannie there's a burglar hiding in the closet. The coats swayed. Get your father at once.

Fannie knew exactly why the coats were swaying. She hadn't heard her mother in time to give a warning, but she had had a glimpse of the culprits as they dashed for cover. Not knowing what had happened to them and fearing the worst, she thought fast. "Mama, it's only Whiskers. That old tomcat loves to sleep in the closet. Here's your sweater, dear. Do finish your sprinkling so you can help me fit my new dress."

Nancy gave her daughter a searching glance, not too convinced it was old Whiskers.

When they were sure their mother had returned to her garden, the three culprits rolled out of the closet on their knees, kissing Fannie. "Oh Fan, you're a peach!"

"Get up those stairs before I have to tell another lie to save your hides. And I want a full report."

The kids took the stairs two at a time just as their mother came in to make herself a cup of tea.

Later in the day, Dr. Andrus, having found his patient doing well, was tying Molly to the home hitching post when his wife rushed out the door. Breathlessly meeting him on the porch steps and wringing her hands, she cried, "Nelson, Reverend Meade is here and oh, I think he's dying."

"Nancy, calm yourself. Fetch a glass of warm water."

Striding into the parlor, he found the good reverend rolling on the floor in agony. Maybelle was trying to keep a cold cloth on his head, Fannie was taking off his shoes, and Mae was struggling to get a pillow under his head. The other girls were unsuccessfully trying to calm his wife. Between groans, Reverend Meade was praying "Oh God, have mercy, don't take me now, I...I have five dear little children. Oh, God, don't..."

"Meade, you're not going to meet your Maker yet," Doc assured his patient.

The suffering man moaned, "Don't know what's the matter with me."

Nancy gave the glass of warm water to her husband. He took it and immediately, sprinkled in some powdered slippery elm, and had the distraught man drink the contents. In a few moments the preacher had some relief and sat up. "Never hurt so badly. Don't know what's the matter."

"Give me your handkerchief," Doc requested, holding out his hand.

Reluctantly the parson pulled out a large white square of cloth, heavily embroidered in one corner with a cross, saying, "I use it for snuffin'."

The girls, huddling in the doorway, were familiar as to what was going to happen.

Closing his eyes while fingering the edge of the handkerchief, the doctor seemed to be in deep concentration.

All eyes were glued on this man of medicine with fascination and expectancy. When he gave a loud grunt, they jumped. To their amazement, Doc started laughing. "Meade, aren't you grown up enough to know not to eat green apples? Go home; your bellyache will be better in a few moments, but keep taking a teaspoon of this powder on the hour for the rest of the day."

The girls rushed up the stairs to gather in Amy and Fannie's bedroom. Amy gave a snort. "I think Papa is faking hocus-pocus stuff just to impress the reverend in case he ever has to be prayed for."

"He knew about the green apples," Anna timidly defended her father.

"That was just a wild guess," Amy insisted.

"But how could he have known about the green apples if he hadn't seen inside the reverend's stomach?" puzzled Fannie.

"Let's test Papa," Nettie suggested.

"How?" they asked, intrigued with the idea.

Anna's eyes snapped. "I know. Each of us will give a few hairs from our heads and put them all together."

"Then what?" they asked.

"Why, one of us will take the hairs to Papa and ask him to see what is wrong," Anna grinned, pleased with her idea.

"You mean one of us will pretend to be sick?"

"Exactly."

"Anna, you're the one who thought of it, so you be the one to give Papa our hair."

"There's nothing wrong with me," Anna hedged.

"There's nothing wrong with any of us. Anna, you'll just have to make up something. You could pretend to have a bellyache."

"No, Reverend Meade had that and Papa would give me that horrid-tasting stuff to drink."

Maybelle piped up, "Have bronchitis and Papa will give you that good-tasting wild cherry cough syrup."

Anna shook her head. "More likely he'd put a mustard plaster on my chest that would leave a red mark, and I couldn't wear my new evening gown."

"You have to think of something," Mae said.

"I'll think of something," Anna said knowing her sisters' determination.

Thinking Anna's idea a splendid one, they giggled and snickered as they pulled out a few hairs from their heads. Nettie thought of going to their mother's dressing table to collect her hair kept in an ornate meisson receptacle with a hole in the lid to poke in hair combings.

Anna was about to take their hair downstairs when Fannie exclaimed, "We don't have Charlie's hair."

"He isn't here."

"Where is he?"

"He's taking that snobbish Tilly Blane to the ice cream parlor."

"If we don't keep better watch on him, he's going to marry someone we'll all hate."

"Even if he were here, we couldn't yank any hair from his head or he'd be suspicious something was up."

"He's so stupid about women, but he always seems to know when we are up to something."

Nettie laughed, "We don't need Charlie. Remember the picture of hair flowers Mama made of Charlie's baby hair when she cut off his curls?"

Tiptoeing into their mother's room, they took the picture of hair flowers from the wall and carefully pulled out a few of Charlie's baby hairs, then braided all the hair together.

On the upper stair landing, the girls huddled together to watch their sister slowly descend the stairs to confront their father. They had several misgivings as to whether it was right to fool poor Papa.

The girls held their skirts over their mouths to suppress gleeful giggles. Rather sheepishly, Anna approached her unsuspecting father. "Papa, I don't feel very well."

"What seems to be the trouble?" her father asked, putting some paper in a file.

"I...I think I have...I have a..."

Her sisters doubled over with mirth. Anna gave them a desperate glance. Seeing them vigorously nodding their heads, she took courage. "I think I have spinal meningitis."

The girls groaned. Anna handed her father the braided lock of hair. Without a word Dr. Andrus took the lock of hair and started concentrating. His daughters almost collapsed in fits of smothered laughter. Anna pressed her lips tightly together, digging her fingernails into the palm of her hand. She didn't know whether to laugh or feel sorry for poor Papa.

Solemnly opening his eyes, his mouth gave a quirk, "If you had gotten the dog's hair, you would have gotten the whole damn family."

The girls were crestfallen. Looking at each other in amazement, they slunk back up the stairs while Anna turned and dashed up the steps, sobbing, "He really saw the green apples!"

Never again did the girls doubt their father's ability to diagnose a patient.

That evening at supper they ware finishing dessert when Doc leaned back, stroking his chin with a speculative eye on his children. He cleared his throat before carefully choosing his words. "Before I started for home, I had a very interesting case come into my office. The way the bump on his head was swelling, someone must have hit him with a cast-iron stove. He also had purple welts across his face. I told him to go home and keep an ice pack on his head, gave him some salve for his face and something for his pain. He wouldn't tell me who had worked him over, but when he was leaving, he said that at the basket social someone was going to pay for all his suffering."

Amy and Nettie quickly looked away from each other, shuddering. Late that night was heard the leather bag hitting the attic wall as Charlie practiced his punches.

The next Sunday, from the pulpit, Reverend Meade paid tribute to the doctor. He thundered, "Every member of this congregation is blessed in having Lord Nelson Andrus in our midst giving comfort and aid to the sick and elderly citizens of our town. Our loving God sent him to us. Hallelujah."

"Hallelujah," echoed the congregation.

The reverend continued with his veneration for their beloved doctor. "Many of you would not be enjoying life. You would not be savoring the bountiful blessings God has rained down upon you, if not for this man dedicated to saving your lives. You would have left your dear children in desolation, your friends in sorrow. You would be in heaven."

"Or hell," someone murmured.

Doc was beginning to squirm under such adulation and breathed a sigh of relief when Reverend Meade closed with a blessing. "May the Almighty pour down on Dr. Andrus and his family the abundance of our Creator."

"Amen" loudly echoed from the stained-glass windows of Christ, and those in the congregation who had reasons to be grateful for the saving administrations of Dr. Andrus shouted, "Amen!"

The minister cleared his throat. "And now I have an important announcement to make that will please you young folks. Right after the basket social there will be a dance. Jake French will be on the violin, Tom Hepner the accordion, and Mrs. Fairweather will play the piano. Randy Jackson will call for the square dances. There will also be waltzes for the older people."

Mrs. Aims leaped to her feet; a dance to be held in church was too shocking for her to bear. The daisies on her hat quivered as she pointed an indignant finger at Reverend Meade. "Not in this church will there be a dance!"

The congregation groaned. They were used to Mrs. Aims' wrath of righteousness. Before the congregation could shout her down, as was their custom, Reverend Meade hurriedly assured the vexed woman, "Mrs. Aims, the dance will be held in the basement."

"Makes no difference. You preach God is everywhere, so God is in the basement and we are sinners if we insult the Almighty by having a sinful dance in the basement."

Someone in the back pew yelled, "God or no God, there's going to be a dance in the basement!"

Mrs. Aims slammed the hymnbook down. "May the hell fire of Satan burn you to a crisp." Indignantly, she stalked out with the daisies on her hat shuddering.

The dance announcement sent the Andrus girls into a swirl of taffetas, silks, tulles, satins, valenciennes laces, and yards of velvet ribbons. Their mother shook her head in perplexity. "I can't see why the dresses you were to wear for the basket social aren't good enough for the dance."

"Oh, Mama, don't you realize a dance is more formal, and besides, some of Charlie's Walla Walla fraternity brothers are coming," Mae explained.

Nancy sighed. "I suppose Charlie talked Elder Rankin into inviting them."

"Of course, and his college friends are pretty sophisticated," Mae said.

"Mae, I didn't know you knew such big words. I'd call them plain snooty," Amy chided her sister.

Mae flared, "I know bigger words. You're a...a...a..."

"Ah, ah...don't say it," Amy cautioned. "Not if you want me to help you with your new basque."

Maybelle piped up, "Mama, may I wear a bustle?"

"You certainly may not."

"But the boys all make fun of my pantalets."

Teasing their sister, Mae, Anna, and Nettie lifted their skirts, kicking and singing:

> "Come the dainty dimpled pets,
> With their tresses all in nets,
> Their peeping pantalets in view,
> Oh, the pretty little dears,
> Shedding waterfalls of tears,
> For their pantalets are in view."

"Mama, make them stop," wailed Maybelle sobbing.

"That's enough girls," said their mother, starting down the stairs. Then turning, she reminded, "One of you girls must run over to Abigale's and borrow her cherry pitter. Mine is broken and she's the only other person in town who has one."

"Mama, we're so busy. We are going to have to work every minute to finish our dresses in time."

"Never mind about your dresses. Your father has asked for a cherry pie. It's his favorite."

"Oh, all right, I guess it's me. I'm the only one who can't thread a needle." Peevishly, Nettie flounced down the stairs and out into the bright sunshine. Teddy wagged his tail begging to go along. "No, Teddy, you stay home. I don't feel like getting into a dog fight today to save your hide."

Paying no heed to Nettie, Teddy trotted at her heels. Passing a yard of clipped hedges bordering a blooming rambler rose, a large dog ran out snarling. Nettie grabbed Teddy and, running back to the house, dumped him inside the door, admonishing him, "I told you, you can't go. Why do big dogs always pick on you? It's because you're so little they think they can lick you. Now stay home."

# Chapter 4

# Doc Objects to the Caprice of Fashion

Abigale, answering the brass door-knocker, exclaimed, "Why, Nettie, what a pleasant surprise."

"Mama wants to borrow your cherry pitter and I'm afraid I'm in an awful hurry."

"Of course you may, but you must take time to meet my guest." Nettie was led into the front parlor, overflowing with exotic plants. "I want you to meet my dear friend, Cynthia Lynn."

"What a charming young lady," Miss Lynn smiled warmly, holding out her hand.

Nettie stared wide-eyed at the most fashionable and sophisticated woman she had ever seen. "D...did you say Cynthia Lynn?" Before she could be answered, Nettie bubbled excitedly, "I know you. You're the editor of Frank Leslie's *Gazette*. You write those wonderful fashion and etiquette columns."

"Guilty," laughed Miss Lynn.

Abigale stared at her friend in shock. "You never told me you were an editor. You only said you had taken up journalism."

"My dear, I didn't think it important."

"Important!" shrieked Abigale.

Nettie laughed, "She knows everything about etiquette. How things should be done. I read all her columns."

Horrified, Abigale stared at her guest, wondering if she had correctly set the table. Had she set the salad plate in the right place, had she...Abigale threw up her hands. "I suppose I've done everything wrong."

Cynthia put her arms around her friend. "No, you silly goose. Now stop this nonsense. You are giving me what the French would call 'Cuisine de tendress,' roughly translated means 'esteem, affection, and delightful tranquility to the soul.' My dear, that is a thousand times more meaningful than correctly setting the table as fashion dictates. I can't thank you enough for this wonderful vacation. I'm tired of telling people not to eat peas with their knifes." They laughed and Nettie invited them for tea the following afternoon.

Fannie was meticulous making her dress. It had to be French seamed. The lavish trim of tiny chenile balls, simulating pearls, had to be spaced exactly an eighth of an inch apart. She was driving her sisters crazy.

Maybelle snickered, "Fannie is fussy because she's stuck on Papa's new patient."

"Mind your own business," Fannie snapped.

Fannie had met her father's new patient while attending a band concert in the park. This bronzed Apollo had retrieved her hat when a sudden gust of wind blew her beribboned and flower-bedecked chapeau from her head and sailed it across the grass. He quickly caught up with it and, bowing low, returned it with an infectious grin.

"Good old Mother Nature has introduced us so it's proper for me to sit beside you. May I?" he asked, indicating the seat beside her.

Fannie nodded, mumbling "thank you" as she adjusted her chapeau, anchoring it with a long, pearl-studded hatpin.

"Very becoming," he said with sincerity, but seeing Fannie frown and turn her back to him, he refrained from expressing any further admiration, and asked, "Have you lived here long?"

"All my life," she answered casting a shy glance at him over her shoulder.

"I wish I could say the same, but I'm a roving cowboy."

"It must be very hard work, with much exposure to the weather."

"That's why I'm going to Dr. Andrus."

"He's my father."

"Yes, I know. I saw you with your father in the ice cream parlor and I said to myself, 'That's the girl of my dreams.' "

Fannie jumped up, coldly saying, "I...I hope your health improves."

"So do I. You've made me think of making plans."

Fannie fumed all the way home. He was much too brash for her liking.

That evening she shyly went to her father on the pretense of offering to help him in the office. Dr. Andrus gave his daughter a penetrating look. "If you're wondering if my new tuberculosis patient is well enough to take you to the dance, why..."

"Papa, I wasn't thinking of that."

"He is."

"PAPA!!"

Doc smiled to himself. Yes, his daughter was interested in John Baker.

Fannie floated up the stairs. Amy, looking up from her sewing and seeing her sister's glowing face, said, "Fan...you have that falling-in-love look."

"Me? Falling in love? Ridiculous!"

"And that's a sure sign that you have." Amy held up fifteen yards of rose taffeta, "Well, I've finished the chenille around the bottom of the skirt. Now try on your dress."

The lustrous material floated over Fannie's head, but she fumed as she fastened the waistband. "The waist is too large."

Amy, with vexation, said, "I know you want to show off that eighteen-inch waist you haven't got. Your waist is twenty-one inches."

Fannie pursed her lips. "I'll have an eighteen-inch waist when I wear my new corset."

"You know Papa will be furious when he finds out how you're squeezing yourself."

"Never mind what Papa says."

"You better pay attention to what Papa says. He has warned you that it deforms your ribs and deranges your digestive organs; then how are you going to have a baby?"

"Amy! How can you be so vulgar? When it comes to that time, I'll..."

"You won't live that long if you keep cinching yourself."

Fannie stomped her foot, persisting, "Corsets make a woman walk gracefully and sit without slouching."

"Yes and stop her breathing," Amy added, sticking to her point.

So was Fannie. "If you get your corset right, you can freely move and it pulls your waist into the most fabulous shape."

Amy's eyes flared. "Papa says corsets are a crime against women."

"And Papa loves to take us downtown to show us off. Why? Because we don't have thick, lumpy waists and that's because we wear corsets. So there!"

Amy tried another tactic. "Fannie dear, if you'll add more petticoats, it'll..."

"I'm wearing four now."

"Wear six and trim them with lots of ruffled lace so they will billow out. That will make your waist look just as small."

"No it won't."

At three o'clock the next day, Abigale and Miss Lynn were preparing to visit Nancy when Abigale noticed Cynthia slipping buttons from a jewel box into her purse. "What are you going to do with those beautiful buttons?"

"In New York and Boston, button memory strings are all the rage. They are unknown here, so I thought I'd give each of the Andrus girls a button to start their own memory string."

"What a lovely idea! Your ceramic buttons are a work of art."

"Yes, aren't they? Buttons also come in brass, horn, and ivory, but I prefer the ceramics depicting children's fairy tales. Isn't it strange that buttons were merely an ornament for clothes until the eighteenth century, when they started to be used to join clothes together?"

"I'm sure the girls will be delighted with your gift. I have some buttons that look like little churches. Would they do?"

"They would be perfect."

Nancy greeted them in the foyer and they dutifully placed their elaborately engraved calling cards on a majolica tray. Later Nancy would paste them in her scrap book as a fashionable record of their visit.

Nancy ushered them into the front parlor filled with botanical wonders. It was popular to have jungles growing among the dark hardwood Victorian furniture. Palms, African violets, ferns, and aspidistras competed for the sunlight filtering through lace curtains. After dutifully admiring the clivias and hibiscus and sedately commenting upon the weather, Abigale timidly inquired about the family's clever seamstress.

Nancy smiled, "Oh, you mean Fannie. She is upstairs with her sisters furiously sewing. They insist on having new dresses for the dance."

Abigale hesitated. "Is it permissible to see her?"

"If you don't mind the clutter."

"Not at all and we have a small gift for them."

Up the stairs they hastened to find Anna in her corset, chemise, and drawers, stepping out of a mound of pale turquoise mousseline de soe. She hastily grabbed her matinée, shrugging into it while apologizing, "We weren't expecting you just yet."

"We have brought you each a small gift, but we won't stay, knowing how busy you are. See, some buttons for you to start a memory string."

"What beautiful buttons!" exclaimed Anna.

"You are supposed to collect one of a kind until you have 999."

"We could never collect that many," doubted Mae.

"You will be surprised how quickly your strings will grow when you display them in the parlor where guests can see them."

"Why 999 and not a thousand?" asked Fannie, fingering her button with admiration.

"Because, my dear, Prince Charming is to add the thousandth button."

"Oh, how romantic!" Anna exclaimed then asked, "Please tell us of the latest fashion in Boston."

Miss Lynn shook her head. "Girls, I'll return another time and tell you when the rush is over."

"We want to know now," the girls begged.

"You must tell us," Nettie insisted "My gown isn't cut out yet and I want to know the latest."

Miss Lynn picked up some chartreuse crêpe de Chine material. "What luxurious cloth."

"That's going to be my new dress." Nettie proudly held up several lengths of yardage. "Now what style should it be?"

"The *Harper's Bazaar* is now on the newsstand for ten cents a copy, and it features the latest designs by Mr. Worth," Miss Lynn told them.

Maybelle excitedly jumped up and down. "Oh, I know him! He dresses princesses, queens, and all sorts of very rich people."

Miss Lynn smiled over the fresh display of girlishness. "Yes, he has established the popular French couture."

The two visitors stood up. "We must go or you won't get your dresses finished for the social. We will return next week to see your new dresses."

The girls begged their mother to send Charlie down to the store for the latest copy of *Harper's Bazaar*. Charlie grumpily consented if they gave him two bits. The girls howled their protest. Charlie flopped into a chair saying, "Okay, no go."

The girls squabbled among themselves as to whether they should give in to their brother's demand. At last Nettie threw a quarter at her brother. "You're nothing but a skinflint!"

Charlie caught the coin, and shrugging he said, "I'm wearing out a buck of shoe leather just to get your damn magazine. Why don't you have just one style for dresses like men have for pants?"

"Oh, such a stupid male like you would never understand," Nettie flared.

By afternoon the girls were exhausted from sewing since the early morning, when they heard their mother call, "Will one of you girls please go down to the basement for a jar of peaches? I want to take it over to dear Mrs. Miller who isn't feeling well."

The girls were arguing as to who should go when Amy dropped the skirt she was hemming. "Oh, all right, I guess it will have to be me."

In the kitchen Nancy handed her a bowl, saying, "While you are down there, skim the milk pans. We need whipping cream for dessert tonight."

"Yes, Mama." Amy felt miserable—her back ached, her head throbbed.

On the stone ledge of the walled-in spring were several large pans of jersey milk a local farmer had brought the day before. Her mother always insisted the thick yellow cream rising in rich folds was much easier to whip then separated cream. Amy groaned as she started skimming off the cream. Her head was killing her. She glanced up at a tin cup hanging on the wall then at four crocks of her father's elderberry wine, used only for its curative properties. Mrs. Aldridge, who often helped her father prepare his herbal medicines, once told her, "Elderberries are rich in organic iron, excellent for anemia and especially good as a curative for headaches."

Without hesitation Amy dipped the cup into the wine, hoping to get some relief. Between sips, she skimmed cream. The wine had such a pleasant aroma and tasted delightfully smooth and cool. By the fourth cup she felt much better. She took a hurried last sip before climbing the cellar steps. As she entered the kitchen, she felt flushed and slightly dizzy.

One glance at her daughter and Nancy's eyes blazed. "Amy, have you been into your father's elderberry wine?"

"Mama, I had such a headache."

"You know your father keeps wine strictly for medicinal purposes. This is the third time you've been into his wine. I see I can't trust you. I'm leaving now for Mrs. Miller's and I'm taking the cellar key with me."

"Yes, Mama. Tell Mrs. Miller I hope she feels better soon."

Feeling refreshed, Amy joined her sisters, telling them, "Well, I feel much better. In fact I'm no longer tired. I feel great."

"Oh, Amy, what makes you feel so good? We feel so tired. What did you do?"

"I drank pints of elderberry wine."

Shocked, they exclaimed, "Amy, that's for Papa's sick patients!"

"Well, I was sick."

"And you're not tired anymore?" they asked, not believing their sister's quick recovery.

"No, I'm not," Amy reassured them.

"Would it help us?"

"Of course it would."

"Let's go," they shouted in unison, leaping to their feet.

Amy shook her head. "Not so fast. Mama has locked the cellar door."

"Oh pooh," Nettie laughed, "we can slide down the coal chute."

"How can we get back up?" Mae asked. "It's awfully steep."

"Stupid," Nettie sneered, "tie a rope to the apple tree and throw the other end down the cellar. We can use that to pull ourselves out."

"Let's go," Maybelle yelled, leading the way.

"I think you're too little to go," Amy warned.

"If I can't go, I'll tell on you," Maybelle threatened.

Amy relented. "Oh, all right, but only one small cup of wine for you."

They gaily whooped and hollered as they slide down the coal chute, but only after tying one end of the rope to the old apple tree and throwing down the other end.

Sitting on the cool stone floor they took turns drinking from the one tin cup. The ruby-red, full-bodied wine was aromatic and tasted delightfully refreshing. After several rounds had been drunk, Maybelle remonstrated, "You're drinking too much."

"You're just mad because we won't let you have any more," Nettie told her.

They eased their conscience of drinking their father's medicine by reminding each other how hard they had worked when helping Papa gather the berries for the wine.

"Yes, and it was dangerous too," piped up Anna.

Fanny shuddered. "The rattlesnakes were so thick we could have been bitten and died."

Remembering her own narrow escape, Amy took a big gulp of wine before telling of her near-death experience. "When I was at the spring, I flopped on the ground to take a drink when I felt something touch the top of my head. Looking up I saw two rattlesnakes curled up in the bushes overhead. I was so terrified I dove right into the icy-cold spring."

Mae closed her eyes tightly at the still frightening memory. "I had a close call with a snake and would have been bitten had not it had a bird in its mouth."

Maybelle, wide-eyed, shivered. "And all those wild cattle. Remember the big old bull that chased us up the tree?"

"See," Amy laughed, "there's no need to feel guilty over a few cups of wine. We've earned every drop."

Anna took the empty cup for a refill. She lifted the lid of the crock and her face paled. "We've emptied the crock!"

They giggled. "Stupid," said Nettie, her tongue thick, "dip in the other crock. Is anyone feeling tired now?"

"No," they tittered.

Mae was uneasy. "Maybe we better be going. It's about time for Mama to come back."

Maybelle murmured, "I feel awfully dizzy."

"Don't be silly, you've only had one cup," Amy told her.

Anna groaned, "I feel sort of sick to my stomach."

"A minute ago, you said you were feeling fine," Amy frowned.

"Not now," murmured Anna, and then started retching.

Fannie weaved to her feet. "Let's get out of here."

"Yes, before Mama gets back," said Nettie trying to stand up.

Amy was getting scared. "Nettie find the rope. You're the one who threw it down."

Nettie wailed, "I can't find it."

"You're not that drunk," speculated Amy.

They were all groping around for the rope, when they heard masculine laughter. A wail shot up from the cellar. "CHARLIE!" they screamed. "Throw the rope down."

Charlie, who had been returning from playing ball, was heading for the kitchen to raid the ice box before taking off again, when he tripped over a rope, landing in his mother's prized pink petunias. Leaping up and cussing over the stupidity of anyone leaving a rope stretched across a well-traveled path, he started coiling up the rope when he heard giggles, laughter, and moans. He knelt, peering down into the cellar's gloom.

"What in blazes is going on down there?" he asked himself. He was all too familiar with the high-keyed laughter and slurred words. "I don't believe it. How is it possible for my sisters to be swacked?"

"Oh Chashy, plish get ush out."

"My God, you've hung one on. Stupids, climb the stairs and open the door."

"Dorsh locked," they wailed.

"I would say, my dear sisters, you're in one helluva a fix. Wait until Mama and Papa find you down there soused."

"Chrish!" they screamed. "Hulp ush otsh!"

"I might consider it if..."

"Don't you dare pull any sly stuff on us," Amy, the most coherent, admonished.

"You're in no position to quibble with me."

"We didn't dwink mush," Nettie said.

Charlie threw back his head and roared with laughter. "You're so damn tipsy, you must have emptied a couple of crocks."

"Oh, I'm feeling turrible," Nettie groaned.

"You're going to feel a helluva a lot more terrible in the morning," Charlie predicted.

"Stop your palavering and get us out!" Amy screamed.

"On one condition."

"What?"

"Get me a date with the new sheriff's delectable daughter."

"Don't know her."

"Very well. No deal." Charlie started to walk away.

A wail of despair from below engulfed him, then a weak voice acquiesced, "Wesh get date."

Charlie slid down the cellar chute with the rope and tied one end around Fannie's waist. He skidded back up, pulling her with him where she collapsed on the grass, moaning. One by one he brought them all out. Mae was last and so sick Charlie had to carry her while the girls pulled them both up. Just then the front door slammed shut.

"Oh, God!" Charlie swore.

"Mama's home," sobbed Maybelle.

"Now whash we do?" asked Anna weaving on her feet.

Charlie hesitated. "Keep your promise?"

"Corsh we will," snapped Amy.

"Very well, my darling sisters, your beloved brother will rescue you from a fate worse than death, if Papa should find out."

Charlie herded his sisters to the far side of the house where there grew a large black walnut tree; its thickly gnarled branches towered over the roof. As kids, they had shinnied up and down the old tree, playing pirates on the high seas. From the highest branch they spotted golden galleons to plunder. The upper bedroom window was the captain's bridge. The girls had clambered up and down the tree as agile as the boys, but today in their inebriated condition it was not only unsafe, but impossible. Charlie ran back for the rope while devising a plan of rescue. Returning, he tied the rope around Anna's waist, instructing her, "Try to climb as you use to. If you slip, I'll haul you up the rest of the way."

"I'm scared."

"Buck up, your boarding a pirate's ship remember."

Charlie swung up the tree and through the bedroom window, pulling the rope. Halfway up Anna's foot slipped, and he had to haul her the rest of the way.

While waiting their turn, the girls lay on the grass vowing to never touch another drop of elderberry wine. They wondered how it was possible to get so intoxicated. Amy explained, "It zoomed straight to our heads because our stomachs were empty. We should have eaten something first."

"Now is a fine time to tell us," the others sniffed.

They looked up into the leafy branches of the old black walnut tree with both love and hate. In the fall when its harvest of nuts lay thick on the ground, they had the dreadful and hated task of husking and shelling, digging out the precious and delicious nut meats from its intricate sections. It took weeks to get the dark brown stain off their hands. Only old Mrs. Aldridge was happy as she used the husks to dye the wool she spun for knitting; but the loathsome task was forgotten when Mama made a black walnut cake, as no other nut had the same delicious flavor.

Charlie called for Amy to tie on the rope. As she was the largest and heaviest of the girls, he had to exert all his strength to get her up and through the window. Even with Amy's help, he had to give a tremendous yank. Amy tumbled through the window, hitting the floor with a thud, knocking Charlie over so that they both plopped heavily onto the floor.

At just that moment, Nancy returned home, pausing in the hall. She thought the silence strange. Usually the house was clamoring with girlish chatter. Taking off her coat, she was startled when a loud thud overhead rocked the hall chandelier.

Going to the foot of the stairs, she called, "Who is up there and what made that noise"

To her surprise, Charlie popped in sight at the head of the stairs. "Hi, Mom. Have a nice visit?"

"Charlie, you are not to bother the girls when they are so busy."

"Sure thing, Mom."

Nancy was puzzled; her son looked disheveled and sweat rolled down his face. "I think I'll come up and have a look." Nancy started up the stairs, picking up a dropped glove. She did not see the look of panic cross her son's face.

"Mama, please, I feel beat. It was a tough ball game. Make me some coffee. I'll be down in a jake."

Nancy gave him a questioning look, but headed for the kitchen. Charlie never drank coffee. She turned back to the stairs calling, "Anna, it's your turn to help with supper." There was a faint muffled reply.

When his mother's footsteps assured him she was in the kitchen, he raced back to the window and thanked God the others were able to help for he was exhausted. Nettie, being the last, stood looking up pleading, "Cawlie, gish me up before pa comsh."

"Sis," Charlie whispered, "you're going to have to help."

"Ish come by my shelf."

"Damn it you're too drunk."

"Nosh much." Nettie highly amused started singing, "Ish a piwate on..."

"Shut up! You want Mama to hear you? Can you tie on the rope?"

"Sure, I'sh a jolly piwate."

Charlie was pulling with all his remaining strength when three-quarters of the way up Nettie's dress caught on a jagged branch. Charlie gave a desperate yank. A loud ripping sound made him groan.

Nettie screamed, "Stopsh, yush terr'n mu dresh ofsh."

"Is mademoiselle going up or coming down?" asked an amused masculine voice.

Looking down into a dark handsome face, Nettie blurted, "Whosh yoush?"

"I'm a pirate roaming the high seas in search of damsels in distress."

"Go wash."

"And leave a fair lady to plunge to her death? Never! Charlie, ease up on the rope so I can get your sister's dress unhooked."

Charlie stuck his head further out the window. "Bob!!! What brings you here?"

"Never mind. Is the lady going up or coming down?"

"Up."

Deftly a young man of medium height with dark, chestnut hair and a handsome profile swung himself branch over branch until he was on the same snag holding Nettie's dress. He unhooked it and caught her around the waist with one arm. He grabbed the rope with the other arm, calling to Charlie, "Keep the rope tight!" He swung Nettie, seemingly with no effort, up and through the window, climbing in after her. Nettie, frustrated and confused, tried pulling her skirt together, saying, "Wash you know bout piwates?"

"Why, Captain Andrus has regaled me with your exploits of high adventure. Apparently this one ran into a snag."

Charlie grabbed his friend's hand. "God, Bob, I'm glad to see you! Of course, you'll stay for a visit?"

"Not through the bedroom; later by the front door. I'm curious as to how the lady fell into the pirate's rum barrel, but I have to dash to get to the store before it closes. See you tomorrow." Bob swung out through the window and was partly hidden by the leafy branches when Nettie leaned out so far out the window she almost tumbled over. "Piwate meet lady tree tomorowsh at ish cwim parlo."

Bob looked up, and gaily laughing, answered, "I'll be there."

"EEEEEeeeee," Nettie screamed as she suddenly disappeared with Charlie's arm around her neck. Gritting his teeth, Charlie spat, "If I didn't know you had a crock of wine in you, I'd say you're a slut. Of all the brazen brass I ever saw..."

"Oh, Charlish, I luf him."

"When you get sober, you're going to be so ashamed, you won't ever want to see him again."

## Chapter 5

# All in the Family

Old Molly, a gray mare showing pale markings of appaloosa ancestry, had faithfully pulled the Andrus family around for many happy years and, along with Teddy, was considered a beloved member of the clan. If she made a mistake and took the wrong route home as she occasionally did, Teddy made it known by barking attention to the fact. Knowing these two pals would get him safely home left Doctor free to ponder on Mrs. James' refusal to take some of his bitter herbs when she was suffering from a bout of erysipelas.

When Molly stopped at the cast-iron hitching post, he sat for a few moments, looking at his home. Luckily the black walnut tree, with all its action, was on the opposite side of the house. Dr. Andrus was proud of his home, having had it built for his large family. His wife, Nancy, admired anything Victorian so he had chosen the architectural style of Queen Anne, as it was the most Victorian, with its wraparound porch and gingerbread trim. Through the stained-glass front door, one entered a large, mirrored foyer, from which ascended a winding staircase leading up to five commodious bedrooms. He hoped, as brides, his daughters would some day descend the spiral stairs to enter the bay-windowed front parlor to be wed. An ornate arch separated the parlor from the family's sitting room. Oak double doors opened into a spacious dining room. Swinging doors led to the kitchen and pantry. A door from the family room opened into his study and to the master bedroom.

He saw the lace curtains part and knew his wife was looking for him. With a sigh of contentment, he tied Molly to the hitching post. A stable boy would pick her up later. The stables were certainly making money off of him as he kept a couple of teams there as well. As usual, Nancy met him at the door with a kiss. When hanging up his coat, she was surprised to see Charlie dash past, taking the stairs two at a time with a steaming pot of coffee. How strange, she thought, following her husband into the family sitting room.

Dr. Andrus looked at his wife with adoration. He was not a sentimental man, but had deep admiration and appreciation for the woman he had chosen to accompany him on life's sometimes difficult journey. She had born him seven healthy, intelligent children and no woman could be more efficient in managing his home. In cooking, she was more concerned in proper nutrition for the children than over-taxing their systems with sweet desserts. She always provided loyal support, helping him in his practice. He knew she was an authentic pioneer, in a latent sense, being in the womb when her family crossed the continent, traveling partly on the old Oregon Trail in a Conestoga wagon. She had been born east of Canby, Oregon, as the wagon train was circling, preparing to camp for the night.

Nancy had no coarseness, as so many pioneer women had. She displayed a refinement that reached beyond the rough frontier. She was always well groomed, never leaving the bedroom in the morning before slipping into a freshly laundered and starched dress and tidily arranging her hair. As if fortifying herself for the day, she always gave herself a quick spray of French Jicky's eau de toilette, a blend of rosewood, rosemary, and bergamot, which wafted after her, bringing an essence of eternal spring. Yes, to show such refinement she must be of cultured breeding inherited from an ancestral lineage. He was sure the family guarded a secret. He must remember to question her about a nobleman connected with the royal court of France.

They had first met in Canby, when Nancy was three and he was twenty-three. With his Stevens 22 rifle he was out hunting grouse. While stalking a bird in a wild rose hedge, hoping to flush it out, he heard a snake buzzing its rattles; then to his horror he heard a small child laughing and clapping. He parted the bushes to see a little girl gleefully circling the snake, delightfully clapping her hands whenever it rattled the buttons on the end of its tail. The snake's head was raised, turning as the child danced around it. Nelson knew at any moment the snake would strike. Quickly raising the rifle to his shoulder he fired. The snake uncurled. The child seemed surprised to see her playmate writhing on the ground and started towards it. Nelson snatched her up into his arms which frightened the child, and she started screaming. A woman came running through the trees. Nelson held out the child, pointing to the snake. The woman cuddled her daughter. "Nancy, please shut up, you'll have every Indian in the country attacking."

"Ma'am, she was playing with the rattlesnake."

"Nancy, how could you, when you've been warned so often to stay away from snakes!" The woman held out her hand. "I'm Mrs. Melancon and I'm deeply indebted to you for saving my disobedient child. We were just going to sit down to supper. Won't you join us?"

"Thank you. I've been so busy hunting I haven't had time to eat."

"Then you must have supper with us. We are going to have roast elk."

"I couldn't turn that down."

Nelson followed her to a brightly burning campfire beside a covered wagon. She explained they were soon moving to a new house her husband was building. She laughed when she saw his amazement upon noticing a four-poster canopy bed, sheltered under a canvas tarp. He was also surprised when he was offered a Louis XV chair, lavishly upholstered in sprays of needlepoint roses. Mrs. Melancon smiled. "We brought everything. We couldn't bear to leave behind things we knew would soften the severity of pioneering."

Nelson assured his hostess, "I understand perfectly. It's just so incongruous to see such luxury on a rough frontier, but I'm sure your cherished belongings will make life in this wilderness much easier."

"You're very kind. Excuse me for a moment." She walked over to her maid who was kneeling beside the campfire ironing a ruffled garment with a fluted hand iron. The maid stood up and soon brought him a plate of meat, wild yams, rice, and cornbread, asking him his preference of coffee or tea. His preference was coffee. When the maid brought his coffee on a silver tray, he noticed the pattern of the cup and saucer, as it was the same pattern of Meissen china his grandmother had owned. The cutlery she handed him was of sterling and the napkin of linen. His hostess returned, sitting down beside him offering him pickles and relishes. She told him, "It took us four months, such a long trip. At times I thought we wouldn't make it. Some of the rivers were so deep and swift and the mountain passes had so much snow. Once I thought we would have to throw some of our things away, but we hung onto everything and here we are, grateful we finally arrived safely."

He looked at her with admiration. "In the years ahead, it will be worth it. I assure you this raw West needs the refinement you have brought."

"Yes, already I feel comforted sleeping in my grandmother's four-poster bed when the wolves are howling at night."

The maid brought a wild strawberry dessert and after accepting a second cup of coffee, Nelson arose, thanking his hostess. Nancy was too shy to say goodbye. He left with a feeling there was a secret in the family, for he knew some of the luxury came only from European aristocracy.

The following day Nelson left for the East, then on to Scotland where he entered medical college. He was convinced the frontier was in need of qualified physicians. His studies took longer than he expected for he had signed for extra courses in surgery, pediatrics, and even a short course in dentistry as he planned to fulfill all the needs of small western communities.

Twelve years later when he returned to Canby, Oregon, his first patient was a lovely fifteen-year-old girl with a broken arm. While he was setting the bone and applying the plaster-of-Paris cast, he said to her mother, "I've never forgotten your kindness in feeding a very hungry man, Mrs. Melancon."

"But you don't seem to remember Nancy, whom you saved from the rattlesnake."

"It's hard to believe it's the same little girl. What a difference a few years make! Nancy, I wish I had been here to save you from breaking your arm. It's a bad break. How did it happen?"

She spoke with some embarrassment. "A horse kicked me when I was trying to hook him up to the buggy."

Her mother explained, "My husband is working in Portland for a few months and Nancy and I don't seem to be successful in handling our horse. Stricker knows he can bluff us by kicking."

The doctor thought for a moment. "Years ago when I was traveling through southern Idaho, I had stopped at a ranch to ask directions when I saw a cowboy breaking a wild cayuse. Every time the horse turned its rump to the cowboy to kick him, the man lashed him with a long snake whip. After the fifth try, the horse stopped kicking and I congratulated the cowboy, who laughed and told me, 'Oh, he ain't broke yet. It'll take a few more days before it sinks into his knot head, he ain't suppose to kick.'"

Nancy spoke up, "That's exactly what Stricker needs, a good licking."

Her mother agreed. "He does need to be disciplined."

"Would you like me to try and break your horse?" asked Nelson.

"I would be most grateful," Mrs. Melancon assured him.

"Tomorrow is Sunday. How about three in the afternoon?"

"I want to see him get what he deserves," said Nancy.

Before visiting the Melancons on the next day, Nelson borrowed a drover's whip. Arriving at their place, Nelson found Nancy sitting on the top rail of the corral, waiting for him. He told her, "Better not watch, he might squall."

"I hope he does and I hope it hurts, because my arm has been hurting all day."

"Let me check and see if the bandage has slipped."

Nancy held out her arm, saying, "I wish it hadn't been my right arm."

Nelson carefully checked the bandage. "Seems all right. It might help if you went in and rested your arm on a pillow."

"No, I want to see him get what he deserves."

As soon as Nelson entered the corral, Stricker whirled, backing up to kick him. Nelson let the whip snap across the horse's hindquarters. The horse was a beautiful Morgan gelding, his name very appropriate since Stricker seemed determined to keep kicking. Several more times Stricker tried to kick and each time received a lashing. Finally it began to sink in that he wasn't to kick, but Nelson knew it would take several more days to fully break the horse. After an hour of training, both the horse and Nelson were sweating and Nelson decided it was enough for the day as he didn't want to break the horse's spirit.

Nelson leaned against the corral, coiling the whip, looking up at Nancy. The bright sun turned her golden curls into a halo and her dark blue eyes shown with such adoration, he turned quickly away. For the first time he felt old, all of his thirty-five years, and she radiated the youthfulness of fifteen.

Nancy smiled, "Do come in and have some cool lemonade and cookies."

"Sorry, I have a patient to see."

"You'll come tomorrow?"

"A friend will take over Stricker's lessons."

He fled from the hurt and disappointment in her eyes. She was of an age to be his daughter. For days he struggled with himself. After all, he had saved her, why couldn't she belong to him?  He wanted her as he had never wanted anything else in his life.  No, it wouldn't be fair to her, and she was much too young to decide for herself.  No, the whole thing was impossible.  When a letter came offering him a physician post in Eastern Washington, he accepted without hesitation.

A few days later while he was hurriedly packing his office equipment in preparation for his departure, the office door slowly opened.  He turned and dropped a packing box.  "Nancy!!"  He rushed to her side.  "What has happened?"

She sobbed brokenheartedly, holding out her arm to show him her broken cast.  Trying to calm her he said, "You seem to have a penchant for getting hurt.  I think I'll have to be your protector and…"

"I don't want you to ever go away."

"Nancy, do you know what you are saying?"

"Yes, I do.  I love you.  I want to be with you always."

"But I'm so much older than you."

She looked at him defiantly.  "I don't think love knows anything about age."

It had happened so many years ago and somehow she had been right.

The difference in their ages never had mattered.  Their marriage had brought them untold happiness.  Nelson took his wife in his arms.  "My dear, if you hadn't broken the cast on your arm, we would never have had all these happy years and wonderful children."

Nancy snuggled under his chin.  "You were leaving and I was desperate."

"My dear, if such a thing is possible, I want you for my wife for eternity."

"Nelson, love is eternal so I'll always be by your side."

Nelson bent his head, kissing her.  "You are a blessing from the Creator and I love you."

Nancy happily laughed.  "Now that's settled, how about some food?"

"Good idea."

Nancy stood at the foot of the stairs, calling, "Anna, come at once, your father is famished."

To her surprise Charlie came leaping down the stairs. "Mama, let me help, the girls are busy."

She was amazed to see her son vigorously mashing potatoes; she had never seen him even peel a potato. When everything was on the table she asked, "Aren't the girls coming?"

"No, Mama, you know how determined they are to outshine all the other girls with their bizarre fashions."

"You mean it's your fraternity brothers they want to impress. But they must eat."

Charlie spoke firmly. "The girls are busy."

The girls were sprawled on their beds, feeling woozy and dizzy. The coffee had helped and Charlie had promised to bring them another pot.

Nancy shook her head. "Maybe later the girls will take time to eat. Meanwhile, you, your father, and I won't wait."

"You and Papa go ahead. I promised to take them another pot of coffee."

Doctor seemed to be fascinated with his pork chop. Suddenly, looking up at his son, he said, "Take them tomato juice with some lemon."

Charlie froze. He knew it was the usual drink to regain sobriety when one had overindulged. How could his father possible know? Charlie panicked and made for the kitchen, his father calling after him, "And take down that confounded rope dangling out the window. Makes the house look like a jail with inmates escaping."

"Yes, sir," Charlie fled, groaning. Why did he have a father who knew everything?

The next day dawned on a quiet household. The sun shone through cumulus clouds, gilding the breakfast table with dancing sunbeams sifting through breeze-tossed locust leaves. Home-born happiness radiated on family faces. Only Charlie had a frown of displeasure as he anxiously scanned his sisters' faces with surprise and annoyance. He expected to see bags under their eyes, but they showed no sign of yesterday's indiscretion. How was it possible they could look so demure and innocent? It went to prove, Charlie decided, you couldn't trust women.

Nancy smiled lovingly at her husband. "Nelson, I can tell you have something on your mind."

"Yes, my dear, you are very observing. I was going to say in a few moments there will be a surprise."

They looked at each other, wondering what it could be.

It was a timeless tradition for the doctor to give a special blessing at the breakfast table. They bowed their heads and the doctor cleared his throat. "Heavenly Father…"

Bang! Bang! the front door knocker loudly clanged. Doc paused. "Amy, will you answer the door?"

"Yes, Papa."

Maybelle whispered, "It must be the surprise."

Nancy worriedly glanced at her husband. "Someone must be ill. Nelson, do eat your breakfast before you have to leave."

They were astonished when Amy returned carrying a very long and narrow beautifully beribboned box. She smirked, "It seems a messenger of affection has brought a gift for Nettie."

"I know of no one who has affection for me," Nettie said stiffly.

"Then it's mine. Many are dying with affection for me," Amy said starting to rip off the ribbons.

Nettie jumped up, grabbing the box. Amy hung on and in the tussle, the lid flew off and a cascade of red roses fell to the floor.

"Roses!" exclaimed everyone. Amy grabbed the fluttering note, pretending to read, "Kiss my lips the …"

"Stop!" Nettie lunged for the note. Amy, being the taller, held the note above her head continuing to tease, "My love for you is undying and…"

Nettie was furious. "Mama, make her give it to me!"

But it was her father who sternly commanded, "Amy, it belongs to Nettie."

Amy reluctantly handed over the note, saying, "It must be that hooked-nose Jake who is so smitten with you."

Nettie hastily gathered the roses and fled up the stairs to her room, locking the door behind her. With trembling hands, she unfolded the tissue-thin note:

Damsel of my Heart
A reminder of our rendezvous at three
This afternoon
Your devoted pirate
Bob

Nettie rapturously flung herself across the bed. It was the first time in her whole life any romantic thing had ever happened. She hugged the roses and tenderly kissed them with tears of joy. It was overwhelming to think someone cared so much as to send her roses. She hugged the roses to her breast. She would press them and keep them forever.

A knock at the door interrupted her reverie. "Go away," Nettie sniffed.

"But I've brought a vase of water for your roses," Maybelle pled. "Please open the door."

"Oh, all right." Nettie reluctantly opened the door.

Together they arranged the fragrant roses in the vase. Abruptly dropping a rose, Nettie slumped on the bed clutching a hand to her forehead. "Oohhh!"

Maybelle rushed to her with concern. "What's the matter?"

"I just remembered."

"What?"

"You remember what happened yesterday?"

"How could I forget?"

"Bob is the one who unhooked my dress from the snag and carried me safely up to my room."

"Is he the one who sent you the roses?"

Nettie nodded. "You know how boozed up we were."

"Oh, you make it sound so terrible."

"It was worse than terrible. He can only think of me as a hussy—or worse."

"He sent you the roses. Maybe he's forgotten."

"No, the roses are just to entice me to meet him so he can make improper advances."

"How do you know all that?"

"Amy. She's so worldly. She knows everything about men."

"Only because she reads those books Mama and Papa say she is not to read."

"I can't take a chance. I can't meet him and, oh Maybelle, he's so handsome. I always dreamed of having a sweetheart like him. Oh, my life is ruined, yes ruined, all because of Papa's horrid intoxicating medicine!" Nettie flung herself on the bed and sobbed brokenheartedly.

Maybelle shook her sister. "You're being silly. Those roses must have cost a fortune coming all the way from Walla Walla. No man would spend that much money just to entice. He sent them because he likes you very much and would never say anything to offend you."

Nettie, hiccupping, raised a tear-drenched face. "But…but no man can respect an intoxicated woman and I…I…I was so drunk." She flung herself back onto the pillow, weeping.

Maybelle, being unable to console her sister, left to confront Amy about her stupid revelations of men, which would probably have the effect of making Nettie an old maid for life.

After looking in all the rooms, Maybelle was about to give up finding Amy when she thought of the grape arbor. Skipping down the garden path, she came upon Amy sitting on a bench almost hidden by grapevines. Maybelle wasn't fooled to see her sister holding up a *New Christian Youth* periodical. Amy, deeply engrossed in her reading, didn't hear her sister approach until she was beside her. Startled, Amy jumped and a book fell from behind the Christian magazine. She quickly snatched up the book and sat on it. "Well, what are you snooping around for?"

"I'm going to tell Mama you're reading that horrid book again."

"You do and I'll tell Mama you've lost her cameo brooch you borrowed from her."

"Amy, your reading trash that will ruin your whole life and it's ruining Nettie's life now. You told her…"

"Nonsense. I only told her…"

"Enough to make her an old maid for life."

"Little sister, you're too young to have any understanding about life."

"I'm old enough to know what life is about."

"What is it about?" Amy challenged.

"It's about love, wonderful miracles, and…"

"Ha, ha, do you ever have a lot to learn. This is real life. Listen to this." Amy opened the book, starting to read, "'His passion was devouring her…'."

"Stop, stop!" shouted Maybelle putting both hands over her ears. " I don't want to hear anymore of that slushy stuff. That's not love."

"Why isn't it love?"

"Passion isn't love, it…it's animalism."

Amy sneered, "Sounds like Papa. Since you know so much, then what is love?"

"It's heaps of affection, kindness, cherishing…"

"And simmering passion," Amy glowed at the thought.

"Amy, something terrible is going to happen to you for disobeying Mama and Papa. You are filling your mind with stuff that's going to make trouble for you."

"Go and peddle your opinions some other place."

"All right, I will." Maybelle went to hunt for her brother who was rummaging through the kitchen cupboards for something to eat.

"Charlie," said Maybelle.

"Yeah?"

"Charlie, Nettie's whole life is ruined and you've got to do something about it."

"Never, never bother a starving man with such a momentous problem."

"Would a piece of strawberry cream pie help?"

"Make it two pieces and the problem is solved."

Charlie followed Maybelle into the pantry. Since her sister faced the catastrophe of being a spinster for life, Maybelle didn't hesitate cutting into a freshly baked pie when she knew she was going to have to face punishment for the act.

While Charlie wolfed down the pie, savoring each luscious bit, Maybelle poured out the whole dreadful situation. Charlie tried to look concerned and nodded his head from time to time, afraid if he didn't show a proper degree of solicitude he would be deprived of the second piece of pie.

After she told him the main details, Maybelle looked fiercely at her brother. "You've got to think of something."

"How about bringing one of my fraternity brothers around for her?"

"That's out. She's in love with Bob."

"She can't be. No one can fall in love in two minutes."

"Nettie did."

"Then it's just puppy love and won't last. She'll be over it by tomorrow."

"Not Nettie."

"What do you want me to do, for Pete's sake?"

"Bring Bob here."

"Nothing doing."

"Why not?"

"Because I'm not going to implicate a fraternity brother."

"But he wants to be implicated."

"How are you so sure?"

"Don't the roses prove it?"

"I'm not sure."

"You're always complaining about not having a brother. Well, if Bob were your brother-in-law, he would almost be your brother."

"Sis, you're getting way ahead of the game."

"No, I'm not."

"Cut me another piece of pie."

"Not until you promise to do something."

Charlie tried to evade the issue but under his sister's determined attack, he finally promised to confront Nettie's heartthrob. "Oh, all right, I'll meet him at the ice cream parlor this afternoon."

Maybelle flung her arms around her brother, giving him a warm kiss. "Oh Charlie, I knew you'd think of the right thing to do."

"Yeah, and maybe it ain't."

# Chapter 6

# Cupid Strikes

At three sharp that afternoon, Charlie was at Neville's Ice Cream Parlor thinking that if Bob spent that much dough on such a noncommittal thing as roses he was sure to be there. Just as he had expected, as soon as he entered, he saw Bob's mop of wavy, brown hair rise above the back of the booth. Charlie slid in beside in him and delivered the news. "She isn't coming."

Bob grinned. "Of course."

"Why in the hell did you come then?"

"I want my wife to know I kept our first date."

"Have you gone balmy? You only saw Nettie once and she was drunk. Besides, you're too old for her," Charlie frowned, shaking his head.

Bob gave a snort. "Your father is twenty years older than your mother."

"How do you know?"

"Information travels."

"Nettie is just fourteen."

"I can wait. I'm twenty-one, giving me a seniority edge of seven years, enough to make me boss."

"Cripes, you're as eccentric as Papa. I've had enough." As Charlie got up to leave, Bob said brightly, "Thanks, old man, for inviting me to dinner tonight."

"I said no such thing."

"I thought you said to be there at six o'clock sharp."

"You're a weirdo," Charlie shouted back as he flung himself out the door.

The laughter following him sounded demonic to Charlie. He had had enough of screwballs for one day. Remembering his father had known about the roses several minutes before they arrived, and now one of his best friends appeared to have gone bonkers, Charlie decided it was too much for him to bear. As a freshman in college, he always looked up to Bob, a senior who had seemed to be so brilliantly intellectual. Now he turned out to be a nut.

Charlie strode up the street like a man with a definite destination. He was going to find some answers or he was going to be just as screwy. Charlie was thinking so intently about his problem, he failed to notice a passing carriage with a lovely girl curiously watching him. Nor did he hear Mrs. Metcalf calling him, asking him to take a jar of her famous mincemeat to his mother. He passed the ballpark without a glance. At last he opened an iron gate and walked up a pansy-bordered walk to a white-washed, green-shuttered house and banged the brass knocker without hesitation.

Professor Hoagland opened the door. "Well, young man, what can I do for you?"

"Please, may I come in? I have a very serious matter to discuss."

"By all means, come in. I only hope I'm up to the honor of your visit."

Charlie knew from the talk in town that if anyone could give him some answers, it was this highly educated man. He had been a professor of physics and philosophy in some Eastern university until he retired. He had come out West to visit his sister and had remained.

Charlie wasted no time in stating the reason for his visit. "There is something wrong with my father."

"I hope it's not serious. Is his health failing?"

"No, it's not that. It's worse. I fear it's his mind."

"What seems to be the problem?"

"It's sort of hard to explain. He sees things no one else sees and he knows things no one else knows."

Professor Hoagland thoughtfully rubbed his chin. Looking at the young man's troubled face, he knew the respect of a son for his father was at stake. Years ago when his sister had been dying of pneumonia, Dr. Andrus had saved her life. Every since he had wanted to do something for this fine physician in appreciation. Paying the doctor bill had not been enough. Perhaps this was his opportunity. Dr. Andrus was too fine a man to lose the esteem of his only son.

Charlie nervously clasped and unclasped his hands. "Some folks whisper it's the devil that tells him things; others say it's dead people coming back. Do you think that's true?"

"Young man there is intelligence way beyond our knowing. The whole universe is run by law. It's within the confines of law when a certain note is played, say on a violin. The vibration is transmuted through the air and produces a resonating vibration in another object, for an example let's say a glass goblet. If the goblet is not flexible enough to respond, it shatters. Everything operates in a sonic range of vibration. Do you follow me?"

"Well, sort of."

"Resonance can occur in buildings, animals, humans. In fact, everything."

"What has that got to do with my father?"

"Your father has what is called Cosmic Sensory Perception. Little is known about it now, but it works in anyone that is in resonance with the transmission. In other words, Cosmic Sensory Perception is the resonance of one individual who may be in resonance with another person, object, or event, regardless of distance or time."

"That's pretty heavy stuff."

"You've read the Bible?"

"My father reads it every night."

"Then you know about the prophets of olden days?"

"Yeah, they knew about things before they happened and warned people."

"Exactly, because they had Cosmic Sensory Perception like your father. Prophets are men chosen and blessed by God. We can safely say your father is a prophet."

The professor watched the boy's face struggling for comprehension. In fact, Charlie was overwhelmed, thinking one moment his father was crazy and now finding he was up there next to God. He said, "I'm soon going back to school, and I'm going to study all about that resonance stuff you talk about so I can understand by father better."

"Young man, that's a splendid idea, but unfortunately it's not being taught in any Western college."

Just then Henrietta, the professor's sister, came in carrying the tea tray. "Charlie, you must join us. I've made a delicious spiced pound cake from your mother's recipe."

"Thanks, I'd like that."

She cozily sat down beside him, smiling warmly. "Have any of your sisters any amorettos as yet?"

"I...I'm not sure."

"Oh well, they are still young. I was talking to Mrs. Aims just yesterday and she told me she has some very fine young men lined up for your sisters."

Charlie gave a groan, but wanting to be polite said, "Who does she have for Amy?"

"Let's see, now who was it? Oh yes, she mentioned Jake."

"But his nose is awfully large and crooked."

"He's a very fine young man and he's going to inherit his father's pig farm."

Charlie tried desperately to stay calm. "Who does she have for Mae?"

"Neville, of course."

"But Papa won't even allow him to date Mae."

"Mrs. Aims knows all about that and says she plans to make your father come around."

In a weak voice Charlie said, "I hope she doesn't have anyone for me."

"Oh, but she does—lovely Mary Ann."

Charlie choked and the professor had to pound him on the back before he could get his breath. The professor turned to his sister. "I believe that's enough matchmaking."

When he was breathing again, Charlie made an observation that was well known by the whole town. "Mrs. Aims seems to have an awfully lot to do with everyone's business."

"Much too much," the professor said, frowning.

Henrietta sniffed, "I was just warning Charlie what Mrs. Aims was up to."

Her brother turned to Charlie. "Young man, you might inherit your father's gift for cosmic perception."

Charlie shook his head. "I don't believe I'd want it. It would be pretty terrible to know that the next day you were going to fall in the river and drown."

"It does takes a man with great inner strength and discipline to handle such a gift," the professor acknowledged.

"I guess my father is pretty great," Charlie said.

"Indeed he is, and don't you ever forget it." In a kinder tone, Professor Hoagland added, "I'm proud to know such a distinguished man as your father."

Charlie quickly finished his cup of tea, thanked his hostess, and shook hands with the professor, saying, "You're a highly intelligent man, Professor, and I sure appreciate your explaining everything to me. I'm afraid I only understood half of what you told me."

Professor Hoagland handed him a large, black, gold-lettered volume, saying, "Take this, young man. It will teach you some very interesting things pertaining to your father. Anything you don't understand, feel free to consult me."

"Gee, that's great. Thanks." With a final goodbye, Charlie bounded down the steps, relieved that his father was okay, but some of the things the professor had told him gave him other worries. He knew his father believed there were other planets with intelligent life. What if they were so intelligent they could resonate with some bonehead on earth who couldn't resonate back and the whole earth would explode like the glass goblet?

Charlie shook his head in perplexity. Things were getting complicated. He turned into his home street and suddenly stopped at the thought of Bob. He certainly wasn't smart enough to resonate when he was dumb enough to fall for his fickle sister in two minutes. Charlie kicked a stone from the walk, trying to do some strenuous thinking. On the other hand, if Bob resonated at the same time his sister resonated... Charlie suddenly stopped, letting his breath out with a hiss. My God, then Bob would be his brother-in-law! Charlie picked up a rock and threw it across the street. Not a chance. He didn't want Bob around to make him feel stupid. He was okay as a friend, but at a distance and definitely not in the family.

Charlie started running down the street, determined that if Bob crashed dinner tonight, he'd throw him out. Going into the house he decided he'd perk up his low feelings by calling on Tilly and went to the hall closet for his fraternity jacket. A tortured bellow practically shook the house. Nancy came running to find her son holding up his jacket as he roared, "Who stole the buttons off my jacket?"

In disgust, his mother said, "It has buttons."

"My jacket had *brass* buttons."

"I simply don't understand what all the fuss is about," said Nancy, following Charlie into the parlor.

"I think I smell a rat!" Charlie shouted as he stalked to where the girls' button memory strings were on display. "Ah ha, there they are." Charlie pointed an accusing finger at buttons glistening on six memory strings. "My thieving sisters have stolen my buttons for their damn strings."

His mother admonished, "Charlie, there will be no swearing in this house."

Mae, peering over the banister, called down, "Charlie, we sewed on good, serviceable buttons."

"Oh yeah, old, chipped, bone buttons."

"Why are you complaining? They hold your jacket together better than your old tarnished brass buttons."

"Of all the stupid remarks I've ever heard and after all I've done for you!"

"Not much."

"If it's the last thing I do in my life, I'll get even with you."

Mae's pleading voice warned, "No date if..."

"No, I won't tell."

Nancy's eyes flared. "I demand to know what you won't tell."

"W...why, nothing much, just th...th...that." Charlie was floundering.

"We emptied the cookie jar," Mae's urgent voice piped.

Nancy wasn't fooled, but she didn't press the matter.

Shrugging into his jacket and jamming on his cap, Charlie stomped out as Nancy called after him, "Charlie, don't be late for supper."

She could bet he wasn't going to be late, Charlie assured his mother, determined to be home just in case that fool showed up.

Charlie didn't know what do to with himself. He was out of the mood to see Tilly, and his sisters screamed at him every time he asked them to go fishing with him. Bob was a sickening bore being so love-smitten with Nettie. Oh, he liked Bob, as long as there was no chance of him horning into the family. Charlie wouldn't admit it, but be wanted to be the only one adored by his sisters. It hurt like hell that Bob was handsomer and smarter, and since women were inclined to be fickle, his sisters were sure to cling to Bob's coattail like simpering little fools. No, he'd keep Bob as a friend, but at a distance.

He could take Tilly to Neville's for ice cream, but she'd expect him to pay for it and he was broke. What a crazy custom, women expecting a man to pay for their treats; why couldn't they take their turn to pay? He walked past his father's office without stopping. He had already spent his allowance in advance and he

## Chapter 6 - Cupid Strikes

had to wait another week for more money. His father was really too strict about such matters. He would have to find some way to earn some money. He was trying to figure out how when a "Hiss!" behind him whirled him around. A short, dumpy, ruddy-faced, middle-aged man caught up with him.

"Sonny, want to earn ten smackers?"

"Sorry, I don't rob banks."

"Stop trying to be smart. I mean real dough. Interested?"

"Doing what?"

"Come on, kid. Follow me."

"Where to?" Looking at this greasy, bald-headed, pot-bellied quirk, Charlie felt skeptical. "Maybe you don't even have the dough."

"Don't I?" blustered the man pulling out of his pocket a handful of silver dollars. Juggling them in the air while looking at Charlie with a speculative eye, he enticed, "They're yours, kid, if you do me a little favor."

"What kind of favor?"

The little guy jerked his head, motioning Charlie up the street. "Come on."

Those gleaming silver dollars had an electrifying effect on Charlie, so he followed him up the street. They turned into a side land where a gaudily painted covered wagon stood in the shade. Charlie's eyes popped as he stared with fascination at the colorful pictures painted on the wagon's canvas cover. Awed by the pictures he commented, "Those girls are sure pretty."

"Yeah, they recovered their health by taking Dr. Cooper's cure-all medicine."

"Oh, so *you're* the medicine man who shoved into town early this morning."

"Yeah, but be more respectful. I'm Dr. Cooper."

"Well, Doc, what's your deal?"

"All you have to do when I introduce you is to stand on the wagon seat, flex your muscles, and tell the towns folk how you recovered from lumbago, boils, runny nose…oh hell, anything else you can think of that could go wrong with you. Ten bucks to start and for every extra bellyache or whatever, I'll add another smacker."

This was too good to be true, and Charlie did some fast figuring. He'd think up enough ailments to make twenty dollars. This would be the easiest money he had ever earned.

Out of curiosity, the townspeople began to gather. To bring them in faster, Dr. Cooper struck a large, iron triangle, hissing to Charlie to stand on the wagon seat and take off his shirt. Charlie didn't hesitate to rip off his shirt and flex his muscles while Dr. Cooper stood beside him holding high a red-and-yellow-labeled bottle.

"LADIES AND GENTLEMEN, by taking Dr. Cooper's famous medicine, this young man fully recovered his health after suffering untold agony from…" The quack gave a vigorous nod to Charlie who energetically took his cue. "I was about to die from lumbago, arthritis, meningitis, St. Vitus' dance, chilblains…" Charlie was counting dollars in his head. He needed five more ailments to make twenty dollars. His mind seemed to go blank. Wildly fumbling for another ailment, he blurted, "…worms, lice, and…"

Dr. Cooper gave Charlie a dirty look. He then turned to his audience broadly smiling. "That's enough to assure you good people of Dayton what tremendous healing powers are in Dr. Cooper's cure-all medicine, able to restore this once emasculated man to full vigor and virility and make him the healthy, handsome man he is today. Tell them, young man, to what do you owe your vigorous health?"

Charlie held up a bottle of the medicine man's brew and took a big gulp. Then flexing his muscles, he said, "To Dr. Cooper's med..." Hearing hilarious laughter, he looked down into a pair of highly amused violet eyes. The word stuck in his throat, and he dove off the wagon seat as if propelled out of a cannon. Slinking down an alley, he felt like an idiot, a cad. Even his sisters, with all their persuasiveness, would never be able now to get him a date with the only girl who could make his heart flip. Lucky her father wasn't there to arrest him. Wearing a sheriff's badge gave him the authority to put any fraud in jail.

Charlie's belly began hurting and he cursed himself for drinking the quack's rotgut. "Ohhhhh," he groaned, grabbing his stomach and running for home.

Dr. Andrus ushered Mrs. Delany out of his counseling room, saying, "You had a light stroke. You will recover, but you must stop eating so much fat pork."

"Thank you, Doctor, and I will certainly follow your advice."

Dr. Andrus motioned for his next patient. "All right, Mrs. Lee, come in."

Just then the outside door was flung open and Mrs. Aims breezed in, looking neither to the left nor right, and marched right past the doctor and Mrs. Lee into his private office. Doc remonstrated, "I'm sorry, but Mrs. Lee is next."

Mrs. Aims sniffed, seating herself across from the desk. "Makes no difference, won't hurt her to wait. I come with a life and death matter." She adjusted her hat so the daisies were in alignment with her right ear before she gave her startling news. "Charlie is going to die. I saw with my own eyes him drinking that quack's painkiller. He's your very own son," Mrs. Aims choked, her eyes ablaze. "Your son had the nerve to say no doctor, and you're the only doctor in town, could cure him of St. Vitus' dance, but Dr. Cooper's medicine made him a healthy man again. Then do you know what he did?"

"I have no idea."

"He drank that quack's painkiller to show how it killed the pain of his arthritis, then he flexed his muscles, which he ain't got, and danced on the wagon seat like a fool. What do you think of that?"

Doc thoughtfully rubbed his chin. "At least, Mrs. Aims, with that powerful painkiller in him he will die without pain." Then knowing Mrs. Aims' longevity in pursuing a subject, he escorted her to the reception room, thanking her for her concern.

With the daisies on her hat quivering, she huffed out the door. "Don't say I didn't warn you!"

John Baker stood up. Doc was surprised. "I was expecting Mrs. Lee to be next."

John grinned. "I'm afraid she was offended when you took Mrs. Aims before her. She left a message. She's not coming back."

"She'll be back when her tooth starts acting up again. Come on in, John." Doc closed the door then seated himself at his desk, motioning John to sit opposite of him. "John, I believe you're making progress. How are you feeling now?"

"Great, just great."

Dr. Andrus wryly smiled. "Hmmm, strange how the upcoming dance has perked you up."

John blushed. "I thought it a courtesy to ask your permission."

"Fannie has passed her eighteenth birthday."

John bowed his head. "I wouldn't think of anything serious until you have me a clean bill of health."

"I respect you for that. Then what?"

"I have an uncle in Arizona who owns a large cattle ranch. For some time he's wanted me to be his head foreman and manage the place. I wouldn't be busting horses or driving cattle. Mainly doing office work."

"That will give you plenty of time to recover."

"That's what I thought, sir."

Doc stood up. "You don't have to dance every dance. You'll make Fannie's evening."

John grabbed Doc's hand, joyfully pumping it up and down.

Doc grew serious. "John, will you drop by the house and tell my wife I want Charlie in my study by five o'clock?"

"I'd be happy to," said John, and with a wave of his hand he went out into the street.

Doc decided to walk home, which would give him more time to think what he could say to Charlie to head him in the right direction.

Nancy met him at the door. "I've never seen Charlie so downcast."

"He's probably doing some rethinking of his actions."

"Nelson, it was really an insult to you."

"No, my dear, he wasn't thinking of me. It was his ego that tripped him up."

"The girls say Charlie told them he thought it to be a good business adventure and he could make some money. But it went bust, as he expressed it."

"He's learning the hard way what every entrepreneur comes up against 'Caveat Emptor.'"

Nancy looked up anxiously at her husband. "He is in your study, reading a book Professor Hoagland has loaned him."

"Hopefully it will be something beneficial." Doc pecked his wife on the cheek and entered his study.

Charlie, ensconced in an over-sized wing chair, was reading voraciously a subject well over his head. Pretending nonchalance to his father's presence, he stood up and respectfully said, "Yes, sir?"

Charlie had expected a roar of denouncement and he felt a little deflated under his father's stern glance. He shivered with fear. That no-nonsense look was a bad sign and he felt it was a preamble to a scathing accusation. Charlie nervously hitched up his pants, giving him time to assemble his defense. Holding up the book Professor Hoagland had loaned him, he said, "Sir, it's about cosmic perception."

The doctor took the book, examining it. "Rather a paradoxical subject. Why are you interested in such advanced scientific study?"

Not having yet acquired the suave tactfulness of more mature minds, Charlie blurted, "I thought, sir, that you were possessed or afflicted or something, what with all your knowing stuff no one else knew, so I went to the professor for some answers."

Doc lifted an inquiring eyebrow. "And?"

"I found you were next to God."

"I hope your further studies will be more enlightening."

Charlie eagerly said, "The professor is going to help me understand you better."

"My son, I believe you are the one who needs to better understand yourself."

Charlie inwardly shivered, thinking now was coming the reprimand. He beat his father to the punch. "I know I'm a stupid ass to have bamboozled into such an idiotic thing."

"Haven't I told you this earth is a schoolhouse where we learn our lessons about life?"

"Oh, God, I must be in kindergarten."

"Our Creator has given you freedom to choose between what is rational and what isn't."

"How do I know what isn't rational?"

"What is irrational is out of sync with the Creator's creation and will destroy you. Making rational choices is in harmony with Creation and will guide and protect you. What you did today, was that rational?"

"Oh, God, no!"

"But you're learning. Always remember to check before any action taken and decide whether or not your action will be good for all of Creation."

Charlie threw his arms around his father. "This planet is sure one tough schoolhouse."

Doc gave his son a pat as Nancy called, "Supper."

## Chapter 7

# Miracles by the Minute

The members of the family were seating themselves at the old claw-foot oak dining table with the expectancy of savoring Amy's specialty of chicken dumplings when they were startled by a vigorous pounding on the front door.

"Drat it," Amy snapped with exasperation. "The dumplings will fall flat if they are kept waiting."

Charlie flung down his napkin and jumped to his feet, certain it was Bob, who no doubt thought he had cleverly manipulated a way to see Nettie. Charlie's muscles twitched, thinking how quickly this uninvited guest was going to land in his mother's bed of peonies.

Nancy hurriedly waved her son back, saying, "Never mind, I'll get the door. I have to find the relish anyway." Charlie slumped back in his chair with a groan.

Nancy opened the door. Her voice gave an upward lilt, questioning, "Yes?" Not the kind of greeting for an expected guest.

The young man placed his hand against the porch pillar as if in need of support. He nervously cleared his throat. "Good evening, Mrs. Andrus. I'm Bob Allen, a close friend of your son, who has generously invited me to have dinner with him."

He was so nice looking with beautiful wavy, chestnut-brown hair and midnight-blue eyes magnetically captivating her that she opened the door wider. Later she would deal with Charlie for inviting a dinner guest without first consulting her.

Nettie, recognizing the voice, panicked and while all eyes were expectantly looking at the hall doorway, she slid under the table, carefully crawled over several pairs of feet, then lunged for the kitchen door and escaped down the cellar steps.

A meaningful look from his mother forced Charlie to make the introductions, which he did with cool formality. An extra plate was set and Charlie could only grit his teeth as the family, rising to the occasion, politely became acquainted with their unexpected guest. Charlie clenched his fists as Bob poured on the charm, fielding the barrage of questions with friendly, open answers, which captivated his family.

"Yes," Bob smiled, "during the Civil War my family moved from South Carolina, where they had kept slaves, to the state of Ohio."

Maybelle excitedly asked, "Did you live in a large white mansion with tall white pillars?"

Bob nodded, amused, "And all thirty-two rooms had the luxury of a fireplace."

Dr. Andrus spoke up. "Of course, when they moved north, they freed their slaves?"

"Better than that. After they moved, they ran what is known as the Underground Railroad and helped hundreds of Negroes fleeing slavery and the war in the South to freedom in the North."

"Very commendable," Doctor conceded. "Did the war break up your family as it did so many others?"

"Unfortunately, it did."

"Should I be proud of a relative of mine who marched with General Sherman to the sea?"

"It depends, sir, which side you're on" Bob replied, looking keenly at his host.

The doctor turned to Maybelle. "Get the small metal box from my desk, if you would."

"Yes, Papa."

Bob continued the trend of their conversation. "Many will disagree with me but I think Sherman was the greatest of the generals."

The doctor, deep in thought, spoke slowly. "If I recall correctly, he forecast the outcome of the Civil War before it even started."

"Indeed he did. He warned one of his Southern friends that in all of history, no agriculture nation ever won over a mechanized nation and he assured him that the South would fail."

"Which they certainly did, and rightly so, although it still bothers me so many Confederate soldiers starved."

"The citizens suffered just as much because General Sherman strongly believed war must not be waged only between armies but against the citizens as well."

Bob was surprised when the doctor replied with strong criticism. "I feel President Lincoln was much too harsh in his second inaugural address. In talking about eradicating the evils of slavery, he said, 'For every drop of blood with the lash shall be paid by another drawn by the sword'."

Bob clenched his fist. "The irony of it is, sir, most of the lashes were given by Negro foremen to their own people."

Maybelle came carrying a small, battered, metal box, "Papa, is this what you wanted?"

"Yes, my dear, thank you." Almost reverently the doctor took from the old, metal box a scarred and faded tintype picture of a Union soldier and his wife. "My cousin. You will notice a dent in the center of the picture. The story is, during the siege of Atlanta he was carrying this picture in his breast pocket when he was shot, and this tintype saved his life."

Bob, looking intently at the picture, gravely remarked, "The fall of Atlanta destroyed the Confederate confidence."

Dr. Andrus nodded. "I've been told the impact of its fall was greater psychologically than materially."

"Yes, I think that is so. Your relative must have been in the thick of it, marching through Georgia with General Sherman to the sea. The Southerners will never forgive them for burning their corn and cotton fields, their mansions, barns, and stables. They say smoke could be seen from horizon to horizon."

"What happened to Savannah?" asked the doctor.

"The city fell during the holidays and General Sherman wired President Lincoln, giving the city to him for a Christmas present. What the army didn't loot, the stragglers and carpetbaggers did."

The doctor lifted from the box a beautiful diamond and ruby brooch, saying, "If I knew my cousin had looted this piece of jewelry, I wouldn't value it so much."

Maybelle took the brooch, holding it up to the light, and in fascination watched the jewels sparkle. Watching her, Bob said, "It could have been donated by some Southern belle, for the Confederate treasury appealed for contributions to help pay for the war."

The doctor took the brooch, placed it back in the box, and said, "There is a strange rumor going around."

"What is that, sir?"

"That the Civil War was instigated by European financial powers to get control of the wealth of the cotton industry."

"Then it wasn't to free the slaves?" Bob gasped.

"Apparently not. To stop slavery was only a front to get the North into war, according to the rumors now circulating."

Bob's face turned livid. "Generations of Southerners will never forgive the destruction of their way of life."

The doctor thoughtfully fingered his fork. "One of my friends says the war isn't over yet. If America ever has an outside enemy, the South will join them in retaliation."

"Sir, your friend must be a Southerner."

Nancy started laughing. "If you two keep on this war talk, we'll all have indigestion."

"You are right, my dear."

Amy grabbed up the tureen of chicken dumplings. "Have a second helping while they are still hot," she urged. "Nothing is more detestable than cold dumplings."

"Your dumplings are delicious, Miss Amy," Bob's warm smile made her blush.

"Thank you. I'm glad you are enjoying them."

Taking a second helping, Dr. Andrus asked, "I understand you're graduating from college this year."

"Yes, my degree will be in architectonics, and I plan to have my own construction company."

"You will return to your home in Ohio?"

"No, I plan to remain in the college town. Statistics list Walla Walla as having more millionaires per ratio to its population than any other town in the States."

"That should make it fertile ground for your business."

A broad smile lit up Bob's handsome face. "That's what I was thinking."

Nancy turned to Bob. "I believe I heard you are the guest of the McGown's."

"Yes, such a wonderful couple."

Doctor patted his mouth with a monogrammed napkin. "And she is an excellent patient."

Charlie could take no more. Bob's charm was churning his stomach. While waiting for dessert, Charlie suggested, "Bob, come with me to the cellar and see the salmon I caught yesterday. I have it on a block of ice. It's sure to win the fish derby."

His mother lifted a warning eyebrow that he was boasting. Inwardly Charlie fumed. Damn it, why couldn't he brag? He couldn't build mansions like Bob intended to, but he could sure catch fish.

An impish impulse overcame Bob's better judgement. "I like fishing myself. When does the derby close?"

"Saturday night at the basket social when prizes will be awarded at the dance. Still time for you to win the booby prize for catching the smallest fish," Charlie chided.

"Mmm, not much time is there?"

"Right, but to make it more interesting, how about a little side wager?" Charlie suggested eyeing the large signet ring on

Bob's finger, which he had coveted for some time. "Say your ring and..."

"And?" Bob's jaw tightened.

"And what? Oh you mean my wager, w...why, how about my solid gold pocket watch?"

Nancy remonstrated, "Your uncle gave it to you when you graduated from high school."

"Don't worry, Mama, it took me a week to catch my prize-winner. Bob can't be that lucky."

Nancy sensed undercurrent of hostility. "Remember that you're friends."

"Mama, we're just having fun."

Nancy wished her husband hadn't retired to his study; he surely wouldn't approve of Charlie's actions.

Bob patted Charlie good-naturedly on the back while reaching for the cellar doorknob as he laughingly challenged, "Show me the monster I have to defeat."

Nettie, hearing the cellar door open, fled over the morning's delivery of coal, heaped in the chute. Slipping and clawing over the large lumps of coal, she emerged in the backyard with her face, dress, and hands streaked with black coal dust.

As the boys started down the stairs, Nancy stopped them "Charlie the cook stove is out of wood. Would you please bring in an armload?"

"Of course, Mama. Bob, I'll be right back."

Bob, stealing glances around, suffered bitter disappointment. Damn it, where was Nettie?

Nancy fully aware as to why this young man was here gave a deep sigh. With six very attractive daughters, how was she going to cope with the droves of enamoured young men until the girls were all married? She turned to Bob. "You must be very fond of flowers sending such beautiful roses to my daughter."

"Yes...yes of course. In fact immensely," he mumbled.

"Maybelle," Nancy called. "Take Bob out to see my prized peonies. It will be a few minutes before dessert is ready."

"Yes, Mama." Maybelle, overwhelmed with the chance of escorting such a handsome man out to see the flowers, chattered incessantly. On the porch she abruptly stopped with a breathless "Ooooh," clapping her hands in ecstasy. "Thank you God for the miracle."

Puzzled, Bob asked, "What miracle?"

"Don't you hear the meadowlark?"

Bob listened. In the distance a bird was trilling a lilting tune. "You call that a miracle?"

"Oh, yes. Think of all the dangers for it, owls and hawks. Yet it keeps on singing so beautifully," she explained, then shyly said, "You see, I collect miracles. They are gifts from God."

"I thought girls collected diamonds."

"Nettie collects diamonds, only she hasn't found any yet. She says she doesn't care about silly birds, moonbeams, or..."

"Who started you collecting such ephemeral things as what you call miracles?"

"Papa taught me to collect them and store them away in my memory chest, then when bad times comes, to take them out and I won't feel so sad."

"Sorry, I don't follow you."

"Let's say you died."

"Let's not be so specific; it makes me uncomfortable."

"Well, let's say Teddy died." Teddy, who was taking a nap on the top step, upon hearing the sound of his name perked up his ear. "I would feel very, very sad to not have Teddy anymore, but I would take from my memory chest a beautiful star-filled night when I was swinging in the old apple tree. I was swinging so high I felt I would soar right into a bowl of stars and..."

"And you didn't feel so sad."

"Exactly. Papa says to start each day asking God to show me His miracles. He says miracles will do me more good in life than being in a stuffy church shouting 'hallelujah.'"

"Your father is against religion?"

"Yes and no. He believes cluttering up dear Mother Earth with all those church monstrosities is an insult to creation.

"You mean cathedrals?"

Maybelle nodded. "All of them. He believes in worshiping like the ancients did by making a circle of stones and stepping inside to say one's prayers. Papa thinks walls of churches shut God out, that in fact one is closer to the Creator when you have His beautiful blue skies above your head and your feet on dear Mother Earth."

Thoughtfully, Bob said, "That takes some heavy-duty thinking. Look, there's a bluebird. Could that be a miracle?"

"Oh, yes. Miracles happen every minute."

"While you're collecting miracles, find one for me," Bob said dejectedly.

"Ooohhh!" Maybelle's mouth flew open, her eyes stared with astonishment at the apparition rounding the corner of the house, then bursting into giggles she pointed behind Bob. "There's your miracle," she blurted, choking with laughter.

Bob whirled around and for a moment was stunned at the sight of the most disheveled, despicable, dirty bit of femininity he had ever seen.

Nettie, shocked at the unexpected sight of them on the porch, gathered up her skirts and fled up the street.

Bob leaped over Teddy to chase after her. Teddy, delighted with all the action, barked excitedly and danced in circles, tangling with Bob's long legs. By the time Bob had thrown a stick for Teddy to fetch, Nettie had gained half a block. Bob took off, his athletic legs stretching out. Nettie, quickly glancing back and seeing she was losing ground, turned and dashed up a flower-bordered walk and into a yellow-trimmed Gothic house, slamming the door behind her.

Bob knocked rapidly. When Abigale opened it with a smile, Bob blurted, "You are harboring a…"

"The alley," Abigale said, hearing the back door slam.

"Thanks!" Bob sprinted around the house to the alley.

Abigale's friend came into the hall with the accusation, "You told him where she was."

Abigale shrugged. "Sometimes Cupid needs an assistant."

"But she doesn't want to see him."

"Cynthia, do look out the back door and see what's doing in the alley. I haven't the nerve. I want things to go rightly so very much."

Just yesterday, Nettie had been over and sobbed out her girlish grief. It was shame that kept her from seeing the young man whom Abigale greatly admired and she encouraged his pursuit of the girl she felt ideal for him.

Cynthia with her head stuck out the back door kept saying, "Oh...oh...dear."

Abigale jumped up. "For heaven's sakes, Cynthia, what is happening?"

In the alley, Bob easily gained on the tiring girl. Teddy had joined in the chase and Bob shouted to him, "Catch her, Teddy!"

Teddy bounced, barking around her billowing skirts. "No, no, Teddy!" she screamed. Teddy sprang against her and down she sprawled in the dust. Bob skidded beside her and lifted her, pinning her flaying arms and holding her tightly against his chest.

Nettie, desperately trying to escape, gave a shove, leaving large black smudges on Bob's immaculately white shirt. Bob yanked her back into his arms. "I never thought I'd be proposing to a girl looking such a mess."

Nettie stopped her struggling, looking up at him stunned. "W...w...what did you say?"

"I said I wanted to marry you," Bob almost shouted.

Wide-eyed with shock, Nettie murmured, "We haven't even been properly introduced."

Bob released her and, stepping aside, ruffled his hair into a shaggy jumble, lowered his eyebrows into the vicinity of his nose, bowed low, and said in a gruff voice, "Miss Andrus, allow me to introduce the illustrious and world-famous architect, Mr. Robert William Allen. Mr. Allen, the gorgeous beauty of Dayton."

In spite of herself, Nettie started laughing. "But you don't know anything about me."

"I know everything about you. You once crawled to the cat's dish and drank all its milk, you bit your brother on the nose to get his teddy bear, you made a cake putting in garlic sauce instead of vanilla. You broke your mother's prized cranberry hobnail bowl throwing it at Charlie and you..."

"Stop! I don't want to hear any more of Charlie's blabbering and I hate you."

"Prove it," Bob snapped and leaning over placed his lips firmly on hers. Several moments passed before he raised his head. His eyes were shining as he happily laughed, "That wasn't a kiss of hate if I know anything about kissing."

"It proves you don't respect me."

"For heaven's sake, why not?"

"You kissed me without asking and men don't respect a woman who gets drunk."

Bob's patience was collapsing. "When I kiss I don't ask, and besides, I've gotten drunk myself."

"But I'm a woman."

"Lucky for me. Your sister tells me you want to collect diamonds. Well, here's your chance. Meet me tomorrow afternoon at Jefferson's jewelry store and start your collection."

"It's not proper to accept such a gift from a gentleman."

"It is when you're going to marry him."

"You know Papa's rules."

"Oh, we're old Civil War buddies. He'll agree."

"Don't be so sure, and besides, I want to be courted before I say yes."

"I'm courting right now."

"No flowers."

"A whole drayload of roses are on the way now from Walla Walla."

"No candy."

"Right now Neville is making your favorite chocolates."

"No presents."

"Would you prefer a shiny new sports carriage or a castle by a lake?"

"Oh, Bob, a castle would be impossible."

"Not when you're marrying a man who is an architect."

Nettie hesitated. "You'll have to ask Papa."

"At once."

"No, not now. All day he's been upset and angry."

"He seemed calm and pleasant at dinner."

"Of course. He wouldn't let company know he's annoyed."

"Explain."

"One of those quack medicine men has arrived in town and Papa says he sells rotgut and..."

"Makes him a lot of sick patients?"

Nettie nodded. "How can people be so stupid as to buy that horrible stuff?"

"Those charlatans are clever in hawking their fraudulent medicine. Have you seen his wagon?"

Nettie shook her head. "No."

"When I saw a large crowd gathered around a canvas-covered wagon, I stopped to see what they were gawking at. Flamboyant pictures were painted in garish colors decorating the canvas top advertising the miracles of his cure-all medicine. One picture showed a young woman, skeleton-thin, pale as a ghost. The next picture was of the same girl after taking the cure for a week, looking radiantly healthy and beautiful."

"Oh, how deceitful," Nettie grimaced.

"But listen to his sales pitch: 'A cure for fifty-two maladies, ranging from heartaches to bone grumblings.' Guess who was shelling out a dollar to buy a bottle?"

"Old Tony, he's bent over with rheumatism."

Bob shook his head. "Abigale."

"Oh no, she can't get sick. She has to help us dress for the dance."

"Don't worry, she has a strong constitution. At the chatauqua I saw her eat three of those indigestible spun-sugar cones."

"Next week Papa is going to Walla Walla to a big medical convention to stop the sale of rotgut."

"I believe he will be successful. Some woman bought a bottle, took some, and fainted."

"Who was it?"

"I don't know, but they carried her to your father's office"

"Poor Papa."

"Darling, tomorrow I'm going fishing. Will you go with me?"

"You know Papa doesn't allow us to date until we're eighteen."

"We won't be dating, just fishing."

"I'm so scared of rattlesnakes," Nettie shuddered.

Bob said, "Take Teddy. He's a rattlesnake killer."

"There's wild range cattle. They're mean and I'm afraid of them."

"This time of year they're up in the hills. Please, darling."

"Well, you'll have to get Papa's blessing—and that means Mother's too."

# Chapter 8

# Surprise Encounter

Bob went to a trusted friend with his concern. Abigale thought it a splendid idea for Nettie to go fishing with him, but she knew Nancy would never allow her daughter to go out alone with a young man. She said, "It will give you a chance to get better acquainted. Never mind the obstacles, I'm sure they can be overcome. Let's see…let me think…"

While Abigale was in deep concentration, Bob's eyes fastened on her with hope. Suddenly snapping her fingers, she laughed, "I have it. Cynthia and I will go with you for a day's outing and we'll get Nancy's permission for Nettie and Maybelle to go along. But," Abigale's eyes twinkled, "when we reach the Swanson's farm, I will suddenly remember I had promised Jane we would visit her, so…we will leave you and the girls to be on your way fishing."

"Maybelle goes too?" Bob asked, sounding disappointed.

"Yes, if Nancy ever found out Nettie had been with you alone, she would never forgive me." True to her word Abigale manipulated arrangements for what should have been a perfect day.

The next morning, when Bob drove the two-seated fringed surrey to the front of the Andrus home, Nettie and Maybelle gaily tripped down the porch steps with Teddy bouncing after them. He was to be the official rattlesnake exterminator. It had taken a whole sausage to convince Teddy to follow them instead of his master.

At the sight of Nettie, dressed in a soft, rose, ruffled voile dress, her curls topped by a wide-brimmed, leghorn picture hat adorned with swirls of ribbons and sweetheart roses, and carrying a matching parasol, Bob caught his breath. She was his dream girl. Cynthia leaned forward from the back seat. "My dear, you look ravishingly beautiful."

"It's something new in fishing outfits I've not seen before," Abigale teased.

Nettie blushed. "A suntan would look simply terrible with my new ball gown, so I have to be protected from the sun."

"Of course," Abigale smiled.

Bob lifted the girls up to their seats. Teddy sat whining; he wanted to be lifted up too. Bob laughed, "Teddy, you're a scalawag, you could jump, but up you go," and he heaved the little dog up beside the girls.

Nancy came out the door, waving to her friends, calling, "Have a wonderful day."

"It's a shame you can't go with us," Abigale said, waving her kerchief and feeling a little guilty over her hypocrisy.

Nancy shook her head. "Today is Nelson's birthday and I must bake him his favorite whipped cream cake." She stood on the drive waving until they were out of sight. Going back into the house, she felt a little depressed. Amy should have stayed and helped with the family washing, but she had insisted on visiting her friend Sally, and the other girls were madly sewing on their new gowns. Thinking maybe a hot drink would give her a needed lift, she went into the kitchen and made a cup of chamomile tea.

Bob's passengers were having a gay time chattering when suddenly they stopped to stare at a fast approaching buggy. The fiery black horse was being driven into a gallop. As the rig flashed past, they had a glimpse of a red-headed man and a girl, almost obscured by her parasol.

"Who is that?" Nettie demanded

Abigale frowned. "He's the son of the McCall's, a wealthy wheat rancher, living on the other side of Walla Walla."

"And a wild one they say," added Cynthia.

"And who is that girl? She seems to be trying to hide herself," Nettie asked, turning in the seat for another look.

"Don't you know your own sister? It's Amy. I recognize the violet ruffled dress she put on this morning," Maybelle answered with certainty.

Nettie shook her head. "It can't be, she told Mama she would be with Sally all day."

"Well, it is Amy and she lied to Mama and I'm going to tell," Maybelle threatened.

Abigale leaned forward. "Maybe it's best not to tell, considering we might not have told all either."

Maybelle looked at her wide-eyed. "What do you mean?"

Abigale winced, thinking, Drat it. I let my tongue slip. Out loud she said, "I...I mean we didn't exactly tell your mother we were going fishing, did we?"

"No, maybe you're right. I guess I won't tell."

Bob knew exactly where they were going and gave the delivery barn team a swat with the reins. In a swirl of dust they came to the old, log-covered bridge. At the entrance, a large, hand-lettered poster read "FISH DERBY"; below that, words written in smaller letters were indistinguishable.

Nettie pointed at the sign. "My brother is going to win first prize."

Bob, acting uninterested, casually asked, "Just what is the first prize?"

Maybelle blurted, "Nettie don't tell. It's a secret."

"It is not! Most everyone knows it's going to be one of Mr. Heins' registered black Morgan mares and Judge Frankland is coming all the way from Walla Walla just to do the judging."

Bob turned to smile at Maybelle. "You know, I have a feeling, this is going to be a great day for miracles."

"Oh, I do hope so," Maybelle replied brightly.

Ten miles out of town, Abigale touched Bob's shoulder. "I just remembered I promised Jane that Cynthia and I would spend the day with her. Their farmhouse is just around the bend."

Both of the Andrus girls chorused in surprise, "Aren't you going fishing with us?"

Abigale gave them her most winning smile. "I'm sure you can catch fish without us, and I did promise Jane."

The girls weren't too sure they liked the turn of events. Abigale patted them reassuringly and, stepping down to the ground, looked up sternly. "Bob, I have explicit confidence that you are a gentleman of sound morals."

Bob grinned. "Don't worry. Today my mind is strictly on fish. I'll remember to get you back at the proper time." Bob clucked to the team and with a slap of the reins, they were off in a cloud of dust. Cynthia and Abigale stood waving and calling, "Have a wonderful day."

An hour's more driving and Bob turned the team off the main highway onto a dim wagon road. He was relieved to see no wheel tracks. He wanted this bit of paradise he was headed for all to himself. Last fall, when the sumac were bright crimson and the birch leaves were fluttering flakes of burnished gold, Abigale had taken him to see an old homestead. It had been abandoned after the cedar-shake roof of the log cabin caught fire, and only one charred log remained, slowly rotting back into the bosom of Mother Earth.

In their ramblings they discovered an old orchard with branches gnarled with age, surprising two deer nibbling on the fallen shriveled fruit. Finding a few petite prunes and an old variety of apples still clinging to the branches, they gorged themselves on the sweetness of the fruit. A balmy, fragrant breeze stirred the meadow grass, thick with goldenrod, making it a waving carpet of flaming gold. Feeling adventuresome, they followed a worn overgrown path, pushing aside tangles of stickery bushes, heavy with globes of ruby red rose hips. The trail meandered on through a wild berry patch, the branches drooping with large clusters of red currants, and as they brushed against them the fruit had fallen under their feet, leaving dark red splotches on the ground.

Bob had been holding back a branch of tamarack for Abigale to precede him when she gave a surprised gasp. He quickly stepped to her side. Before them was a large shaded pool of dark, emerald-green water. Tall feathery ferns were mirrored in lacy patterns of the still surface.

The beauty of the scene held them in silent rapture. As they looked on, a covey of quail scurried down to drink. Then from the dark cool depths came a swirl of ripples and a large silvery fin surfaced, its speckled body arching in a breathless leap above an indigo-blue shadow.

Bob gasped, "My God, what an enormous fish!"

Abigale whispered, "We have found old man Curl's secret joy. They are his pets."

Bob spoke low, "There's a feeling of holiness here."

Abigale spoke softly with sadness. "I wish old Curl was still here."

"You knew him?"

Abigale nodded. "For years I visited him and his wife, bringing them small treats from town. He built all the log buildings himself with only a broad axe and a cross-cut saw. He loved this place so very much."

"It's a paradise," Bob said with a deep sense of contentment.

"I felt as badly as he did when he was forced to leave because of the fire and old age." Tears glistened on her cheek and she choked. "For years I have hoped someone would come along to restore the old homestead and love it as he did."

Bob said nothing, but in his heart he knew he was the man who could.

Hearing the horse loudly whinnying, they reluctantly hurried back, frightening several Chinese pheasants, their bright garish plumage, giving life to the dead grass.

They found the horse objecting to the nearness of a browsing elk. Abigale paused beside the buggy. "It makes me sad to leave. It's like parting from an old friend." She climbed into the buggy, looking back. "It's amazing how the lilacs survived the fire. You must see them when they are in full bloom. How beautiful they would be adorning a church for a wedding, masses and masses of heavenly, fragrant, lavender blooms adorning the altar and pews." Turning to Bob, she placed her hand on his shoulder whispering, "Bob, maybe you're the one to make it come true."

An impish grin lit up his face. "Abigale, are you proposing to me?"

Because of their age differences, they both gaily laughed as if the idea were preposterous.

Maybelle brought Bob back from his reverie by expressing her delight in the surrounding country. The road twisted and wound along the banks of a gurgling stream as it tumbled down into little water falls on its way to join the mighty Columbia River.

Teddy's excited barking drew their attention to a brown bear ambling into the shade of a tall fir tree. Now and then, grouse whirred up from the roadside, startling the horses.

Bob clucked to the team and lightly touched them with the buggy whip until they broke into a trot. He was anxious to see the old homestead. His heart beat faster when they came to a tumbled-down rail fence with wild roses in full bloom softening its decay. The strong scent of lilacs wafted on a rising breeze, intoxicating them into breathing deeply of their fragrance. As they rounded a bend, Maybelle jumped to her, feet crying in wonder, "A sea of lavender lilacs! How gorgeous !!!"

Bob smiled at the excited girl. "They have survived the fire to bring you their beauty and fragrance. I guess you can chalk that up as being the day's first miracle."

Maybelle cast a sly glance at him. "I believe you've become a miracle-seeker yourself."

"Maybe I have."

Nettie gave a disgusted sniff. "I think both of you are silly."

Bob tied the horse's reins to a fence post and gathered up his fishing gear, telling the girls, "You can follow me until your tired, then you can come back and pick a bouquet of lilacs to take home."

Bob donned his rubber waders and they followed him to the gurgling stream, rushing clear and glacier-cold over the colored pebbles below. Maybelle started lifting larger rocks along the misted shore. She held up a small wiggly, yellow worm she had pulled from its pebbly shell. "Bob, I'll keep you supplied with periwinkles so you'll catch lots of fish."

Nettie scowled and shivered. "I hate wiggly, crawly things."

To the girls' delight, wild syringas bent their waxy, white, fragrant clusters of blossoms over the rippling water stirred by a southern zephyr. They gathered small nosegays, tucking them into their hair. When Bob heard their shrieks of girlish laughter he looked up to see a small, black-tail deer eating the flowers from their hair.

When the girls tired, Bob walked them back to the carriage and spread a blanket on the grass. From his pocket he took out a small book and handed it to Nettie, commenting, "When one is in the outdoors, William Cullen Bryant brings one closer to nature with his wonderful poem *Thanatopsis*." Smiling down he quoted, "He who in the love of nature, holds communion with her invisible forces, she speaks a various language." He bent and kissed her curls. "You will enjoy the sublimity of his poetry while you're waiting. I won't be long."

Maybelle went to see if she could find any owls' nests in the rafters of the old barn.

After reading a couple of pages, Nettie threw down the book of poetry with a ladylike snort. She much preferred the romances of E. P. Roe.

Bob disappeared down the creek until the charred remains of the cabin were out of sight. He searched for the old trail, his memory guiding him through the field and berry patches until thrusting his way past the fir tree, he came out beside the pool. It was even lovelier today, with the wild syringas swaying wandlike over the still surface mirroring cumulus clouds lazily floating across the fathomless blue sky. Quietly he knelt beside the still pool. A shadow slowly passed. Another darker shadow split the still surface, then rose in one mighty leap, majestically arching above the water, lingering for one magic moment before splashing back into the shadowy part of the pool. Bob hardly breathed. He had no idea how many large trout there were or how long they had lived in the pool's protected shelter. For several moments he lay beside the pool, thinking. Yes, he was going to buy the old homestead. What an ideal place for the horse he hoped to win, for a summer home, for the family he someday hoped to have. What a wonderful place for children. A loud splash drew his attention back to the pool. In a way he hated the thought of what he was about to do.

Teddy had found something to play with—a large, white, range bull he had teased into charging him. They kept circling each other with Teddy barking challenges until the bull gouged him with the tip of its horn, sending Teddy yelping for help.

Nettie, who was gathering wildflowers in the meadow, looked up and panicked. Teddy was dashing straight for her with the large, white animal gaining ground behind him. Nettie threw down the flowers, gathered up her skirts, and fled to the nearest tree. Teddy's frenzied barking and the bull's bellowing terrified her, but she managed to climb through the lower branches just as Teddy, with a desperate leap, hid himself behind the tree. The bull lowered his head and charged the tree, swaying the branches. Nettie screamed and scrambled higher, yelling to Teddy, "Shut up, you little fool!"

She was too scared to call for help, but Bob heard Teddy's frenzied barking and came running. He dropped his fishing gear and the large fish he had caught. Picking up rocks, he ran closer and bombarded the angry animal. He knew range bulls had nasty tempers and were known to even chase men on horseback. He was uncertain if the animal would charge him. Picking up a larger rock and hurling it with all his strength, he hit the bull between the eyes. The bull dazedly shook his head, then docilely trotted down the road.

Bob looked up into the tear-drenched face of the girl he adored. She was hysterically sobbing. He tried to calm her by teasing,

"Well, well, just imagine my luck to again find a beautiful damsel in a tree to be rescued."

"Oh, Bob, look at my arms, all skinned up and I have to wear a ball gown tomorrow night."

"If you try to shinny down the tree trunk, you're going to get skinned up even more. Climb down to the lowest branch, then jump. I'll catch you. Come on. I have something to show you."

When Nettie finally fell safely into his arms, he kissed away the tears then carried her over to where he had dropped his fishing gear. In the grass lay something dark, shiny, and enormous. Nettie gasped, "Oh, ohhh." Angrily stomping her foot she snapped, "Throw it back."

"For heaven's sake, why?"

"B...because it's bigger than Charlie's."

"It's up to the judge to decide that."

"If your fish wins, I'll never speak to you again. For the last time I'm telling you to throw it back."

For a moment Bob stood looking down at the beautifully speckled Dolly Varden, a monster of its species. He looked up at Nettie's distorted, flushed face, his own turning to an angry red. "I'll be damned if I'll throw it back."

With blazing eyes she faced him. "I'll never marry you, never, never, NEVER!"

Abigale was surprised to see them back so early and more so when she had to sit beside Bob in the front seat, Nettie frigidly refusing to do so. "Oh dear," thought Abigale, "what possibly could have gone wrong?"

As they silently drove back, a balmy sweet-scented breeze stirred the leaves of the old locust trees. A full mellow moon tipping the horizon silhouetted the dark fringe of pine trees. Abigale's jaws clenched and she was determined not to waste the gorgeous night while someone pouted provokingly. She threw back her head and in her deep contralto voice sang, "Down by the old mill stream. Where I first met you." Abigale stopped. "I'm not going to sing a solo. Come on, let's sing." Again she started singing.

Bob was surprised hearing Abigale's lovely voice. When Cynthia joined in with her soprano and Maybelle with her girlish high notes, the strained air began to lighten.

Maybelle turned to Bob. "You have to sing too."

"Can't carry a tune."

"Oh yes you can. I heard you singing in church. Then she lowered her voice."Please," she whispered, "help us out."

To her delight Bob started singing in a mocking lilt.

> Nettie, Nettie give me your answer, do
> I'm half crazy over my love for you
> It won't be a stylish marriage
> I can't afford a carriage
> But you'll look sweet upon the seat of a bicycle
>     built for two

There was silence, crackling with ice. Abigale whispered, "Oh dear," and wondered what would save them from this horrible impasse.

Maybelle, full of disdain for her sister's conduct, flung her arms mischievously around Bob's neck, nuzzling his cheek much to Bob's amazement, then cuddled against him and sang in a giggly voice:

> Bob dear, Bob dear, this is your answer true
> I won't marry such as the likes of you
> If you can't afford a carriage
> There won't be any marriage
> For I'll be switched, if I'll be hitched
> On a bicycle built for two

Loud clapping and laughter startled them. They were surprised to see they were surrounded by several buggies whose occupants joined in singing the popular songs of the day. Sopranos, tenors, contraltos, and a couple of baritones joined into a harmonious blend of voices as they sang.

> There's a long, long trail a winding
> Into the land of my dreams
> Where the nightingales are singing
> And a white moon beams

More and more buggies were stopping to join the musical cavalcade as they slowly wound their way toward the Andrus home beneath the canopy of locust trees sifting bright moonlight into magical lacy shadows.

Maybelle grabbed the buggy whip, using it as a baton to direct the many voices that kept joining in the sing-along fest. She led them into singing some of her favorites.

> Let me call you "sweetheart," I'm in love with you
> Let me hear you whisper that you love me too
> Keep the love light glowing in your eyes so blue
> Let me call you "sweetheart," I'm in love with you

Upon seeing their church choir conductor, Maybelle loudly announced, "We will now have a solo from our noted soprano, Mrs. Delany." Two men hoisted her up onto the top of a carriage and someone produced an accordion. The crowd hushed as her thrilling notes soared over the treetops, then she motioned for them all to join her, and in a rollicking mood they sang with gusto.

> In the good old summertime
> In the good old summertime
> Strolling down the shady lane, with that baby mine
> You hold her hand and she holds yours
>     and that's a very good sign
> That she's your tootsie wootsie
>     in the good old summertime

Hoots and shouts of gaiety brought people out of their houses, some joining them walking along the wooden sidewalks. Nancy, hearing the commotion, ran out then dashed back in calling to the girls, "Come down quickly! Company's coming."

When Bob tied the team to the Andrus hitching post, the doctor came out and invited everyone for cookies and lemonade.

Teddy, tired from bull fighting, had fallen asleep with his head on Abigale's lap. He now awoke with a sniff and a growl. Seeing an intruder peeing on his mistress's peonies brought out his guarding instincts and he leaped to the ground. A large hound had followed one of the buggies and was making himself at home on the Andrus lawn. With all of his twenty pounds, Teddy waded into the scruffy-looking hound. People screamed as Teddy and the hound turned into a whirling mess of flying hair. Teddy refused to listen to Doc calling him. A loud sharp voice yelled, "FETCH!" The hound dutifully picked Teddy up by the scruff of his neck and brought the yelping, kicking Teddy to his master. Old man Cryder released Teddy from his hound's mouth and chuckled, "It's a good thing I have old Mike trained to mind me or he could have killed your stupid mutt. You better start teaching your dog manners."

After Doc thanked the old man for rescuing Teddy, he challenged him. "Training dogs isn't my profession; how about you training him?"

Cryder snorted, "No thanks, he ain't worth it."

Blankets were spread on the lawn and all the occupants of the carriages and buggies gathered for refreshments. Nancy and the girls passed cookies and when they ran out, they raided the pantry for cakes and pies. Everyone was in a gay mood, laughing and chatting—everyone but Nettie who flounced into the house without a word.

Brushing the cake crumbs from her lap, Abigale rose, saying it was late and she would like to go home. Immediately Bob led her and Cynthia to the carriage. In spite of the jolly time they had had, they rode in silence. When they reached the yellow, Gothic cottage, Abigale alighted and turned to Bob. "Would you like to come in?"

Bob tied the reins to a post, thanking her.

In the hall Cynthia gave her hand to Bob and said, "It's been a long day. If you'll excuse me, I'm going to retire."

Bob shook her hand warmly. "Thank you for coming."

Abigale went to the kitchen to make coffee. Bob sat with his head in his hands. When she returned with two steaming cups of coffee, Bob said in a husky voice, "Thank you, dear friend, for saving the day from total disaster."

He went on to tell her what had happened. "I admire her for being loyal to her brother, but as her future husband, I felt she should be loyal to me."

Abigale patted his hand again. "But remember, you're not yet her husband. After you're married, I'm sure she will be just as loyal to you."

"What will I do at the judging? She told me she wouldn't marry me if her brother didn't win first prize."

"Suppose you ask God to show you what to do. Sometimes the Almighty has other plans for us." Abigale stood up, holding out her hand. "Goodnight, my friend."

# Chapter 9

# Preparation for Trouble

In spite of Mrs. Aims' threat to blow up the church with stump powder if the hellish dance of iniquity was held in the church basement, preparations continued at a frantic pace.

Charlie, loudly protesting he wasn't going to be inducted into any decorating committee, found himself climbing wobbly ladders to hang festoons of gaily colored paper streamers and strings of mystic Japanese lanterns across the ceiling under the dictatorial eye of Mary Ann, whom he could barely tolerate.

At last the great day arrived. The gowns were finished down to the last pearl button. The girls arose early and excitedly gushed as they put their hair up in crimping pins, then rushed downstairs to make cream puffs for their baskets. After searching the pantry and ice box and finding no butter to make their cream puffs, they sent Charlie to the creamery to buy a couple of pounds.

Charlie drove old Molly as fast as she could plod along the road to the creamery which wound through a park of quiet beauty. Trunks of birch and maple were entwined with clinging vines of ivy. Large beds of ferns grew in the shade of fir trees; wildflowers carpeted vast areas. A deer bounded away. Edging the park, a mountain stream rushed over a giant wooden water wheel, sending cool mist upon breeze-tossed elms. Wild ducks rose up from still pools below. At one time the water wheel had powered a flour mill. Now it powered the creamery. Every morning farmers brought large cans of milk, jars of cream, and baskets of fresh eggs to be made into butter, cheese, and six flavors of ice cream, all of which were peddled on the streets by a white-cab ice cream wagon whose presence was announced by a clanging bell, collecting more children than the Pied Piper of fairy tales.

Charlie was hastening out the door with his purchase when a dog barked at Molly's heels. Using it as an excuse, the old mare took off as if running for her life. She ignored Charlie's dire threats, shouted at the top of his lungs as he gave chase. When two pounds of butter hit her flank, she doubled her speed. The buggy thundered over the bridge. Even though Charlie was proud of his track record, he couldn't catch up with Molly. Stopping to catch his breath, he wished for Teddy to catch the culprit.

From a side street rode a girl on a gray mare. Seeing the runaway, she gave her mount a whack with her riding whip and disappeared behind Molly around the corner.

Kicking the dust in his fury, Charlie was about to hike to the livery stable for another horse to chase Molly when the gray mare reappeared around the bend with Molly docilely trotting behind. No angel could have looked more divine: dressed in a forest green riding habit, gracefully seated on a side saddle, her high, top hat swathed in veiling, jauntily tilted on blond curls, shading dancing dark violet eyes. Laughing, she handed Charlie Molly's reins, saying, "You better tie her up next time; she can't be trusted." Giving her mount a nudge with her riding crop, she galloped up the road, leaving Charlie in shock. He couldn't believe it possible that the toughest and most feared sheriff of Columbia County could have sired such loveliness.

Charlie walked into the kitchen in a daze. Amy, tying a large red bow to the handle of her basket, called over her shoulder, "Put the butter near the stove so it'll be soft enough to cream for puffs." Hearing no reply she turned. "Where's the butter?"

"Y…you see, there…"

"Charlie, you forgot!"

"I threw the butter at Molly and..."

"I always knew you were weak in the upper story. Now I know it. Anna!" Amy called. "Come with me to the creamery."

With Amy holding the reins, Molly made the trip to the creamery in record time. Returning, they saw a man leaning against the fence as if in need of support. He was racked with coughing. Anna jumped down, running over to him. "Do you need help?"

He nodded, raising his head. Anna recognized him as the man her sister was infatuated with. Hoarsely, he whispered, "Take me to Doc Andrus."

Although Molly resented the whip, she kept up a good clip. They arrived at their father's office to find it surrounded by buggies. In spite of the crowded waiting room, however, Doc motioned them into his private office and immediately took charge. "John, I've warned you not to get tired. You've overtaxed yourself by building Mrs. Aims' fence around her garden. You must learn to take rest spells. You're not over the hump yet, my boy."

"Will he be able to go to the dance?" Anna anxiously asked, knowing how much Fannie was planning on his presence.

"It depends," answered her father moving the stethoscope across John's chest.

Amy asked, "Papa, why are there so many people waiting to see you?"

"Because they've been fools enough to take rotgut."

"Will they die?"

"They're sick enough to wish they could."

"Why can't the medicine show be stopped?"

"That's exactly what I hope to do when I attend the medical convention in a couple of weeks."

"Will John be all right?" Anna anxiously asked. Her father nodded.

The girls hurried home, Anna saying, "Fannie will be heartbroken if John is unable to go to the dance."

"Let's not tell her how sick we found him," Amy advised.

Anna nodded. "Yes, that's best."

The cream puffs were in the oven and the girls were decorating their baskets. Mae, remembering Neville's note with his instructions, sighed, "I do hope Neville knows lavender is almost purple. There's not a purple ribbon in town."

Maybelle had trouble getting a stuffed bird to stay on the handle of her basket. They teased Amy over the huge red bow she had tied on her basket. Maybelle snickered, "That would sure stop a train or make that mean old bull at the homestead charge."

Charlie popped in carrying the little wooden pig with a red ribbon around its neck. "You forgot Sam's pig."

"Get out!" they yelled. "We had it hid. Where did you find it?"

"Easy."

"Throw it away."

"You're going to break Sam's heart."

"Will you leave us alone or do I have to kick you out?" Amy sputtered.

Charlie went into the parlor and slumped into a chair. His father came home to get an ice pack for John and was on his way to the kitchen when he paused beside his son's chair. Laying his hand on the boy's shoulder, he said, "Having a problem, my son?"

Charlie shook his head. He didn't have one problem, he had six problems. As if that weren't bad enough, he had an uncomfortable feeling he never had before.

Doc patted his son's shoulder. "A great man, I believe it was Emerson, once said, 'A man's value depends on his capacity to face adverse situations rapidly.' I think you're man enough to face yours successfully." Doc gave Charlie an encouraging smile and walked on into the kitchen, asking his wife, "What's wrong with Charlie? Never saw his looking so glum."

Nancy laughed. "Oh, he has an idiotic idea he's in love."

Doc chuckled, "He better get used to that feeling. He'll probably have a dozen rounds of puppy love before he's married."

The girls had just gone up to rest when their mother called, "Mary Ann is here to see you."

"Send her up."

Mary Ann, head of the dance as well as the decorating committee, looked around at the satin-and-lace-trimmed gowns before she smugly announced, "Plans for the dance have been changed. It is now to be a masquerade and you can't wear formal attire. Wear any old rag and put a brown paper sack over your heads so you won't be recognized."

Amy's face turned to a dull red with rage. "Mary Ann, I know your scheme. You don't have a new gown to wear so you don't want us to wear our new ones. You're the most miserable, selfish, hateful person I know."

Mary Ann thrust out her chin, smirking, "Well, you can't get in unless you're masqueraded, so there." She fled before a book hit the door behind her with a thud.

"Drat it," Amy snapped. "I've got to practice so I can throw faster."

The girls were seething with disappointment when Abigale and Cynthia came, bringing exquisite maline lace handkerchiefs for them to carry. The two women listened in sympathy as the girls indignantly told of Mary Ann's latest dictate.

Cynthia started laughing and clapped her hands. "Girls, you can still go to the masquerade wearing your gowns and have oodles of fun."

"How?" they chorused.

"Wear a mask."

"What's a mask?" Fannie asked looking puzzled.

"It's a piece of material covering the upper part of the face, with slits for the eyes. They can be beautifully made of satin or velvet and trimmed with lace, ribbons, and feathers to match your dresses." Cynthia snatched up a piece of black lace and held it under her eyes. "See how provocative and romantic it can make one look and you can flirt outrageously because no one recognizes you."

The girls started laughing. "It sounds like fun!"

Cynthia shed her coat. "It's more than fun. You can still wear your gowns when you're masked. We'll make them elegant to

### Chapter 9 - Preparation for Trouble

match your dresses." With merry laughter, she went into action, instructing the others how to help. The girls hunted up scraps of material, lace, and ribbons left over from their dresses. Cynthia did the cutting. Abigale sewed on trimmings of lace, flowers, and feathers. Anna and Fannie made the linings, while the others sewed on ribbon ties. When they finished, the girls tried them on, giggling with delight.

Abigale and Cynthia went downstairs to have tea with Nancy while the girls rested. Later the girls would call them to help them get buttoned into their ball gowns.

Charlie, restless and bored while waiting to escort his sisters to the dance, wandered into the pantry, hoping to find a leftover cream puff. Six beautifully decorated baskets for the social were in a neat row on the lower shelf. The temptation was too much. Hurriedly glancing around to see if the coast was clear, he ripped off the purple ribbons, and pulling from his pocket the little red-ribboned pig, tied it on the basket handle. Working with haste, he switched trimmings on the other baskets, then sauntering into the dining room, he bumped into Amy in her dressing gown, holding a feathered white dove with the intention of adding it to the red bow on her basket. Charlie offered his assistance. "Sis, you're busy. I'll put it on for you."

"You're a dear," Amy said, dashing back up the stairs.

Charlie promptly tore off the pink roses on Fannie's basket, replacing it with the dove. He smiled smugly to himself, thinking this would even the score of his stolen brass buttons, then nonchalantly he strolled to his room to read the latest issue of the *Scam* magazine until time to escort his sisters.

When the doorbell rang, Nancy excused herself to answer. A messenger boy handed her a florist box, asking her to sign for it. After doing so, she called, "Nettie, something for you. Please come and get it."

Nettie tripped down the stairs, thanked her mother, and raced back up, the package in hand. Her sisters excitedly gathered around her with curiosity as Nettie took from crushed white tissue paper a fragile, iridescent, pale lavender flower. Anna gasped, "It's an orchid."

In wonder Mae whispered, "It's a corsage for you to wear on your gown tonight, I'll bet."

Nettie found a small card tucked in the tissue and read, "Save the first dance for me. Bob."

Nettie was infuriated that he would dare send her a flower after refusing to throw back the fish. She fiercely threw it into the waste basket.

Amy snatched it out saying, "If you aren't going to wear it, I will. It will complement my gown to perfection."

After another short rest, the girls decided it was time to put on their undergarments before calling their two friends to help button them into their gowns. Amy flatly refused to pull Fannie's corset laces any tighter. Fannie, determined to have an eighteen-inch waist, flung the corset strings around the bedpost and pulled back until she almost fainted. The other girls were more lenient with their waists.

Taffetas rustled as the girls stepped into lavishly lace-trimmed petticoats. Amy tied on the largest bustle, which made Maybelle envious and she crossly lamented, "Why do I have to wear these hateful pantalets when I'm almost as tall as you?"

"Your day is coming," Amy said to soothe her sister.

Hearing their names called, Abigale and Cynthia hurried up the stairs. Nancy promised to come up later. Nettie took one look at Abigale's pale face and said, "You're sick."

Abigale held her hand to her forehead. "Just an upset stomach."

"When did you take that vile quack stuff? Don't deny it. Bob saw you buy it," Nettie accused her.

"Just before I came over. I was feeling tired and thought it would perk me up a bit."

Alarmed, Nettie said, "You can't get sick now. Come." Grabbing Abigale by the arm, she rushed her down the stairs and on down to the cellar. She plunged the tin cup into the crock of elderberry wine, handing it to Abigale with a curt, "Drink it."

Abigale rebelled. "You're not going to get me drunk."

"It's an antidote for the rotgut you took."

Upstairs, plans were percolating. Cynthia was explaining to the girls how Charles Frederic Worth had instigated the idea of showing his fashions on live mannequins at organized fashionable style shows. "Girls, your gowns merit just such a showing. Why not a private style show for your mother?"

While plans for the style show were enthusiastically progressing, down in the cellar Nettie was worried. Abigale was not responding to the elderberry wine cure as she had expected. Nettie decided Abigale had to be rushed to her father. Up the cellar stairs they went, stopping long enough to shrug into their coats. Abigale exclaimed, "Nettie! Your coat doesn't cover your chemise!"

Nettie grabbed her brother's coat, which dragged on the ground as they dashed out the door. Luckily, Molly was waiting, harnessed to take them to the ball. Once at the office, Nettie marched her patient right through the crowded waiting room into her father's private office. They had to wait while the doctor finished pulling a tooth. Her father took one look at Abigale and shook his head. "Abigale, you'll have to take an emetic."

While Nettie nervously paced, Abigale parted with the rotgut. Doctor ordered his daughter, "Take her home and give her some milk toast."

After downing two bowls of Doc's recommendation, which restored Abigale to feeling almost normal, she felt well enough to join Nancy who had just been called to attend the amateur style show.

They were given swing rocker orchestra seats in front of Edison's morning glory phonograph, where they waited in uncertain expectancy. Cynthia selected a cylinder record and at the wheezing sound of a fiddle, Cynthia took her place beside the bedroom door behind which there issued nervous giggles. Sedately, Cynthia fingered her notes. Having been to many style shows both in Boston and New York, she sounded very professional as she started to announce the first live mannequin.

Cynthia intoned, "This evening we present the latest in evening toilette. Our first model..." She paused. Mae came through the door, which was speedily slammed behind her so the nervous titters of the other models waiting their turn could not be heard.

With dignity Mae coasted into the room then correctly pivoted to better show her gown as Cynthia started describing it. "The skirt is of gold short lavender faille, trimmed with three pinked flounces of mist green toile. The overskirt is of point lace draped behind in a panier. The basque is of purple grosgrain, while lace is swagged holding a cluster of pink roses."

The front door knocker and the back doorbell rang simultaneously. Charlie yelled "I'll get it" and ran to the front door accepting a small white box from the messenger who widely grinned. "Big splash tonight?"

"Yeah," Charlie answered, then dashed to the back door to accept another small white box. Taking the stairs two steps at a time, he delivered one box to Mae, who was ecstatic over the gift Neville had sent. With shiny eyes she let Abigale help her pin to the basque a dainty corsage of violets.

"You have a very thoughtful young man with good taste," Abigale remarked.

"Oh yes, yes he is," Mae happily replied.

Charlie yelled, "Come on out, Fan, flowers for you."

Fannie rushed out. "Oh...oh," she gasped, jerking off the white lid, then kissing a spray of lilies. "Dear, dear John remembered."

Abigale leaned over, whispering to Nancy. "Dayton has no florist shop. How did they come?"

"Judge Frankland brought them from the florist in Walla Walla. He is to judge the fish derby tonight, you know," Nancy replied.

Charlie turned to leave and Mae told him, "You can stay if you'd like and see the other gowns."

"Naw, I'll see enough of them tonight at the dance," he shrugged, then left to kill time by scrounging in the kitchen for something to stick to his ribs. He wasn't going to trust to luck his getting a basket that would substantially satisfy his appetite.

Cynthia continued with the style show, describing Fannie's gown. "This flattering style shows an artistic flare of a talented seamstress. A full dress of chartreuse-colored faille, it has an elaborate trimming of white chenille balls and simulated pearls, edged with point lace." Fannie proudly pivoted then joined the audience.

Anna appeared, fluttering her handkerchief. Cynthia warmly intoned, "This exquisite diaphanous evening dress is made of pink tulle and trimmed with Valenciennes lace with silk burnt-orange zinnias tucked into a large ribbon bow."

The cylinder record had to be changed and as the plaintive strains of a waltz started, Nettie entered with assumed dignity she wasn't feeling. She realized her gown would be more becoming had the gorgeous orchid adorned the bodice. Since Amy had laid claim to it, she knew it would be impossible to reclaim it. Cynthia started to describe the gown. "This gay toilette has a basque of cream-colored poult de soie with pale sprays of heather and an overskirt of cream-tinted Flanders lace. The skirt has lace pleating headed by a shell ruche of lace. The overskirt made of lace is draped in full pleats edged with a frill of lace. The sleeves have lace puffs. Her coiffure is elegant and simple."

Nancy whispered to her friend, "In my mind these styles are much too sophisticated for girls so young, but my husband spoils them, saying they are only young once and to let them have what they want."

Abigale nodded. "I understand your feelings. To me, it seems they should all still be in pantalets."

Amy swished in, dramatically fluttering a feathered fan. Cynthia glanced fearfully at Nancy before describing the gown. "This elegant fire-engine-red faille gown has a front of black lace and is richly embroidered with gold fringe. The low corsage is decorated with rows of Venetian pearl beads on black lace."

A stunned silence filled the room and Cynthia could think of no words to break the dreadful quiet.

Finally, Nancy said, "Girls, your gowns are beautiful, but Amy, your low corsage is unacceptable. It's indecent. Fannie, see if you can find a piece of black lace to cover Amy's bosom."

"Mama...," wailed Amy, "That will make me look like an old lady."

"Better to look like an old lady than a young whore."

"Oh, Mama, please, a low bodice won't make me look like a whore."

"It will put you well on the road to being one."

"Papa said we could have anything we wanted."

"Your father underestimated your taste."

"I like my gown just as it is," Amy persisted.

"You're not leaving this house until your bosom has more covering. Fannie, see that the neckline of your sister's dress is extended."

"Yes, Mama," Fannie answered wondering how she was going to do it with Amy in rebellion.

Nancy pursed her lips. "Amy, I want you to remember what your grandmother once told you: 'It takes seven generations to make a woman a lady, but only one generation to make her a whore.' I'm going to see that no whore comes out of your generation."

Fannie took this opportunity to get even with Amy for not helping her with her corset, so she found a piece of black lace and stitched it up to her sister's chin, inwardly grinning at Amy's remonstration.

There came a scream from the other room and the door was kicked open by a very angry little sister. Sobbing heartbrokenly, Maybelle cried, "You forgot me, just because I had to wear pantalets. Only bustles count with you!"

Fannie ran to her, taking her in her arms. "Darling, of course we didn't forget you. We were just delayed. Now hush up so Cynthia can describe your lovely dress."

Maybelle dabbed at her eyes. "No dress is lovely with pantalets."

Cynthia informed the rebellious young lady, "Pantalets have a stunning style of their own."

Maybelle wasn't deceived by this subterfuge and tears again spurted as she enviously eyed her sisters' bustles.

Cynthia brought out the masks and amid giggles, the girls donned them, eyeing each other with hysterical laughter, but were very pleased with the effect. Each mask was different and complemented their gowns. They doubted their identity would be a mystery, but at least Mary Ann couldn't kick them out for not being masqueraded.

Charlie was waiting for them in the front hall and started clowning as soon as the girls appeared on the stairs. Giving a shrill whistle, he feigned to be trying to guess which one was who.

Nancy was proud of her daughters but knew her husband would see the deforming aspects of their attire. Their waists did seem unusually small and their bustles unusually large.

Opening the hall door for her brood to leave, Nancy expressed her concern. "I do hope no one brings any homemade brew tonight."

Charlie reassured his mother, saying, "With Mrs. Aims appointing herself as chief chaperone, there won't be a drop."

Maybelle wailed, "She might bring stump powder and blow up the church."

Charlie guffawed, "Not a chance! Old Mac is going to frisk her before he lets her in."

Just then their father came up the porch steps surprising them. "Papa!" they cried.

Doc beamed, "These can't be my babies."

"Papa, we're all grown up!"

"Indeed you are." He keenly looked at his daughters with displeasure, but love kept him silent. Then turning to his son, he said, "You're the man in this outfit, so I expect you to take good care of the ladies you are escorting."

"Trust me," Charlie grinned. "Let any guy look at them twice and I'll pop him on the beaner."

The girls groaned. "Why couldn't we go by ourselves?"

Charlie laughed, "Because it's going to take a real man to look after six feather-brained females."

They were going down the porch steps when Mae exclaimed, "We've forgotten our baskets."

"My darling sister, I have taken care of everything. Your baskets are in the carriage covered with newspapers so their beauty won't be dulled by the dust."

Mae sniffed, "I...I...well it's hard to admit, but I guess you are a dear and thoughtful brother after all."

Charlie made a deep bow in acknowledgement of the compliment then bid his father, mother, and their guests a pleasant evening.

Their father, having seen them off for their first dance, was returning to his office and would be unable to join his wife and her guests for dinner.

# Chapter 10

# Rotgut for the Gullible

Back in his office Doc took a moment to relax. It had been an unusually grueling day. He sat staring at a motto on the wall. He himself had penned the ornate lettering, which several of his patients had requested him to remove, because they found it embarrassing. He read the motto with amusement, for it was so true of human nature.

> God and the Doctor we alike adore
> Just at the brink of danger, not before

The rest of the motto was hidden by a large stack of black medical books on his desk.

The motto's frame of black filigree wrought iron was probably too heavy for the delicate flow of Spencerian script, but he was proud of the resplendent penmanship. It relaxed him to make those bold flourishes of the chirographic art. He had a passion for ornamenting the borders of this letters with graceful ethereal doves and fish with vaporous fins. Doc bemoaned that he was unable to cut his own pens out of goose quills, as did the genius and legendary penman Plott Roger Spencer, but had to satisfy himself with an obique pen as his profession prevented him from practicing the many hours it took to become a master of the Spencerian art.

Right now he would like to take his pen and draw flowing lines, but needed research necessitated him to burrow into the formidable medical jargon and he reached for a volume. Papers started slithering off his desk and he swiveled around to see his old friend Professor Hoagland quickly shutting the door behind him. "Nelson, I saw your light and thought I'd stop in to say hello."

"Glad you did. Are you out for a drive this evening?"

"Yes. I thought I'd check in on the young folks at the dance to see how things were going."

"And?"

"Under Mrs. Aims' stern, righteous eyes, it couldn't be anything but staid and proper."

"And dull, Professor. She is only one of millions who are misguided by ignoramus preachers into believing hell fire and brimstone."

Professor Hoagland smiled, knowing of his friend's strong opinions on religious matters. "She doesn't plan on going to where it's hot. She's going to sit on the right hand of God and do nothing."

Doc gritted his teeth. "Because the Lord has washed all her sins away with his blood, I suppose."

The professor nodded but remained silent, not wanting to get his friend fired up. He tried to change the subject, but Doc was not going to drop it. He hit the desk with his fist. "Don't you see how that totally disregards the awesome machinery of Cosmic Law? America once had a great reformer and writer who I believe expressed it best when he wrote, 'According to man's good and evil deeds, words, thoughts, and actions whilst on earth, even so shall he inherit in heaven, light or darkness, joy or unhappiness.'"

"You're quoting from Thomas Paine's famous doctrine, I believe."

"Yes, and he further stated 'Man's belief of a Savior is unjust that no honest man should accept another dying for him.'"

The professor nodded. "Paine is sort of hero of yours, isn't he?"

"Indeed he is. When George Washington was retreating with his ragged army, during the American Revolution, it was Paine who gave the rallying cry that turned the tide and won him the victory."

"How was that?" the professor asked.

Doc cleared his throat, stood up and, dramatically raising his arm, thundered, "'These are the times that try men's souls. Those who fight for liberty deserve the thanks of every woman and man. Tyranny, like hell, is not easily conquered, yet we have the consolation with us, that the harder the conflict, the more glorious the triumph.'" Doc sank back down in his chair saying, "Oh, Paine was a great American."

The professor grimaced. "No doubt, no doubt. He was sure full of fire and guts."

Thumbing some papers on his desk, Doc agreed, "Yes, and we need more men like him to fight this damnable takeover by the quacks, peddling their fraudulent medicine."

The professor struck a match on his pants and lit his cigar before commenting. "Nelson, you have some fine-looking daughters. You won't be able to keep them home much longer."

"No, I suppose not."

"With that stack of medical books, you must be searching for information."

"Antidotes."

"I hear the perjurer is doing a lucrative business. What do you suppose is in his medicine?"

"Could be a crude alcohol, cocaine, or heroin. The latest report lists arsenic trioxide."

"Good Lord, that's rat poisoning! Their cure-all is certainly getting more potent."

Doc gave a disgusted grunt. "And more dangerous."

"Say, Nelson, do you recall that rascal who called himself Dr. Jenkins, about three years ago?"

"Two."

"He sold snake oil for rheumatism and chicken feathers as a sex amphetamine."

Doc smiled wryly and nodded. "I remember well. Young Jake Thompson bought a jar of chicken feathers and an adhesive on his wedding day. The old sorcerer had persuaded Jake it would be more effective if the feathers were glued to his gluteus maximus. I had a helluva a time removing the feathers. They must have been stuck on with pitch. Had to use kerosene to remove them."

"Bet he was blistered."

"Wedding day had to be postponed."

The two friends chuckled, then Doc grew serious. "They are getting further away from the teachings of Hippocrates all the time."

The professor flicked the ashes from his cigar into the spittoon. "He was called "the father of medicine" wasn't he?" Doc nodded and his friend tried to recall what his nephew had told him. "I remember Dan saying he had to take Hippocrates' oath before he could graduate from medical school. Let's see now, what was it?"

"To do no harm."

Professor nodded. "Yes, that was it."

Doc gave a wry smile. "He believed in using natural means only for treatment."

The professor threw his cigar into the spittoon. "What made the establishment swerve away from using herbs?"

"Money. The law says you can't patent herbs, so it loses them the monopoly and cornering the market's lucrative business."

"Which means these peddlers of dubious medicine are the forerunners of a big drug industry."

"Exactly."

"Can't someone do something about it?"

"Someone did try, back when the American government was being formed. A highly respected physician, Dr. Benjamin Rush, made a supreme effort to protect the people when the constitution was being written."

Doc pulled a volume from the stack and adjusted his glasses. "Here is his speech to Congress. 'Unless we put medical freedom in the Constitution, the time will come when the medical profession will organize into an undercover dictatorship. The Constitution of the Republic should make special provision for medical freedom as well as religious freedom.' "

"What happened?"

"Medical lobbyists defeated the bill."

"They can't gain a monopoly."

"The already have. In 1849, a group of medical physicians formed the American Medical Association for the purpose of destroying the Hippocratic method of treating by natural means."

"That's preposterous!"

"Professor, there is a war being fought. Why people aren't aware of it is because it's being fought with theories, between the followers of Hippocrates, who believe totally in bringing the body back to health by natural methods, and those opposing this method, who are the followers of the Greek philosopher, Aristotle, whose theory was to fight disease by such methods as bleeding, violent laxatives, and strong emetics."

"They can't get away with it."

"They already have, during George Washington's last illness. His highly respected orthodox medical physicians bled him of ninety ounces of blood and injected him with several doses of calomel and large amounts of emetic tartar. They had him inhale vapors of vinegar and applied mustard poultices to his already blistered body. Within twenty-four hours, the first president of the United States was dead; and all he had was a sore throat."

With disbelief, the professor asked, "Nelson, can this really be true? It's so preposterous."

Doc emphatically nodded. "It's all recorded in the Library of Congress."

"When will this horrendous trend stop?"

"When money no longer has any power and people wake up to fight for their lives."

"They better wake up fast."

"Unfortunately, millions will die before the public realizes how the orthodox doctors are killing them."

"Right now, Nelson, you better stop this peddler before he kills some one."

"He has his peddler's license, so the law protects him."

"I have a feeling something will happen that will force you to chase him out."

Suddenly, the door was flung open and a women staggered in, sobbing, "Dr. Andrus, help me. I'm so sick."

Doc jumped up, helping her to a chair. "Mary, did you buy any medicine from the peddler?" She nodded and he asked, "How long since you took it?"

"I don't remember."

The professor rose to leave. Doc stopped him. "Wait." Turning back to the woman, he asked, "Mary where is the bottle now?"

"Home."

"Is there anyone there?"

"No."

"Where is the medicine?"

"On the kitchen table."

"Hoagland, would you be kind enough to bring the bottle? Take Molly and the buggy, it's faster."

Hoagland grabbed his hat and coat. Dr. Andrus guided Mary to a cot in the hall, kept for just such an emergency. Mary held out her trembling hand. "It won't stop shaking, and my head won't either."

"Don't worry, Mary," Doc reassured her, then called after the professor, "Fetch Nancy and tell her to bring all the thick cream she has."

Bending over Mary, Doc gave her a thorough examination with avuncular professionalism. He feared the neurotransmitter was affected and neurosurgery would be necessary.

Mary's whole body was quivering. He gave her two tablespoons of olive oil, fearing to give her an antidote of any strength before he knew for sure what the nostrum contained.

Teddy kept scratching at the door, wanting in. Doc hurriedly opened the door and went back to Mary, finding her whole left side paralyzed. He started to massage her body with his own ointment, trying to have hope where there was doubt.

At Mary's house, Professor Hoagland was having difficulty locating the medicine. It was not on the kitchen table. He flung open cupboard doors. Row on row of bottles with nondescript labels filled the shelves. He shook his head. None looked like the flamboyantly labeled bottles the peddler would be selling. In desperation he rushed into the bedroom. On the night table was a bottle with a bright, garish label, just the kind the charlatan would be hawking. Grabbing it up, he hurried to pick up Nancy.

As they were driving to the office, he told Nancy the circumstances. She was deeply distressed. "Oh, the poor dear. When she was younger she was a concert pianist and is now our church organist. Oh, what a shame."

"Try to calm her. She is very upset."

"I'll do my best."

They were passing a bilious green house when Nancy said "STOP, oh, please stop, I'll only be a minute." She jumped down and dashed up the steps, yanking the bell cord. Mrs. Aims opened the door a crack and peeked at her with a critical eye. "What you want?"

"Mrs. Aims, I know you believe in prayer."

The door opened wider. "Of course, I do."

Nancy hurriedly told her about Mary. "Please, oh, please Mrs. Aims, gather the Baptist church ladies together and pray for Mary."

"What's wrong with her, did you say?"

"I haven't time to tell you but she is dying from gut rot the peddler sold her."

"He'll go to hell for sure."

"Please pray."

"Don't worry no more, Mrs. Andrus, our prayers can pull her right out of the grave."

"Thank you."

At the office, Doc took the bottle and emptied the contents into a granite cup and placed it over a gas jet flame, commenting, "I'm reducing it by over half."

Nancy rushed to Mary. "My dear, you're going to be all right."

Mary stretched out her trembling hand to Nancy, sobbing.

Soon Doc poured the concentrated liquid back into the bottle, instructing his wife to administer the cream. "Keep giving it to her until I get back."

Turning to the professor, he said, "Come with me to Cryder's farm. May need you to witness."

Luckily, Molly's rheumatism was better and she trotted at a brisk pace instead of her usual plodding. Teddy sat quietly between them, seeming to know there was an emergency.

Reaching the weathered farmhouse, Doc pounded on the door loudly, knowing the farmer retired early. Old Cryder came to the door in his long johns and Doc immediately made his request. "Cryder, I want to buy a pig."

"What in hell, I'm already in bed! Come back tomorrow." Cryder started to close the door.

"Cryder, I have to have the pig now."

"Don't tell me you're that hungry."

"No, I have to run a test on the pig. May save Mary Hunter's life."

Cryder leaned against the door casing. "Suppose you tell me what's up."

"The medicine peddler is in town."

"Yeah, I know all about that crackpot."

"His medicine may have arsenic in it."

"You mean that stuff that's damn rough on rats?"

"I won't know until I make the test. Then I'll know which antidote to give her."

"In that case, come on down to the barn."

"You better get something warmer on."

"Naw, these red woolies keep me from freezin' even if hell was freezin' over."

They trooped past an old well with the wooden bucket on the stone ledge and walked between several dilapidated out-buildings until they came to a long, low-roofed hog barn. Cryder spoke sharply. "Keep your dog out. He'll rile my pigs."

Doc, unaware Teddy had followed them, spoke kindly to the little dog. "Teddy, go back to the buggy. You're not wanted." Teddy obediently trotted away.

As they passed a heavily boarded fence enclosure, Cryder pointed at the huge, white-girthed hog rooting in the sawdust, "That's the son-of-a-gun that messed me up."

Doc shook his head. "Well, don't let him work you over again. You might not be so lucky next time."

"I'd sure as hell shoot him if he wasn't such a good breeder."

"His tusks came close to one of your vital organs. It was a close call."

"You sure did a swell job of patchin' me up. My backside is almost healed. What kind of pig you want, big or small?"

"Medium. Here's ten dollars for him."

"Forget it. You never charged to patch me up."

"Will you hold him while I give him the dose?"

"Sure thing." Cryder firmly held the squealing pig.

Doc looked up at the professor. "It shouldn't take long to find out if it's what I'm suspecting."

Doc took out his pocket watch and started counting the minutes. After three minutes the pig started shaking, two more and it went into convulsions. A few horses galloped into the barnyard and the three men looked up. When they glanced back down at the pig it was dead.

Doc nodded his head. "Just as I suspected. Strychnine. In diluted doses the American medicals recommend it as a stimulating tonic. This batch wasn't diluted enough and is highly toxic."

Angrily the professor chomped his cigar. "It's damnable to think they would jeopardize lives by such a recommendation."

"Remember a war is going on and people will be used as guinea pigs until the whole thing blows up."

Cryder fiercely asked, "Mary goin' to make it?"

Doc shook his head. "She won't recover fully. Her hands will probably tremble for the rest of her life."

Cryder's fury was mounting. "That damn peddler needs to be shot."

"Calm down, Cryder. He has his license and is protected by the law."

But Cryder wasn't calming down. "I say run the damn varmint out of town with buckshot in his pants. Don't forget I'm one of your vigilantes. You two go ahead. I'll dress, saddle my horse, and meet you at your office in a jake."

They found Mary no better. Doc rummaged around his large medicine chest until he found the antidote he was seeking. He poured some opaque powder in a glass of water, instructing his wife, "Give her another dose in half an hour."

Doc left to join the professor who had insisted on joining them and was holding the reins of a couple of horses. While they were mounting, Cryder rode up with three more vigilantes. Cryder bellowed, "We'll show that god damn killer out of town with his death wagon."

When they rode up to the ornately decorated medicine wagon, a boy stood leaning against the front wheel. Cryder bellowed, "Where's that swindler?"

The boy nonchalantly eyed them. "You mean Dr. Cooper. He's sure a nice man. He gave me twenty-five cents to watch his wagon and another twenty-five cents to not tell where he's going."

"Well, where did he go?"

The kid grinned. "Mister, that will cost you twenty-five cents."

Cryder howled, "You damn little squirt, you're not going to play your con game on a vigilante." Cryder reached down and grabbed the youngster by his collar and shook him until Doc intervened.

"Stop! I don't want another patient."

"Doc, don't worry about havin' another patient. It's the undertaker he's needin' when I'm done with him." Cryder dangled the boy kicking and yelling in the air, giving him a shake and demanding, "Now where is he?"

"H...h...he said he was g...going to the shindig a...at the church and get himself a c...c...cutie."

Cryder threw the boy against the wagon's canvas cover and ordered, "Harness up them nags. Your benefactor is hittin' the road damn fast."

When they rode up to the church, Old Mac, acting as doorman, grinned at them. "I know who you are looking for. Well, he ain't here. I wouldn't let him in. Widow Kerns was walking past and he grabbed her arm and walked off with her. I don't know whether she went willingly or not."

They spurred their horses back to the wagon, only to see a dust cloud up the road. Cryder swore. "That no good scamp tipped him off."

The branches of a nearby elm tree parted and the boy peeked out jeering, "Ha, ha, bet you can't catch him."

"I'll catch you and beat the hell out of you."

"I'm going to tell my pa on you."

"Go ahead. I've licked him before." Cryder jerked his horse around and yelled, "Come on, let's catch him and tell him to stay out of Dayton or we'll kill him."

They spurred their horses over the bridge and rode past several farmhouses. They seemed to get no nearer to the swaying bouncing wagon. Cryder snarled, "Damn it, he's gotta slow down." Jerking his rifle from his scabbard he fired a couple of shots that brought yells of fury from the front of the wagon.

Doc knew Cryder's temper was on a short fuse and reined in his horse. "Come on, let's go back. He knows now he's not wanted and I have to get back and check on Mary."

Cryder turned in his saddle and glared at Doc. "I never knew before for you to chicken out when there justice to be done."

"Come on, Cryder, let's go back," Doc insisted.

"Not a damn sight. He may be kidnappin' widow Kerns."

"Cryder, you're being melodramatic. I know widow Kerns would never have anything to do with a man like the peddler."

Cryder sneered, "And you're supposed to be so smart. Any woman would fall for the kind of sweet talk that guy cooks up."

Doc was losing his patience with his hot-headed deputy. "As head of the vigilantes, I say we go back."

"And I say we catch him and work him over until he squawks. And I want to give him a knockout punch for Mary."

Doc whirled his horse around and without looking back headed for his office to sit by Mary's bedside for the rest of the night.

## Chapter 11

## Fish Folly

    *N*ancy stood on the porch with her two devoted friends, proudly waving to her children, who were tucking themselves into the white-fringed surrey. They were laughing and scintillating with the effervescence of youth, while nervously fluttering with anticipation for a romantic evening. She winced when she heard Amy loudly ordering her brother not to drive fast as she feared losing some of their fragile accoutrements if the horses were to trot. She shuddered when her son shouted back, "I'll drive as I damn well please!" Grabbing the buggy whip, he snapped it over the backs of the team, making them lunge, and they took off with a lurch, the girls screaming.

    Nancy shook her head. "I'm afraid with Charlie in such a bad mood, it won't be a peaceful evening."

    Abigale asked with concern, "What seems to be the trouble?"

    "Oh, it's so ridiculous. Charlie thinks his best friend has caught the larger fish and his heart is set on winning the grand prize."

    "I understand the prize is to be a horse."

    "And we don't need another horse, but you know how young

people are. Let's go in to dinner. We won't wait for Nelson. He'll be late. Abigale, I've made your favorite dish."

Abigale clapped her hands with delight. "Fromage de Telte?"

Nancy nodded. "Yes and knowing your fondness for it, I doubled the recipe so you can take some home for tomorrow."

Abigale beamed. "You truly are a dear. It's asbolutely delectable but the recipe is so complicated I never make it."

The three friends chatted vivaciously as they sat down to dinner. Abigale, taking a large bite of the treat, closed her eyes, savoring the subtle blend of spices. "Nancy, no one can make Fromage de Telte as flavorful as you do."

Nancy, quite pleased with the compliment, smiled. "And no one can make lemon chiffon pie as zestful as you do."

They both laughed, looking tenderly at each other. Cynthia set down her teacup, saying, "The girls looked adorable in their bustles."

"I'm afraid bustles are too sophisticated for girls so young, but Nelson spoils them dreadfully and lets them wear whatever pleases them. He says youth never lasts long enough, but of course he had no idea they would choose bustles, he so hates them."

"For goodness' sake, why?" Cynthia asked with a puzzled frown.

"Nelson claims bustles are deforming and are bad for a woman's health."

"But they are so stylish and graceful," Cynthia insisted.

Nancy nodded. "I agree with you." She deeply sighed, "But it makes them grow up too fast. It seems only yesterday that they were just little girls wearing pantalets. Tonight it was a shock to see them as grown-up ladies."

Abigale sympathetically patted her friend, "My dear, they will always be your little girls, always needing your guidance and advice."

Nancy shook her head. "Which they don't always take."

"They will as they grow older. They will come to rely more and more on your wisdom," Abigale assured her.

Cynthia, buttering her crescent roll, said, "Your daughters are so very pretty. I vouch you will have your hands full of admiring suitors before they are all married."

"That is what I fear," replied Nancy, and she told them about Bob crashing in on their dinner.

Cynthia laughed. "I admire his ingenuity."

Abigale lowered her voice. "Have you heard about poor Mrs. Miller's distress and humiliation?"

Nancy's fork paused in midair. "Whatever are you talking about?"

Abigale blushed. "It's really too vulgar even to mention."

Nancy shook her head. "I've heard nothing."

Abigale stammered, "H...h...her daughter is in the family way."

"Are you sure? Nelson has mentioned nothing about it."

"I'm afraid it's true; she's starting to show. They went to a doctor in Walla Walla."

"But she is only fourteen!" Nancy exclaimed.

Abigale shook her head. "So tragic, but Nancy you won't have to worry about your girls. You and your husband have brought them up so properly."

"Yes, I have no fear that marriage will come first," Nancy replied. "But sometimes I worry Nelson isn't strict enough. He indulges them so."

Cynthia asked uneasily, "Has anyone mentioned who the man is?"

Abigale gave a deep sigh, "Mrs. Aims says she would swear over her dead body it's that charlatan of the medicine show."

Cynthia leaned forward with interest. "But he's only been here a couple of weeks and they say she is showing."

Abigale shrugged, "He was here for a week several months ago. Don't ask me any more about it. I...it's so sordid."

Still curious, Cynthia said, "You can be sure Mrs. Aims will have all the details."

"Girls, girls, I'm afraid we are gossiping about something that doesn't concern us. Shall we discuss the next meeting of the Baptist missionary society?" Nancy suggested.

Cynthia gave her a look of resigned acquiescence. "Nothing could be duller to talk about."

Abigale casually mentioned, "Since her daughter's plight, Mrs. Miller refuses to attend any meetings and she is the president, so it will be difficult to carry on with proceedings."

"Be that as it may," Nancy reasoned, "the clothing we have collected for the poor South Africans must be mailed immediately."

Meanwhile, as the three women were discussing the matter, Charlie sat hunched over, holding the reins tightly clutched in his hands, scowling formidably. Escorting six uninteresting sisters was exasperating when he was besotted with the provocative possibility of escorting the luscious and desirable blonde, violet-eyed daughter of the former major general of the Civil War's losing side. Ironically, he was now the feared sheriff of Dayton, a Yankee stronghold still rehashing the pros and cons of the war that divided a nation. It was well known the old warrior had a strong aversion to becoming the father-in-law to a Yankee and he was adept in vanquishing all lovesick swains. Charlie couldn't understand why the South was defeated when such a belligerent combatant had fought for their cause.

Slapping the reins over the backs of the team, Charlie decided love could hurdle all obstacles and dreamed how walking with Elaine would be like strolling among the stars. All he had to do was outmaneuver her father. He had made plans to dazzle her. Already he had succeeded in outshining his sisters. He had spent his whole month's allowance to buy some steel buttons for his waistcoat that brilliantly sparkled by reflected light. The salesman had positively assured him the glittering buttons would attract the feminine eye and mesmerize any girl. Also to give a boost to his sagging morale, he had spent five bucks at a Walla Walla haberdashery to rent a black swallow-tailed suit. Not for him a pirate or scarecrow costume with a paper sack over his head. Fannie had made him an elegant black-satin mask and he hoped to God his eyelashes wouldn't tangle in the lace she had insisted on sewing around the eye slits.

While his sisters chattered about all the romantic potentials for the evening, Maybelle sat silent in the corner of the seat wrapped in misty dreams. She knew for a certainty that the night would bring her a special miracle. She shivered with anticipation.

With a flourish Charlie drew the team up to the front of the church. Already the steps were crowded with Cinderellas, clowns, and scarecrows, all with paper sacks over their heads. Only one other had defied the edict of the dance chairman and come in formal attire. High-pitched laughter and nervous giggles floated on the soft evening air.

Charlie turned to face his sisters with a stern admonition. "If you giggle you won't have a chance with my fraternity brothers."

Amy snorted, "We aren't infantiles," then gave a loud giggle.

Charlie wryly smiled when he saw Mrs. Aims standing like a hawk ready to pounce on anyone who might be carrying a bottle of home brew. He and a couple of his fraternity brothers had met the night before and decided Mrs. Aims had to be eliminated early in the evening.

As befitted a proper escort, Charlie dutifully helped each sister to alight, then sprang into the carriage and swiftly disappeared around the corner with the girls screaming for their baskets.

Charlie was desperate not to be present when Amy made her grand entrance. She had been practicing for days trying to emulate the elegant poses of Lillian Russell, as pictured in the *Today's Lady* magazine. What Amy failed to comprehend was that she had neither the beauty nor the charisma of the opulent actress to make the same kind of grand entrance.

Charlie stopped at a side entrance leading to a small Sunday school room, being used this night as a depository for the baskets. He flung the reins to the stable boy hired for the evening and, making three trips, safely placed the lovingly bedecked baskets on the table beside a very unusual basket, a ship in full sail with a tiny bisque sailor boy on the lid's deck.

For a moment Charlie stood pondering over his brass buttons being stolen by his sisters for their memory strings. Sam's pig, which he had put on Mae's basket, would ruin her evening if she had to eat with him. No, he decided, after all, she had always saved an extra piece of pie for him. He just couldn't do that to her, so he replaced the sailor on the ship basket with the pig. His other sisters had never done anything special for him so he left his rearrangement on their baskets unchanged.

Hearing the door open behind him he slipped the sailor into his pocket. When he turned around his face blanched. In strolled a blonde girl dressed as a doll in a short, pink, ruffled costume sashed with a blue ribbon tied in a large bow. A matching bow held back long curls. A baby's pacifier was in her mouth and she held a teddy bear.

Charlie's heart gave a flip. Although she wore a mask, no one but Elaine could look so adorable. She walked quickly to the table then whirled to glare at him. "Who put that nasty little pig on my basket?"

Charlie started stuttering and she angrily flared, "That was a horrid thing, to steal my little sailor! Where is he?"

Charlie suddenly realized he had to say something. "Mmmmmaybe he fell overboard."

Guiltily fingering the sailor in his pocket, he dived under the table, showing great effort in diligently searching. Down she dropped beside him, saying, "He has to be somewhere near if he fell off."

The nearness of the girl he wanted more than anything else in the world and her heavenly perfume made him want to gather her in his arms and it strained his self-control beyond endurance. He was about to unleash his passion for a kiss when the outside door banged open and a stately figure of authority stalked in. He took one look at the baby-doll slippers and the shiny black, patent-leather oxfords protruding from under the table and roared, "What is the meaning of this?" in a voice that must have sent many a man to face the firing squad.

Both pairs of shoes scuttled from under the table. Breathlessly, Elaine hurriedly explained, "Papa, my little sailor boy fell off and we were trying to find him."

"And I found him," Charlie mumbled, while discreetly pulling the little sailor from his pocket.

Elaine gave a delighted squeal and placed the tiny sailor back on board her ship.

Mrs. Aims came in to check on the number of baskets and was immediately recruited by the sheriff. "I want you to personally see that my daughter is properly chaperoned until I return for her."

Mrs. Aims proudly threw back her shoulders and, with a fierce gleam in her eyes, promised, "Your honor, I shall take care of her as if she were my own daughter." Since Mrs. Aims had no children, this was not too reassuring for the sheriff.

Charlie groaned as Mrs. Aims marched his adored doll off to stand beside her by the punch bowl.

As Charlie was striding across the dance floor, a shrill whistle from a fraternity brother stopped him. "Well, chum, we better get started on our maneuver or it will to too late."

Charlie glanced at the well-guarded punch bowl. Mrs. Aims' shifty eyes were on the alert and his adorable doll looked bored. Charlie hissed, "Give me five minutes before I signal." Then he swiftly strode to where his sisters were seated at one of the small tables circling the dance floor. For once he thanked God he had sisters.

Amy was in tears. Many in the room had snickered at her grand entrance, which she had thought to be the best of Lillian Russell's poses. Amy had indeed drawn all eyes to her when she swished her train dramatically around and fluttered her fan. When her fan waved with increasing velocity Maybelle had looked around to see whom Amy was trying to attract. At the far end of the room her glance riveted on a massive crop of red hair. She was sure it was the same man she had seen driving with her sister the day they went fishing. He was dressed as the Jack of Spades, and his mask merely a pair of dark glasses. He was surveying a long table holding huge trays of cracked ice displaying the fish competing for the grand prize. Hearing amused tittering, he turned to find the source. Seeing him turn, Amy frantically waved her fan in a manner usually used to signal a passing ship. The redhead disappeared as if swallowed up by the sea.

Charlie bent over his sister Anna, whispering. Soon she was seen leading Elaine over to their table with Mrs. Aims' watchful eyes following them.

Charlie dashed to the cloakroom and returned carrying under his arm a paper sack. He gave an owl hoot and immediately a fight started at the far end of the basement. Mrs. Aims deserted the punch bowl with a rush, followed by everyone else. Charlie hastily made his way to the refreshment table and deftly poured two bottles of Jake's best home brew into the large milk-glass punch bowl. Giving a quick stir with his finger, he gave a shrill whistle and made fast tracks away from the scene of his transgression.

Mrs. Aims returned to her vigil, heaving from her exertion and pleased with herself for breaking up the fight. Dabbing at her perspiring forehead, she reached for a cup, dipping it into the sparkling ruby-red fruit punch. Not until the third cup did she feel any cooler.

Mayor Allison, coming in for a quick look, was offered a glass of punch by the gracious chaperone. He insisted she join him in a toast to a successful evening. She declined, but he insisted. "Come, my dear Mrs. Aims, you can't refuse a mayor's request."

"Oh, very well, just one."

That one had a dreadful effect on her eyes. She couldn't focus them to see the whereabouts of her charge.

Bob, looking even more handsome than usual in his black tuxedo and white tie, was receiving congratulations on his extraordinarily large fish. Seeing Bob's popularity, Charlie strode over to the table. Taking one look at Bob's fish, his face turned livid as he shouted, "This is a salmon derby and your fish is a Dolly Varden. It doesn't qualify!"

Bob calmly walked out the door, ripped a poster from the outside wall, came back and thrust it under Charlie's nose. "You will note. It plainly says 'fish.'"

Charlie, flushed with rage, yelled, "That's because the old goat couldn't spell salmon!"

Bob spoke dangerously low. "Posters all over Columbia County say fish. However, I leave the decision to the honorable Judge Frankland."

The judge stroked his chin. He hadn't anticipated any controversy in the judging. Three men had been appointed to do the weighing and measuring and had handed him the results. Bob definitely had caught the largest fish. It was simply a misunderstanding due to old Josh's lack of education.

Mrs. Aims, who usually had her nose into every one else's business, wasn't going to miss this opportunity to stick her proboscis into this hot argument. "Well if you ask me..." she started.

"No one is asking you," Charlie snapped, wounding the old lady's ego. Recovering she spat, "Well, your fish looks like a minnow beside Bob's."

Charlie howled with rage over the insult.

Judge Frankland wasn't the only one faced with a tough decision. Bob looked up and met Nettie's cold stare. His eyes shifted to Charlie's face distorted with malfeasance, then to Judge Frankland who was showing no emotion.

Bob admired Nettie for being loyal to her brother, but he was deeply hurt for she showed no consideration for him. Some people uneasily shifted their feet, while others nervously coughed.

Judge Frankland scanned the face of the son of one of his best friends. Would their friendship be at stake if he made his decision in favor of the young man whose integrity showed with clarity on his handsome face? The judge hesitated as he looked at the anxious faces of the young people surrounding him. Low whispering and murmuring were growing louder by those who were taking sides. He realized his decision must be made quickly before animosity grew to the point of breaking up the party. Not yet knowing how to resolve the issue, he started to speak; but Bob, realizing if he had any chance at all of winning Nettie for his wife, he would have to capitulate, spoke first. He turned to the Judge, "Sir, I believe negotiations are in order."

Judge nodded. "You are quite right."

There was a hushed silence in the crowd as they wondered how he was going to bargain. Bob avoided looking at Nettie as he spoke. "Due to a misunderstanding, I concede the victory to my friend, Charlie." The silence in the room erupted into excited chattering. Bob cleared his throat and added, "As for the horse, Charlie, you have honorably won it, but I would greatly appreciate it if you would accept my check for a thousand dollars for its purchase."

A ripple of astonishment swept over the ballroom. They had never heard of such a preposterous offer for a horse.

Charlie, taken by surprise, hesitated. He also did a quick calculation of his finances, which were in the red. Looking around and seeing Nettie give a slight nod, he slowly reached out his hand, barely touching Bob's, who noticed his signet ring was already on Charlie's index finger.

Feeling the crowd was on Bob's side, Charlie snapped, "No check, chum. I want cold cash."

Bob chillily replied, "Very well. Meet me at the bank in the morning and you will get your cold cash." He turned to walk away when he felt a light touch on his arm. He looked down into Nettie's stormy eyes.

"I still won't marry you," she told him coldly.

Indifferently, he replied, "I'll abide by the lady's decision," and he made his way through the crowd, out to see the horse he had just purchased. The only thing easing his aching heart was the thought of this beautiful animal running free in the meadows of the old homestead he had acquired that morning.

The mare whinnied and rubbed her velvet-soft nose against his cheek. As he stroked the satiny, warm skin of her neck, he felt she was returning his affection. He dreaded returning to the

## Chapter 11 - Fish Folly

ballroom. To the stable boy standing by he gave instructions to keep the mare in the livery stable for the night and take her out to the homestead in the morning. He would ask Abigale to go with him and also take a man out to repair the fence.

For a long time he sat by the mare, petting her and making plans for his homestead, wishing old man Curl was still living so he could help him in the reconstruction of the old place. Doc Andrus had once told him there was no death. The spirit energy giving life to the human body lives on in a higher rate of vibrations, and that love is eternal. For some time he sat thinking of other things this wonderful physician had told him. One remark that stuck in Bob's mind was to every day thank the Creator for the precious gift of life, to meet every problem as a challenge to be overcome. Bob felt his whole world had collapsed. The mare nudged him and he stood up wondering how in the hell was he going to face the crowd that had seen him jilted. Bob reentered the basement. Seeing Maybelle sitting alone at one of the tables, he strode over to sit down beside her. "Well, little miracle finder, are you enjoying the party?"

"Oh, it's heavenly. Bob, you're so noble, the way you handled everything. I'm truly ashamed Charlie is my brother." In girlish admiration, Maybelle gushed, "You're like a knight in shiny armor."

Bob shook his head, sighing, "I'm afraid my armor needs polishing."

Maybelle sympathetically touched his shoulder. "You were so chivalrous, but my sister is a stupid boob."

Bob's head sunk in his hands, but he said nothing. Suddenly, Maybelle leaned close to him. "Could you pretend I'm your little sister?"

"Easily," Bob replied without hesitation.

"Bid on the basket that looks like a ship and win it. Eat with the girl, make goo-goo eyes at her, dance every dance with her, hold her tight, and smooch her."

"That's pretty strong advice."

"Do it and Nettie will fall like a ripe peach into your arms."

"Do you guarantee the results?"

"Teetotally."

"There is one thing you haven't considered. I am no longer interested."

"Pooh, of course you are or you wouldn't be so hurt as you are now."

"I've decided to be a bachelor for life."

Maybelle's peal of laughter drew others' attention. "Oh, Bob, you're being so ridiculously funny. Do you think the girls would let any man so handsome go unmarried?"

"I was unaware my looks would have such an effect on the gentler sex."

"Of course they would. Now go this minute. The bidding on the baskets is about to start."

"Did you say the basket with the ship?"

Maybelle vigorously nodded. "Yes, now go and stand close to the auctioneer."

On his way to the auctioneer's table, he was accosted by Charlie in a rare case of embarrassment. "Bob, old boy, could you advance me a few shekels?"

Now that Charlie was civilly speaking to him, Bob didn't hesitate to pull out a few dollars from his pocket and hand them to him. Charlie snatched the money and rushed off without even a thank you.

Bob proceeded as he had been directed and stood with some dubious feelings beside the auctioneer.

Back at the office, Dr. Andrus was spending the rest of the night monitoring Mary's condition when his office door was violently kicked open and Cryder came in carrying a man who appeared to be dead. "Doc, I was on my way to see Sam about buyin' a sow and..."

"At this time of night?"

"Well, yeah...you see..."

Doc looked sharply at Cryder who hurried to explain. "I was ridin' along, enjoyin' the moonlight when I looked down and see this guy lyin' in a mud hole. Not wantin' to leave him in the mud, I brought him to you."

"Who is he?"

"Damned if I know. A horse must have run over him to mess him up like this."

"Doc turned up the man's bleeding face and exclaimed, "My God, it's the peddler!"

"Do tell? Well, well, what a coincidence," Cryder said, feigning innocence.

"Yes, quite a coincidence, Cryder. You've made me a lot of work."

"Don't ketch your drift."

"It means I have to take the time to sew him up when all my time is needed to be with Mary."

"In that case, I'll throw him back in the mud hole," Cryder started backing out the door.

"Stop. You sit by Mary and if you see any change in her breathing, let me know at once."

"If she stops breathin', I'll kill the bastard."

In a tender, motherly way, Cryder sat by Mary, patting her hand as big tears trickled down his weathered cheek. He was nodding with fatigue when Doc staggered from his operating room. "My God, Cryder, what you did to that man."

Cryder jerked his head up in defiance. "You heard what he did to Mrs. Miller's little Susie?" Doc silently nodded. Cryder spat out his snuff. "Well, I fixed him Indian way so he ain't goin' to rape any other little girl."

# Chapter 12

# Battle for the Baskets

Bob nervously shifted his feet and cursed himself for not having asked Maybelle whose basket he was to bid on. He hoped it would be someone who felt amiable towards the world and tenderhearted towards mankind. He had had enough of animosity for the evening. He knew another snub would have him walking out.

A boy looking like one-eyed Dick brought the first basket embellished with a stuffed bird on the handle. Before handing it to the auctioneer, he pressed his nose in the basket and sniffed. "Something in here smells like fried chicken."

The auctioneer took the basket holding it high over his head. "Hear that folks? This olfactory connoisseur says he smells fried chicken. Now what am I bid?"

"Fifteen cents," an adolescent voice croaked.

The auctioneer exploded. "Your bid is an insult to fried chicken!"

The same voice yelled, "I ain't insultin'. I ain't got no more money."

"Sorry, my boy, you're out of luck."

"I ain't neither. Pa just gave me one buck."

"You bid one buck?"

"Yeah, you fleecer."

The auctioneer yelled, "One buck. Do I hear three?"

Bob glanced over at Maybelle's hanging head and knew it was her basket and she was extremely embarrassed. Bob tugged at the auctioneer's sleeve, whispering. The auctioneer whirled the basket over his head. "I have a bid of five dollars, going, going..."

Maybelle was reacting with vigorous shaking of her head which Bob ignored and was about to claim the basket when a boy about Maybelle's age, dressed as a knight complete with shiny sword, yelled, "Six dollars." Maybelle started nodding her head and Bob let the knight proudly claim her basket.

Knowing Maybelle was determined for him to bid on the ship basket, Bob fumed as he waited for a long procession of baskets to be auctioned off, and he began wishing the ship had sunk. Bidding was going slowly and the auctioneer was exasperated. He began to berate the crowd. He held up a basket cleverly decorated with an assortment of cheeses and ingeniously topped by a bottle of wine, which seemed to inspire the auctioneer.

"Folks, here's a chance to get a real meal which would cost you five bucks in the best restaurant. Now let's hear some real bidding. Don't forget, your bids will help the church get a new roof."

"Ah, let the roof leak," some disgruntled voice blurted. "Baptize the sinners with the holy rain."

"I will ignore that ignoramus remark," sputtered the auctioneer.

Mrs. Aims sidled up to him, whispering. Straightening up, he thundered, "We have fifteen more baskets left to auction, all the delicious meals just waiting for some lucky bidder." Holding up a lavender-ribbon-bedecked basket, he intoned, "Come on, who's going to be the lucky bidder?"

In spite of his promotional pitch the bidding went slowly. Bob grew impatient and had decided to walk out; just then the same pirate brought out the ship basket. He glanced at Maybelle, who was gleefully and vigorously nodding. Before the basket was even in the auctioneer's hand, a voice rang out loudly, "Five dollars!"

Bob was stunned when he recognized the voice. It was the last person in the world he wanted to bid against. He took another quick look at Maybelle, who was jumping up and down and making a queer movement with her mouth, which he translated to mean "Bid, bid." Bob spoke so low that the auctioneer told him to speak up. He took a deep breath. "Ten dollars."

"Twenty dollars!" rang out the same voice, sounding more determined. Mentally, Bob took a quick inventory of his finances, wondering just how much he had given Charlie and, more important, how much he had left.

The auctioneer was beaming "If this bidding keeps up the church will have a new roof and..."

"Thirty dollars!" Bob interrupted, not daring to look at Maybelle.

The same voice, now sounding desperate, shouted, "Fifty dollars!"

The auctioneer seemed to have lost his voice and didn't acknowledge the bid at once. The voice, now angry, repeated, "I said fifty dollars!"

"Yes, yes," the befuddled auctioneer rasped. "Sold for fifty dollars."

After a glimpse of Maybelle squealing her encouragement, Bob raised a hand, objecting, "Not so fast. There is another bid. I raise it to sixty dollars." he intoned.

"Going once, going twice..."

Before the auctioneer could bring down his gavel to announce "Sold," there was a commotion in the back as Charlie made his way to the auction table. He held out Bob's signet ring to the auctioneer who shook his head. "Sorry, that won't put a roof on the church. Sold to this gentleman for sixty dollars."

Bob accepted the ship basket and made his way through the crowd to Maybelle, who threw her arms around his neck and kissed his cheek.

Bob grabbed her shoulders, fiercely looking at her. "Whose is it?"

"Open the basket and find out."

Under the ship's lid rested a dainty pink slip. In violet ink was faintly scribbled "Elaine."

Bob felt a cold chill. Would this jeopardize his deal for the horse? He slumped into a chair. "Why did you do this to your brother?"

"I did it for you. Everyone knows you won the fish derby. Charlie doesn't deserve to win."

"Your brother will kill me. I'll give him the basket."

"Oh no you won't!" Maybelle grabbed the basket. "I won't let you chicken out. Go claim your dinner partner, bring her here, and we'll have oodles of fun."

Elaine was delighted to have the most popular young man in town escort her to his table. She glowed with elation. Her basket had brought the highest bid in the history of basket socials in Dayton.

It was a schoolmate of Maybelle's who had successfully bid on her basket. They were starting to eat when a shrill scream shattered the hum of voices. A burly lumberjack had Amy under the arm and was carrying a basket trimmed with a bunch of straw flowers, on the other. Maybelle jumped up to confront him. "What are you doing with my sister? That's not her basket."

"Oh yeah?" he snarled, thrusting a slip of paper under her nose. Maybelle couldn't believe her eyes. It was Amy's name. What had happened? Amy's basket had had a big bow. She quickly glanced around and saw Anna beside a red-bowed basket eating with the school principal. She knew Anna's basket had been decorated with red straw flowers. How did they get mixed up? She glanced over at Charlie who was howling with laughter.

"Oh dear," Maybelle lamented.

Through clenched teeth, Amy yelled, "I'm not going to eat with you, you big mutt."

"Your goin' to eat and like it."

Bob hurriedly shoved back his chair, ready for action. Maybelle grabbed the drumstick out of Bob's hand and waved it in the air. "Come on, Sis, join us. The more the merrier." Bob pulled a chair from the next table, offering it to Amy.

"That's a great idea." The lumberjack plunked the angry girl in the offered chair. Amy sat down with a curt "Thank you."

Mrs. Aims came over to inquire, "Are you children enjoying yourselves? Hot chocolate is being served in the Sunday school room. Oh, Elaine, I see your mother has made her famous-raisin filled cookies. May I have one?" Before Elaine could consent, Mrs. Aims helped herself to a handful, then took after the auctioneer, who was starting to get the orchestra together. She hailed him as he was going out the door. "Oh, Mr. Delany, you were wonderful. You sold every one of the baskets and not only did we make enough to shingle the church's roof, but there was enough to buy a rug for the aisle."

"Well, I'm sure pleased to hear that. Now I must hurry and get Tom Hepmer. He's to play the accordion, you know."

"He won't be playing anything. He's drunk."

"He promised he'd stay sober."

"Well, he broke his promise. He found out old man Smith is selling his new batch of home brew behind the livery stable."

The auctioneer shook his head ruefully. "The dance music won't be good without him."

"Old Josh can play better."

"Good. I'll go get him."

"Don't think he'll come."

"Why not?"

"He's mad because he was insulted when he couldn't spell salmon on the posters he lettered for the fish derby."

"He's coming if I have to drag him."

"Good luck. He's as stubborn as a mule."

Fannie left her supper partner as soon as they finished eating. She was too depressed to talk to anyone and found a chair behind the church organ to nurse her bitter disappointment over John's failure to come to the dance. She had received several compliments on her lovely gown, but she took no pleasure in the admiration. She felt all the hard work on her gown was for nothing when John wasn't there to admire her tiny waist. And she didn't feel good. At times she felt dizzy. Since John hadn't come she was anxious to go home.

Across from her Mae and Anna seemed to be having a good time with the Anderson brothers who were well known for their practical jokes. Suddenly, pandemonium broke loose. Bustles and trains didn't prevent Anna and Mae from leaping up onto their chairs, screaming. Two frightened garter snakes slithered across the dance floor and the whole room broke into a riot. The two brothers' hilarious laughter soon turned into howls of protest when Mrs. Aims descended on them with the janitor's broom. Order was restored when Mrs. Aims grabbed the two culprits by the ears. She dragged them out of the ballroom. Some had to admit Mrs. Aims was handling her chaperone duties with commendable proficiency.

The violinist had finished tuning up. Mrs. Fairweather struck several rollicking chords on the piano, but Josh stood immobile with his accordion. The two musicians started to play again, but Josh still stood motionless. In exasperation Mrs. Aims stomped up to him.

"You old cuss! What's the matter with you? Ain't you goin' to play?"

"I ain't playin' until I get an apology."

"What for?"

"For sayin' I couldn't spell salmon."

"Well, you couldn't, could you?"

"That ain't the point. I didn't have to be insulted."

Mrs. Aims huffed with disgust. "Very well, I apologize."

"Ain't you. It's that young whippersnapper of Doc's."

All eyes turned to Charlie, whose face was turning to a bright sunset crimson. "I'm not apologizing to that old goat," he protested.

"Then I ain't playin'."

The crowd groaned. It was the accordion that put the pep into the music. Bob walked over to Josh, bowing low. "I humbly apologize for anyone who has hurt your feelings."

Josh shook his head. "No, gotta be him. He's the one who was insultin'."

Someone in the crowd shouted, "Come on, Charlie, be a good sport. It will take only a minute then we can get on with our dancing. It's no good without Josh."

Others started pleading with Josh who only shook his head.

Amy's supper partner jerked off his lumber jacket and walked up to Charlie. "You apologize or I'll finish the fight you once started."

Mrs. Aims was losing her patience. "You two fools are goin' to ruin the party."

A sweet voice rang out, "It's going to be a lovely party because Charlie is going to apologize, aren't you dear?" Elaine was now by Charlie's side, snuggling up to him, looking tenderly into his face.

Astonished gasps erupted from the crowd. "I...I...w...was just going to," stammered Charlie.

"Of course you were." Elaine raised on tiptoe to kiss his cheek.

Mrs. Aims' eyes popped with horror and fury. What would the sheriff think of his daughter's outlandish conduct? And she had promised to guard her. "Ohhh!" Mrs. Aims wailed, wondering if the sheriff would jail her for not attending to her duties as she had promised him.

Charlie was almost choking as he apologized. Josh said nothing but turned and picked up his accordion. Immediately, the three-piece orchestra struck up a lively two-step and the jovial couples crowded onto the dance floor.

Now that Bob had lost his partner, Maybelle timidly smiled up at him. Bob held out his arms. Maybelle hesitated. "I'm sorry you're disappointed."

Bob looked down at her. "Disappointed? Not at all. I'd much rather dance with my little sister."

"You fib beautifully."

He swung her out onto the dance floor, side-stepping to avoid bumping into Charlie and Elaine, both of whom seemed to be in a world all their own. He was surprised the couple behind them seemed to be having trouble. He recognized Amy's voice. "You big lug. You're stepping on my feet."

"What's the beef? After the horse whipping you gave me, it's coming to you," answered a husky voice.

Unsteady peels of laughter kept drifting across the dance floor. Maybelle looked questioningly up at Bob. "It sort of sounds like someone is drunk."

Whirling her around so the punch bowl was in his line of vision, Bob saw Mrs. Aims was still guarding it while Nettie was unsteadily walking away with a glass of punch. Bob grew suspicious. When the violin gave a sharp twang ending the dance, Bob escorted Maybelle back to Amy and headed for the punch bowl. He dipped a cup into the ruby red punch, took a couple of swallows, then turned to Mrs. Aims. "Have you at any time left this punch bowl unguarded?"

Mrs. Aims gave him a quizzical glance and pursed her lips, declaring, "No, I have NOT."

"This punch has been spiked," Bob told her.

Shocked, Mrs. Aims insisted, "I've been here all the time."

"How about when there was a fight?"

"Oh yes, I remember I did leave to break up the fight, but I was gone only for a minute."

"Long enough for some one to give the fruit juice a real jolt."

"But surely not enough to get anyone drunk?" Mrs. Aims anxiously asked.

Bob pointed. "There's your answer."

Nettie was coming with unsteady steps for another glass of punch. Bob stepped in front of the punch bowl. "I think you've had enough."

"Enough fruit juice? Don't be silly," Nettie hiccupped.

Bob told her, "Someone has spiked it and given it a kick."

Nettie shrugged. "Who cares? I'm hot and I'm thirsty and I'm going to have another glass." She staggered over to the punch bowl. Horrified, Mrs. Aims grabbed up the punch bowl and elbowed her way through the dancers. Once outside she dumped the contents into a ditch.

Bob snatched Nettie's arm, pulling her protesting across the crowded dance floor. Outside he tossed her into a buggy, grabbing the reins from a surprised livery stable boy, and snapped the horse with a whip.

Nettie screamed, "Where are you taking me?"

"To Neville's for a sobering cup of coffee."

"He's closed."

"Then to Abigale's."

"Sh... She's with Mother."

"Not now."

The buggy wheels squeaked to a stop in front of the same Gothic cottage. Forcefully pulling Nettie along, he stalked to the door and banged the knocker. Abigale came to the door in her dressing gown. She feigned delight on seeing them but knew something was terrible wrong.

Nettie tried to wrench her hand free, but Bob's grip tightened. "Dear friend, may we have a cup of coffee?" asked Bob.

"Of course. Come in."

Abigale made no mention of Nettie's unsteadiness and ignored Bob's sternness. Instead, she headed for the kitchen, asking, "Do you want your coffee weak or strong?"

"So it will float an axe," Bob replied with a grim laugh.

When Abigale returned with three steaming cups of coffee, she found Bob still staring at the wall and Nettie on the sofa with her head buried in a pillow. "Well," Abigale forced herself to ask brightly, "whose basket did you bid on Bob?"

Nettie's head shot up from the pillow. "That bleached, blonde-headed, simpering..."

"Elaine's," Bob said with a warning look at Nettie.

Oh dear, Abigale thought. What can I do, what can I say to calm the trouble waters? Taking a deep breath, she said, "Oh, she's such a snooty little snip, all because she's the sheriff's daughter. Bob, how could you?"

### Chapter 12 - Battle for the Baskets

"Exactly." Nettie brightened considerably.

Bob was so dumbfounded he dropped his coffee cup. Never, ever before had he heard Abigale make a derogatory remark about anyone, and more astonishing, she was blaming him. Nor had he ever heard her chatter as she was now. Abigale had never been the chattering kind.

The two friends struggled to carry on a conversation while Nettie sat silent with glaring eyes. Finally, Abigale could no longer take it and after both refused a second cup of coffee, she rose, saying, "The night is still young and so are you, so scoot back to the dance. Bob, see that you behave yourself and dance every dance with Nettie. Goodnight, my darlings."

Upon leaving, Bob gave Abigale a withering look that left her quaking. Hurriedly closing the door, she rushed upstairs to the guest room. Cynthia glanced up at her friend's stricken face and dropped the magazine she had been reading.

"My dear, what happened? What's wrong?"

"Something terrible has happened between Nettie and Bob. I was trying so hard to make things right between them, but I think I've messed up everything."

"Perhaps you should just let them sort out things by themselves."

Abigale sighed, sobbing, "You're right, but I guess I want them to marry so very much." Abigale dabbed her eyes. "I know I've hurt Bob's feelings."

Cynthia started reading again. "Just give them time to iron out their troubles."

Returning to the church, Bob was accosted by Maybelle. "Oh, Bob, Amy has been gone for an hour and I can't find her anyplace."

"When did you see her last?" Bob asked with concern.

"She was dancing with that Walla Walla boy, the same one we saw her with when we went fishing. As soon as they finished dancing I was going to tell Amy to stop snuggling up to him, but Fannie came to tell me she was leaving and when I looked up they were gone."

Bob swore under his breath but reassuringly patted Maybelle's shoulder. "Don't worry, I'll have a look around." However, Bob himself was worried. In college Dick Horton had none too good a reputation. When he found Dick's carriage gone, he borrowed a saddle horse for a faster search.

Fannie was telling Maybelle, "John hasn't come so I'm leaving."

Maybelle laughed. "Bet you aren't. Look!"

Fannie, turning to look, saw John entering, and she rushed to meet him. He gave her a happy grin and, taking her in his arms, swung her out onto the dance floor. Fannie bubbled with joy. "Your coming makes my evening."

"Mine too," he softly whispered against her cheek.

Fannie anxiously asked, "You're feeling much better?"

John nuzzled her ear. "The minute you were in my arms I felt great."

Fannie happily snuggled under his chin. "Papa warned me not to let you get tired."

John grinned, "With you in my arms, I'll never get tired."

Shyly, Fannie looked up into his admiring eyes and asked, "Do you like my new gown?"

"I like your beautiful blue eyes best."

John made a quick side-step to avoid the janitor carrying a bucket of coal to stoke the large potbellied stove. Fannie remonstrated, "It's too hot in here now!"

John tried to stop the old man from putting more coal into the stove, but the janitor shook his head. "I'm paid to shovel coal into this coal-eatin' burner, so I gotter do it."

Twice more the lovers circled the floor, engrossed in each other when John felt his sweetheart go slack in his arms. He looked down with concern. "Dear, are you all right?"

"I...I...I think so. I...I feel so strange." Then she collapsed.

Alarmed, John lifted her in his arms, heading for the hall. Jerking down coats from the hooks, he spread them on the floor and lay Fannie down carefully. She looked deadly pale. He bent his head to her breast. There was scarcely a heartbeat and she was not breathing. Remembering his sister in just such a situation due to a tight corset string, he reached for his pocketknife. Unbuttoning her basque, he was cutting the corset string when Mrs. Aims came through the door. John's frightened eyes looked up into Mrs. Aims' horrified stare. For one frozen moment she stood, then dashed screaming among the dancers yelling, "Murder! Murder! Help, Fannie's being murdered!"

At that moment an explosion sent the stove lid into the air, sending soot and ashes over the room. Someone yelled, "Get out! Get out! Mrs. Aims has blown up the church!"

"You fool!" yelled Mrs. Aims. "It's the devil that done it. I warned you."

Fearful the church would catch on fire, John carried Fannie outside and laid her down on a buggy seat. While rubbing her wrist he saw color coming back into her face. Her eyelids began to flutter and she took several deep breaths. "Darling, I think you fainted."

"How silly of me," she said sitting up.

"I'm taking you to your father's office at once."

"No, just take me home. I'm all right, really I am."

John helped her out of the buggy and as she looked down to alight she saw her open basque and cut corset string. Appalled she looked at John with dismay. "How dare you! How dare you!" Jumping down she started running for home with John swiftly following, pleading his cause.

Back in the basement, the janitor was trying to calm down the panic by explaining, "It weren't Satan, it was me forgettin' to open the damper."

Mrs. Aims disagreed. "It was the devil himself that done it and the smoke is straight from hell."

Nancy waited up to hear about her children's good time and was aghast on seeing their black-streaked cloths and hearing their teary laments. Only Charlie radiated cheerfulness for he had danced every dance with his adored doll.

Fannie wept uncontrollably. "I'll hate John for the rest of my life. How dare he be so brazen! Oh, I'm so humiliated and disgraced, yes disgraced. Oh, how I detest him!"

Amy hobbled through the door, flopping down in a chair. "That brute walked all over my feet on purpose. I'll be crippled for the rest of my life. I should have killed him with the buggy whip. The next time I will."

Mae and Anna bemoaned their ruined dresses. Nancy was shocked seeing their soot-smudged gowns. "And how did you tear them?" asked their mother.

Weeping, they explained, "Snakes were chasing us and we had to jump up on chairs or get bitten."

"It's unbelievable," Nancy exclaimed.

Just then Nettie staggered in falling on the sofa. "Bob never danced one dance with me. My very own sister is a traitor. She danced every dance with him. I'll never trust her again."

Maybelle bristled. "Of course he didn't want to dance with you when you were staggering all over the place."

"That's a lie," Nettie yelled.

"You were drunk," Maybelle accused.

"Drunk on fruit juice? You're crazy."

"I am not. Oh, Mama," Maybelle sobbed, "there wasn't even one little miracle."

# Chapter 13

# Challenging the AMA

A morning of weeping clouds and dripping locust leaves reflected the mood of the Andrus family at breakfast. Doc, taking his napkin from its ring, looked across at the empty seat opposite him and asked his children, "Your mother, isn't she coming to breakfast?"

"No, Papa," Anna glumly replied. "She's not feeling well."

Doc immediately rose from the table and went to his wife. "My dear, why didn't you tell me last night you weren't feeling well?"

"I didn't want to disturb your sleep. You work so hard and it seems a number of your patients imposed on you too much."

"Surely you must know you mean more to me than any patient. Now let's see why you're feeling ill."

After examining the woman he loved more each day, he stood up, looking sympathetically down into tear-filled eyes, shaking his head. "My dear, I'm afraid you're having another bout of erysipelas. The children have been putting too much strain on your nervous system. You must have more rest. The girls are old enough now to take over the household duties and I'll take Charlie back to college on my way to the medical convention. That will eliminate some of the stress."

"Nelson, what is wrong with the children? They seem not to get along with anyone and never want to listen to me."

Doc smiled. "My dear, it's all a part of growing up. You can't reproach the young because they are searching to find better ways."

"But we have suffered so many hardships to make a good life for them and they don't seem to appreciate it. Frankly, Nelson, I don't think I can take much more, as they no longer want to listen to advice."

"If our children complied with all of our counseling, they would cease to be youths. Youth must search, quest, and rebel."

"I don't mind the search so much as the constant rebelling, which makes it so difficult."

Doc took his wife's hand, caressing it. "I think the whole family needs a vacation."

"Yes, and Anna most of all. Have you noticed how she's drooping?"

He nodded. "Mrs. Aldridge has made a new tonic I believe will help her. How would you like a camping trip, say to the Blue Mountains?"

"Oh yes, that would be wonderful. The children could work off some of their energy by hiking and swimming."

"Then it's settled."

Nancy nodded. "How soon can we go?"

"As soon as I return. Now don't worry. Next year will be much easier. By then the school will be rebuilt and all the children will be back in school."

"What is John going to do without you while you're gone?"

"I'll only be away a week."

"He's coughing more and getting so thin."

"He'll come around as soon as Fannie makes up with him."

"She's still very angry."

"Probably more embarrassed than anything."

"You must admit it was a very ungentlemanly thing to do."

"A very sensible thing to do. A brain deprived of oxygen very long can be severely damaged."

"Is that what caused her to faint?"

Her husband nodded. "She couldn't get enough air because of her infernal, tight corset. Her stupid vanity is to blame."

"But surely there was some other way so as not to expose her." Nancy laid her head back against the pillow.

Doc sat down on the edge of the bed. "After the dance, John, seeing a light in my office, came in to explain the situation. He said Fannie was turning blue and he thought she was dying. He had two sisters and knew all about corsets causing fainting and surmised what was wrong. He felt it urgent to get air into her lungs, so in desperation he cut her corset strings."

"She says she'll never forgive him."

"She will, because I think she really loves him."

Nancy heaved a sigh, smiling at her husband. "It seems true love travels a rocky road."

Doc stood up. "True love grows on life's challenges. We have survived in pretty good shape."

Nancy laughed, "Because, dear, you removed most of the rocks."

Doc leaned down to kiss his wife. "Ask the girls to hire two more teams and a couple of teamsters. Have them pack enough food for a couple of weeks and get all the camping gear together. As soon as I return we'll head for the Blue Mountains."

Two days later, after dropping Charlie off at the college, Dr. Andrus drove to the law office of his friend, Judge Frankland, who quickly rose from his chair to warmly greet him. "Nelson, it's good to see you. Our fair city doesn't see you very often."

"I'm afraid I wouldn't be here now, had not the Medical Association invited me to speak at their convention."

"Yes, I saw in the papers that you were to speak. Well, my friend, give them hell!"

"I'll at least give them something to think about."

"Knowing you as well as I do, I know you'll shake them up. They are headed in the wrong direction."

"I've come to congratulate you on your decision to run for governor. But I confess I'm surprised."

"Why surprised? You don't think I have the qualifications?"

"No, no, nothing like that, but you always admired Emerson's philosophy."

"And I still do."

"You will recall he believed the less government the better."

"That's exactly why I'm running."

"But the papers stated that if you were elected, you would create a new social service department."

"It would eliminate five other departments and consolidate them into one department, thus less government and fewer drones on the payroll for their votes."

"You'll make a great governor for the first term, but I doubt you'll get a second term."

"Why not? I intend to keep to the principles of our Founding Fathers who created this nation a republic, a rule by law."

"That's exactly why it will be difficult for you to get a second term. There are politicians who want to turn this nation into a democracy, a rule by men. History has proved a democracy is always short-lived and ends in a bloodbath."

"You paint a grim picture."

"It is that, but a true one. Mankind seems never to learn from history." The doctor, taking his gold-plated watch from his vest pocket, glanced at it. Then snapping it shut, he said, "If I'm to make the meeting on time, I must be leaving." He held out his hand. "Good luck. I'll see that Columbia County supports you. I only wish all my children were old enough to vote for you."

"Nelson, I fully appreciate you support. By the way, a few of my medical friends are attending the convention. They, too, agree with the Hippocratic Doctrine."

"I'm glad someone will be there who's in accord with it."

"And they will stand by you."

"I'll probably need all the support I can get. The next time you're in Dayton, be sure to stop and have dinner with us."

"Thank you. I'll look forward to it. Good luck."

Dr. Andrus left for the governor's mansion where the convention was being held. As the carriage drove up the driveway to a large turreted mansion, four large Airedales bounded out to greet him, followed by a tiny Pekinese which belonged to the governor's granddaughter. The large dogs seemed to be protecting the pup and no one dared to get near the little thing without a savage growl of warning from the bristling Airedales.

The governor himself came to the top of the porch steps to greet him. Warmly holding out his hand, he said, "So glad you were able to come, Dr. Andrus. I feel your presence will be greatly needed to balance the meeting."

As Dr. Andrus entered the crowded ballroom, he was surrounded by those who wished to meet this man whose healing fame was drawing patients from all over the States and as far away as Europe. They little suspected they would soon be writhing under his accusations.

Dr. Lally, a flushed-faced physician from Illinois, stepped to the podium to make the introductions. One by one he introduced the physicians who were focusing on individual parts of the human anatomy. Because each speech was limited to fifteen minutes, they gave only a brief résumé of their specialization. Nothing was mentioned about treating the cause of the disorder afflicting the human body and it brought a frown of disapproval from Dr. Andrus and some good ammunition for his speech.

Again Dr. Lally stepped forward. "Gentlemen, tonight we are privileged to have a distinguished physician with us. It gives me great pleasure to introduce to you Lord Nelson Andrus."

Polite clapping followed Dr. Andrus to the podium. For a moment he stood surveying his audience, then he spoke sternly. "When man was created, he was formed gently, fragilely, and as an exceedingly complex being. He was given the gift of life and governed by cosmic forces. The physician has a great responsibility when called upon to deal with the elementary part of the body, the machine itself. In order to help correct any malfunctioning, he must fully understand the working of forces carried by rays. Positive forces will induce growths while negative forces repel them. All rays carry forces. A force carried by a particular blue ray induces sleep and unconsciousness to pain. Sunstroke is caused by a certain ray penetrating the cerebral cord. A red cloth covering the back of the neck stops the force from penetrating the cloth and prevents sunstroke."

A murmur of surprise swept through his audience. Dr. Andrus continued, "A simple experiment can show you the working of one force. Place two blocks of ice of the same size in the sun for an hour. Cover one with a black cloth, the other with a white cloth. The one under the black cloth will be completely melted while the one under the white will only be half melted. This occurrence is caused by black being affinitive to heat force, while white is a repellent. Nobody of matter can make changes without the action of forces. After a force has passed through the system it becomes exhausted and should pass unobstructed from the body through the pores of the skin. Perspiration, being mostly of water, is a powerful affinitive to attract, collect, and carry off exhausted forces, which frees the channels for fresh forces for their rejuvenating action. If the channels remain clogged, then the exhausted forces back up and in many cases cause heart attacks. The use of water to keep free the channels for exhausted forces to be eliminated was well known by the Ancients but forgotten or opposed by modern medicals.

"Four hundred years before Christ, Hippocrates, the father of medicine, knew the value of the water cure. Moses under divine instruction commanded the Israelites to bathe once a day. Ancient Persians erected elaborate and magnificent public bathing facilities to keep their population healthy. Two thousand years ago, a couple of noted physicians, Celus and Galan, exalted and praised the bath as being invaluable to the body's well-being. History tells us Emperor Augustus was cured by water of a disease that thwarted his physicians.

"In the fifteenth century in Constantinople, the Turkish baths were used extensively with excellent results.

"In 1840 the water cure spread to America and became popular. But in 1854," Doctor Nelson thundered, "American doctors eliminated any practice that allowed the public to use remedies in the home that were inexpensive, and in 1879 they successfully passed medical law prohibiting the water cure in America. It was no longer legal to assist the body with water to eliminate exhausted forces for restoring the body to health."

Dr. Andrus pounded the podium. "What right have you to deny people the means to recover their health?"

A pompous physician from Ohio arose. "If you will pardon the interruption, the law was enacted to protect the advance of the science of medicine."

The doctor's eyes blazed with contempt. "Do you dare to call it an advancement in the science of medicine when physicians bled a patient of ninety ounces of blood, injected several grains of calomel which is a compound of the deadly mercury, administered poultices of vinegar to already existing blisters, had him breathe vapors of vinegar, gave him strong emetic powers—and in twenty-four hours, the patient, the first president of the United States, was dead? And all he had wrong was a sore throat! Is that progress in medical science. I ask you. IS IT?"

"I question the authenticity of your accusation Dr. Andrus," said a physician from Idaho leaping to his feet.

The stillness in the room was almost suffocating as they waited for Dr. Andrus to give proof of the accusations, he had flung at his audience. His soft, low voice was more effective than if he had he shouted when he replied, "You will find it all recorded in the Congressional records in their library."

There was a nervous and embarrassed shuffling of feet among the association's members. Dr. Andrus stood immobile. He wanted the horrendous actions of their colleagues to sink in. When he spoke again it was with bitterness and sadness. "When our President was dying, he asked his physicians to be allowed to die without interruption."

It was plain the members refused to be humiliated when one rose to his feet to address the speaker in a hard and forceful voice. "Dr. Andrus, you have not taken into consideration how we have advanced."

"Have you?" the doctor shot back. "When you do nothing to stop the deplorable hawking by unprofessionals of questionable nostrums? Several of my patients have taken their so-called cures which have so damaged their nervous systems, they will never recover from tremors."

A man whom the doctor knew to be a highly respected physician and a friend of Judge Frankland rose to comment. "Dr. Andrus, we physicians have come to rely upon these men for some of our medicine."

"I don't doubt it at all," the doctor quietly replied. "And I warn you, because of economic self-interest, this questionable business of the medicine-show men will grow until it's in full control of the medical establishment with their consent."

The same physician stood to ask, "Can't something be done to protect the people?"

"Yes. Force your government to give the same freedom of choice for alternative medicine as they did for religion in the nation's constitution."

"You mean the freedom to choose between natural means and poison?"

Dr. Andrus smiled. "If you want to put it that way, yes, but I would prefer to refer to it between orthodox and alternative medicine. Someday your very life may depend on it."

Someone in the back shouted, "We aren't going to swallow..."

"You're going to swallow a lot more before I'm through with you," interrupted the doctor and spent the rest of his allotted time exposing the charlatans of the medicine shows. He finished with the admonishment, "Stop these hucksters from selling quack medicine laced with alcohol, cocaine, heroin, to name but a few of the poisons they use. Stop the obscenities practiced by these hucksters or it will be the forerunner of a lucrative orthodox business, ruling your practice with an iron hand because money will rule."

There was murmuring in the audience as Dr. Andrus shuffled his notes. "In closing I wish to predict the future uses of forces to replace the knife in surgery and to some degree replace medicine as we know it. Thank you, gentlemen, for your attention."

As Dr. Andrus was making his way from the podium, Dr. Lally intercepted him with a request. "Doctor, several members in the audience have requested a period for questions. If you would consent to answer them, it would be greatly appreciated."

"I would be most happy to comply; unfortunately I have an appointment to see a very ill patient."

After seeing the patient, he went to his hotel room to rest and was surprised when his son bounced into the room. "Papa, you almost caused a riot! In fact you stirred up a hornet's nest."

"How so?"

"My roommate's father is a doctor and Ralph says he's been pacing the floor since hearing your speech. Boy is he mad! He thinks you should be lynched. What did you say that caused such a uproar?"

"Only the truth."

"Well, it surely upset his apple cart."

"It's regrettable they won't learn from the truth and advance their medical knowledge into avenues that will benefit their patients."

"That's because they are selfish and greedy, thinking more about making money than getting their patients well," Charlie venomously declared.

His father smiled, shaking his head. "My son, know this: Humanity usually fights evolving into higher realms of development. It takes eons of time for the human race to evolve."

Charlie hung his head in contemplation, then jerking it up he said, "Yeah, I know. They burned one guy at the stake for saying something that was true and another guy they hung for saying the truth about something else. Well, anyway, they better wake up fast or they'll get killed by all those phony quacks."

His father smiled at his son's lack of specifics, saying, "People probably won't change for a century or more."

A knock sounded and the doctor nodded for Charlie to open the door. He quickly arose when Judge Frankland walked in with outstretched hand, vigorously shaking the doctor's. "Nelson, you really jolted them. Congratulations! My friends tell me you gave an outstanding speech."

"I hope I wasn't too severe on them."

"That would be impossible. It takes some strong veracity to pierce through their tough medical hides. They are going to have to change directions or we'll all be in for it."

"I fear that will take a long time."

"Nelson, I've come to tell you I'm putting a guard at your door for the night."

"That won't be necessary."

"Maybe not, but I'm not taking chances. Some of my medical friends tell me that some of the physicians are having your practitioner's license annulled and..."

A knock interrupted the judge. Charlie went to the door. A bellhop presented a note. Charlie handed it to his father who read the missal with amusement. Turning to the waiting boy, he said, "Tell the gentlemen I'll be right down."

"Yes sir. They are waiting in the reception hall." Then the boy grinned. "They sure look mad!"

Doc turned to his friend. "I'll handle this alone. It won't do you any good to get mixed up in this just before the election."

The judge shook his head. "I'll get mixed up in more provocative situations than this before I'm through with politics. Lead the way."

As they entered the reception room, five professional men stood up, their attitude bristling. There was no offer to shake hands, only scowls of indignation.

"Gentlemen, what can I do for you?" Doc asked with a smile.

"We have come to inform you that your license is being revoked."

"On what premises?"

"On false statements."

"Everything I've said is substantiated by facts."

"On the contrary, you made unfounded accusations and you can no longer practice."

Judge Frankland stepped forward, "Gentlemen, to make that valid it has to go through the legal system. Show Dr. Andrus the necessary legal papers to take away his license."

"Well, we are getting them tomorrow."

"By law, you have no right to threaten an American citizen and can be persecuted of which I have the authority to have you arrested for intimidating an innocent man."

All five men shifted uneasily on their feet. "It was just a warning," one mumbled.

"It was a threat," snapped the judge.

Charlie, red-faced, shouted, "You better apologize to my father!"

"Charlie, that's enough," his father warned.

One of the physicians blustered, "No doctor killed George Washington."

"The Congressional Library is open for your research."

Judge Frankland spoke severely. "And now, gentlemen, without further inconvenience to Dr. Andrus, we will call this matter closed."

In the hotel room, Doc shook his friend's hand. "I've changed my mind. The way you handled this matter I predict you'll win six terms."

They both laughed and the judge departed with the promise of having dinner with the Andrus family soon.

As he fell asleep, Charlie informed his father, "I'm going back with you and help you pack for your vacation."

Doc yawned. "Well, son, how about your agriculture class?"

"Oh heck, it shouldn't be too hard to learn how to grow tomatoes."

## Chapter 14

# Mrs. Aims on the Attack

While the doctor was away, Mrs. Aldridge came every day to treat Nancy with a new ointment she had made of chickweed. It greatly eased the pain and itching of the swellings Nancy was suffering from, keeping her in bed. The girls had taken over the house duties, but there was quarreling between them as they felt Amy wasn't doing her part. They accused her of being lazy, which she vigorously denied. "I am doing more than my share, so there."

"You haven't done a thing to help all morning," Fannie accused.

Amy burst into tears. "You're all hateful, and…"

"Is a referee needed?" a boyish voice inquired.

Startled, Mae dropped a basket of freshly laundered clothes and Maybelle, squealing with delight, ran with open arms, exclaiming, "Charlie! What are you doing back? You're supposed to be growing tomatoes."

"I'm here unofficially as a bodyguard."

"Bodyguard! Whatever do you mean?"

"Papa stirred up a hornet's nest at the medical convention and they are mad enough to kill him."

Wide-eyed, the girls were horrified. "Kill him! Ohhh!"

"Well, they made some pretty strong threats."

"Is Papa really in danger?" asked Anna, putting an apple pie in the oven.

Charlie slammed his fist on the table. "You bet he is with those scalp-wielders after him, so I'm here to protect him."

"Pooh. What could you do to protect Papa?" Anna challenged.

For an answer, Charlie drew a knife from his pocket. He pressed the bone handle and a sharp blade sprang out. "That should cut them into ribbons," Charlie said, looking smug.

Doc, after spending a few minutes with his wife, went to his study next to their bedroom to catch up on some office work that needed to be done before leaving for the mountains. Mae stuck her head in. "Papa, Mrs. Aims is here to see you and she looks ready to explode."

Dr. Andrus gave a deep sigh of resignation. Dropping his pen, he said, "In one of her self-righteous moods, I suppose." He hated to be interrupted. Swiveling his chair around, he nodded. "Show her in."

Teddy, sleeping at his master's feet, leaped up snarling and snapping at the church's main proponent of heaven and hell. Every daisy on her hat bounced and every floorboard creaked as she stomped to a chair. "Get that varmint out of my way!"

"Teddy is one of the family."

"Learn him some manners then."

Quietly doctor spoke to Teddy and the little dog obediently tucked himself under the desk. Doc shuffled some papers on his desk, asking, "Well, Mrs. Aims, what can I do for you?"

"Nothing, just nothin', but I can do somethin' for you. I can have you put in jail, but seein' how you cured my niece Sadie of her lumbago, I won't."

"What seems to be the problem?"

"Your sinful daughter is headed straight for hell."

"I am unaware that any of my daughters are sinful."

"Ha!" Mrs. Aims threw back her shoulders and squinted shrewdly. "Your daughter Nettie has Satan right on her heels."

Doc thoughtfully rubbed his chin as he watched the daisies shiver.

"Nettie has stolen ten dollars from my niece. Ten Dollars! And them bein' so poor! They could have bought five pairs of shoes, a sack of sugar, and a hog."

"You're making rather serious allegations, Mrs. Aims."

"Nettie told Sadie dead spirits would tell her who she would marry if Sadie gave her ten dollars."

"You may be sure, Nettie will be reprimanded and the ten dollars will be returned. Here, I happen to have a ten-dollar gold piece in my pocket."

"I knew, Dr. Andrus, you would make it right, but do you know who Nettie told Sadie she would marry?"

Doc shook his head. "I have no idea."

Mrs. Aims spat, "That miserable, no good, jackass Ernie Peepers."

"I'm very sorry this has happened."

"You gotta stop tellin' her dead spirits know everythin'. They are demons."

"Mrs. Aims, I never have anything to do with dead spirits. I work with cosmic energy."

"That energy stuff is over my head, but I know if you'd taught her about the good Lord willin' to wash away her sins with gallons of his blood, she'd…"

"A savior, no matter how holy, can not save a person from reaping the result of his wrongdoing. It would annul the cosmic law of cause and effect, which would be impossible."

Mrs. Aims fiercely sputtered, but before she could speak, the doctor gently reminded her, "Even your Bible upholds this cosmic law for it says, 'As ye sow, so shall ye reap.'"

Mrs. Aims pounced on the word reap. "Reap! Your daughter is goin' to reap hail and brimstone for her sins. If you'd teach her religion, she'd…"

"Religion has instigated more wars, inquisitions, and ignorance that any other factor."

Nancy, hearing every word, was about to leap out of bed to confront the two antagonists when Mae came in, carrying the tea tray. Seeing her mother's distressed face, she anxiously asked, "Mother, what's wrong?"

"Shut the door, dear, before I lose my mind."

Mae set the tray down and shut the door. "Has Mrs. Aims sent Papa to hell again?"

"Why does your father infuriate her by saying the Bible is fabricated by unprincipled priests?"

"Mama, it's well known that Ezra didn't know how to translate the Old Testament."

"You sound like your father."

"I believe Papa is right when he says true religion has to come from the heart by doing good deeds and having kind thoughts."

Nancy sighed. "Be that as it may, he doesn't have to rub her the wrong way."

"Is truth ever offensive?" asked Mae.

Nancy shrugged. "What is this about Nettie?"

When Mae remained silent, Nancy keenly looked at her daughter. "Well? What is she up to?"

"Mama, you've always told us not to tattle on each other."

"This is a serious matter and I should know."

"Nettie says she is going to be a witch and make a lot of money."

"A witch?"

"Well…not exactly a witch. She's really called a medium."

"What in heaven's sake is a medium?"

"Dead Indian spirits come to her and tell her things."

"What things?"

"Whom people are to marry, how to get money, all sorts of things."

"How did Nettie get this idea?"

"Charlie said this medium came to Walla Walla about a month ago and he thinks she's great. She told his fraternity brothers they would win the next ball game."

"Did they?"

"They haven't played it yet. Charlie says mediums make a lot of money and Nettie swears she's going to be a medium, but she liked the sound of 'witch' better."

"I'll have to talk to her father about this." Nancy finished her cup of tea. Just then the door slammed. Mae opened the bedroom door a crack and peeked out. Turning, she whispered, "Mrs. Aims is gone and Papa is staring at the wall."

Dr. Andrus was indeed in deep concentration, wondering how to make Nettie see the error of her ways. At a faint knock at the door, he swiveled his chair around. "Come in."

Maybelle tiptoed in, throwing her arms around her father, and kissing him on the cheek. "Papa, I'm so worried."

"Tell Papa," he encouraged.

"Amy is retching."

"Probably an upset stomach."

"But she's been retching every morning for over two weeks."

"Why hasn't she come to me?"

"She doesn't want anyone to know."

"Tell Amy I want to see her at once."

"Yes, Papa," Maybelle left skipping up the stairs and in a few moments skipped back down. "Amy says she can't come."

"Very well, I'll go to her." The girls were surprised to see their father, he so seldom came upstairs. Because he asked to see Amy alone, they went to their rooms, glancing back with curiosity. They huddled together in Fannie and Mae's room, speculating. Mae frowned. "She must have done something terribly wrong."

Maybelle piped up, "Could it be something to do with those horrible books she reads?"

Fannie thought differently. "Maybe she has appendicitis."

When they heard Amy's door open, Nettie peeked out and whispered to the others, "Papa looks so serious and Amy is with him and her eyes are all swollen and red."

Downstairs, Doc shrugged into his overcoat and went to see his wife. "Dear, I'm taking Amy to the office and if we aren't back in time, don't have the girls wait dinner for us."

"Nelson, is something wrong?"

"Have the girls make you a bowl of chicken soup. You must keep up your strength for out trip." Pecking her on the cheek, he left with Amy.

The girls were all in the kitchen making rolls, stirring up a cake, and teasing Charlie, who had come to pilfer anything that looked tempting. Anna chided him, "Charlie, why do you want to be a poor, old farmer? You don't know a potato from a rutabaga. Come with us to the mountains. It will be so much fun."

"Fun for who? It means I would have to cut all the wood for the campfires, carry hundreds of pails of water from the spring, and kill all the snakes. You're so squeamish. Yeah, fun for who? Not me. I prefer to grow tomatoes for my fun."

"Charlie, we will miss you so much," they wailed.

"Don't pull that soft stuff on me. It won't work."

Anna reminded them, "We better start getting ready for the mountains. Charlie, you round up the tents. I think they're in the shed. Mae, how about you getting all the blanket rolls together? Nettie, you pack the camping equipment."

Mae pursed her lips. "Are you just going to sit there giving orders?"

"Don't be so catty. I have the worst job of all, putting the supply of food in boxes."

Maybelle complained, "Aren't you going to give me anything to do?"

"Of course, dear. Pack Teddy's food and put in plenty of bacon cracklings to mix with his dried fish."

They were so busy getting the camping gear together, before they knew it, it was time to get dinner. They planned an easy dinner of meatballs and spaghetti and were just finishing eating a vinegar-pie dessert when their father and sister returned. Amy dashed upstairs, while the doctor, without a word, went directly to his wife, closing the door behind him. With puzzled glances they looked at each other but said nothing.

Doc stood with his back to the bed and faced the window with his hands clasped behind him. Nancy knew so well by his demeanor something was amiss. "Nelson, do you have something to tell me?"

"Yes, my dear, yes I do, but you mustn't let it worry you. Everything will work out all right."

"Nelson, stop being evasive and tell me what you are trying to break gently to me."

"Dear, the girls are grown-up enough to take care of everything. You needn't do a thing."

"Nelson, tell me what it is."

"In a couple of weeks there's going to be a wedding."

"Whose wedding?"

"Amy's."

"She isn't even engaged."

"She is now." He turned, smiling. "She is very excited about it."

"What are you trying to hide from me?"

Doctor sat on the edge of the bed, taking his wife's hand. He talked calmly and matter of factly. She listened wide-eyed with disbelief. There was a catch in her voice. "Oh, Nelson, you could save us from this disgrace. You could..."

"But I won't. I won't destroy life because of Amy's indiscretion. Life starts at conception."

"Never, never did I ever think I would have to go through the humiliation poor Mrs. Miller went through."

"No one need know."

"Nelson, you know better. In a town this small everyone knows everyone else's business. How are we going to tell the girls?"

"Mae seems to be the most mature. She's diplomatic and can be depended on to handle things with her sisters."

"I...I...hope you're right because I don't have the strength to prepare for the wedding."

Doc left to see Mae. Finding her alone, and after divulging the matter, he went to his study to finish his paperwork.

He had only been working for about an hour when the door burst open and Nettie stood before him with blazing eyes. "I was supposed to be the first one married in our home. I wanted to be first to come down the stairs in my bridal veil trailing, and now Amy has spoiled everything! Oh, I hate her!"

The doctor calmly shuffled some papers. "My dear, we have more serious things to discuss than your petty peeve. How can you possibly steal ten dollars from Mrs. Aims' niece, claiming dead spirits told her to marry Mr. Peepers?"

"I didn't steal it," Nettle snapped. "You consult dead spirits all the time."

"Never have I ever done such a thing."

"Lots of people say you do."

"That doesn't make it true. I work with cosmic energies only."

"Charlie says there's a woman in Walla Walla called a medium and she makes a lot of money from dead spirits so I thought I'd go and learn how."

"We sent a letter for your enrollment to Missouri's nursing college. I thought your intent was to eventually become my nurse, helping me in my practice."

"But Papa, that was ages ago and I thought if they wouldn't accept me…well…I had to do something and mediums make money."

"There hasn't been time to hear from them. Missouri is a long ways from here and the mail may have to go part way by stagecoach. So while you're waiting I suggest you learn some proven natural healing processes from Mrs. Aldridge, those not taught in nursing college."

"What kind of healing processes?"

"Reiki, for one. A powerful healing technique rediscovered in ancient Sanskrit manuscripts."

"What's it about?"

"The hands are used to remove blockage of energy in the body, which can have its root in the body itself or at the emotional and spiritual level."

"You mean you have to rub a patient with your hands?"

"Gently."

"Ugh! What if the patient is a big, hairy-chested man? I couldn't do it. I'd have to give him a pill and let it go at that."

"In nursing, you will have to face many unpleasant things not of your liking. You will have to have a tremendous love for humanity and not fall prey to your scruples."

"Maybe I should be a midwife and help cute little babies into the world."

"That will take extensive training and a longer time in college to qualify."

"Then that's out. I want to stay away from home as short a time as possible. It makes me homesick just to think of being away from you and Mama."

"There's always the time when birds must fly from the nest."

"Well, this bird wants to stick to the nest."

Doc stood up and patted his daughter's head. "I'm depending on you to be my nurse."

"I suppose the hardest part is the first jump from the nest."

Her father laughed. "But think how nice it will be to fly."

An hour before bedtime Anna, Mae, Fannie, Nettie, and Maybelle snuck down to the cellar and huddled, whispering. Fannie remonstrated, "Maybelle, you're too young to even hear about…about certain things. You go and keep Mama company until we come up to bed."

Maybelle objected, "I'm grown-up too."

"Not this grown-up," Fannie assured her. "Run along like a good girl."

"Oh, all right, but I know something you don't know. Now I won't tell," she taunted and flounced up the stairs.

As the sisters huddled together whispering, Anna voiced concern. "Strange no one mentioned who the groom is."

Nettie sounded certain. "Of course it's that red-headed guy she was riding with in the buggy, dancing with at the basket social, holding hands with at the movies, and…"

Fannie shook her head. "I think Mama is making a mistake by not letting Amy wear white for her wedding gown."

"For heaven's sake, what else could she wear at her wedding?"

"Mama says it has to be lavender, mint green, or pale rose."

"That's like Amy wearing a sign saying 'I am a tainted bride.' No she definitely has to wear white," Nettie said with conviction.

"And Mama says she can't wear a veil, only a perky little hat with no flowers on it and definitely no train, just a walking dress."

"How horrible! It takes a train swishing down the stairs to be romantic."

"Who says anything about romance? I think it's a shotgun wedding."

"Whatever is *that* and where did you hear about it?"

"In one of Amy's forbidden books, she keeps hidden. I…it says…oh, this is too embarrassing."

"You can't stop now."

"It told about a girl getting in the family way and…and her father took a shotgun to the man who got her that way and made him marry her."

"I didn't see Papa take a gun."

"Maybe he used a knife. He has some for operating you know."

Anna shook her head. "I always thought Amy was the smartest of any of us, but now she turns out to be the dumbest."

Mae came to her sister's defense. "I wouldn't call her dumb."

"What would you call her?" Anna challenged.

"Naive," Mae said.

Her sisters hooted. "Innocent after reading those passionate love stories? Don't be so silly. We still say she's dumb. Maybe 'stupid' is a better word."

Fannie groaned, "It doesn't matter what word you want to use. She's humiliated us all."

Mae, the practical one, snapped, "No, she hasn't. We are going to stick together and carry off this wedding with a flourish, with our heads held high." She turned to Fannie. "Of course, you'll start making her wedding dress in the morning."

"I suppose so," Fannie replied without enthusiasm.

"Make it ivory. That's almost white and no one will notice the difference," Anna suggested.

Nettie dabbed her eyes, sniffing, "Never, NEVER, will I ever forgive Amy for being first to be married in our dear home."

Fannie patted her sister. "Dry your eyes, dear one, you're not even going to be second."

Nettie stared at her sister. "What are you talking about?"

"I've decided to marry John."

"You aren't even speaking to him."

"I've decided it was prudish of me to act the way I did, but you'll have to admit how embarrassing it was to have him see me naked."

"You weren't naked. You had your corset cover on."

"Well, he had no right to cut my corset strings."

"I suppose it would have been better for him to let you die."

Maybelle came tripping down the stairs. "Mama wants you all to come to bed right now."

They shook their heads. "We have more planning to do."

Maybelle warned, "Charlie is snooping around and you know what that means!"

Mae, having been put in charge of the wedding arrangements, took it seriously. "Go back to Mama and keep her busy until we finish planning. We have to get it done before Amy butts in. You know Amy."

Anna chimed in, "Oh yes, we know Amy, she would want her wedding as if she were the Queen of England."

"And we can't afford it," said Nettie.

Mae reminded them, "This is the only place we can have secrets without Charlie barging in. Talk about women gossiping, they can't compare to men. Charlie would trumpet our plans all over town. Please, dear, go up and keep Mama happy for just a few minutes more."

"But I want to plan too," Maybelle pleaded.

"We are the oldest and have the most to do."

"Oh all right, but you have to let me do something."

"You may be the flower girl."

"That's just dandy. I'll throw dandelions at the bride."

"Show your sister more respect," Mae told her.

"Respect," Maybelle snorted and skipped back up the stairs.

Mae started allocating the different duties. "Fannie, you'll have to make the dress on your own. Amy is too ill to help."

"I suppose I'll have to make the dress with elastic at the waist," Fannie giggled.

Mae went on making appointments. "Anna, you make the most divine angel food cake."

This was greeted by a chorus of protests. "Not angel food!"

"What kind do you suggest then?"

Most wanted devil's food.

"But that's a dark cake," Mae objected.

"Well, it's going to be a dark wedding," Nettie said flippantly.

Anna timidly suggested, "I could make an applesauce or spice cake."

"That's it, spice cake. Very appropriate. The bride must have had a lot of spice to get in this fix." Nettie threw back her head, laughing.

"Girls," Mae scolded, "show your sister more respect."

"Respect!" they shrieked. "Are you kidding?"

Again Mae scolded, "You're discussing your sister as...as if she were a whore."

Nettie pursed her lips. "What's the difference between a whore and a tainted bride?"

Fannie ventured to answer. "I...I think a whore takes money and the tainted bride doesn't, and since Amy didn't take any money, she's not a whore."

"How do you know?" Nettie flared. "All she talks about now is the big house he's building her, a fancy carriage all her own, and..."

"Stop it," Mae ordered. "We haven't decided yet on the decorations for the parlor."

"I suggest thistles for the wedding bower," Nettie snickered.

"Just because you're mad at Amy for being the first bride to be married in our home, you needn't be so catty," Mae said.

"Why can't she be married someplace else? How about the church?" Nettie suggested with hope.

Fannie sounded horrified. "A tainted bride in church. Never!"

"Nettie, I appoint you head of the decorating committee and NO thistles," Mae warned

Maybelle came thumping back down the stairs. "I can't keep Mama contented another minute and Charlie suspects something."

"All right. Tell Mama we are coming up." Mae gave last-minute advice. "We are going to do everything one is suppose to do at weddings and there will be no smudge on our family." But they climbed up the stairs with heavy hearts.

# Chapter 15

# Soiled Wedding Day

Amy's wedding day dawned with a drizzle, splashing silvery droplets on the locust leaves, and from board sidewalks across to board sidewalks, large puddles dotted the dirt road, sending up sprays of muddy water with every passing carriage wheel.

Mae stood by the archway, wearing a dress she hated. In the catalogue it had looked elegant, a soft rose foulard, but when it came and she opened the box and saw it was a murky pink, she almost cried. There was no time to exchange it and Fannie hadn't had the time to make her a new dress. The dress she had worn at the basket social dance was spotted with cinder burns and smeared with soot. Feeling miserable and unhappy, she made a final check on the arrangements.

Abigale, seated at the organ, was waiting to start the wedding march. Doc stood at the foot of the stairs, ready to escort his daughter to the altar. Judge Frankland had just arrived to perform the ceremony and Teddy was quietly sitting with the wedding ring tied around his neck. Only a few close friends had been invited, and they were sitting with what Mae was sure were strained smiles.

Upstairs, Fannie was in hysterics, sewing the last pearl button on the wedding dress, while in the kitchen Anna was in tears. She had finished spreading white icing on the wedding cake and was arranging the white sugar roses Neville had made when her mother came in to inspect. Nancy, still feeling ill and furious over the whole situation, took one look at the cake with Anna placing the last rose on top of the third layer and said, "That will never do. I thought I plainly said no white is to be used at this wedding."

"But Mama it's finished," Anna said with a sob.

"I'm sorry, Anna, but I forbid white to be used."

Anna ran out of the kitchen dabbing at her eyes. Just then Maybelle came in and having heard her mother begged, "Mama, I know how to make chocolate icing."

"Very well, ice it again as quickly as you can and don't use the roses."

"What will I use?"

For a moment Nancy stood considering, then making up her mind she jerked off a branch from the ivy plant in the window. "Here, string that around the cake."

Nettie put the last bouquet of peonies in the vases forming a small altar. Their mother had refused to let them use her prized fiery white, so they used the less beautiful pink with its burgundy blotches, which her mother raised for their fragrance.

Mae wondered if she were imagining the guests were uneasy, for they kept shifting in their seats and nervously glancing around. Did they know the truth? She shuddered and thought what good had it been for their father to instill in them the seriousness of their actions so they would reap an effect that would make them happy.

Suddenly, Mae felt furious. She had an overpowering desire to tear the flowers to pieces, smash the wedding cake, and tell the guests to go home. Instead she went to answer the doorbell to let in a late guest. Through the door's stained-glass window, she saw a bunch of daisies and groaned. Before she could open the door, it was thrust wide and Mrs. Aims walked in.

"You forgot to invite me and I couldn't miss being at the first wedding in the Andrus family." Without waiting for Charlie to usher her to a seat, she appropriated the seat the Judge had just vacated to quickly confer with the organist.

At the signal from the top of the stairs, Abigale struck the first cord of Mendelssohn's march. The guests murmured as Amy appeared. The light filtering through the curtains cast dark shadows on the wedding gown, turning it into shades of gray. Before descending, Amy hesitated. Charlie tensed, thinking, "My God, is she going to try to give one of Lillian Russell's poses?" The groom, whom no one knew, stood uneasily in a burgundy suit, wearing a cravat of bright purple which clashed with his thick crop of red hair. Bob, the best man, standing by his side, nervously toyed with his pearl-studded cuff links.

Amy paused on each step to prolong the attention every bride savors from the attentive guests. Nancy felt an overwhelming pride in her husband as he offered his arm with such poise and dignity to the bride. Tears stung her eyes as Judge Frankland solemnly started the ceremony with much sincerity. At the right time, a low command came from his master, and Teddy trotted up to the altar; but he didn't want to part with the ring and growled a warning to the groom when he tried to remove it. Not until the doctor intervened was the groom able to place the plain gold band on his bride's finger.

As soon as the bride was kissed, Mae fled to the kitchen, grabbed a dishtowel, covered her face and wept. After thanking the guests for coming, Nancy went back to bed unable to attend the reception. The guests mingled and chatted and were much too polite for Mae's comfort and as soon as the duty of throwing rice after the newlyweds was over and they had departed for Walla Walla where they were to make their home, Mae breathed a sigh of relief.

Abigale asked Bob to take her home. Reaching her cottage, Bob asked permission to come in. Abigale felt tired and nervous but smiled. "Of course, do come in and help me get over these wedding jitters. I shouldn't feel so depressed, but I...I...feel..."

"Let down," Bob said.

"With a jolt, " Abigale laughed. "I'll make us a strong cup of tea."

When she returned, she found Bob pacing the floor. He turned and took the teacup from her. Setting it down on the coffee table he asked, "I believe you think a lot of my homestead, don't you?"

"I love it. How is the mare liking it?"

"Oh, she's having a fine time jumping fences to join the elk. The wedding has delayed me from going out sooner to fix the fence again so the elk won't be able to knock it down. Will you go with me tomorrow?"

"I'll be delighted."

"Abigale, have you ever thought you might marry a younger man?"

"I have, but I won't."

"Abigale, we are made for each other. I'm asking you to marry me."

Abigale nervously fingered the edge of her handkerchief. "It might work beautifully for a few years but, say, in twenty years, I would be an old woman and you still a young man. No, it wouldn't work."

"You are too hasty with your answer."

"Bob, Nettie is waiting."

"But I'm not. Love can be killed and mine is stone dead."

"Give it more time to heal."

"No."

"You know, Bob, there is another one in the family who adores you and, with a little tender care, it could grow into a love purer and more steadfast than Nettie could ever give you."

Bob lifted a startled eyebrow and fastened questioning eyes on Abigale's serious face.

Abigale poured him another cup of tea. She was afraid to look at him. Finally, she took a deep breath before whispering, "Maybelle."

Bob looked at Abigale unbelievingly with amazement as if he hadn't heard right. "She is a child!"

"Children have a way of growing up very quickly. She is crazy about your homestead, crazy over everything about you. Think about it and don't let such purity and loveliness slip out of your life. Now, my dear friend, I must go to bed before I drop and I'll be most happy to go tomorrow with you and Maybelle to the old homestead. Goodnight, dear friend."

"Maybelle!" Bob exclaimed taken by surprise. "I...I thought just you and I."

Abigale shook her head. "No, I think we both need a day with the vivacity of youth."

The next day the family decided to postpone their vacation again so as to give them a rest and agreeably consented for Maybelle to join Bob and Abigale to spend a day at the homestead. On the way to the homestead, Bob tried to share in the chatter but he felt uneasy. Maybelle was her usual sweet self.

Nettie was miffed she hadn't been invited and restlessly flounced around annoying the rest of the family. Mae grew restless with unhappiness and went out on the porch to lean against a pillar. She gazed up into the great vastness of the cosmos, shimmering with sunshine. Here her father found her.

"Your mother wants you. What are you doing out here all alone?"

"I'm wishing it had never happened."

Through the years their father had often played games of make-believe with them. Now he assumed a husky, playful voice. "I am the great magician from Mars, and I have the power to grant one wish. What is yours?"

Mae gave a delighted laugh. "Oh, Great One, I wish the future to bring a pure and happy wedding to this great house, the bride to be virtuous and the groom to be upright in God's sight. The bridal flowers and the wedding cake to be all white and everyone to be truly and joyously happy."

There was an overwhelming silence between them as the doctor grew thoughtful, realizing the family's one stray lamb had indeed left a blemish on his children. At last he spoke. "Mae, what has happened will be ordinary in the next century. Enjoy and appreciate this golden age, for in the future America will become the second Babylon with all its decadence, debauchery, power, lust, and greed."

"Oh, Papa, not America. It's so young."

"In the hoary history of the past, whenever a nation puts love of money and power before the love of the Creator, that nation is doomed to be destroyed."

With horror filling her eyes Mae asked, "Will I live to see it?"

Doc shook his head. "No, but your great-grandchildren will."

Mae tried to speak lightly. "Papa, I'm afraid you are not lifting my blue mood."

"No, I suppose not."

"With such a wicked future, what will become of Maybelle, so pure, innocent, and sweet?"

"It is not Maybelle I fear for, but Nettie."

"What about Fannie and Annie?"

"Our trip to the Blue Mountains will bring a happy beginning for Fannie."

"And Anna?"

"She will be the happiest of all with a man of another race."

"And me?" Mae timidly asked.

Her father laughed. "You want a few surprises, don't you?"

Going back into the house Doc retired to his study, shuffled through the unopened mail until he came to one postmarked Missouri, the one he had been waiting for. Opening it, he was satisfied with its message and took it in to his wife. "Dear, I believe our problem with Nettie is solved. The college of nursing will accept her."

"Oh, Nelson, that's wonderful!"

"She can leave for Kansas City as soon as we return from the mountains."

"What a relief to get her away from that ridiculous idea of becoming a witch."

"Not only that, but she will be of invaluable help in my practice."

"Amy wasn't hurt when you refused to take her case?"

"On the contrary, she seemed to be excited to have a Walla Walla physician."

On the way to the homestead, the three friends were taking turns holding onto the halter rope of a beautiful Arabian mare they were taking for companionship for Bob's Morgan mare. Now and then Bob would stop for Maybelle to jump out to gather grass to feed her, and when they came to a stream, they let her drink. Maybelle fell so in love with the gentleness of the horse, she begged Bob to let her ride her, but Bob shook his head. "Not now. Later when she is well broken and I have purchased a saddle for her."

Maybelle squealed her delight. "I hope your horse will like this playmate and stop jumping fences."

They were eating lunch by the charred remains of the old cabin when Bob suddenly said, "Maybelle, if you were reconstructing this old place, what changes would you make?"

Maybelle surprised them both when she unexpectedly said, "That would be up to Mr. Curl, and he's not happy where he is. He wants to come home."

Bob and Abigale were so dumbfounded, they could think of nothing to say, but Maybelle had a lot more to say. "He needs to be closer to tell us what to do. Oh, Bob, please bring him home."

Bob turned to Abigale. "Where does he lie?"

"In the old graveyard about five miles on the other side of town."

Maybelle leaped to her feet, pointing. "He needs to be back where he belongs, right there under that big spruce tree by the pool. Oh, Bob, please. Then everything will be all right."

Bob's eyes were misty as he spoke. "Very well, as soon as you return from your vacation, we will bring him home and you must be here to welcome him back."

Maybelle dropped to her knees, throwing her arms around his neck, "Thank you, thank you." Leaping to her feet, she gaily whirled around and around, ending in a cartwheel, the lace on her pantalets fluttering. Bob, wanting to tease her, burst into song.

"Oh, the darling dimpled little girl
"With pigtails down her neck
"Male hearts by the score, she wrecks
"Pantalets, pantalets, she wears
"She's so cute who cares."

With blazing eyes Maybelle stood before him. "That's a horrid song and you made it up."

"Guilty," admitted Bob choking with laughter, but when he saw tears in her eyes he jumped up taking her hand. "I'm truly sorry, but you looked so adorable I couldn't resist teasing you."

"I hate pantalets!"

"What do you want to wear?" Bob asked seriously.

"Bustles!" Maybelle burst out.

Abigale asked, "Don't you think you're too young?"

"No, I'm not. It's these silly pantalets that make me look so childish and I'm really grown-up. In fact, I'm getting old."

"Madam," Bob bowed low before offering his arm, "allow me to assist you to the carriage."

"Not that old," Maybelle snickered.

Abigale started putting on her sweater and picked up the picnic hamper. "Yes, we must go. It'll be dark before we get home."

Maybelle wailed, "Not yet. I haven't fed Tommy and Tubby."

"For heaven's sake, who are they?" Abigale asked.

Grabbing a piece of bread from the hamper, Maybelle ran down the path, calling over her shoulder, "Come on, I'll introduce you."

Standing beside the clear-blue depths of the pool, Maybelle knelt down, rippling the water with her fingers, then held a bite-size piece of bread inches above the water. Some movement below made ripples on the surface. More splashing with the fingers, followed by a large dark body breaking the surface, and the piece of bread was gone. "That's Tubby," Maybelle explained.

Abigale started to speak but Maybelle held a finger to her lips. "Shhhhh."

Again Maybelle fluttered her fingers in the water. In a moment there was a flash of silver as a large trout gracefully curved above the pool and the bread disappeared. "That's Tommy," Maybelle said.

"How can you tell the difference?" asked Abigale

"Didn't you notice Tubby is fatter?"

"No, I did not. They are just fish to me."

"But they have different personalities. Didn't you see Tommy is more graceful while Tubby just grabs?"

"I'm sorry, but I'm not as attuned to fish as you are."

Bob asked, "Do you count them as one of your miracles?"

"Oh, yes, but much more. They are my very own dear friends and they know me. Oh, Bob, you'll never fish here again, will you? Oh, please?" she pled.

Instead of saying no as she hoped, Bob looked intently at the sweet girlishness and his heart flipped. Abigale saw the look in his eyes and smiled to herself.

"I demand penance for their lives. " Bob sounded so dead-serious Maybelle snapped her eyes open wider.

Breathlessly, she whispered, "What?"

"What are you prepared to give?"

Abigale grew tense as she watched the anxiety grow in the girl's eyes. "W...why most anything."

The moment was so intense Abigale would have trembled had she not been positively sure of Bob's moral integrity. She breathed a sigh of relief when Bob said, "Very well, in order to save the lives of your fishy friends, you are to plan the log home I'm building here."

Maybelle gave a squeal of delight. "Oh, Bob, I'd love to! You mean, I can plan it any way I want to?" she anxiously asked.

Bob nodded. "The deal is, you are to supervise the whole building process and tell the carpenters just what you want."

"That will be duck soup," boasted Maybelle as she unleashed her enthusiasm.

Bob grinned at Abigale. "She's pretty young."

"Not too young," Abigale replied.

On the way back home, Maybelle talked Bob into letting her drive the team. She had just taken the reins when a covey of quail whirled up under the horses, startling them and they took off on a dead run, unmindful of Maybelle hollering "WHOA!" while pulling the reins back with all her strength. The team swerved off the road, dodging trees and pulling the carriage over windfalls with lunges, jolting Abigale half out of the seat. Trying to grab her hat as it flew off, she clung on for dear life. After four attempts, Bob finally was able to get hold of the reins while hanging onto Maybelle, who was dangling over the front wheel. A frightened deer, not knowing where to run for safety, kept leaping in front of the team. Before they caught up with the terrorized animal, it dashed into a rose thicket. Slowly Bob brought the team under control, but was unable to stop them until they came to a fallen log across the forest aisle. Snorting and heaving, unable to jump the large log, the horses stopped.

"Whew!!!" Maybelle gasped. "That was a thriller!"

Abigale could hardly speak. "I...I can do nicely without thrills."

Bob, holding the horses by their bits, turned them around and led them back to the road. Climbing back into the carriage, he grinned at the frightened girl. "Want to try again?"

"Indeed she won't or I'm getting out," declared Abigale.

"Singing calms the nerves," Maybelle said and started singing a soft lullaby. Abigale laughed. "I think Wagner's "Valkyries" is more in tune with my nerves."

"Oh, that would just stir them up," Maybelle affirmed.

Bob settled the argument by singing in his rich tenor. "Oh, Abiding Light."

All the way back to the Andrus home they sang old hymns. Maybelle thanked Bob for a lovely day and kissed Abigale.

Running up the porch steps, she turned and, waving goodbye, blew a kiss.

Abigale touched Bob on the shoulder. "Did you catch that kiss?"

"Right on the smacker," Bob laughed.

Arriving at Abigale's place, Bob stood beside the carriage waiting for an invitation. Abigale shook her head, "Not tonight. I feel I have some bruises and I'm going to jump into a tub of hot scalding water, hoping I won't have purple splotches."

Bursting into the house, Maybelle found Mae conferring with her mother on the last minute traveling preparations, so she rushed to the kitchen to find Anna. Fannie and Nettie were with her, packing of groceries. Maybelle gushed, "Oh, Bob is so wonderful! You should have seen how strong he is. He lifted a great big log and he stopped the horses when they were running away and he chased a big bull right out of the field and...."

"Stop!" shouted all three girls as they turned to look at Maybelle.

Startled, Maybelle asked, "What's the matter?"

Nettie pointed an accusing finger at her. "You've fallen in love."

Maybelle stomped her foot. "I have not! Of all the crazy things I've ever heard! Bob is just a good friend."

Anna snorted, "Oh yeah, where have I heard that line before? It's always a sure sign of being in love."

"I AM NOT!"

"I can recognize love when I see it," Anna vouched.

"All right, what is love, if you're so smart?" Maybelle challenged.

Anna sang in a mimicking staccato, "Love is a whirl-a-gig twirling you to the stars."

"Love is a cyclone turning your world upside-down," piped Fannie.

"Love is a pain in the gizzard," sang Nettie in the highest notes she could reach.

"Well, my gizzard is okay," snapped Maybelle as she flounced out of the kitchen.

"Girls," came their mother's voice, "if we are to get an early start in the morning, you must get to bed."

"Yes, Mother, we're on our way."

They were starting up the stairs when old man Cryder staggered through the front door, trailing blood. "Tell your pa I'm in a bad way. That old boar got me again and for sure he killed me this time."

Nettie ran for her father, Anna ran for towels to mop up blood, and Fannie helped the fainting man to a chair.

Doc had retired for the night but came in wearing his bathrobe and took charge. "Cryder, I thought I warned you to stay away from that big pig."

Cryder weakly shook his head. "H...he got out and I had to put him back in."

"You'll bleed to death if I try to get you to my operating room. Nettie, I've taught you the things I need. Go as fast as you can and bring all that is necessary to patch up this stubborn cuss."

Nettie dashed out the door started hurrying up the sidewalk when Bob drove past. Seeing the running girl, he stopped. "You seem to be in a hurry to get somewhere."

"Oh, Bob, take me to father's office. Cryder is bleeding to death. Hurry!"

Bob reached down and quickly pulled her into the buggy, then snapped his whip over the horses' backs. On the way Nettie explained the emergency and also the fact she was going to attend nurse's college in Kansas City. Bob's only comment was to wish her every success. He waited for her while she hurriedly collected what she needed, then drove her back, simply saying goodbye as he tipped his hat.

After Cryder had been sewn up and eaten a bowl of chicken soup, he began to take an interest in the plans being made concerning his future.

It was decided it would be impossible to postpone their vacation yet again, and Cryder's bandages were too tricky for anyone else but the doctor to change twice a day, so Doc decided they would have to take the patient along.

Nancy remonstrated, "Sitting in a seat, he'll be jolted to pieces and open up his wound."

"No, we'll throw on a mattress and he can ride on top of the wagon load," Doc decided.

Old Cryder raised his head. "I ain't goin' unless I can take my pigs."

Doc shook his head. "I'd think you'd have had enough of pigs the way you're butchered up."

"Oh, that was only the old boar. I'll leave him home, but I know you're goin' to where there's some big diamondback rattlers and my pigs will clean out them varmints and make camp safe."

# Chapter 16

# Redskin Savior

The morning's dew-drenched grass sparkled in the early dawn as the golden orb peeked above the horizon, parting the pale amber-tinted curtain of clouds in the east. Already the Andrus family was bustling about with activity in the last-minute loading of the wagons. Cryder's son arrived with a crate-load of pigs to accompany his father, who was already encamped on a mattress surmounting an overloaded baggage van. At the last minute, Doc decided to ride on top of the load with his patient to assure himself the old man was riding comfortably.

After traveling for several miles through the countryside, passing small farms where already the farmers were out doing their chores, Doc began to fear John, who was driving the carriage team, might be tiring and start hemorrhaging. He leaned over, asking Cryder, "Think you'll be all right if I spell John off and drive for a while?"

"Hell, yes. I don't need a babysitter."

"Can I trust you to lie still so you don't open up your wounds? I know this part of the road has always been rough."

"You know why?" Cryder said in scorn. "It's that Miller. The cuss uses the road to drive his combine on to his other field and it digs up the road."

"Well, hang on tight and do the best you can. As soon as we hit the forest road, it'll be easier." Doc jumped down but met protest from John when he tried to take over the reins. He didn't understand until he saw the only vacant seat was beside Fannie.

In the first place it had been difficult to persuade John to come on the trip as Fannie still wasn't speaking to him, but Doc had persisted knowing how beneficial the cool pine-scented mountain air would be for him.

When they gained the foothills of the Blue Mountains, Cryder insisted he was well enough to ride in the buggy. For several miles John had been coughing, and when blood appeared on his handkerchief, Doc ordered John to exchange places with Cryder, much to the old man's delight, as he could then keep better check on his pigs.

After they crossed several gushing mountain streams, the forest became dense and shut out the sunlight; scrub brush was replaced by majestic, tall trees. As the road climbed, the pine trees gave way to heavy stands of balsam. Coming to Godman Springs, they stopped for lunch. John wasn't doing well and again started spitting blood. Doc took a teaspoon and small bottle from a hamper and went in search of a balsam tree with sap-filled blisters. Finding what he needed, he pierced the bottom of the blisters with the end of the spoon and collected sticky yellow sap with a highly poignant fragrance. This he mixed with unpasteurized honey one of the farmers had supplied him with for combining with his natural remedies. Giving John a teaspoonful, followed by a cup of hot ginger tea, soon relieved him, and he was able to ride with some comfort on top of the mattress.

The teamsters had gone ahead with all the camping gear to set up camp at the doctor's favorite camping place on the bank of the Tucannon River, well-known to fishermen for Dolly Varden trout and the elusive rainbows.

When the Andrus family arrived at dusk, the green-and-white-stripped tents were pitched and coffee was perking on a campfire much to their delight, for it had been a long, tiring day. Maybelle sniffed deeply of the pine-scented mountain air, exclaiming, "It's great to be here where God lives!"

Doc was soon busy around the campfire. Kneeling on the pine needles, he claimed, "I'm an old hand at making bannock," and raking out a few glowing coals to the side of the campfire, he slapped on a black cast-iron skillet. Searching through the supplies, he returned with a sack of flour. Rolling back the top he started mixing the bannock; then, pouring the dough into the sizzling, smoking skillet, he waited for it to bubble before taking a spatula and turning up its golden crispness. Teddy, patiently sitting by, begged for one, but Doc shook his head. "You'll have to wait your turn, Teddy my boy."

On the other side of the campfire, Mae was frying steaks. Enticed by the delicious smells of perking coffee and sizzling steaks, the others stopped their camp duties to gather around the fire. Soon plates were heaped with Doc's golden-brown specialty topped with homemade strawberry jam, bringing sighs of pure enjoyment, reassuring Doc that he had not lost his touch. At last everyone was too full of camp cooking to eat more, but they lingered around the fire, relaxing and watching a full moon slowly rising above a forested mountain ridge, picoting the horizon with lacy silhouettes of trees. Frogs croaked in stranded pools. In the distance coyotes serenaded the moon and owls hooted to each other from swaying treetops. But for the breeze cooled by the gurgling stream, the night would have been hot. The peace and quiet of the evening was broken by a shrill scream, as if a woman were in agony. Cryder stood up saying, "Them damn cats give me the creeps."

Nancy asked anxiously, "Are there many cougars up here?"

"Too many to suit me," Cryder said, going to collect his gear.

Nancy was surprised when the two teamsters rose, saying, "We can make it to Godman's Springs before it gets real dark."

"Can't you wait until morning and start after you've had breakfast?" Nancy asked.

"Nope, gotta go or our wives will give us hell for not getting back in time to take them to church." Good grazing was scarce so they took all the horses, leaving only one in case of an emergency.

The night filled them with nature's contentment and they lingered around the glowing coals, watching sparks drift slowly upward, sifting between the overhanging branches of fir. At last, one by one, they succumbed to tiredness and retired to their tents, where they fell into a deep reviving slumber.

They awoke the next morning to the olfactory delight of perking coffee and frying bacon and were amazed to see old Cryder busy around the campfire flipping buckwheat hot cakes. He happily grinned at them. "Used to be a camp cook for a big-game outfitter. Thought I'd try my hand at flapjacks again. Knew you'd still be tired after your trip. These stacks of hots should start your day right."

Grabbing a plate, Doc forked a stack onto it, remarking, "Cryder, you have to be a lot better to get up so early." He stuffed a bite of the hot cakes in his mouth and remarked, "I sure like this maple syrup."

"Made that to," beamed Cryder.

"I thought it came from trees," Doc said.

Cryder grinned. "When there ain't maple trees around, you make it."

"Sure hits the spot. Recipe a secret?" asked Doc.

"Nope, just brown sugar, mapeline, water, and gobs of butter."

"Fooled me. Tastes like the real McCoy."

"Yup, they all say that."

The others sleepily started to emerge from their tents and, to the old man's delight, they complimented him on his culinary expertise.

Each had their own way of spending the day. John and the doctor went fishing. Cryder went with them to hunt for periwinkles under the wet stones to furnish them with fish bait. Nancy and the girls felt more inclined to relax around the camp.

Two days after their arrival, Anna mysteriously came down with a high fever and was kept to her camp cot. Her father could find no cause for such a high temperature and she began wasting away. Her sisters took turns bathing her with cold water in an effort to bring down her temperature. Doc tried one medication after another but to no avail.

One night he was sitting alone by the campfire, pondering Anna's illness when suddenly a dark figure stood in the firelight. He was a handsome young Indian, over six feet tall. He wore fringed buckskin pants and several strings of beads over his bare, bronzed chest. His raven black hair was in shoulder-length braids topped by an eagle feather. His features were more aquiline than that of a full blood. He was a splendid specimen of a young Indian brave, standing with all the dignity and virility of his race.

He held out a few thick-leafed branches, saying, "The West Wind whispers a white girl is sick."

Doc rose to take the branches. "Yes, my daughter is very ill."

For a moment the young Indian stood silent. When he spoke it was with deep sincerity. "My mother sends Indian medicine to make tea, the Great Spirit say heals."

Doc motioned him to a seat. "I am most grateful to your mother. Will you join me for tea?"

"Thank you, another time. Our camp is upriver. We come to pick huckleberries and gig for salmon. Our treaty give us that right. My mother and my sister with her baby camp with me. The baby has new teeth and her crying attracts cougar. I must hurry back."

With a soft-spoken "Good night," he melted into the shadows.

Fannie came out of the tent, settling herself down on a log. "Papa, I thought I heard you talking to someone."

"Strangely, an Indian was here bringing Indian medicine to heal Anna."

"How did he know Anna was sick?"

"It is my belief Indians are so in tune with cosmic forces, they can contact an energy we know so little about which gives them an awareness of things beyond our dulled civilized senses."

"Anna's fever remains high."

Doc handed his daughter the branches given him. "If you will make a strong tea of this, it might be an answer to our search for a remedy."

"I hope so as she is burning up with fever and out of her head. She keeps babbling about a teepee with red hands painted over it." Fannie hurried away, then returned with a blue-granite teakettle of water which she placed on the grill over the fire. Sitting by her father, waiting for the kettle to boil, she remarked, "Papa, don't you think it rather strange, Anna raving about a teepee and here comes an Indian? Do you think it just a coincidence or do you think it has a meaning we are not aware of?"

Doc took a few moments to reflect before he spoke. "I believe there are cosmic forces all around us that are working to direct our destinies."

For some time they discussed this mystery of life, until the teakettle boiled over and Fannie dashed with it into the kitchen tent. She made the tea very strong, but when she took it to her sister, Anna weakly protested, "I don't want any more of those horrid brews."

"But, darling, an Indian brought it saying it would cure you. Please be a sweet dear and drink it," Fannie coaxed.

Although Anna tossed restlessly all night, in the morning her temperature was down two degrees. After that, she drank the Indian tea without complaining, showing an improvement each day until the thermometer registered normal and she began to take interest in the camp's activities.

One night after supper, she didn't retire with the others when the hour was late but instead sat alone by the campfire, pondering on the strange dreams she had been having, wondering why she kept dreaming of Indians. She had read about them and their nomadic life. Though she lived in a frontier town, to her knowledge she had never seen an Indian and wondered why she kept seeing them in her dreams.

While she was wondering about the strangeness of it, she suddenly felt she was not alone. In alarm she rose, ready to flee to the safety of her tent, when out of the shadows stepped an apparition that made her gasp. Was she dreaming? He stepped closer to the fire and its light illuminated his dusky face. Clutching her hand to her breast, she whispered, "I have seen you in my dreams."

He spoke low. "Yes, I came to give you of my strength."

"You brought the healing herbs?"

He bowed his assent. Anna spoke with tears in her eyes. "I would surely have died had you not brought your healing medicine. A fire inside was burning me up."

"It is best you keep taking tea, sickness still in you."

"You are a stranger. How did you know I was sick?"

"Owl maybe tell me."

Anna's eyes opened wide with surprise. "Can owls really talk?"

"Owls messengers of forest."

"I do not understand but it's a lovely thought."

"To understand you must know of Great Spirit."

Anna spoke sincerely, "I would so like to know."

From his beaded jacket he drew out a package. He stepped closer, handing it to her. Curiously, she took it and carefully unwrapped the soft doeskin, revealing a pair of beautifully beaded moccasins.

"Oh, how lovely," she said admiringly.

"Soft for feet. Mother Earth take you closer to her breast."

Anna held the moccasins to her cheek. "I love the smoke smell from their tanning." She shyly looked up at him. "Thank you."

He stepped back. "Three days I come when there are no shadows. You be better, take for walk." Before Anna could reply, he was gone.

That night sleep deserted Anna. Why did she have such a strong feeling for this...this savage? Of course he was a savage;

for one thing he wore beads. On the other hand, he did show he was a gentleman, so he really wasn't a savage. When dawn tinted the sky, Anna felt so mixed up she decided not to go for a walk with this stranger.

Near breakfast time Nancy stepped out of their sleeping tent and just as quickly stepped back in. John was passing with a bucket of water that seemed much too heavy for him. Never had she seen him look so frail. She felt an overpowering fury. Her husband was doing everything to save this fine young man and Fannie was doing nothing to help. In fact, she felt it was her daughter's fault that John's health was declining. Not yet had Fannie told him he was forgiven. With determination to end this impasse, Nancy headed for the girls' tent. She found them happily chatting. She wasted no time. "Fannie, you are causing pain to the man you profess to love. I demand you go to him at once and tell him he is forgiven."

"That's what we have been telling her," Nettie said.

"Oh, Mama, how can I? I'm still so embarrassed."

Nettie's eyes blazed at her sister. "If you're such a prude and won't tell him, I will," she declared and dashed out the tent with Fannie racing after her.

They found John seated on a log watching a covey of quail scratching a rotten log for insects. He raised his head, looking surprised. Standing with both hands on her hips, Nettie informed him, "Fannie has something to say to you."

Fannie came up to him with hanging head. He stood, holding out his hand. Nettie left, only to hide behind a nearby tree. For several moments they just stood there until Nettie was boiling with aggravation and was about to confront them with their stupidity when she saw her sister collapse in the arms of the man she loved. Satisfied all was well, Nettie went to pester Cryder about his pigs.

Nancy left the girls' tent to start breakfast and was astonished to see a haunch of venison on a bed of fir boughs in front of the kitchen tent. Doc strode up, looking for some fishing tackle. Nancy pointed at the meat. " Nelson, what does this mean?"

The doctor smiled. "It means someone is kind enough to be feeding us."

Nancy shook her head. "Yesterday it was grouse, the day before it was salmon, and now this...this..."

"Best eating there is. Nothing better than venison. Have one of the girls roast some for supper."

"Nelson, is that all you have to say about this?"

"I would guess someone is courting in an honorable way."

"Courting?" Nancy was shocked. "Y...you mean..."

"I mean I would be proud to have a dusky-skinned son-in-law."

"You can't be serious."

"Well, the Andrus family could stand a squirt of stronger blood."

"Nelson, you're impossible."

Her husband replied seriously, "Don't forget, all my treatment to cure Anna was to no avail. It was his herbal remedy that brought her back to health."

"But why bring so much meat?"

"His way, I suppose, of showing his devotion."

Nancy turned away. First it was Amy, then it was Fannie, and now this impossible situation with Anna. She began to wonder if she was going to be able to cope until her girls were married.

Just then, Nancy had to jump aside to avoid being rammed by a squealing pig dashing past. Teddy was standing on top of the picnic table, barking his head off at a crate-load of pigs just released.

Cryder came up to her, explaining, "Saw one of them big rattlers curled up near the kitchen tent and I had to let the pigs go after him so..."

"So you turned all the pigs loose," Nancy said accusingly.

"Yep, that's about it. They'll clean out them varmints so you needn't be scared."

Slowly the days passed for Anna. No, she would not take a walk with...this...this savage. But she had been so sick and he...he did help her. Maybe she would take just a short walk with him. After a few moments, she decided she wouldn't. She had read about Indians killing white people. On the other hand, she felt Indians had been badly treated by the white people. She finally decided she would stay in the tent and not see him. But on the day he had told her he would come when there were no shadows, she carefully dressed, putting on her favorite blue voil and tied blue ribbons in her hair. To get it just right, she kept retying it, then sat outside anxiously watching the winding trail she was sure he had come on before. Impatiently she waited, then decided she might not be looking her best and returned to her tent. She removed the blue ribbons and let her golden tresses flow over her shoulder. She stood looking critically at herself in the mirror. Did this make her look too childish? She piled her hair on top of her head and held it with two tortoise-shell combs. Looking again in the mirror she scowled and took out the combs, wondering if braids would be more suitable. She took up the blue ribbon again and tied it in a bow around a strand of hair, letting it coyly peek above her ear. She returned to her vigil, watching the trail where it disappeared behind a grove of pine trees. The sun was high overhead. Anna started to fume. Didn't he know there were no shadows?

But he came on a trail behind her. In spite of the warm day, he wore a full suit of buckskin. Without greeting, he held out his hand to her. "Come, we go."

"Where are we going?" Anna asked, looking timidly up at him.

"Where the singing water runs cool and shady," he replied. They went but a short distance when he parted a clump of willows beside the trail and led her to a large rock jutting out over the stream. She sat down on its smooth surface. A breeze stirred the leaves, tossing her curls above her forehead. He silently stood beside her.

Anna nervously laughed. "I...I don't even know your name."

"My Indian name too hard for tongue."

"Try me," Anna challenged.

"Tomoetcheeketa."

"Yes, it is a bit long."

"Call James."

Anna shook her head. "No, I like your Indian name best, but you are right, it would be hard for me to say your Indian name, so I will call you by the first part—Tomo. It sounds nice and friendly. Does that please?"

His face softened. "It please." From the fringes of his jacket he drew out a small packet he handed her. "You please?"

Anna looked at him with questioning eyes and slowly undid the buckskin ties, unfolded the soft doeskin, and gasped with pleasure. "Oh, how beautiful!"

"Earrings my sister made for you."

Girlishly excited, she waved them above her head to watch the beads sparkle in the sunlight. Suddenly she grew serious. "I love everything about Indians and their ways. Many times I have wondered why I was born white."

He sat down beside her. "Maybe Indian way too hard for you."

Anna shook her head. "Oh no. To live in a teepee, with clean fresh air, I would grow strong. To live a nomadic life would be so much fun. One week hunting in the mountains. The next week down on the river fishing. Fall time gathering berries in the foothills and digging camus roots on the flats. Oh, it would be great to live so free." She flung wide her lifted arms, her face glowing.

Silently he bowed his head, then sadly looked at her. Slowly she lowered her arms. "Tomo, you do not like that kind of life?"

His chest heaved with heaviness he could not hide. "Great Spirit made man be free to roam as he wish. White man say no."

"That's wicked for any man to say how another man must live. He must be free to choose how he will live." Anna was unaware that she was beginning to speak the native way.

"That way Indian think but white man say live on reservation. Reservation death to Indian."

Incensed at such injustice, Anna clenched a fringe on his jacket. "What you say, Tomo, makes me ashamed to be white."

He bowed his head and remained silent. Anna tilted her head, looking up at his somber face and thoughtfully said, "But the reservation is in Idaho and you are here."

He raised his head. "Only short time."

"What do you do on the reservation?" she asked.

"Interpreter for government. Many times go to Washington for my people."

Anna was all interest and asked, "The Nez Perce?"

He nodded but said nothing and Anna pondered, "When you think about it, the name Nez Perce is an odd name for so noble a people."

"It mean, hole in nose."

Anna gasped, "But only cannibals have holes in their noses."

"With my people, mean great chiefs."

"Do you mean royalty, like kings and queens?"

He nodded and Anna was puzzled. "I do not understand."

"The story is long."

"Oh, Tomo, please tell me."

"Long before white man, strange men came from far away, wear iron, carry big cross, kill Big Chief."

Anna interrupted to ask, "Could you mean Montezuma?"

He nodded and continued. "Few of his people escape. They ride many moons on spotted horses till they come to great land of salmon. Here they stay. To not forget they come from Great Chief they wear flowers, wampum in nose."

"To denote they are of royal blood?" Anna asked.

"Yes," he replied in assent. Anna lifted shiny eyes to his, asking, " Oh, Tomo, you are so noble. Could you be of royalty?"

For answer, he took from his jacket a skin pouch and from it an ornament which he slipped into the septum of his nose. Anna excitedly clapped her hands. "I just knew all the time you were royal."

He gave a slight smile over her girlishness. "How know?"

"In a dream, a very old Indian put a large war bonnet on your head and bowed to you."

"Great Spirit talk to you."

"Tomo," she anxiously asked, "tell me really and truly how you knew I was sick."

"Great Spirit say, half your heart dying, go."

"Oh, Tomo, you came just in time. I really was dying."

He rose, saying, "Sickness still inside. No good get tired. We go."

"I don't want to go. I'm having such a lovely time."

"Kuuts Kuuts, come."

"You call me Indian name! What does it mean?"

He made no reply but parted the flaming red branches of sumac bushes for her to pass. Silently his moccasins treaded beside her and Anna felt a communion between them that made words superfluous. His presence thrilled her until her blood seemed to race through her veins. He left her at the edge of the campground, saying, "Tomorrow when sun leaves no shadows, I come."

Anna ran into camp, calling, "Mama, Papa."

Nettie stuck her head through the tent flaps. "They have gone for a walk. Anna, your face is glowing. You have fully recovered. You had us so worried."

Anna sat down beside her. "Where did they go?"

For some time Doc had wanted to take Nancy to a place that was sacred to him. Today seemed to be the opportune time and he was anxious for his wife to share with him one of his deepest feelings. He led her on a dim trail for several miles. Finally he made her sit down on a log to rest before he parted branches of a thick alder, opening onto a stand of forest giants. Winter snows had lain deep in this low ravine and their trunks were bare of branches for thirty and forty feet up. They stood stately tall and majestic, overpowering in their colossal height. Nancy tilted her head far back, her eyes traveling far up their trunks until their tops seemed to be holding up the azure-blue sky. "Nelson, what majestic trees! What are they"?

"They are the Creator's cathedrals."

"No, I mean what species are they?"

"Tamarac, the American larch."

Nancy felt overwhelmed by their magnificence. "Look how gracefully they sway in the breeze. Their branches look so feathery and lacy."

Doc had taken off his hat in reverence to these mighty giants.

"My dear, don't you see how standing among them, one is closer to one's Maker than in any church?"

"But, Nelson, we need the churches to show us the way to heaven when we die."

"Why wait for heaven? Why not enjoy heaven here and now?"

"We need preachers to teach us..."

"Nature with all her wondrous creations can teach you more than any preacher."

"For heaven's sake, Nelson, do you want me to be a heathen?"

"No, I want you to fully realize that the great Creator has given us everything to make this earth a heaven." For some time they sat hand in hand on a log, contemplating the age of these mighty trees, but Doc was dissatisfied and, to a small degree, disappointed that his wife had not fully embraced his view of Earth's holiness.

The next day, when Tomo failed to show up as he had promised, Anna grew restless. When she couldn't wait another minute, she tied on her wide-brimmed, leghorn-straw hat, and picking up a few things she thought would please his mother and sister, she started up the trail she assumed would lead her to his camp. After walking for what seemed hours, she realized she had lost sight of Oregon Butte, the steep-cliffed mountain that rose from the valley floor and served as a landmark. On she plodded, feeling more unsure with every step. A snake buzzed his rattles beside her and she gathered up her skirts and ran. Further on she sat down to rest, but when an elk bugled, the eerie sound echoed through the forest and she took flight again. She had long lost sight of the mountain stream she had started to follow. Not knowing which direction to go, she trudged on, hoping for a sight of his camp. Now frightened, she rounded a sharp bend in the game trail and jumped, screaming. Standing in front of her was Tomo, arms folded and looking stern.

"You were going where?"

"W...why I was going to thank your sister for the beautiful earrings."

"Camp is where?"

Anna pointed behind him. He turned to look then facing her, said, "Strange, camp move. I not know."

Anna felt annoyed and with her chin held high demanded, "Let me pass."

Nimbly he stepped aside and she ignored him as she walked past. Further up the trail she quickly glanced back but he was gone. Suddenly she felt terribly alone. She was growing so hot and tired. She rounded a clump of sumac only to face Tomo again. She held out a rag doll. "I have made the baby a toy and I want to give it to her."

"Another time. Too far."

"Tomo, I like you very much, but you are getting too bossy."

"Another fever, you die."

"Oh, so you're afraid I might get sick again. Well, your fears are ungrounded. I'm as strong as...as...a…"

"Yes?"

"As a horse."

"Think not."

"I'm going to your camp just the same." She screamed "Let me go" as he swept her up in his arms, and with a clenched fist she pounded his chest. He swiftly bent his head. His braids touched her cheek. His lips touched hers until she went limp with astonishment. She had never been kissed by a man before and she was shocked into silence. He carried her all the way back to camp and set her down in front of her tent.

Nettie, looking up from her reading, saw the Indian's stern face, and chided her sister, "So, the big chief wouldn't let you have your own way."

"Oh, shut up," Anna said and went looking for her mother.

Unexpectedly, the next day Tomo showed up very early. Finding only Maybelle by the campfire, he told her, "Good day to come to camp. Big salmon run."

Maybelle jumped up. "Oh, I'll go and tell Anna. May I come too?"

He nodded. Soon Maybelle was back, followed by Anna. They followed the river, now and then stopping to watch the salmon digging in the stream's gravel bottom. They thrashed back and forth with their nose to dig a place to lay their eggs where it was clear of the river's settlement.

Arriving at his camp, they were introduced to his mother and sister. Their camp was spotlessly clean. The baby was in a snowy white dress embroidered with flowers. She was only eight months old and smiled and cooed as they talked to her. Maybelle stayed to play with the baby while Anna went to watch Tomo gig for salmon. He had built a crude platform over the river where he knelt with a sharp, forked-speared gig held high over his head. She watched a large salmon swim under the platform and in a flash he thrust down his spear. Heaving the thrashing salmon up, he threw it on the bank, where his mother took it, placing it on a canvas and cutting it into narrow widths. She then put the long strips on pine poles over a fence to dry. Fascinated, Anna went to watch the Indian woman deftly scoring the fish and was told it was done to prevent spoilage. Anna wanted to help, as the Indian woman couldn't keep up with all the salmon Tomo was catching. Soon she was cutting fish and having a hard time doing it as his mother taught her. Her spacing of the cuts was too narrow and pieces of fish were dropping from the drying pole. She was deeply engrossed in the difficult job when she heard a soft laugh. As she looked up into Tomo's amused face, her knife slipped and cut her finger. He quickly stanched the blood by gathering willow leaves and wrapping them her finger, saying, "My mother has good helper."

Walking back to camp, Tomo explained how important the salmon were to his people, for in time of poor hunting the dried fish provided well for them.

That night when the moon was full, Anna woke up with a start. A man's shadow was on the tent wall. Quickly slipping into her wrapper, she grabbed her parasol and crept out of the tent, staying close to the canvas wall. As she raised the parasol and rounded the corner of the tent, a hand snatched her parasol and covered her mouth. A low voice said, "Tomo. Be quiet."

"Oh, how you frightened me!" Anna whispered.

"Kuuts Kuuts, you are very brave."

"Why are you here?"

"Cougar kill fisherman's boy. His tracks come here."

"Oh, how terrible!"

"Do not be afraid. Tonight I watch."

"But your sister and mother are alone."

"No, my father come to take us home."

"Oh, Tomo, you'll be gone," wailed Anna.

"Your father say, you go tomorrow."

"Won't I ever see you again?" Anna's voice quivered.

"Kuuts Kuuts, when shadows cross the trail, I come."

Towards evening he came carrying a roll of white doeskin. Everyone admired the hide's softness. Fannie wanted a piece of it to make a shopping bag, but he shook his head, remaining silent. Finally, the family drifted away leaving them alone. Tomo surprised Anna by stretching the skin on the ground and asking her to lie down on it. Anna hesitated, thinking it a queer request but she finally complied. Picking up a piece of charcoal from the edge of the campfire he deftly drew an outline of her slender form on the skin. Puzzled, Anna asked, "What does this mean?"

"Kuuts Kuuts say she want Indian dress. I make."

Anna's eyes flew wide open. "You make me a dress?"

He nodded, and in amazement Anna said, "I simply can't believe you can make me a dress."

"My mother do beading."

"But, Tomo, I can't accept such a valuable gift unless I give you something. Would you like a new hunting knife?"

"Tomo tell you when time come."

Anna stood up with tears in her eyes, "Tomo, won't I ever see you again? I...I can't say good-bye."

"Never good-bye Kuuts Kuuts, never." He Looked deeply into her eyes, then turning, he walked away, leaving Anna feeling desolate and wondering about the meaning of Kuuts Kuuts, which he had refused to tell her. Teddy came whining up to her and she threw her arms around his neck, sobbing out her grief. "Oh, Teddy, maybe I'll never see him again." As if in sympathy, Teddy licked her cheek.

## Chapter 17

# Fulfillment of Dreams

Back home Fannie put away her preparations for her marriage to help Nettie get ready for her trip east. Since making up with John before leaving the Blue Mountains, she had seen a dramatic change in him. Gone were the dark circles under his eyes and the hollows in his cheeks had filled out. Her father expressed relief over his patient's improvement. But something was worrying Fannie and she made up her mind that as soon as Nettie was gone, she would go to their dear and close family friend and ask Abigale's advice.

Fannie worked diligently at the sewing machine, getting Nettie's wardrobe ready for her trip to and residence at the nursing college. She made several lovely blouses to wear with one serviceable skirt. For her sister's traveling attire, she made a stunning and stylish wine-colored suit trimmed in lynx fur, which suited Nettie's auburn hair and fair complexion. Fannie told her, "In this suit you are a raving beauty and sure to catch a husband."

"Stop flattering me, Fannie dear. You know I'm destined to be an old maid."

Fannie hooted with laughter. "Don't feed me that trip trap. You'll be married before I am."

"Me married before you? I don't even have a beau and you're soon to married."

"Things can happen fast. Wearing this suit, your fairy godmother will whisk you up to the altar."

"Alone?"

"No, silly."

Just before Nettie was leaving to catch the train, her father called her into his study. Nettie was excited. "Oh, Papa, what a thrill to be going away on a train."

"Yes. One of the first things Judge Frankland did when he became governor was to get the Northern Pacific into Dayton. It was a reward for my strong support for his governorship."

"Papa, I'm going to become the best nurse you've ever had and I will lighten your work a lot."

"My dear, you're going to be faced with many choices. Before you decide anything, remember to always consider your motive. If your motive is rational, following the Golden Rule, things will turn out satisfactorily."

"Oh, Papa, don't worry about me."

"I do, because you are young and without any experience of the world."

Nettie fondly kissed him, "Dear Papa, I'll think what you would do and do it."

Doc shook his head. " No, my dear, follow your conscience. It's the voice that will guide you and protect you, if you will listen and follow its advice."

"Oh I will, I will, I promise." Nettie gave her father a big hug. "If I don't hurry I'll miss my train."

The family went down to the train to see Nettie off. Mrs. Aims, considering herself one of the family, arrived to give Nettie a Bible and some advice. "I hope you've asked Jesus to forgive you of all your sins includin' the time you took some of my best dishes to your playhouse and broke them. You need a clean slate to start out with; only the good Lord knows what the devil has in store for you. You be careful. Satan knows how to set traps you don't suspect. Stick to your learnin' and no playin' around."

Nettie graciously kissed the old lady and assured her, "Oh, Mrs. Aims, I promise to be on the alert for the devil, just like you."

This pleased God's most ardent helper. "See that you do," she commanded and pecked the cheek of the girl she always thought she was saving from the fiery furnace of hell.

Nettie sat at the train window, waving until the train had puffed around the bend and Dayton was out of sight. She dabbed at her tears, then sitting up straight she scolded herself, "Don't blubber when you've barely gotten started."

As soon as the train disappeared, Fannie headed straight for Abigale's house. Abigale came to the door, warmly greeting her. "Fannie, dear, you look tired."

"I'm beat. Why weren't you down to see Nettie off?"

"Such an occasion is just for family."

"Mrs. Aims didn't think so," Fannie frowned.

"Came with a lot of advice, did she?"

"Oh, definitely."

"Which Nettie will ignore."

"Of course. Abigale, now that your friend has returned to Boston, are you lonely?"

Abigale cheerily smiled. "Oh, a bit, but not too much when I have such wonderful friends as your family."

"Yes, but one by one we are slowly leaving."

"Fannie, are you leaving?"

"John and I are going to be married."

"Wonderful!"

Fannie fumbled with her gloves, sounding worried. "I...I don't know."

"What seems to be the trouble?" Abigale asked anxiously.

"Well, my sisters are already planning a large wedding for us and neither John nor I want one."

"How about just a small church wedding?" Abigale suggested.

Fannie shook her head. "Even that, I'm afraid, would put too much strain on John. You see, he hasn't fully recovered."

For a few moments they both sat contemplating a solution. Finally, Abigale looked inquiringly at Fannie. "Would you consider quietly going to the Justice of the Peace with a couple members of your family to be married? I could give a lovely luncheon for you and your family afterwards."

Fannie threw her arms around Abigale. "Oh, dear friend, I just knew you would figure things out for us. That is exactly what John and I would like. Then afterwards, without any fuss, we can board the train and be on our way to Arizona. You knew John's uncle has given him an office job on his large cattle ranch?"

"Yes, your mother told me. It sounds perfect for your fiancé until he is fully recovered."

"Papa thinks the hot and dry climate of the Southwest is just what John needs."

"How soon do you and John want to be married?" Abigale asked.

"As soon as possible. John's uncle is anxious for him to come."

"Give me a week to make the luncheon arrangements."

"I know John will want Bob to be with him. They have become such close friends," said Fannie, looking vastly relieved.

Abigale frowned. "I'm not sure where Bob is just now. Did you know Amy's husband had given Bob a contract to design and build their new home?"

"I had heard rumors, but I wasn't sure."

"Bob came to see me a few days ago and told me. He had conferred with Amy and from what he said, it's to be a large mansion, in fact a showcase for Walla Walla."

Fannie shook her head. "Can they afford such a home?"

"Seems that Amy's husband has inherited a large fortune from his father who has recently died."

Fannie drew a deep breath. "I cannot understand Amy's craze for the opulent. You can be sure Amy will furnish this mansion lavishly."

Abigale nodded. "One good thing, she has excellent taste."

Getting up to leave, Fannie asked, "How are we going to find Bob?"

Abigale said with certainty, "Neville has to make a hurried trip to Walla Walla tomorrow for supplies and he can hunt Bob down and give him your message. Do you want him to tell Charlie to come too?"

"Oh, heavens no! Charlie would cook up some big surprise to celebrate our wedding and our nice quiet affair would turn into a riot."

"Mrs. Aims' roses are in full bloom, and they are gorgeous and..." Abigale hesitated, not knowing how her suggestion would be accepted.

"Stop, Stop!" Fannie implored, jumping to her feet. "You would have to invite her if you asked for some roses."

"Her gorgeous damask roses would look lovely on the luncheon table." Abigale was almost pleading.

"John would rather have cactus on the table than to have Mrs. Aims at our wedding."

Abigale shrugged. "They would have looked lovely."

Fannie started to leave. "It's impossible. They had a falling out because she got mad at John for not putting her garden fence exactly where she wanted it."

"So be it. How is your mother today? She had a migraine headache yesterday."

"I wish Papa would retire. His patients expect too much of him and the extra work falls on Mama."

"The next time I see your father, I'll mention his retirement," Abigale suggested.

"I warn you, he may not like the idea. I'll let you know the day we want to be married as soon as I talk with John."

"Splendid. See you later," Abigale said, watching Fannie trip happily down the walk.

The following week, Doc was unable to cancel patient appointments and Nancy was too busy doing Fannie's last minute packing, so Mae and Anna accompanied the couple to the Justice of the Peace. Afterwards, both Doc and Nancy made time to attend the luncheon.

## Chapter 17 - Fulfillment of Dreams

Just as Abilgale always did everything well, the luncheon was beautifully planned. As they were just sitting down to partake of a dainty menu, the door flew open and behind a huge bouquet of exquisite roses they saw a bunch of bobbing daisies. Mrs. Aims stalked in, thrusting the roses into Abigale's arms. Then she turned to John. "I forgive that stupid idea of yours, puttin' the fence in the wrong place. But, I couldn't see you get away without wishin' you well on your weddin' day. The good Lord told me to forgive you. Well here I am, forgivin'. Looks like you have some good eatin'."

Abigale was so shocked, she could find no words, but looked fearfully at John. Mrs. Aims walked over to survey the wedding cake. "Them sugared violets sure look pretty on that white icin'." Turning she said, "You better put my roses in water before they wilt."

Abigale rushed into the kitchen for a vase of water, followed by Fannie. Abigale was in tears, wringing her hands. "How could she, how could she," the hostess repeated, "be so brazen?"

Fannie took Abigale into her arms. "Dear, it isn't as bad as you think. John is about to bust at the seams with laughter and you *did* get your roses."

"What will I do?"

"Have her join us. John and I can then start on our journey with her full instructions on how to escape the devil." Fannie started to laugh.

Mrs. Aims joined the family to see the newlyweds off on the southbound train with the advice: "See that you stay married until death and no splittin' up over a little argument."

John, almost choking with laughter, shocked the old lady by saying, "I'll sock her in the eye the first time she disagrees with me!"

As the engine started puffing and moving the cars, Mrs. Aims still gasping and shaking her head, exclaimed, "I ain't so sure that marriage is goin' to last."

Nancy took her arm. "John was only teasing you."

"I ain't so sure." Mrs. Aims gave a worried look at the departing train.

The weeks flew by as the Andrus family adjusted to the absence of Fannie and Nettie. One day, Mae made the observation, "Charlie seems to have vanished into history."

Her father replied, "Judge Frankland is keeping a friendly eye on him and tells me Charlie has a new girlfriend, a beauty with large brown eyes."

Mae gave a snort. "Strange. It has always been violet eyes. Has he gone colorblind?"

Doctor smiled. "He gave up on violet eyes after her father told Charlie that he wasn't the man for his daughter."

"I've never known Charlie to give up that easy," Mae said.

Doc chuckled, "Because he found brown eyes preferable. Her father owns several large greenhouses five miles on the other side of Walla Walla and has given Charlie a good summer job."

"So that's why he has extended his college courses to include agriculture."

Doc nodded. "I'm proud to say he has been promised managership as soon as he finishes college."

Mae shook her head. "It's hard to believe he could stay in one spot long enough to grow a tomato."

Doc laughed. "I think Charlie is finally growing up. At least he's taking things more seriously."

"How seriously?" Mae asked.

"He's asking me about the facts of life," Doc answered.

"Oh-oh," Mae scoffed. "If that means wedding bells, I hope they ring in Walla Walla. I'm bored with weddings."

Just then, Teddy came sniffing around the room. Doc said, "He misses Nettie. She roughhoused with him and he loved the rough-and-tumble play." He spoke to the dog, "Teddy, one thing in life you can always count on and that's change. You'll just have to get used to the girls going." Teddy came up to him whining. Doc patted Teddy's head and the little dog continued searching for his boisterous playmate.

## Chapter 17 - Fulfillment of Dreams

The family began to notice Anna's frequent trips to the post office and her downcast expression when she returned with mail only for the rest of the family. She began to grow thin and pale. Worried that Anna's illness was returning, Nancy went to see Abigale. "I just don't know what to do. Anna hardly eats at all and she just mopes around with no interest in anything."

Abigale reminded her friend, "I'm told she grew very fond of the Indian who brought her the herbs that broke her fever. Has she ever heard from him?"

Nancy shook her head. "No, I don't believe so."

Abigale made a suggestion. "Instead of Anna waiting around hoping to hear from him, why doesn't she go to the homestead with us? Bob has invited Maybelle, Mae, and me to go stay with him for a few days next week while he does some work at the old homestead before returning to finish Amy's house."

Nancy sighed. "At least it would get her out of the house and into the cooler mountain air. But will she go?"

"Of course she will when I tell her we're going to sleep under the stars and cook over the campfire. Nettie told me how Anna has become very interested in the way Indians live, and what could be more Indian-like?" Abigale laughed.

The following week, they arrived in the evening at Curl's old homestead. Bob built the campfire and helped the girls set up their tent. He insisted on cooking supper over the campfire and surprised them by cutting and sharpening twigs. He then speared one end of each twig into a steak, anchoring the other end in the ground, so that the meat roasted over the glowing coals. After he buried potatoes in the ashes, the steaks began to sizzle. He did allow the girls to make the salad while he manned the cooking of the steaks. While they were eating, to their surprise and delight, a white-tail deer stepped daintily into the firelight and lay down. Abigale smiled with sadness. "That's old Curl's pet. He called her Sadie."

Mae somberly observed, "It's been two years since he died, and she hasn't forgotten."

Maybelle spoke up. "Do you know what I think? I think old Curl brought her to us to say hello."

Mae exclaimed, "But he's dead!"

Maybelle affirmed with certainty, "Just his body is dead. His spirit energy, which is the real him, is just as alive as ever."

Mae shuddered. "Where did you hear all that stuff?"

"Papa, and if we had a wider range of vision, we could see him."

Bob looked keenly at the girl, thinking she was much more grown-up than her years.

The doe seemed perfectly at home and nibbled at the grass around her. Now and then she perked her ears to listen to the night sounds, once leaping up when a coyote howled; then, hearing it no more, settled back down to doze. The rest of the party being tired, took the hint and reluctantly took a last look at the star-studded night before saying good night.

The next morning they found Sadie in their outdoor kitchen having breakfast on the leftover salad. In the distance they heard grouse drumming on a log. A mother quail, with her tiny brood, strutted into camp to peck at fallen breadcrumbs, sending Maybelle into peals of soft laughter at their perky feathers sticking straight up from their little heads. Later a small, black-tail deer showed off her young, spotted twins, by leading them through camp. All day Bob would suggest things to be done and most always Maybelle would reply "I don't think old Curl would like that" or "I think old Curl would want it this way" until Bob was getting tired of hearing about old Curl. It was a relief to him when one day Maybelle came up to him, saying, "Mr. Curl says you have to take the responsibility of your place as he has other things to do." Mr. Curl was never mentioned again.

But Maybelle herself found something to be tiresome. Bob was always saying, "Well, little sister, what do you think of this?"

One day Maybelle, having had enough of the little-sister routine, told him, "I'm tired of all that sister stuff."

"You're the one who thought of it," Bob reminded her.

"I know and it was stupid."

"Well, what do you want me to call you?"

Maybelle seemed tongue-tied and Bob looked at her quizzically.

She refused to lift her downcast eyes when she finally stammered, "C...c...could we pretend?"

"Pretend what?" Bob asked with interest.

Maybelle was finding it hard to answer. Bob looked keenly at her, thinking how much she had grown since he last saw her. The top of her head now reached his chin and there were other revealing changes that surprised him.

"Well, what do you want to pretend?" Bob repeated.

She jumped to her feet. "C...could we pretend we're...we're sweethearts?" Gathering her skirts above the lace on her pantalets, she ran as fast as she could. For a moment Bob sat stunned, then in a flash of merriment took after her, easily catching up with Maybelle and tripping her. They both sprawled on the grass.

Abigale, coming out of the tent, exclaimed, "For heaven's sake what does this mean?"

Bob was laughing so hard he could hardly speak. "This minx has just proposed to me."

Maybelle leaping up, stamped her foot, her face a fiery red. "I did no such thing. I...I...just said…"

"Yes, what did you say?" Abigale questioned.

"Oh, forget the whole thing!" Maybelle snapped. She ran to the creek and waded in, splashing.

When she was gone, Abigale raised her eyebrow. "Well?"

Bob rocked back on his heels. "My friend, I believe you're right."

"Yes?" Abigale questioned.

"I believe kids do grow up and pretty fast at that."

"It took you a darn long time to wake up to that fact."

The next day Bob became aware that Maybelle was taking every precaution to avoid him. The easy camaraderie they had shared was gone. As usual he went to Abigale with his problem, but Abigale shook her head. "This time, my boy, you're on your own."

At last he hit on a scheme to break the impasse. He went to Maybelle, who refused to look at him. "My dear little friend, I'm so busy with Amy's house, I find I won't have the time to plan my own. Could you be so good as to sketch out a floor plan for the cabin? Remember, we once made a deal: you were to draw the plans, if I wouldn't fish Curl's pond."

"How many children are you going to have?" She seriously asked.

Bob was taken back by this unexpected question. "Well, I believe marriage comes first and I haven't found anyone yet who would have me."

He kept silent, letting that sink in. She gave him a quick glance.

"Unless," he spoke low, "unless we pretended we were married and decided how many children we wanted. Would that help you make the cabin plans?" Seeing this girl, who flipped his heart, blush and turn away, he quickly added, "Of course it's just pretend."

She spoke so low, he could hardly hear her. "Two makes a nice family."

Bob spoke matter-of-factly. "Two it is. Now you can start sketching the floor plan."

"Are you sure you really want me to plan the house you'll be living in forever?"

"Absolutely. You're the only one who knows my tastes."

"It would be nice for you to have a study to do your work."

"A splendid idea," Bob enthused.

Maybelle began to warm up to the idea and for the next hour the two talked over the plans for the cabin. At last she left to make tea and Bob sauntered over to the fishpond congratulating himself on how cleverly his scheme had worked. He threw himself on the ground, lying on his back, watching the cumulus white clouds pile up on the horizon. He decided he wouldn't clean up the charred logs of the old cabin that day as he was expecting his workman to come any time, bringing old Curl's coffin to be laid to rest as Maybelle had requested. Yes, he thought, Maybelle had definitely outgrown her pantalets and should be wearing petticoats and bustles like her sisters. He tried to picture how she would look without her braids and her hair up in combs. Strange how her adorable smile kept flashing in front of him, whether he was at his desk or attending social events. When in Walla Walla he missed her more than he cared to admit. So absorbed was he in his thoughts, he never heard her until she suddenly stood beside him, throwing the cabin plans in his lap.

"I can't do it!"

Bob leaped to his feet. "What's the matter?"

"I'm not going to plan a beautiful home for someone else."

"But it's for me," Bob said, puzzled over this turn of events.

"No, it isn't. You'll find a girl and a...a...ask her."

"What?" Bob asked curiously.

"You know." Maybelle flushed, turning to walk away.

Bob caught up with her. "I think this pretending has gone far enough."

Maybelle gave him a quick glance. "You don't want to pretend anymore?"

"That's right, I want it to be real. I'm asking you to marry me."

For a moment Maybelle looked wide-eyed, then that adorable smile spread across her face and she threw her arms around his neck. "Oh, Bob, I thought you'd never ask."

"You little minx, you deserve a spanking."

"I'll settle for a kiss," she smiled and held up her lips.

After he raised his head, Bob looked deeply into her eyes. "Your tactics couldn't be more grown-up."

"Why did you take so long?"

"Because I thought of you as a little, little girl."

Maybelle stepped back and held wide her arms. "And I'm a big, big girl."

Bob gathered her back into his arms. "Not that big, and I suggest you ditch those pantalets so I won't feel like I'm engaged to a kid."

Maybelle giggled. "Let's keep it a secret until I'm wearing bustles."

"How long is that going to be?"

"Tomorrow. I can snitch one of Anna's dresses, it just fits."

Just then, Bob's workmen came carrying Curl's coffin. Maybelle directed them to a spruce tree by the pool where several trout were rising to the surface catching grasshoppers being blown by a gust of wind down on the emerald-green water.

The workmen had dug the grave the day before and now they lowered the coffin as the girls threw wildflowers they had gathered. Bob nailed a copper plaque engraved with the old man's name and date of birth and death on the gnarled trunk of the old spruce tree. Anna read the Ninety-First Psalm, and Mae gave a beautiful benediction. In a tearful voice, Maybelle said, "Welcome back home, dear Mr. Curl. We want you to be very happy. God bless you." With these last words, she ran away to hide. Bob found her dabbing at her eyes, and his heart gave a lurch as he looked into the somber face of the girl who was unaware how deeply she had intruded into his life. Looking up with tears streaming down her face, she asked, "Oh, Bob, do you think he's happy now?"

That evening the girls argued between themselves as to whether they should go ahead with the entertainment they had planned around the campfire that night or spend the evening in traditional mourning for old Curl.

Maybelle emphatically decided, "We are going to have fun just like we planned. He's happy now and that is exactly what he would want." When the night blanketed the earth with stars and the campfire leaped with glowing flames, they gathered, with Sadie joining them. Anna commented that it was a good thing they had left Teddy at home or Sadie would have had no peace. Before they left home they had debated on whether to let him come, then remembering how he had baited the bull on the fishing trip, they unanimously decided not to run another risk as no one wanted to climb a tree.

Maybelle started the entertainment by wrapping herself in a Pendleton Indian blanket, and after sticking a grouse feather in her hair, started dancing around the fire. Mae, having been coached beforehand, brought out a tin pan and pounded a tom-tom rhythm on it with an iron ladle.  Crow-hopping, Maybelle started singing a very old song almost lost in history and taught to her by an old trapper, one of her father's patients.

> On an Indian reservation
> Far away from civilization
> Where the feet of pale face seldom trod
> White man went to fish one summer
> Met an Indian maid a hummer
> Daughter of the big chief Spare the Rod
> White man cast some loving glances
> Took this maid into war dances
> Smoked the pipe of peace took chances
> Living in a teepee made of fur
> Rode with her on an Indian pony
> Gave to her diamond rings a-phony
> Then he sang these loving words to her
> Won't you be my little Napanee
> Won't you take a chance and marry me
> Though you are a little Indian maid
> I'll soon turn to a darker shade
> I'll wear feathers in my hair
> Paint my cheeks an Indian red
> If you'll only be my Napanee
> Soon papooses came in numbers
> Red skin yells disturbed his slumbers

Here Maybelle fluttered her hands over her mouth giving several war whoops, which sent her audience into peals of laughter.

> White man wondered he had blundered
> Now the feathers droop upon his head
> And he's wishing he'd never gone a-fishing
> And had said those loving words to her

Maybelle collapsed on the ground. "I can't sing another note. I'm bushed."

"Is there another verse?" Mae asked.

Maybelle nodded. "But I've lost my voice."

Anna piped up, "You can finish your song tomorrow night. It's a great song."

"Well, I sang it just for you," Maybelle said.

Just then they heard hoof beats and a rider came into the clearing. As soon as he dismounted, he strode over to Bob, handing him a note.

Mae said, "I'll bet it's from Amy."

Bob finished reading the note, "You're right. It's from your sister, ordering me back at once to see to the installing of the gasoliers."

"Why couldn't she have waited? I'm not ready to leave." Anna sounded disgusted.

"It seems she is giving a house party soon and needs the lights." Bob, too, sounded disappointed.

"As usual, she is just thinking of herself." Mae sounded very put out.

"It's my job and she's the boss," Bob said.

In the morning they were up at dawn to get an early start back. Bob wanted to make it to Walla Walla the same day. He told Maybelle, "If I don't go, I won't be able to bring you what I intend to bring you." He looked at her mysteriously.

Maybelle wrinkled her nose. "What?"

"You know what."

Maybelle nodded with a grin. Mae, overhearing the promise, asked, "What are you bringing my little sister?"

Bob laughed. "A lollipop, of course."

## Chapter 18

# Heartbeat of the Tom-Toms

Because of their trip to the homestead, Anna received Tomo's letter almost too late. Had not Amy insisted Bob return at once, she would have missed the one train that could take her in time to meet him. She phoned the Northern Pacific ticket office and was dismayed to learn the only train she could catch, making connections in Walla Walla for points west, was leaving at midnight that night. She immediately sent a telegram to Tomo, giving him the time she and her sisters would be arriving in Pendleton. She sent another telegram to her brother asking him to join them in Walla Walla and continue on with them to the town hosting the famous All Western Round-Up where Tomo's people were gathered to add pageantry to the event.

Tomo's letter had been brief. He had been going to school to learn to speak better English. He had also been to Washington, D.C., to confer with government officials on behalf of his people and was involved in many meetings with the Indian agent to solve some of their problems.

As Anna read his words, she wasn't exactly sure how she felt, perhaps a little hurt and disappointed. Tomo said nothing about the love he had declared for her in the Blue Mountains, nothing about whether he missed her. Then she read these words: " Kuuts Kuuts, all will be said from my heart when we meet. The owl say, all is well. You hold half my heart. We never say good-bye again."

Tears of joy glistened down her cheeks, and after reading his traveling instructions, she tucked her precious letter inside her blouse.

Anna insisted Mae and Maybelle go with her and she also urged her mother to go, but Nancy shook her head. "No, the trip to the Blue Mountains will suffice me for some time."

"But Mama, on the train you'll be able to rest," Anna pled.

"No, my dear. I don't want to go without your father and he can't leave poor Mrs. Aims while she is in so much pain."

"What's wrong with Mrs. Aims?" Mae asked.

"She broke her hip, and it's a dreadful break."

"How on earth did she do that?" Maybelle asked, throwing a carpetbag on the bed.

"She was chasing Teddy out of her yard with the broom and slipped on the wet grass."

Mae was indignant. "She should be happy that Teddy digs the gophers out of her yard."

"She thinks Teddy is a demon. Poor dear, your father says she will be bedridden for several months." Nancy started downstairs. Turning, she warned, "You haven't a minute to lose if you're going to get everything done and make it to the train on time. So hurry."

As the girls were packing, Mae laughed, "If Mrs. Aims is in bed for months, it will give Teddy time to clean her yard of gophers."

Even at that late hour, Abigale came, bringing some fashion magazines her friend Cynthia Lynn had sent from Boston. She thought reading them would help the girls pass the time on the train. They immediately recruited her to help and she unexpectedly found herself sewing on buttons, packing, and helping them dress.

Nancy called up, "Hurry, girls, the carriage is here." Fumbling into jackets and coats, they rushed downstairs, pecked their mother on the cheek, calling back as they tripped down the porch steps, "Tell Papa good-bye."

As the carriage started, Teddy trotted right behind, trying to keep up. Mae knelt on the back seat, waving him back, yelling, "Teddy, go back!" Teddy kept trotting. "Don't you understand? Go back!" The little dog sat down whining.

Abigale and Nancy stood waving until the carriage was out of sight. Teddy sat in the middle of the road with a forlorn look, watching them until they were out of sight, than started running to catch up.

When the girls reached the train depot, great clouds of steam were belching from the train. "Mae, you go get the tickets while we take our bags and get settled," Anna advised.

"Ohhh," Maybelle exclaimed when she saw the bright-red plush seats. She plopped down on one with a bounce, saying, "How elegant." They pushed one of their bags under the seat and shoved a couple overhead.

The conductor swung his red lantern back and forth, calling, "ALLABOARD!"

Alarmed that the train would start before Mae returned, they rushed to the window, trying to see her and wondering why she was taking so long. Again the conductor yelled, "ALLABOARD!" Maybelle dashed down the aisle to search for her sister. Just then, the depot door flew open and Teddy ran out with Mae right behind him, waving her parasol, yelling, "Go home! Home!"

As the train started moving, Mae gave up the chase, ran to jump on the bottom step, clutched at Maybelle's outstretched hand, and was pulled up the steps and into the car.

At the sound of the train wheels clicking on the rails, the girls shivered with excitement, wondering what thrilling adventure awaited them. For miles and miles the girls, unable to sleep, watched the sagebrush bathed in moonlight rush past the windows and tried to spy a jackrabbit, which they had been told could jump ten feet.

Growing tired of the scenery, Mae brought out a basket, saying, "Mama thought we might get hungry and packed a few things she thought we would like." They were starved since they hadn't taken the time to have supper. So they sat back, munching chicken sandwiches, deviled eggs, pickles, and their favorite raisin tarts. When satisfied they could eat no more, they dozed off, only to be awakened by the conductor announcing they were coming to Walla Walla. The girls freshened up the best they could and gazed anxiously out the windows for the first glimpse of Charlie.

Slowly the train moved through the outskirts of Walla Walla, known for its vast surrounding wheat fields which produced enough wealth to make more millionaires per capita than any other town in America. The wealthy wheat ranchers embellished the town with their magnificent mansions. The town was famous for its sweet Spanish onions grown by Italian immigrants and sold as Walla Walla onions to those with gourmet appetites. In earlier days the first missionaries arrived to save the Indians with their religion and were massacred by the Cayuse Indians for bringing small pox to them. A small part of town was known as Chinatown, and now and then a Tong war would break out causing the citizens to demand the government take action and send them back to China.

Three noses pressed against the sooty windows, watching with fascination as the train slowly puffed past the poorer part of town nestled along the railroad tracks. The conductor came down the aisle, telling passengers they would have half an hour for breakfast at the train station's lunch counter. The train slowly ground to a stop and the girls scrambled down the aisle. Maybelle was grabbed from the bottom step and whirled around in the arms of a very handsome young man.

"Bob!" she squealed. "How did you know I was coming?"

"Your brother, of course."

"You're going with us to Pendleton?" She asked.

Bob shook his head. "I'd sure like to, but your sister Amy would exterminate me if I did. The gasoliers have yet to be installed." Grinning, he looked at Maybelle. "You've certainly done a lot of growing up since we were at the homestead. Where are the braids?"

"Under my hat."

He gave her a devilish look. Lifting a quizzical eyebrow. "And?"

She slightly lifted her skirt enough to reveal ruffled petticoats. "You can't sing that horrid song to me ever again."

"What song?" Mae asked curiously.

Bob shook his head. "Your little sister would kill me if I even mentioned it."

After greeting his sisters with a kiss, Charlie herded them to the station's lunch counter, yelling at Bob. "Come on and join us. That tyrant sister of mine can do without her damn gas lights until tomorrow." They merrily chatted and laughed about some of their pranks of earlier days until a blast from the engine warned them it was boarding time. Hurrying back, Maybelle was the last to climb the steps. As the train started moving, Bob ran beside it, holding her hand. "Darling, I didn't get my kiss."

"If you don't let go, you never will," Maybelle warned him, trying to free her hand.

When Bob could no longer keep up, he blew her a kiss. Mae jerked her sister into the coach. "You're going to fall off!"

Once seated the girls started bombarding their brother with questions. To their astonishment, he talked endlessly about his college course in agriculture. It was incredible to them that their brother could be enthusiastic about the whole process of growing tomatoes and other hothouse specialties.

At last Mae blurted, "Now let's hear about *her*."

Charlie actually blushed and started stammering, "Sh...sh...sh...she's wonderful."

Mae laughed. "We already know that, but what is she really like? Knock-kneed? Cross-eyed? Will we like her?"

"You better or I'll knock your heads together," Charlie said, scowling. Then for the next half-hour they heard about nothing but Helen. After telling of his determination to marry her, he suddenly turned to Anna. "How about bringing me up to date on your love life? Will I like him?"

Anna smiled. "You will soon be meeting him and can make up your own mind."

When the train slowly crawled into the Pendleton station, Anna felt suddenly shy and didn't join the others looking out the windows. She felt almost afraid, wondering what he would be like now that he had taken advanced courses in school. Would Charlie take to a man of another race? If not, her brother could be horrid. Anna was trembling as she alighted from the train steps. Nervously glancing around, she could see no man wearing a buckskin suit. They started to walk to the train station, when Anna felt a light touch on her shoulder. She turned to confront a complete stranger.

"Kuuts Kuuts, you do not know me?"

There wasn't one thing about this man that she recognized. He wore a suit more stylish than her brother did. There were no braids, no beads. Anna pressed her lips tightly together. She wanted to cry, and she felt frightened.

Charlie quickly took in the situation and stepped forward. "I believe introductions are in order."

The stranger beside her held out his hand to her brother. "I am James Henry, a friend of your sister's."

It was the first time she had heard his English name. Charlie heartily shook hands saying, "It's about time I met the savior of my sister. I've heard all about how you miraculously cured Anna."

"It was an honor to be of service. Now may I present my sister, Tamera Henry."

A beautifully gowned girl, dressed in the latest fashion, shyly shook their hands. She turned to speak to her brother in their own language. He immediately informed them he had ordered lunch and had booked a hotel room for them that night. He apologized, "I'm sorry our village is in an uproar preparing for the parade and the big potlatch tonight and cannot accommodate you, but we invite you to the potlatch."

"Thank you, we will be delighted to accept," Charlie said, acknowledging the invitation.

The café was small and clean and the food delicious, a roast of elk, with side dishes of tenderly cooked vegetables. Anna kept casting furtive glances at the man who had won her heart, but who was now a stranger. His copper skin revealed he was native, but he wore the clothes of the white man with ease and distinction. He didn't even talk the same. His English seemed even better than her brother's and his table manners certainly were, she thought, watching Charlie reaching across the table to fork a bun.

Seeing her distress, her lover lightly touched her hand. "Soon you will have your old playmate back, then you will not feel so shy and uncertain." Anna gave him a quivering smile. She wasn't sure just how she felt about this stranger.

Before dessert was served, Tomo and his sister excused themselves, saying, "We must go to prepare for the parade. You will enjoy seeing our people in their ceremonial dress. Even the horses will be decorated."

Tamera said, "Grandmother will not join the parade. She ask you to sit with her to watch."

Mae accepted, saying, "Thank your grandmother and tell her we will be delighted to join her."

After brother and sister had left to get ready for the parade, Maybelle accosted her sister. "Anna, what's the matter with you? You haven't said a word since we arrived."

"I...I feel so strange. I'm all mixed up." Anna's voice quavered as she spoke.

Maybelle gushed, "Oh, Anna, he's so splendid, so handsome! You're so lucky."

Tamera had told them they could rest in their hotel room until parade time, then afterward they were to meet them at the Indian village. The girls made their way to the hotel while Charlie went to explore the town.

They had only been resting for an hour when an Indian girl knocked at the door to let them know the parade was about to start. They made their way to the street, now crowded with jostling crowds looking for a place from which to watch the parade. As they stood debating which way to go to find Tomo's grandmother, a small boy tugged at Anna's sleeve and made a sign for her to follow. Charlie found them in the melee of people and they wended their way through the crowd following the boy. He stopped by an elderly Indian woman who looked up and motioned for them to camp chairs she was holding for them. In broken English she told them the tom-toms were telling them the parade had started at the far end of the long street.

The crowd grew excited at the first sight of the marshal leading the parade. The honor had been given to the chief of the Nez Perce. As he drew near, Anna's blood began to race. He rode his fiery appaloosa mount with solemn dignity. Dressed in ceremonial finery, the eagle feathers in his huge magnificent war bonnet fluttered as the high-spirited appaloosa stallion pranced, sending some onlookers standing too far out in the street scurrying, for this horse was known for killing a man.

Tomo's grandmother watched with delight, calling Anna's attention to the parade's marshal. "My father," she said proudly, then loudly called to him in the native tongue. He remained motionless, but his horse jumped to the side.

"He doesn't hear you," Anna said.

The Indian woman nodded her head. "He hear. His horse jump, that mean he hear."

The chief was followed by a band playing a lively military march, then came the floats. A prize was to be given for the most original.

Drawn by four appaloosa horses, a gorgeous float decorated in Indian designs of bright colors brought shouts from the crowd. Several lovely Indian girls were sitting at the foot of an elaborate throne rising from the center of the float. Seated on the throne was another beautiful Indian girl, wearing a dazzling, brilliant crown. Graciously, she waved to the cheering crowd.

Anna's eyes were still following the chief when Charlie gave her a nudge. "Tamera," he said, pointing. Quickly shifting her eyes, she was amazed to see Tomo's sister standing on another float elaborately decorated in an Indian motif, beautifully dressed in a white doeskin garment decorated with elk's teeth. The girl smiled directly at Anna and gave a significant wave in her direction. Anna felt overwhelmed. She frantically waved back, exclaiming, "Tomo's sister is the real queen of the Pendleton round-up." Another band played a stirring march and was followed by a distinctive float depicting a forest setting, where a trapper stood with his dog team of eight ferocious-looking huskies lying at his feet. He held a Sharp's long-barrel rifle that he loaded with powder and fired into the air every few moments.

When a float passed them carrying a huge block of ice with a frozen salmon the size of a small whale, Charlie leaped into the air. "God, if only I had had that monster at the fish derby." One float popular with the crowd was carrying a taxidermist's pride: a full-grown bucking bull, ridden by an authentic cowboy, who kept waving his hat and letting out whoops which frightened the babies along the parade route.

Next a float turned into a river where a placer miner panned for gold. Now and then he tipped his gold pan to display large gold nuggets.

The floats kept coming in varied sizes and themes and the marching bands kept getting louder and Anna grew restless wondering when Tomo would appear. Her eyes were so weary that she had just closed them to rest when the Indian woman beside her made a clicking sound with her tongue to call Anna's attention to an approaching band of Indians in breechcloths. Their faces were painted in bold colors and they carried coop sticks fluttering with feathers. Alone in front of the group rode Tomo. His stolid features gave no expression of emotion as his mount cavorted, his piercing eyes looked neither to the left nor right but solemnly straight ahead. On his horse's flank were painted red hands, which Tomo once told her signified the Power of the Great Spirit.

Maybelle grabbed Anna's arm. "Ohhh, he's magnificent!"

"H...he doesn't see me," Anna spoke plaintively.

"He will, I'm sure he will," Maybelle reassured her.

Just then his horse reared, lifting Tomo high above the crowd, and as he reined it back into formation he looked straight at her, moving his lips, speaking the words that made her heart pound: "Kuuts Kuuts." Anna almost burst into tears. Somehow she no longer felt afraid of him. This was the man she had fallen in love with.

Tomo and the war chiefs rode bareback, but the Indian braves following them rode high pommel saddles over brightly colored saddle blankets reaching almost to the ground. Their faces were hideously painted with streaks of black, red, and orange. They were a boisterous group, war whooping as they rode, making their horses spring to the side and causing the crowd to retreat hastily to the curb.

Behind them the Indian women dressed in intricately beaded buckskin carried gorgeous bags of solid bead work and porcupine quills. Some of the women with babies carried them on their backs in colorful slings.

Tomo's grandmother pointed out Indian women who were outstanding for their bravery. One woman wearing a dress decorated with elk teeth had risked her life by swimming her horse out into dangerous rapids to save a boy who had fallen in the turbulent river. Another woman had defied a rut-maddened elk who was charging a child and was able to save it by throwing a blanket over the animal's head.

Although it was fascinating history, Anna had lost interest as soon as Tomo had passed. The parade ended with a showing of pedigreed livestock and four-hitched teams of Belgian horses. In halting English Tomo's grandmother told them it would be an hour before her people were ready for visitors, so they decided to inspect the pavilions exhibiting produce, poultry, rabbits, and livestock. So fascinating were the agriculture displays of artistically arranged vegetables and fruit of the highest quality, displaying red or blue ribbons that they couldn't get Charlie to leave the building. He stood in awe of a fifty-five-pound pumpkin. When he came to the tomatoes, their size baffled him and he drilled the farmer who raised them as to the exact methods he used to grow such large specimens.

The girls finally left Charlie spellbound, gazing at the tomatoes, to go to the building where poultry was being shown. The girls had no idea there were so many different breeds of fowl. Mae's choice was the Rhode Island Red because they laid brown eggs. Anna preferred the white Leghorns because they were so pure and white. Maybelle fell in love with the tiny Bantams whose chicks were smaller than quail. She decided then and there to have some of her own. "Bob just has to buy some for the homestead. Wouldn't they look cute roosting in the prune trees?"

Charlie came to drag them over to the stock pavilion where they were almost run over by a farmer herding his bull into another pen. There they could see the famous appaloosa horses close up, and again Maybelle said, "Bob just has to have one for his homestead."

Mae reminded her, "He already has two horses."

"Yes, but not as beautiful as these. They are fabulous and have such a wonderful history. Oh, I do want one to ride!"

Mae laughed. "With your persistent ways, you'll get one."

The next building was full of rabbits of all shapes, sizes, and colors. Again, Maybelle expressed her desire to have some for the homestead.

Mae told her, "Let's get out of here before you have the homestead overcrowded with animals."

Charlie looked at his watch. "I think it's about time we started for the Indian village. They must be organized for the festivities by now." Urged by their brother, they directed their steps towards the Indian encampment. First they saw rows and rows of large white teepees, each displaying a shield designating their clan. Some shields were very artistic.

Cooking fires sat in front of many of the teepees, and Indian women were seen scurrying around cutting meat. Ribs of buffalo were staked to roast by the fires and large black pots steamed with choice cuts of elk. Fish had been wrapped in leaves and buried in the ashes to roast. Over a long pit of fire, a whole beef was roasting, dripping fat on hot coals and sending up tantalizing mouth-watering aromas. Tables had been set up holding long trays of huckleberries, roots, and dried salmon. It was a scene of great activity and expectations.

Taking a deep sniff of sizzling meat, Charlie declared, "Boy, I'm starved!"

They had wandered down one lane of teepees, and when no one paid any attention to them they started down another row, weaving their way among Indian children hard at play. Dogs were everywhere, but so well-trained they kept away from the cooking pots. They knew better than to try to snitch a piece of meat, as some of the children carried large sticks and gave a hard whack to any canine that even sniffed too close to the roasting meat.

They had stopped to decide where to go next when Tomo's sister appeared. She spoke to them for a few moments, explaining some aspects of their culture. Charlie was especially interested in the meaning of many of the shields he had noticed in front of their teepees.

Walking to a larger teepee Tamera stepped aside, holding the flap open and motioning to Anna to enter. When the others started to follow, she closed the flap and led them to an adjoining teepee.

Anna stood in the dark, her eyes slowly adjusting from the bright sunlight. Hearing the now familiar native name he called her—"Kuuts Kuuts"—she turned to see him standing in his breechcloth, so virile and handsome, with his arms held wide. Anna flew into his embrace. "Oh, Tomo, I like you best like this."

Her Indian lover held her close. "Too long to be apart."

She leaned her head on his bronzed chest, then shyly looked up, touching his face. "What happened to the paint on your face?"

"Maybe it frighten you."

"Oh no, I thought it looked very pretty. You once told me the paint marks had a meaning. What did yours mean?"

"Another time." He held her away from him, looking deeply into her eyes, speaking seriously. "All my family are now together. It is not always so. Few times there is enough for the Indian wedding. Will you marry me Indian way, then later the way of your people, we will marry?"

"Y...you mean now?"

He nodded. "Yes, all my people are here to wish us well."

"But, Tomo, I have no wedding dress."

He took a few swift strides over to an elk-skin-covered chest and took out a garment of exquisite beauty. Handing it to her, he said, "This is the dress I started to make for you and you asked what you could give me in return. Now I ask for your gift to me. Will you marry me?"

Anna slowly unfolded the dress of white doeskin, richly embroidered at the yoke, with a gorgeous blend of seed beads. A wide strip of beading bordered the sleeves and hem. Long fringe edged the dress.

Anna held it to her breast with shiny eyes. "Oh, Tomo, it's so beautifully made. I love it. Yes, I want to be with you always. Always by your side."

Enfolding her in his arms he tenderly kissed her. Then, lifting his head to listen, he said, "The tom-toms are calling us to our wedding ceremony. I wait outside."

Anna quickly dressed in her wedding gown. She then took the tortoise combs out and let her hair flow over her shoulders. Tamera entered carrying a matching pair of moccasins. She held out a lustrous beaded necklace, fastening it around Anna's neck. Holding a smoking pot of cedar, she blew the smoke over Anna, then kissed her and led her out to her brother, who now stood fully dressed in his buckskin suit. The flash in his eyes told Anna he was pleased.

Tamera led Anna down to a large circle of his people who were moving to the beat of the tom-toms. As they approached the dancers, two women unclasped their hands to include Anna's. Tomo had flung a bright Pendleton blanket around his shoulders and walked to the center of the circle. As the circle revolved around him, his people chanted in quartertones deemed so difficult to the white man's ears. Anna, shuffling her feet in time to the tom-toms, felt as one of them, that this is where she belonged. She felt an exhilaration she had never felt before. She looked at Tomo standing so proud, with such dignity as only an Indian who was truly noble could look. Her breast swelled, thinking she was going to be the wife of this man who would some day, because of his nobility, be chief of the Nez Perce people, known to be the most worthy tribe in America and treated the most shamefully by the United States government.

They had made two full rotations when the tom-toms suddenly stopped. The silence was electric, still the circle rotated. Tomo left the center and stately walked to the circle. Several Indian women shuffled past him; then, with a sudden motion, he drew back his blanket and enfolded Anna, leading her back to the center. Here he completely covered the two, hiding them from the dancers. Clasping her close, he kissed her until she felt drawn into his sinewy, bronze body. Frantic beating on the tom-toms with joyous cheering ended the ceremony. The dancers broke the circle to partake of the wedding feast.

Throwing off the blanket, Tomo took Anna's hand. "Kuuts Kuuts, we are now married Indian way. Tamalait, the Great Spirit, blesses our marriage, but it can't be consummated until we are married by the white man's law."

Anna's brother and sisters now came up to congratulate them. Charlie was exuberant, vigorously shaking the bridegroom's hand and vowing, "Boy, that's the kind of wedding I'd like to have. Means something. You know you're married when you do it the Indian way."

"From ancient time we have claimed our loved one for our own this way, until white man come and made it against the law," Tomo bitterly told them.

Frowning, Charlie said, "Yeah, I know, but my father says the time is coming when retribution will rain down on the white man's head and the Indian people will be vindicated."

Tomo nodded. "If it were not so, the Great Spirit would not be giving justice."

Charlie slapped Tomo on the back. "You're one of the family now."

Tomo smiled. "Not yet. We have yet to be married by a minister."

Charlie rubbed his chin. "Let's see. How about setting the date now and I'll arrange a bang-up wedding in Walla Walla."

Tomo looked at Anna, who was laughing. "Charlie, not too bang-up. We want it to be dignified and meaningful."

"Of course, of course, a church, a minister, the works. I'll arrange everything. Just set the date."

Anna hugged her brother. "I've never loved you so much."

Just then Tamera came to invite them to their feasting and to join in the games. With enthusiasm, Charlie joined in their gambling. Sitting with a row of men on one side, he faced another row opposite. Between them on the blanket were their bets. Charlie's eyes bulged out when he saw expensive blankets, saddles, knives, and moccasins and made up his mind he'd win one of those Pendleton blankets for Helen. He hunched down, concentrating as the bone quickly and mysteriously passed, hopefully unnoticed from hand to hand. When the tom-toms stopped, the trick was to guess who had the bone. The Indians were so clever at manipulating the bone, Charlie found it impossible to keep track of its whereabouts. The game could have gone on all night but for the wedding celebration with a giving of wedding presents to the bride and groom.

The game had to be discontinued until later. Charlie had won a saddle, much to his disappointment. He knew Helen was afraid of horses and would never ride, and he definitely was not a horseman. As he wondered what to do with it, Maybelle suggested, "Oh, Charlie, give it to Bob for a wedding present."

"Yeah, but he has two horses. I better go back and see if I can win another one."

"Oh no you don't!" His sisters warned him.

Anna stood by her Indian husband, hating to say good-bye, but he had an important meeting to attend. He would see them off in the morning and meet them the following week. He understood when he saw tears in her eyes. "It is only for a few days, Kuuts Kuuts. Then I will come for you and we take a honeymoon."

"Tomo! Where?" Anna asked excitedly.

But he only smiled.

# Chapter 19

# Surprising Encounters

A month had passed since the girls had returned home from the Pendleton round-up and Anna's unforgettable Indian wedding. It was difficult, after all the excitement of their trip, to settle back to normal everyday family life. Each day Anna fretted more over Tomo's delay to start on their honeymoon. Serious problems his people were having with the Indian agent detained him. She grew weary waiting and her health began to deteriorate.

One day Maybelle was surprised when Bob arrived unannounced and demanded to know which button string was hers. She hesitated, asking, "What on earth are you up to?"

"Never mind," he replied shedding his overcoat, jacket, and vest.

"Leave on your shirt," Maybelle giggled. "There's no fire in the stove."

Ignoring her, he plopped down on the floor. "Hand over your string."

"I won't unless you tell me what this all means."

"I'm going to finish your button string," Bob answered, pouring a sack of buttons on the floor.

Maybelle burst out laughing. "Oh, Bob, you're so silly!"

"Never call a man in love 'silly.' Come on, gimme," he insisted, reaching out his hand.

Maybelle stood in amazement as the large assortment of buttons of every shape, size, and color rolled across the floor. "You surely didn't bring enough buttons to finish the string," she asked dubiously, handing him her string.

"If there aren't enough I'll murder that salesman. Here, get busy and start stringing," he replied seriously, handing her a handful of buttons.

Laughingly, Maybelle sat down on the floor beside him and started threading buttons on one end of the string while Bob shoved buttons onto the other. "Bob, why do you want to finish my memory string now?"

"Very simple," Bob replied, reaching for a brilliant blue button. "I want to make sure I'm Prince Charming."

"But, Bob, there are only two hundred and sixty-five buttons on the string now."

"Great. That leaves only seven hundred and thirty-five to go."

"It's simply impossible to string that many today."

"If we can't then there's going to be trouble."

"Couldn't you be Prince Charming tomorrow?"

"Nope, got to get back tonight."

Mae came home from visiting Abigale and was astonished to find them on the floor, stringing buttons. Bob looked up grinning. "Important to finish the button string at once."

"Why the hurry?" Mae asked curiously.

"Have to make sure I'm the one and only Prince Charming."

"Has anything happened to make you unsure?" Mae snickered.

"There was a report she was making goo-goo eyes at the milkman."

Mae mischievously grinned. "You never heard about the iceman?"

"Ye gods! The competition is growing."

"Yes," Mae laughed, "and there's a very handsome mail clerk who just came to town and you never can tell."

Maybelle shook her head. "You two are really hatching up trouble for yourselves."

Mae shed her coat. "Since there is need for haste, I better lend a hand or you won't be finished this year."

"Thanks, pal. I always knew I could count on you," Bob said, handing her some buttons.

Mae plopped down on the floor, asking, "How many to go?"

"Last count, six hundred and forty."

Mae shook her head. "You couldn't possible have brought that many buttons."

"If I didn't, everyone is going to lose their buttons," Bob scowled.

They were merrily chatting when Mae suddenly grew wistfully serious. "I wonder if there will ever be a truly perfect wedding in our home. I...I mean everything white and everyone crazy with joy."

Bob chased a button across the floor before asking, "Are you accepting applications now?"

"The earlier the better," Mae replied flippantly.

Bob turned to Maybelle. "Are you interested in applying?"

This was the second time Bob had stunned her with the unexpected. She gave him a serene look while telling Mae, "I will fulfill your dream for a perfect wedding. I'll come down the stairs trailing miles of white veiling. My gown will be whiter than white. I'll cut the tallest, whitest cake with a machete. I'll throw a white satin slipper right at your stubby nose that can't keep out of my affairs." She saucily eyed her sister. "Well, are you going to accept my application?" She dramatically paused before challenging, "That is, of course, if there are enough buttons to proclaim a Prince Charming."

Bob and Mae said nothing but stared at Maybelle with amusement. She glared back at them. "Well, I hear no hurrahs, so I assume my application is rejected."

Bob started to frantically string buttons. At last he held up a huge coat button, yelling, "The thousandth button, proclaim me Prince Charming."

"You cheated!" Maybelle shouted at him accusingly. "There must be at least two hundred more buttons to go."

Bob stood his ground, "I proclaim this the thousandth button." Then he shrugged sheepishly. "The rest can be put on later." He turned to Mae. "Accept your sister's application. Now, my little pixie, you have been put off our wedding long enough. As Prince Charming, I demand that you name the date."

At that moment Nancy came into the room. "For heaven's sake, what are you doing?"

"Planning a wedding," Bob replied rising to his feet, holding out a helping hand to the girls.

"I hope you're not serious," Nancy said.

"Never been more serious," Bob assured her.

"And when is this wedding to take place?"

"It's up to the lady to name the date," Bob answered with a challenging look at Maybelle.

Maybelle gave Bob a withering look and fled the room. Bob watched her go with longing. He turned to Mae. "Will you please tell her I'll see her before I leave?"

That night in their bedroom, Mae accused her sister, "You know you're going to marry him. Why don't you tell him when?"

"Because I want to be courted a long time. I want lots of flowers and candy and..."

"Which shows you're still just a kid. You better grow up before..."

"Before what?" Maybelle asked, studying her sister.

"Before he gets tired of sending flowers and candy and..."

"And?" Maybelle looked at her sister quizzically.

"And finds someone else."

"You can't scare me. I'll get married when I want to."

Mae began thinking aloud. "Charlie is getting married. Anna has to finish getting married and you've promised to get married.

Mama will never survive three weddings. Unless," Mae took a deep breath, "unless, you all get married at once."

"You mean a triple wedding?" Maybelle asked in astonishment.

Mae nodded. "Why not? It would save a lot of work, time, and money."

"I'll think about it."

"Don't think to long. Don't forget Anna is only half married and that's dangerous. We don't want another Amy episode on our hands."

Maybelle flopped over in bed. "Mae, for goodness' sake, go to sleep so I can think."

"Don't say I didn't give a warning," Mae yawned, drawing up the covers.

A couple of weeks later, letters started arriving from Nettie, her scribblings exciting but unbelievable. They whooped when their mother read how Nettie managed to survive a Kansas City cyclone by finding refuge in a storm cellar. They shrieked with mirth when their sister described how the terrible wind drove straws through telephone poles and plucked all the feathers off the chickens.

Mae snorted, "She must think we are a bunch of stupid idiots to believe that."

"Here's her proof," Nancy said handing them photos of the twister's rampage.

One photo showed a straw sticking out on either side of a telephone pole, but that didn't convince them that it wasn't a fake and someone played a prank by gluing a straw on either side of the pole. But when another photo showed naked chickens roosting without a single feather on them, they had to admit Nettie might be telling the truth.

Several weeks later, they received another letter from Nettie with even more fascinating news. Nancy came into the parlor where the girls were working on an elaborate puzzle. Without a word, she thrust an enlarged picture at them. Mae looked closely at it, exclaiming, "When did Charlie have his picture taken?"

Anna scrutinized it even more closely. "I've never seen Charlie in that kind of suit before and he's always hated bow ties. But it's a good picture of him."

Nancy took back the picture. "It's not Charlie."

"Whaaaat?" They exclaimed.

Mae expressed her certainty. "No other person could look that much like Charlie, not even a twin."

Nancy started reading Nettie's letter.

"Dear Mama;

Things have been happening so fast, you won't believe it. The senior nurses gave a large party for the freshmen and invited all the doctors serving their intern requirements at the hospital. I had just finished dancing and looked at the doorway where a man stood watching. I was overwhelmed with joy. I rushed to him and threw my arms around his neck and gave him a big kiss, saying, 'Oh Charlie, how wonderful of you to surprise me! I love you more than ever!' The man looked down at me with twinkling eyes, disentangled my arms around his neck saying, 'Mademoiselle, it is a pleasure to be so warmly greeted since I am a stranger in your country, and I deeply regret I am not Charlie.'"

"Oh, Mama, you can't imagine how embarrassed and confused I was! I backed off as fast as I could, tripped, and would have fallen had he not caught my arm to steady me. He made no effort to unclasp his hand but led me over to a sofa in the corner."

Maybelle interrupted, "Wow, that can be dangerous."

"Shut up," Mae snapped. "Don't butt in when it's getting exciting."

Nancy continued reading. "'We talked for three hours,'" Nettie's letter went on.

"That's long enough to get engaged," Maybelle snickered.

"For the last time, KEEP STILL!" Mae warned.

Their mother turned a page,

"We might have talked all night, had not the matron come to tell us the lights were about to be turned off. Mama, I think in some way we are related. I'm not sure, but we will meet again tomorrow night and I'm sure to find out more. With out knowing it, he gave me a clue. He mentioned that one of his ancestors fled France during the French Revolution. He isn't sure but thinks he might have come to Canada. Oh, it's so exciting!"

Just then Doc came into the room and was told all about Nettie's letter. He stood thinking for a moment before commenting, "My dear, I had all but forgotten about your mysterious ancestor." He looked at the picture long and hard. "There has to be some hereditary connection for such a close resemblance."

Their father had come home early with some distressful news. In the foothills of the Blue Mountains, a family had been burned out of their home. Two of the children were badly burned and had been brought to him for treatment. "There's six in the family and they are living in a tent on the river bank. They lost everything and have no food or bedding."

"Oh, what a terrible thing to happen," Nancy said.

"Yes, and they are a good family," Doc commented.

"They will need help right away," Mae said.

Doc scribbled a note on a scratch pad. "I want you girls to go to the store and buy everything that is needed. Give Jake this note. Get six heavy woolen blankets and enough food for a week. We can get more later. They will also need dishes and pans. I'll leave it to your good judgment to buy the necessary things."

"They'll need lots of soap," Maybelle piped up.

Mae snapped, "Soap! When they haven't anything to eat! You're crazy."

Maybelle defended herself. "Well, living in a tent can be awfully dirty."

Nancy spoke up, "Couldn't they save anything?"

Doc shook his head. "No, everything they owned was lost in the flames. Their home was burned to the ground." He turned to Mae. "My dear, you take charge."

"Yes, Papa, but I don't know how much to buy."

"Later, after you meet the family, you can fill out with other things they might need. I depend on you to be practical."

The girls hurried down to the general store. First they bought three large, wicker clothes hampers. To avoid duplications Mae decided Anna should buy the essential cooking pots and dishes, Maybelle would select the bedding, and Mae herself would buy the staples. When Mae saw Maybelle putting a large box of chocolates in her basket, she immediately went over and put it back on the shelf, admonishing her sister, "Eating that on an empty stomach would kill them."

"But, Mae, they have to have something to cheer them up."

"Well then, buy cookies for the children. You're suppose to be selecting the bedding."

"Oh, all right, but bedding is so uninteresting."

Anna was making sensible selections of kitchenware, but hesitated over the size of pans. A clerk suggested medium-sized pans. They had been shopping for an hour when Mae noticed Anna was having difficulty carrying her basket, complaining it was too heavy. When she started coughing, Mae made her sit down until they were finished.

Mae continued filling her basket with flour, sugar, salt, and then some fruit and vegetables. When they were finished, she ordered a dray to take them down to the river. On the way she had the driver stop at the creamery and ran in to buy butter, milk, cream, and on second thought and against her better judgement, a quart of strawberry ice cream. "Oh heck," she thought, "Maybelle is right. They need something to lift their spirits and it would go nicely with the cookies."

Nearing the riverbank, the girls saw smoke rising out of the tent's stovepipe. Not knowing exactly what they would find, they hesitated in front of the tent. Just then, a woman looked out through the tent flaps. Seeing them she smiled and invited them in and graciously introduced herself as Mrs. Nelson. Pointing to two small boys whose arms were bandaged and a little girl shyly peeking from behind her skirt, the mother smiled. "This is my daughter, Maria, and my sons, Sam and Henry."

The girls were surprised when the boys politely shook their hands, saying, "Pleased to meet you."

Mae told Mrs. Nelson, "We have brought you a few things we hope you'll accept."

"I am most grateful for your help. We've always been able to take care of ourselves until now. The fire was so unexpected and we lost everything."

Mae went outside to have the driver carry in the baskets. As he set them down on the makeshift table, which sagged under their weight, Mrs. Nelson was overwhelmed. "My goodness, you brought so much!" The children talked excitedly as they looked through the baskets. Mrs. Nelson turned to the girls, "You won't mind if I feed the children. They haven't eaten since yesterday."

Anna lifted a loaf of bread, jam, and peanut butter from the baskets, saying, "This always made my favorite sandwich. They probably would like it too."

The children squealed their delight. Mrs. Nelson was so pleased with everything and expressed her gratitude, then insisted the girls have tea with her. Mae was about to refuse, but seeing the eagerness in the woman's eyes, accepted. She was glad they had remembered to buy a teapot.

They all sat down on wooden boxes. Anna commented, "I didn't know how nice and cozy a tent could be."

The woman smiled. "Yes and we are lucky there is plenty of good wood around so we can keep warm all night. Of course, that means a lot of wood chopping, but luckily my husband's brother is staying with us. He keeps the stove well supplied."

Just then a tall, rugged man came in carrying an armload of wood. "Here he is now," Mrs. Nelson said. "Tom, Look at all the wonderful things these good people have brought us."

Setting down the chopped wood, he removed his cap when introduced. "Such help right now is a blessing we deeply appreciate. As soon as possible, it will be repaid."

"You need do no such thing," Mae declared. "Papa always keeps aside a fund to help people in need."

He smiled. "A very thoughtful thing to do. Some things happen to people unexpectedly and they need help."

Mrs. Nelson explained. "We were so blessed to have Tom visiting us from Canada as he's a carpenter. He will stay long enough to help with building us a new house. Right now my husband is at the old home place seeing if there is anything he can salvage from the fire."

Tom left for another load of wood and the girls excused themselves, saying they must get home to help their mother with supper.

Walking back, the girls were discussing the family when Mae remarked, "He isn't handsome, but he doesn't have to be. He has such a strong, rugged look of honesty and integrity."

"From you, that's a real compliment," Anna observed.

Maybelle said, "The children are adorable and they had such nice manners."

"Which proves they are a fine family," Anna agreed.

The next morning a man came to the kitchen door. Mae recognized him at once as being the brother they had met the day before. He removed his cap. "Maybe you have some odd job I could help you with."

Mae hesitated. He was keenly watching her. She started to decline his offer when an inspiration lit up her face. "I don't suppose you would consider doing women's work?"

He smiled. "I used to help my mother in the house."

"I...I...." She glanced quickly at him. "Would you consider shelling black walnuts? It's my sister's birthday and I want to make her a black walnut birthday cake."

The man's smile widened. He knew she hated the arduous task. "Most certainly. I think I've shelled tons of them for my mother."

"Oh really? You won't mind then?"

"I'd love it." They both burst into laughter and Mae invited him in, bringing out the nuts and a hammer. While he was shelling, she stirred up the cake. They visited as if they were old friends.

Maybelle burst into the kitchen. "Where is Anna? Her husband has come."

"She's cleaning out the storage room."

"Oh dear, she won't be looking her best," commented Maybelle, and she rushed out in search of Anna.

# Chapter 20

# Sky Spirits of Salmon River

Tomo knew at once the girl he loved was ill. "Kuuts Kuuts, all not well?" He asked with deep concern.

"Oh Tomo, they want to give us a big wedding and I don't feel like it. I feel I am truly married already. I don't want another wedding."

"But it is important to make it legal to be married by a priest."

"Nothing could be more sacred than the ceremony with your people. I want no other."

"Dear one, I must see your father."

"He is at his office."

"I must go to him. While I am gone, dress in your traveling clothes."

Doc greeted his Indian son-in-law with warmth and respect. He listened intently to the man's request.

"Yes, I have noticed my daughter's condition and I think you are wise to object to the rigors of a formal wedding. A justice of the peace would make it legal and it takes but a short time. I will be glad to accompany you. What do you plan afterwards?"

"In the Bitterroot Mountains is a mineral hot springs my people use for centuries to cure many kinds of sickness. A comfortable cabin by the springs, given to me by an old pioneer, too old now to live in such remoteness. I take your daughter there for a while until she has recovered her health."

Doctor asked with concern, "Would such a life be too rugged for Anna in her present condition?"

"My sister and her family camp near and do all the work as long as needed."

"I have heard from other physicians of the miraculous healing properties of mineral springs. I think you have used great wisdom in such a plan."

"I am grateful you agree. I believe best we leave at once. My brothers wait with their pack train to take us to the springs."

The doctor and Mae accompanied them to the courthouse to stand with them before the justice of the peace. Nancy had prepared a light lunch and the black walnut cake had been decorated with white icing roses. After a toast to the bride and groom, the family escorted them to the stagecoach depot with Nancy shedding tears. "They are going into such a wild country. Will I ever see my daughter again?"

Doc reassured her, "With that husky Indian husband by her side, he'll bring her safely back."

Leaving Dayton, the stagecoach traveled the same route as taken by Lewis and Clark, the first official explorers to the Northwest in 1851. Tomo pointed out a small, grassy meadow by a willow-fringed creek where their exploration party had camped for the night. Anna tried to imagine the thrill of being the first white man scouting out an unmapped wilderness.

The swaying, jolting stagecoach left clouds of dust behind as they lurched over the deeply rutted dirt road. Tomo, showing concern over the discomfort his wife might be feeling, was met with gracious acceptance and a smile. Anna was amused. "At least we have a road. Think of poor Lewis and Clark not having even a trail to follow and having to thrash their way through all that brush."

Tomo tried to entertain his bride by telling her stories about the Nez Perce's tall and dignified chief in whom she had expressed great interest after reading of Chief Joseph's many exploits. Tomo told her, "On our chief's trips to the East, his wit make him popular with reporters. One of his humorous sayings very famous because it is published."

"Oh, what was it?" Anna asked interested.

"'Big name often stands on small legs.'"

Anna clapped her hands with delight. "Oh, how clever."

Tomo cast a quick glance at Anna. "Maybe I shouldn't tell you this one."

"Oh, please do," Anna begged.

"'When you get the last word with an echo, you may do so with your wife.'"

"Oh Tomo, I'll always let you have the last word," Anna promised. "Do tell me more."

Tomo told her about the time their chief was a guest at an Indian exhibition. A young lady, wearing a hat with several large ostrich plumes, came up to him, demanding, "Did you ever scalp anybody?"

The chief had pointed to the woman's fantastic feathered hat and answered through an interpreter, "I have nothing in my collection as fine as that."

Anna convulsed with laughter. Growing serious she wanted to know, "Did Chief Joseph ever meet any of the generals who fought against him?"

"Yes. Once when he was visiting the Carlisle Indian School, he met and shook hands with General Howard. Afterward he told the student body, 'Long time ago I wanted to kill the General.'"

Anna clenched her small hands, pursed her lips, stuck out her chin, and with glittering eyes spat, "Oh, the way he treated the poor Indians, I would want to kill him myself."

Tomo lovingly smiled down on the earnest, flushed face of his wife, saying, "It is good to have such a fierce fighter by my side."

"Tomo, did the Nez Perce ever have a code of laws?"

Tomo nodded. "Yes."

"Do you remember them?" Anna asked.

Tomo said, "'Never tell a lie. Speak only the truth. Treat all men as they treat you. It is a shame to steal a man's property without paying for it. The Great Spirit hears and sees everything. According to his merit a good man gets a good spirit home. A bad man gets a bad spirit home.'"

Anna was surprised. "Why Tomo, it's something like the Ten Commandments of our Bible."

"Yes, it is so."

Anna lovingly kissed his cheek. "I can't get over how well you now speak English."

"Kuuts, Kuuts. I study hard. I knew some day I would be your husband and I wanted my wife to understand me."

Anna shyly glanced at him. "I loved the way you used to talk."

Her stalwart husband shook his head. "No, to live in white man's world, it is best for Indian to talk good English."

They heard the brakes screech and the driver cautioning the team to take it easy. Looking out the coach's windows, they saw they were going down a very steep grade. Soon they saw the sun glinting on the waters of the Snake River. For miles they traveled along the banks of the historic river where once the Indians had to cross at full flood when the United States Army pursued them.

Tomo bitterly told her of the incident, "Much of our stock drowned."

Anna felt distressed. "Oh, the poor, poor animals."

Tomo explained how the Clearwater River empties into the Snake River, making it large enough for very large fish to swim up to the forks. "I have seen them eight feet long. The fishermen caught them and tied them to stakes."

"Papa bought one once, and I think we shared it with most of the town. It was delicious but very fat. I believe they called it a sturgeon."

Tomo nodded. "It take good fishermen to catch one."

The barren, rocky Snake River hills rose on the opposite side of the river. Tomo hated them. During Hasoal, the hottest month of the year, the hills reflected the heat until it was almost unbearable. Seeing his wife getting weary and feeling the heat, he wished for the valley of Winding Waters—Wallowa, with its cool mountain lakes, glacier streams, and vast forests, the home of the Nez Perce who were deprived of their beloved homeland by the invading white man's government.

Noticing her husband's stern face, Anna anxiously asked," You are so silent. Is something troubling you?"

"The Great Spirit never intended one man to rule over another man. Man was meant to be free to choose his own way according to the guidance of the great giver of life."

Anna tenderly leaned her head against his shoulder. "Tomo, someday there will be justice for the Indian, but it will be so terrible I do not want to be around."

"That will not bring back my people they have killed. They will destroy our Earth Mother and defy the Great Spirit who gave them life. No, I see no justice."

"Papa says the Great Cosmic law never fails to bring justice." Anna was perspiring profusely and seemed to wilt under the intense heat. Her husband worried the trip was going to be too hard on her and there was yet a long distance to travel. When they had crossed the Snake River and their stagecoach pulled into Lewiston, Idaho, for the night, Tomo immediately took his wife to the hotel and brought her a dainty meal he thought would please her. But she was too tired to eat. He left to find something cool for her to drink. When he returned he found she had gone to bed. Then he saw all the clothes she had been wearing, and he knew she must wear lighter clothing.

He searched through their luggage until he found her wedding dress of soft doeskin. He held it up. "Kuuts, Kuuts, tomorrow it is best you wear dress I make you. You will feel cooler and not so heavy."

"Oh Tomo, you are so thoughtful. Yes, I will wear it."

The next day she traveled with greater comfort in the lighter weight of the one garment and vowed to never go back to wearing four petticoats, a tight-laced corset, bustle, and several undergarments underneath the heavy eight-yard worsted skirt. She decided then and there, since she had married an Indian, she was going to wear only Indian dresses.

For hours they traveled through dry, hot, rocky country. It depressed her. When they came to a small Indian village, she shuddered, for it was surrounded by barren rocky hills. She thought it a very ugly place. Tomo spoke bitterly, "Lapwai, our reservation. White chief in Washington say my people must live here where there is no game, no camas root, no fish, and no berries. My people will starve."

"Tomo, isn't there anything here?"

"Rattlesnakes," he spat.

Anna was glad when the stagecoach stopped for only a few moments then started climbing out of the hot, sandy valley. The higher they climbed, the cooler the air. Reaching the high plateau was a relief from the sweltering valley below. Now the air had a cool, poignant scent of coniferous trees. Tomo pointed to areas where the women of his tribe dug for camas roots; farther up in the foothills they gathered berries to mix with pounded dry elk meat for pemmican.

Anna wished she had lived with the Indians before the advent of the white people. How free they had lived, respecting their mother, the earth, and giving homage to the Great Spirit. She asked herself, "Why weren't such a peaceful, noble people protected from the onslaught that brought blood, bitterness, and almost annihilation? Why, oh why wasn't there justice?"

At last they descended the Whitebird Grade, named after a chief who had fled to Canada. After traveling several miles across the low lands, they were engulfed by a cloud of dust as the coach came to a stop in front of a few log cabins nestled by the turbulent Salmon River, flowing through the most remote wilderness area of Idaho.

Tomo helped his wife to alight. As her foot touched the ground she staggered with weakness. " Oh Tomo, I feel so terrible I...I think I'm going to die."

"No Kuuts Kuuts, you will see many snows yet to come. Tonight you will breathe the cool mountain air. The hot springs will sweat the poisons out of your body and you will grow strong."

Weeks before, Tomo had sent a messenger to his family requesting his brothers to meet him at the small town of Riggens with their pack train. They would take Anna and Tomo to the hot springs, a journey of thirty miles over a narrow trail, blasted out of the sheer rock cliffs high above the wild Salmon River.

Tomo's keen eyes quickly spotted a string of packhorses across the river waiting for them. His two brothers came walking across the crude bridge to help him carry the luggage to be roped onto the packhorses. They had found a sidesaddle for their brother's wife to ride. Anna was too weak to walk and Tomo carried her across the bridge and helped her to mount. This being the first time his wife had ever ridden a horse, he was concerned she might be frightened. To assure himself of her safety, he rode behind her so he could carefully keep a check on her condition. He had assured her the horses were sure-footed.

Anna clutched the pommel of the saddle with both hands. She squeezed her eyes tightly shut, but could feel by the movement of her horse that they were climbing a very steep trail. Once when her horse stumbled, her eyes flew open and she looked far down onto the raging rapids below. In terror she started to climb off her horse. Quickly Tomo dismounted, rushing to her side to restrain her.

Anna begged, "Oh Tomo, let me walk, please let me walk."

"No, Kuuts Kuuts, the horse is sure-footed and safer." To reassure her, he walked ahead holding the reins of her horse.

When her horse knocked some rocks off the side of the trail and she watched in terror as they rolled down the cliffs, splashing into the boiling rapids far below, she pled, "I can crawl! Please, let me get off."

He shook his head and tried to reassure her. "When the sun sets, you will be happy in your new home."

Mile after mile the pack train plodded through the narrow river canyon. Anna was beyond terror. She was no longer aware of her surroundings. When Tomo saw her weaving in the saddle he ran to her, lifted her out of the saddle, and carried her. His two brothers took turns with him and they carried Anna the rest of the way. They came to an old hay meadow, now being reclaimed by Mother Nature with the wild growth of ferns and wildflowers. Here they had to cross a narrow swinging suspension bridge high above the swiftly flowing Salmon River. They could see on the other side a large hand-hewn log cabin and beyond it steam rose in the cooler air where the hot springs flowed into a roughly made swimming pool. Smoke spiraled from the cabin's stovepipe, assuring Tomo his sister had arrived before them and was now busy preparing a meal.

When they reached the porch, his older sister, Silver Moon, came quickly to the door and gently helped the almost unconscious Anna into a chair. She brought the ailing woman a bowl of steaming venison stew.

Anna gave her a quivering smile. "I'm sorry. I'm too tired to eat."

Silver Moon nodded. She did not speak English, but she understood. Taking the distraught girl by the arm, she led her into an adjoining bedroom and helped her into bed.

Night after night the moon wove its magic, sailing through the clouds, lighting up her room. Day after day sunbeams painted patterns on the coverlet of her bed, but Anna was too sick to take any notice of her surroundings.

One evening Tomo came to her bed bringing a stranger. "Tewats," he said.

Anna looked up at her husband. Understanding her questioning eyes, Tomo told her, "You are not getting better. You are too weak to bathe in the hot springs. I bring our medicine man who has cured many of our people."

Although he was old, the medicine man stood beside her bed with the virility of youth. With aloof dignity he spoke in his native tongue, which Tomo translated. "Tonight, I come as shaman to your campfire. Do not fear. The sky spirits of Tewats will chase away the evil one making you sick. Tamalait, the Great Spirit heals." Saying this with authority, he stalked out of the room.

Tomo remained kneeling beside his wife's bed. "Kuuts Kuuts, tonight I carry you to the sacred fire of my people where Tewats will use his power to heal you."

Anna cried out, "Tomo, anything, anything to make me well so I can be a good wife to you. I want to cut fish, gather berries, and dig camas roots. I want to be free from this burning inside."

That night when the bright moon freed itself from the tree-clad horizon and wove through billowing cumulus clouds to light the land, Tomo carried Anna to the center of a circle of his relatives formed around the campfire. As he knelt with Anna in his arms, the tom-toms began their throbbing beat, stirring the silence of the night. Voices started chanting and the circle slowly moved step by step. Suddenly, with a howl, a hideously painted apparition sprang into the firelight. Leaping around the fire and shaking a feathered rattle, the shaman chanted in weird quarter-tones, "Ahiya, ahiya." Leaping over the flames, he again shook the rattle close to Anna.

Tomo whispered, "He is driving away the evil spirit making you sick."

The shaman squatted beside Anna and took from his medicine pouch several sacred objects. He placed around Anna's neck a necklace of herbs. From a smaller bag he carefully shook out powder into a cup of water Silver Moon had brought him. He motioned Anna to drink it. Without hesitation Anna drank and soon felt a pleasant coolness stealing over her. Again the shaman leaped over the fire, shaking his rattle then with a wild howl he disappeared into the dark shadows.

Rising with Anna in his arms, Tomo spoke in a low voice. "Tamalait, the Great Spirit, say all is well, all is well."

At dawn the next day, Anna startled her husband by meeting him when he returned from bringing in the horses. She smiled and said, "I feel so much better. I believe I'm going to live."

"Kuuts, Kuuts, your moccasins will make many tracks in many snows."

For the next few days, Anna's dark-skinned aristocratic husband stayed within calling distance in case he was needed. The day he felt his wife was strong enough, he led her to the hot springs pool, where they swam together in the invigorating mineral water, which had a slightly acrid smell. It made her feel buoyant and light. Her husband insisted she drink several cups of the mineral water.

In a few days she felt so invigorated, she playfully splashed water on her husband, reassuring him that the Great Spirit had guided him well to have brought her here.

Finally, Tomo felt it safe to go with his brother-in-law to restore the field of alfalfa now overgrown with a tangle of brush. It had been ten years since the old pioneer, had left, leaving his cabin and land. Now, only small patches of alfalfa were growing. He wanted to clear the small field and raise hay for a couple of horses.

Anna now took a keen interest in her surroundings. She was amazed how well the cabin had been constructed with large, hand-hewn spruce logs, but even more surprising was the heating arrangement in the cabin. Pipes had been laid under the floor to carry a flow of water from the hot springs, keeping the cabin at an even temperature without the need of a stove. Hot and cold water had been piped into the kitchen. In the living room large windows looked down on the changing vistas of the river. At one end of the living room, a log spiral stairway led up to two more commodious bedrooms.

Tomo had sent ahead several boxes of supplies for their comfort. Anna felt well enough to start unpacking and was delighted with the bright Indian blankets which she draped over the crude twig chairs the old pioneer had made, their bright colors adding gaiety to the somber log walls, which greatly pleased her.

Tomo took time from his work to take his wife on walks beyond the hot springs. Blue grouse unexpectedly whirred from the dense undergrowth, startling her. Deer stopped to stare then returned to nibbling grass. Once they caught a glimpse of a porcupine as he waddled into a thicket. Tomo pointed to the animal's quills, seeming to shiver over its body. He told her, "Our Indian women sometimes use their quills instead of beads. They sew them onto bags and moccasins. My sister makes necklaces and earrings of them."

"But Tomo, I don't think they are very pretty, just a dull gray."

"Our women dye them beautiful colors with plants."

"I think I'd like a necklace made of them."

"My sister will make you one."

On another day the quietness of their surroundings was shattered by a loud, hoarse bellow, rising to a high-pitched tone then exploding into several eerie grunts. Startled, Anna stopped in dismay. Another louder bellow came from the other side of the trail and Anna snatch up her skirts and ran. Tomo, easily catching her, swung her up into his arms, laughing, "You are some Indian, running away from a good pot of stew."

"What kind of horrible animal made that noise?"

"Come, we sit on log and be quiet. Maybe he will show himself."

They sat for only a few moments when a magnificent animal of enormous size cautiously stalked into the small clearing, tossing its polished rack of sweeping antlers. Stiff-legged, it advanced, then tossing his head up, it bugled.

Anna clutched her husband's arm. "How majestic."

"Big bull elk," he whispered.

"Look," Anna pointed as five smaller animals emerged from the deep shadows of the forest.

Tomo nodded, "His harem. He fights the younger bulls to keep his wives. He is challenging the other bull we have just heard across the creek."

Bugling again, the bull elk crashed through the underbrush, followed by his harem, leaving the meadow in silence.

Anna took a deep breath, "Well, I'm glad there was no fight. It would be a terrible encounter between two such huge animals."

Tomo nodded. "Yes, once I saw two bulls clash. They struggled all day. Finally, one that was being defeated broke off and ran."

Every day Anna took her swim in the pool, but Tomo preferred the sweat lodge he had built near the pool. Anna tried it once but found it much too hot for her.

Each day Silver Moon came to cook and clean, and in the close association Anna grew to love her sister-in-law. Although she spoke no English, somehow they had a silent communion between them that pleased them both. Although at times Anna felt it would be nice if she and her husband were alone so she could cook his meals herself, she deeply regretted when Silver Moon one day indicated she was leaving to have her first child. Anna threw her arms around the lovely Indian girl, kissing her with tears streaming down her face. Turning to Tomo she said, "Tell her how much I'll miss her and I love her like I love my own sisters."

Tomo nodded. "She knows. She now understand English a little."

Now that his sister and family had gone, Tomo didn't want to leave his wife alone for long periods of time. He made it a point to do some of his work while she slept, and during the day took long walks with her, teaching her the wisdom of the wilderness, pointing out the many plants his people used for medicinal purposes. One day Anna had been walking ahead of her husband when she heard a loud buzzing. Looking down, she saw a snake; its coils on the tip of its tail were quivering, sending out a warning rattling. She was bending over, intending to examine it closer when Tomo, with a sweep of his arm, brushed her aside. Snatching a tree branch, he beat the writhing snake until it lay still.

Anna shuddered. "Why did you kill it? It had pretty diamond markings."

"You have much to learn. This diamondback rattler. If it strike you, you might die."

Anna soon learned the place was infested with rattlesnakes. Even the very small ones, which she thought looked harmless and cute, were to be shunned, for they too could strike as lightening fast as the larger snakes. The old pioneer had once exterminated them by bringing in pigs that had cleared out the dangerous crawlers. But the place had been isolated for so long they had returned. Silver Moon's husband promised that when he returned he would bring his dogs, which were even better than pigs in killing snakes.

Now that Anna was taking walks by herself, Tomo taught her to shoot a twenty-two revolver and insisted she carry it with her at all times when walking the forest trails alone. Anna became so adept at shooting the firearm she could shoot the heads off the snakes and then safely remove the rattles. She was proudly filling a wooden box with their small, button-shaped warning system.

Now that the couple was alone, Anna grew to know her husband in ways that were strange and fascinating and drew her closer to him. When he speared salmon in the deep whirlpools below the cabin, she cut them the way she had seen his mother wield the sharp knife when they had been camped on the Tucannon. One day she was cutting the strips very thin when she heard soft laughter and looked up into the amused eyes of her husband. He teased her, "You cut pieces so little, we not have to chew." He picked her up swinging her around, seating her on a nearby log and in a moment he swiftly finished cutting the fish. She was proud of the long strips of deep yellow salmon she hung on the poles over the tangy alder smoke of the drying fire.

When he killed a deer, she learned to notch the edges of each piece of meat so they wouldn't curl and mold. She loved best to pick the wild huckleberries, which she learned to mash into pounded dry meat with melted fat of deer and elk for pemmican, so important to supplement their winter's food in case hunting was poor. Tomo told her he had known of his people starving to death. Because Tomo intended for them to stay for a year before he returned to his interpreting job, Anna worked hard to put up a large supply of food to prevent any such possibility.

Some of Tomo's relatives came to camp up river to hunt elk. They often made trips to Lewiston and when they returned, they brought mail and packages from her family. Fannie had sent several jars of delicious cactus honey from Arizona, with a note saying John had completely recovered his health and had been given a foreman's job with an increase of pay that would enable her to come north for a visit.

Maybelle sent her an adorable kitten to keep her company. Mae sent a pair of beautifully embroidered pillowcases, saying she was soon coming for a visit even if she had to walk all the way. Her mother sent several packets of flower seeds instructing her to plant them all around the cabin. Nettie sent an extravagant, sheer nightgown, trimmed with exquisite French lace, making Tomo wonder about the strange way of white people sending gifts of such little use.

One warm, bright, moonlit night, Anna, in a playful mood, waited until she thought Tomo was asleep, slipped out of bed and put on the sheer white nightgown. Then, running out to the meadow, she started to dance, leaping and swirling in the pure joy of vibrant health. Her gown floated around her in a vaporous ethereal mist. Laughing and whirling, she danced over the patches of moonlight. Suddenly she stopped, breathless, for Tomo stood in his breechcloth with folded arms, watching her. A little embarrassed at being caught doing something he probably thought was childish, she hastily explained, "The night is so beautiful, I am so happy, I...I felt like dancing."

Speaking no word, he lifted her into his arms and strode to where the moss grew soft and lush. Laying her down, he crushed her close, whispering, "Kuuts my wife. You are mine. You come to me, a gift from the Great Spirit. You are half my heart. I love you as the eagle loves to soar, as the owl loves the night, as the deer love their young."

"Oh Tomo, I lived because I love you. Without you I would have died."

"The Great Spirit speaks. We are one." He kissed her until Anna felt a part of him. An unsurpassed joy engulfed her, while an owl hooted its message of the wilderness.

Although the days were filled with happiness for Anna, she thought often of her family. She worried a bit about Amy, for she had heard nothing from her. So many questions filled her mind. Was Amy really happy? Had Bob finished her mansion? Why had Amy sent no gift? None of her family had even mentioned Amy.

One day they heard shouts down by the river. Tomo went out to investigate and soon was helping two men hoist a large wooden crate up the steep bank. It was so heavy they had to hook on one of the horses to pull it all the way to the cabin. Heaving it onto the porch, one of the men called Anna's attention to the large printed letters on the crate. In black ink was written:

"To my sister Anna Andrus,
To be routed down the Salmon River to the Riggen's Hot Springs of Idaho."

Anna was amazed it had found her with such a skimpy address; then she felt angry that her sister hadn't even bothered to find out her married name.

Anna couldn't imagine what such a large crate held for her. On the porch, Tomo took an axe to the wooden crate so that Anna could peek in. Seeing dark, shiny wood, she was more puzzled than ever. Tomo took away more of the boards until Anna gasped with amazement. A piano! And she couldn't even play! What had possessed her sister to ship such an extravagant gift down a treacherous river into such a remote wilderness to a person who couldn't even play a piano? That was Amy. Unpacking it, Tomo handed her a hastily scribbled note.

"Hi, Sis. Surprise!! Living in that Godforsaken heathen country, you'll need something to take your mind off all that desolation. You were always talking about wanting to play a piano. Well here it is, so start learning. The instructions are under the keyboard. Don't expect a visit from me. I hate horses. Be sure and come to Maybelle's wedding at my place. Amy."

## Chapter 20 - Sky Spirits of Salmon River — Why Wait For Heaven

Tomo wondered more than ever about the queer ways of the white man. Because the piano was too heavy for the cabin floor, he had to first put braces underneath before moving the piano inside.

For days Anna only stared at the Baldwin Grand; then slowly she started to study the first sheet music lessons. She waited until Tomo had gone for the day before she attempted to play the first simple notes. At first the notes sounded harsh and out of place for she had grown to love the whisper of the wind through the trees, the soft drumming of the grouse on a log, the blue jays talking to each other. But she kept studying and practicing until one day she could play "Humoresque," which greatly pleased her. She kept thinking while practicing, "Trust Amy to do something unthinkable and outlandish as sending this huge musical instrument into such an isolated, rugged, and remote wilderness."

# Chapter 21

# Changes in Destiny

For a whole year there had been only one letter from Anna, mostly telling about the wilderness life around her, how adept her husband was in keeping them well supplied with meat and fish, and of all the wonderful things Tomo did to make her life comfortable in such remoteness.

Just when Doc had expected them to be returning, he instead received a short note from Tomo inviting him to visit and explaining they were going to stay for another year. Doc laid down the note thoughtfully just as Mae entered his study. Seeing the seriousness of her father's face, she asked, "Papa, what is it?"

"A note from Tomo, inviting me for a visit. They aren't coming out for another year."

"I wonder why they are staying longer."

"He didn't say. I don't think there is anything wrong between them; she is very much in love with him. Mae, why don't you visit them? Find out if everything is all right. Could it be Anna hasn't fully recovered and he doesn't want us to know? A visit will do both you and Anna good."

"Papa, I think she is more fascinated or intrigued. He is the handsomest man I have ever seen. His facial features are not the flat nose and broad face of most Indians."

"I agree. I would say more like an Egyptian Pharaoh."

"He certainly has the dignity and nobility of one."

"I believe royalty is in his blood. The Nez Perce have a fascinating history that goes all the way back to Montezuma, the great Aztec chief. There is also mystery about the Nez Perce; their language has many Latin words."

"How on earth did they ever get Latin words?" Mae asked, puzzled.

"Later perhaps Tomo will be able to shed some light on this. Mae, it is my wish that you go for a visit."

"I'm afraid to."

"Afraid?" Her father asked in astonishment.

Mae nodded. "What does the Bible say about mixed marriages?"

"You'll have to ask your mother about that."

"Well, anyway, I'm against mixed marriages, and I'm not sure I really like him. If I go I might make trouble because if Anna isn't really happy, I'm going to bring her back."

"Things might be very different than you expect. Think about it."

Mae went to find her mother just as Abigale came bringing a freshly baked lemon pie, Nancy's favorite. Maybelle joined them in the parlor for a cup of tea and a piece of pie. Nancy mused aloud, "When Maybelle and Charlie marry, that will finish the weddings."

Abigale spoke up. "You have forgotten Mae," she said, smiling at the girl.

Maybelle reminded them, "She's not even engaged."

Mae glared at her sister. "How do you know so much about my personal affairs?"

"Well, you've been going with Neville for ages and has he proposed yet?"

Mae blushed. "I've found someone I like a lot better, and I don't know how to get rid of Neville."

Maybelle jumped up. "Easy. I'll write a note you can send him that will speed him on his way out of your life."

Mae was dubious. "I'm not sure about that."

Maybelle went to her father's desk. After chewing the end of the pencil for a few moments, she began scribbling without hesitation. She finally flung the pencil down, and snatching up the written missal, she thrust it in front of Abigale, demanding, "Read it."

Abigale gingerly took the paper, hesitating. Maybelle said, "Go ahead, read it. That will get rid of the jerk."

Abigale gave Mae an apprehensive glance before starting to read.

> "For five whole years I've been your dupe
> Your name to me is now poop
> A better man has come my way
> And he's in my heart to stay."

"Stop!" Mae yelled, scandalized. "I couldn't send him that. 'Poop' sounds so unrefined."

Maybelle laughed. "Write 'soup' then."

Later in the day their father requested that Mae and Maybelle visit Mrs. Aims and take her a little treat. He told them, "It's hard on the old lady to be alone and flat on her back and it is our duty to bring comfort where we can."

Both girls winced, neither of them relishing the idea of having to listen to Mrs. Aims' opinions of how most of the town's inhabitants were destined for hell.

After slipping some cookies and a piece of cake into a bag, they started for Mrs. Aims' bilious green house. They tried to console themselves. Mae commented, "Breaking her hip seems to have taken some of the fire out of her. At least she's not so enthusiastic in saving sinners."

"No, she's more interested in how to get to heaven herself," Maybelle observed.

"And she isn't trying to butt in and run other people's business so much," Mae concluded.

They were greeted rather gruffly. "You mean well, but I can't eat a bite of them cookies when all them poor darkie kids are starving in Africa."

The girls looked at each other wondering what to say. It wasn't necessary, for Mrs. Aims had a lot to say. "Imagine me flat on my back when there's a heap of sinners needin' to be saved."

Mae desperately tried to change the subject. "Mrs. Aims, I understand you were one of the first pioneers this far west. It must have been very difficult."

Mrs. Aims gave a derisive grunt. "People now have silver spoons in their mouth compared to what I went through."

"You mean Indians?" Maybelle tentatively asked.

"Nah, rattlesnakes, bears, wolves, and cougars. I shot so many cougars I lost count."

"You didn't have any trouble with Indians then?"

"Well, once I did have to shoot one."

The girls shuddered. They could believe Mrs. Aims really did kill an Indian because they once saw her break her umbrella over the head of their preacher simply because he had misquoted the Bible.

After giving Maybelle a sly look, Mrs. Aims started telling a heart-rending story about a beautiful young girl who kept refusing to marry a very fine man who finally got tired of waiting and married a widow with six kids. The girl who kept putting off the wedding date found she loved him terribly, became an old maid, and died of a broken heart.

Mrs. Aims keenly watched them leave to visit the Nelsons. On their way to the destitute family, Maybelle abruptly stopped. "I don't believe a word of that story about the girl putting off her wedding. I think that old hag made the whole thing up."

"Why would she do that?" Mae asked.

"She is still sticking her nose in other people's business. I wish she had broken her neck."

Mae was shocked. "She means well."

"I tell you, Mae, she is still just a busybody. She was really talking about me, trying to scare me into picking my wedding date."

"But she didn't know about you not naming the date."

"Oh yes she did. In this town you can't forget to wear your bloomers without some blabbermouth gossiping about it."

"She's known you since you were a baby and she wants to see you happy." Mae, in sympathy with Mrs. Aims' illness, tried to calm the troubled waters.

Maybelle fumed, "I'm perfectly capable of taking care of my own happiness."

The Nelsons had moved their tent closer to their half-finished house. Teddy, running ahead of the girls, started barking. The children were playing outside and when they heard Teddy, and saw the girls, they came running, shouting their greeting. Teddy loved to play with the children. They threw sticks for him to chase and played hide and go seek with him. The little dog no longer searched the house for Nettie, for he had found playmates who were even more fun.

Mrs. Nelson always insisted they have tea with her, and Tom was never too busy to join them. Mae was fascinated with Tom's description of life in northern Canada.

"But how can you stand that dreadful cold?" Asked Mae.

"Nothing to it," Tom grinned. "Put on a caribou parka, moose-skin mukluks, lynx mitts, and go out and enjoy fifty below."

Maybelle shuddered. "In one minute, I'd be an icicle."

Mae thoughtfully remarked, "No, I think I'd like it, to watch my breath freeze into little crystals. Yes, I'm sure I'd like it."

Tom was watching her with interest. "The Northern Lights are the most beautiful sight you can see on this earth."

"What are they?" Maybelle queried.

"There are several theories, but I prefer just to think they are a grand show God puts on for us to enjoy."

"I like that idea, but what do they look like?" Mae asked.

"It's hard to describe them, because they are never the same. Some nights they look like waving colored curtains of green, yellow, and pink. Other times they are dazzling white streaks of fire, darting across the sky. They always leave me in awe," Tom concluded, rising to go back to work.

After a full day of roofing and flooring on his brother's new house, Tom would often show up at the Andrus home and find something to fix about the place. One day Nancy remarked to her husband, "I was unaware until recently that our house is falling apart. Tom has replaced the broken board on the porch step, repaired the porch's leaky roof, put a new latch on the pantry door, and he plans on replacing the broken window in the hall. As you know, we've been intending to repair it for ages. Nelson, do you think he's trying to pay us back for the help we have given them?"

"I think we are lucky to be included in his courtship."

Nancy's eyes widened with surprise. "Y...you mean Maybelle?"

"No, Mae. And I'm happy such a fine young man is interested in her."

The Andrus family was hearing fantastic things about Amy. She was importing her rugs for the mansion's living room from the Orient. The wallpaper for the dining room was being custom-made in France. The silk drapes were to be hand-blocked in Ireland. Nancy shook her head, asking, "Where does she get all these opulent ideas? Certainly not from my side of the family."

"Mama, I think it is. You've forgotten your French ancestor coming to Canada," Maybelle reminded her mother.

"He was destitute," Nancy protested.

"Destitute, with all that jewelry he brought with him? He must have been very, very wealthy. Why didn't he stay in France?" Maybelle wondered.

"He would have had his head cut off."

"Only the nobility were guillotined," Maybelle said.

Nancy nodded. "Dear, please get my jewel box."

Maybelle went to her mother's bedroom and quickly returned, holding an elaborately engraved silver casket. Nancy opened it to reveal a rather large ruby brooch on emerald green velvet.

Maybelle exclaimed, "Mama, half of it is gone!"

"Yes, I've always wondered why it had been severed in two."

"You can't wear it that way because the fastener is on the other half," Mae observed.

Maybelle had taken it and, turning it in the light, watched the precious stones glow in a rich, deep, rosy hue. Handing it back, she said, "I think there is a mystery here. I think someone meant for you to look for the other half."

"However could I do that?" Nancy asked. "No doubt the owner has been dead for decades."

"He just might have left heirs he wanted you to find."

One day an Indian runner brought a message to Anna at the Riggen's Hot Springs saying that Mae was on her way to visit. Anna was beside herself with excitement. She couldn't wait for the arrival of her favorite sister and kept running across the swinging bridge to check the trail for the first glimpse of Mae.

At the first sight of a horse plodding up the trail, Anna flew down to meet her sister. Mae almost fell off the horse, vowing, "I'll never be able to walk again."

Kissing and hugging and with arms around each other, they chattered as they walked towards the cabin. Anna was trying to catch up with all the news about the family and Mae was trying to tell her sister all that had happened.

Halfway across the swinging bridge, Mae stopped. "I must wait for the pack train. I have brought a surprise for you."

"Oh. What is it?" Anna happily asked.

"Wait and see."

Anna spotted the packer and his string of horses coming out of a dense stand of fir trees. "Well, I won't have to wait long."

As soon as the pack train came up to them, Mae told Anna, "Open the pack box on the left side of that pie-faced horse and see what I have brought you."

Glancing back at her sister with questioning eyes, Anna ran over to the horses and hurriedly lifted up the lid. Up popped up a little black nose.

Anna squealed "Teddy!" And lifted the little dog out of the pack box. "No, it's to little too be Teddy."

"It's one of his sons."

Anna was delighted and hugged the puppy tenderly. "You couldn't have brought me anything better. I've missed Teddy a lot and now I have his offspring. What joy he'll bring! Oh Mae, only you would be so thoughtful. Thanks heaps," said Anna and she lovingly kissed her sister.

Putting down the three-month-old puppy, Anna watched with delight as it wobbled on shaky legs, then took after a squirrel in its first big adventure. Soon it had to be rescued when it wanted to fight the packer's large husky dog.

Anna laughed, "He's just like his father. Teddy was always getting into fights."

At the cabin Mae marveled at the convenience of the place so far from civilization. She loved the rusticness and the way Anna had arranged the place. Right away Anna suggested a swim in the mineral hot springs pool. "Mae, I know after that trip how dusty and weary you must be. A swim in the pool will refresh you and you'll feel like new."

"I don't know how to swim."

"You can just paddle around, and it'll make you feel so good."

"Very well, but I never thought to bring a swimsuit."

"I just wear a pair of my bloomers and a corset cover."

For an hour they splashed around the pool with the pup on the bank chasing after them until he fell in and had to be saved.

Mae asked, "What name are you going to give him?"

"Nothing but 'Teddy Junior' will do."

Mae was helping Anna start supper when Tomo came in carrying four grouse he had just dressed to be cooked for supper.

There was an awkward moment as they stood staring at each other. The last time Mae had seen her sister's husband, he had been wearing a business suit. The man who stood before her now was wearing only buckskin pants, his hair was long and shaggy, a string of beads hung around his neck. Mae inwardly shuddered, thinking how her sister was living alone out in this wilderness with a savage. She fought to control her trembling and her shock.

Anna was busy pealing potatoes and didn't notice her sister's look of horror, but her husband did. He quietly lay the grouse on the counter, then turned with a gentle smile to face Mae. "It is an honor to have you in our home."

Through trembling lips Mae answered, "Thank you. I've been very homesick to see Anna; we've always been closer than the rest."

Anna picked up the tiny puppy to show her husband and the little thing growled at him.

Tomo showed no emotion, but petted Teddy Junior, saying, "It is well you have a mighty brave guard dog, for coming in I saw fresh grizzly tracks down the trail."

"Which way was it going?" Asked Anna

"Down river."

"Thank goodness it's headed away from us."

At supper Mae felt uncomfortable. Tomo was gracious but mostly silent. Anna seemed not to mind her husband refraining from entering into any conversation with them. Anna was full of stories about things that had happened since they had come to the hot springs, but Mae was glad when at last her sister showed her the guest bedroom. Mae couldn't sleep. How could Anna seem so happy so far away from civilization with a man that Mae found intimidating? She was almost afraid of him. Before she went to sleep she had made up her mind. She was going to take Anna back with her.

The next day Anna had to bake bread. Mae was feeling depressed and wanted to be alone to try and think things through. She said, "I feel like taking a walk."

"Don't go beyond the pool. You heard Tomo say he saw grizzly tracks."

"It was going the other way," Mae reminded her.

"Yes, but it isn't best for you to go outside of the yard. Don't forget you are in a very remote country now with lots of wildlife."

"Don't worry. I won't be gone long, and I'll stay close to the buildings."

Mae felt such relief to get off by herself. She passed the pool's steaming water and a short ways beyond was the cold stream that emptied into the pool to make the temperature of the water comfortable.

There was another aspect to her trip that she had not yet mentioned to her sister. Before leaving home, her father had surprised her by saying, "Mae, you have a good head on you. Look the place over with an eye as to whether or not it would be a good investment for a sanitarium. Instead of holding my clinics at Medical Lake, I could hold them at Riggen's Hot Springs." Mae had assured her father she would carefully look over the situation. She knew now the terrible trail would be too difficult to take very sick patients over it unless a road could be built. That seemed impossible, for the cost would be far to much.

Seeing a covey of quail beyond the creek, she crossed it for a closer look. She was intent on watching the birds scratching among the leaves when a slight noise in the brush made her look up and her heart stood still. Across the small clearing, a huge bear appeared, lumbering out of the shadows. Mae wanted to run but she was frozen to the ground. Seeing her the bear stopped. A slight wind was blowing, ruffling his silvery shaggy fur. Mae was beyond terror, her knees gave way, and she sank onto the wild grass. The bear started towards her and she closed her eyes, waiting for the end.

"Don't move!"

At the sharp command, Mae's eyes flew open to see Tomo standing in front of her holding a large tree branch. She was amazed to hear Tomo speaking to the bear, "My brother, go in peace and no harm will come to you."

Mae, peeking around Tomo's legs, saw the bear rise on its hind legs and shift its head from side to side. Tomo kept quietly talking and the huge beast seemed to be listening. When Tomo stretched out his arm, commanding "Go in peace," the bear dropped down on all fours and leisurely left the meadow.

Tomo turned and held out his hand, lifting Mae from the ground. No words were spoken between them. Mae was too overwhelmed for words.

That evening at supper, Mae was astonished when Tomo appeared in his dress suit, his hair neatly braided. Tomo smiled into Mae's startled eyes. "My sister, I know you were half afraid of the wild man and you were unhappy your sister had married him. Anna is used to me in my native dress, but to you it was a shock. I should know this is so. Let us start over. Now I wear in your honor the white man's dress. Am I forgiven for not first understanding?"

Mae gave a little laugh and said, "Of course you are forgiven. But for you I would not be sitting here now."

Anna dropped her fork. "What happened?"

Mae drew a big breath. "A bear was going to eat me and Tomo talked him out of it."

Anna was almost angry. "When you came back you told me nothing."

"I was too scared even to mention it. Tomo, I think the bear really listened to you."

Anna shot a question at her husband. "Was it the grizzly?"

Her husband nodded. "It was an old silver-tip."

Mae was puzzled. "How did you happen to come?"

"I saw your tracks by the pool and followed them knowing the grizzly was still around."

"And you stood there protecting me with only a wooden club."

Then Tomo told how his people, long before the white man and his guns, killed bears by jumping on their backs and clubbing them between the eyes.

## Chapter 21 - Changes in Destiny

Anna, concerned her sister might be in shock, followed her that night to the guest room and sat on the bed visiting. "Mae, I've always been close to you and I know there is something on your mind. Is it the young man Mama wrote me about?"

Mae nodded. "Yes."

"What seems to be troubling you? Don't you love him?"

"Oh yes, I love Tom more then anyone else in the world, but..."

"You better tell me," Anna insisted.

Mae burst out in agitation. "Anna, Tom lives in just this type of country, where there are lots of bears. After today I don't know whether I'm brave enough."

Anna hugged her sister. "My dear, the only safe place in this world is in a hospital or jail. You could be run over by a train and killed or have someone shoot you. If you really love your Tom, you wouldn't be afraid of dragons."

"Anna, is that the way you feel about Tomo?"

"Yes, I'd die for him."

The rest of Mae's stay, the three spent a great deal of time together, hunting, rafting on the river, and having wonderful meals cooked over campfires.

One day Mae told her sister, "I came to take you back with me, but now I don't want to leave. I'm getting used to this place and have come to love your wild way of life."

"If I'm not mistaken, you'll have one of your own. Tomo and I would love to visit you in the Yukon."

Mae shook her head slightly. " There's a problem. How can I leave Mama and Papa when they need me so much? I'm the only child left."

"It will all work out, so don't worry. I have a feeling you're getting homesick to see someone very special."

Mae laughed. "Have you a crystal ball?"

"No, an owl told Tomo. The Indians, you know believe the owls tell them things and all day the owls have been hooting. Tomo says they are telling of someone who loves you and wants you to come back to him."

They both burst out laughing, and they kissed each other good night.

Upon Mae's return home, she told her father, "Anna has become all Indian. She talks like an Indian, she dresses like an Indian, and her religion has become Indian. I never thought it possible to have such love as they have for each other." Mae gave a little laugh. "And to think I was going to bring her back! If I had tried, I believe he would have killed me, he is so protective of her."

Doc smiled. "It's the way it should be between man and wife."

"But Papa, she has grown so bitter over the way the white people have treated the Indians. She vows the cosmic laws of justice, as you have taught her, will bring retribution upon the heads of the white people, that they will suffer as they made the Indians suffer and be destroyed as they destroyed the buffalo. She is truly great in defending her husband's people, but will terrible things happen to our country?"

"There are many religious leaders with great wisdom and foresight who claim great tribulation will come to America. Even the first U.S. president's orderly related how George Washington had visions of seeing black clouds hovering over America, fighting in the cornfields of the Bible belt, and blood running from sea to shining sea."

"Then it must be going to happen, for didn't George Washington have a vision of winning the war at Valley Forge? And he did," Mae reflected.

Doc nodded. "George Washington was about to suffer defeat when a vision turned the tide for him and gave him victory."

For a few moments the two sat in contemplative silence. The doctor, in his methodical way, finally spoke. "Mae, the cosmic law of justice works with absolute precision. There will be retribution for the wrong done the red man as surely as the sun will rise in the morning."

Mae shuddered. "Oh, Papa, no."

"There would be no justice if it were not so."

"Can't something be done?"

"Our founding fathers did do something. They formed the new country into a republic, rule by law. There are politicians trying to change this country into a democracy, rule by men. A democracy has always been a short-lived proposition and usually ends in a blood bath."

"Papa, you paint a gloomy picture," Mae said with bowed head.

"According to your mother, the Bible supports those same predictions."

Mae rose to her feet. "Well, there's one Indian getting compensation. Anna worships her husband and, best of all, they are going to have a baby. She is hoping for a boy, because she wants to name him, Alokut after Chief Joseph's brother, a great war chief of the Nez Perce." She paused, then changed the subject. "By the way, how is Amy getting along with plans for Bob and Maybelle's nuptials?"

"Fine, I think, but that reminds me. Your sister sent word that she wants you to come as soon as possible to help."

Mae groaned. "I know why. A big bash like she's planning means a lot of hard work. Papa, really and truly, how is Amy getting along? Have you met any of her in-laws yet?"

"We were just beginning to get acquainted with them; in fact they paid us a short visit. They have a very interesting history. Seems they are Germans from the east side of the Volga River, immigrating to America when Amy's husband Jacob was only four years old. The family arrived with but one suitcase and now they own several large wheat ranches out of Walla Walla, as well as a pineapple grove in the Hawaiian Islands. They have worked hard for their wealth and are not too proud to tell how they had arrived in America with almost nothing, which goes to show how industrious they were. When the father died soon after their visit with us, he left a large fortune to his only son."

"Amy's husband?" Mae asked.

Doc nodded. "Yes, but whether or not his inheritance is a blessing remains to be seen."

"He must have been left with a great deal of money, as wheat prices have gone sky high. Well, Amy knows how to help him spend it," Mae said with a sigh.

"It seems he is giving her full rein to do as she pleases as he has many other interests and a hobby that takes up much of his time."

"What kind of hobby?"

"Raising buffalo."

"What ever possessed him to have buffalo?"

"He wants to restore a herd around Walula. But he's having difficulty keeping them fenced. They have so far broken down all the fences he has put up. Now he is building a stronger board fence to keep them securely penned in until the herd is large enough to hold their own with predators. Then they can be released."

"He was wonderful to give Bob the contract to build their home. It must be costing a fortune."

"Well, he has it." Doc, smiling, scratched his beard.

Mae grimaced. "Such is the reward of the transgressors."

"My dear, life is never all roses."

Mae turned the doorknob to leave "Where is Mama?"

"Over at Abigale's. She is helping your mother finish a quilt for Amy. Amy is combining a housewarming with Bob and Maybelle's wedding to create one large affair."

"Why is the wedding at Amy's?"

"Your mother hasn't felt up to another wedding, and Amy wanted a chance to show off her new home. She also felt it was an opportune time to introduce Bob to Walla Walla's rich society who might be interested in giving him some commissions."

"Papa, I'm surprised you gave Maybelle permission to marry so young."

"Mae, life is uncertain at its best. Bob wants to go to New York to study Revival and French Rococo designs, which meant he would be away for a year. That's too long for them to be apart; its not good for either one of them. Maybelle has always been interested in art and New York would offer her the opportunity to study. Later she could help Bob in his work."

"It...it sounds wonderful." Mae hesitated before timidly asking, "H...how is the destitute family?"

Doc smiled. "In other words, how is Tom?"

Mae blushed. "Well, how is he?"

"Lonely, I would say, from the many times he asked when you were coming back."

"Then he hasn't forgotten me?" Mae eagerly asked.

Doc laughed. "At least he won't forget all the black walnuts you had him shell. Why did you have him shell so many? Your mother says there's enough shelled walnuts for a dozen cakes."

"But Papa, he just kept on shelling, even when I tried to stop him."

"Gave him a good reason to stay and enjoy your company."

"He does seem awfully nice."

That evening Tom showed up, grinning. "Want any more black walnuts shelled?"

Mae laughed. "No, but I'd like to hear how the new house is coming along."

"Come for a walk and I'll tell you all about it."

Mae grabbed her paisley shawl, and they strolled out into the soft moonlight, walking through the park which was heavy with the intoxicating scent of nicotina. Tom's voice was virile and masculine as he told of having a job at the lumberyard and working on his brother's house after working hours. Then he talked about the vast open spaces of Canada and his home in the Yukon. Briefly he told about his successful occupation as big game guide and casually mentioned how she would love the great wilderness of the far North.

Mae was so enthralled with his description of Canada, she pelted him with questions. It was late when he walked her back home, and Mae was surprised they had been gone so long. Somehow she didn't want to say good night.

Getting ready for bed, she looked in the mirror. Her face seemed to glow. She asked herself, "Mirror, mirror on the wall, am I really in love?" Jabbing her finger at her reflection, she snapped, "If you are, you better forget it because you're the only child left and Mama and Papa need you."

# Chapter 22

# Spectacular Spectacle

Charlie met Mae at the railway station in Walla Walla and drove her out to Amy's place. He was bubbling over with enthusiasm. "When you see Sis's new home, it will bowl you over." Then he briefly told about his own wedding his in-laws-to-be were planning, the ceremony to be at St. Paul's Episcopalian church with the reception to be held at the country club.

Mae sounded exasperated. "So much for the perfect wedding at home."

"There's yours."

"I'm not even engaged."

"From what I've seen of the walnut cracker, he..."

"Who told you?"

"Never mind about that. While you were visiting Anna, I paid a quick visit home and met him. He seems just right for you. If I'm not mistaken, I saw wedding bells in his eyes."

"He hasn't even kissed me!"

"Get prepared, things can happen fast." Charlie carelessly flicked the buggy whip over the backs of the team. They had been driving down a lane of majestic trees when it opened up into a wide-open space. Mae gasped. In the center of a field of golden wheat stood a glorious, turreted mansion.

Charlie pulled the team to a halt. "Doesn't that just bowl you over?"

Mae was too overwhelmed to say anything, but sat savoring the mansion's elegance.

Charlie said, "They call it a Gothic Revival, but I call it a housekeeper's nightmare. Thirty-two rooms to keep clean. Of course, Amy refuses to rattle around in an empty house, so she has filled it with the contents of several antique shops. I can say this for her husband, he never lets Sis run out of dough. Wait until you see the inside." Again he flicked the buggy whip.

"No, don't drive on yet. I want to take it all in. I love the way they have painted it, cream with burgundy trim."

"You ain't seen nothin' yet," Charlie flippantly quipped.

Mae marveled at Bob's ingenuity. "He's really a top architect."

"No doubt, no doubt, and while I'm grubbing in dirty greenhouses, he'll be hobnobbing with the eccentric rich," Charlie said, slapping the reins over the horses' backs. They proceeded through the wheat field just being landscaped with ornamental shrubs close to the mansion. As the team pranced up to the pillared entrance, a stable boy came running to take the reins and drive the team around to the back.

A maid opened the door. They stepped inside onto an Isfahan oriental rug carpeting a large foyer. At the far end, a magnificent divided stairway led up to the parlor and dining room. The maid ushered them past a vast ballroom, then turned right, opening double doors to the reception room, eloquently papered in embossed gold irises, reflecting rich colors and an intricate pattern of the gasolier shades. Elegant portieres of root-beer-burnished-gold velvet were heavily trimmed with gold fringe and tassels. The impressive furniture was mostly French Rococo. A few pieces of priceless Belter chairs with fragile, wooden-lace trim were prominently displayed. Brilliant Povey stained-glass ornamented the large windows. The ceiling was embossed with hand-painted romantic vignettes of fanciful scenes by Bouche and Fraganard of the baroque period. The room enjoyed the pleasure of an ornate fireplace of Italian marble. Above the mantle Mae was not surprised to see a large portrait of Lillian Russell, as Amy seemed possessed by the voluptuous actress. Everything seemed meant to convey the wealth of the occupants.

Mae, having just returned from visiting Anna's humble log cabin, was overwhelmed by such luxury.

Another maid came to bring an apology from her mistress, saying, "Madam regrets she will not be able to join you until dinner."

Mae was furious and sputtered to Charlie, "I can't stomach all this pretentiousness. I'm leaving."

Charlie chuckled, "Don't you get it? Amy, as always, is trying to get your goat. Don't let her get away with it. Stay and turn the tables on her."

Mae's lips tightened. "I am definitely leaving," she insisted and hurried through the foyer.

"Ah...ah...no you don't." Maybelle came tripping down the stairs, throwing her arms around her sister. "I'm sticking it out and so must you. It really isn't so bad after you get used to all the hoopla."

Mae was grudgingly drawn up the stairs. "I'd a thousand times rather be in Anna's little log cabin than th...this."

"You've got to pretend you are immensely impressed or Amy will have your scalp," Maybelle warned as she led Mae into a sumptuous guest bedroom. "There are a dozen more rooms like this one," she explained.

Mae flopped into a satin slipper chair, shaking her head. "So she couldn't come to say hello. How dare Amy to put on such airs with her own sister."

"Not is all as it seems."

"What does that mean?"

"Never mind. I want to show you my wedding dress Amy had imported from Paris."

Mae thought the gown exquisite, but much too elaborate for a girl so young. She said nothing, however. Just then, the maid knocked at the door to inform them dinner was about to be served.

Mae remonstrated, "I can't go to dinner in my traveling clothes."

"You'll have to. If you're late for Amy's grand entrance, she'll annihilate you."

They entered a walnut-paneled platter-shaped dining room. An immense Rococo revival étagère stood on one side of the room, while on the opposite side was a buffet heavy with a collection of Czechoslovakian crystal. A footman indicated for the guests to be seated, which Mae thought was improper, as the guests were supposed to wait until the hostess was seated. But the hostess was missing. Mae glanced at the dinnerware and knew why Amy had chosen Minton. At home they had one dish of Minton, which their mother had considered too valuable to be used. The cutlery, of course, had to be Grand Baroque, the most embellished of all sterling silver. The centerpiece was a large epergne filled with luscious, long-stemmed apricot-tinged pink talisman roses and sprays of pale lavender Michaelmas daisies. Mae casually looked around to see if she knew a few of the guests. Several she assumed to be Amy's in-laws from abroad, whom Amy was graciously accommodating for her splurge into Walla Walla's high society.

Nervously the guests waited for their hostess to appear. A swish of a fan brought all eyes to the archway. Charlie groaned and half-slid under the table. Amy stood in a grand pose, swishing a plumed fan that once belonged to the great Lillian Russell. Charlie devilishly called, "Hi, Sis. Hurry up or you'll be late for dinner."

Amy angrily snapped her fan closed as she gave her brother a withering look. She flipped her train around, then waited for the footman to seat her.

After indicating to a servant to start serving, she angrily pursed her lips and asked Mae, "What have you heard from Nettie?"

Charlie stabbed an olive. "She's dug up a guy who looks like me. Makes me uncomfortable. What if he commits a crime and he skips? The police will jail me thinking I'm him."

Amy ignored her brother. "Mae, has she found any connection in any relationship with Mama's French ancestor?"

Picking up her cocktail fork, Mae replied, "After climbing around in the family's genealogical tree, they have concluded he might be, but more research needs to be done."

Amy continued to pursue the subject. "Does that mean there is a possibility?"

Mae shrugged. "Nettie says they are going to have to see a lot more of each other for more research."

"Which means," Charlie said, regaining his breath after choking on a gulp of wine, "there's serious stuff cooking."

Charlie was deliberately using language he knew infuriated Amy who irritated him with her high-society airs meant to impress the elite of Walla Walla.

After another wave of her fan, Amy said, "Mae, you were visiting Anna. How is she?"

"Wonderful and happy."

One of the guests made a comment, making Amy wince. "She is married to an Indian, is she not?"

"East Indian," Amy snapped.

"A damn good red Indian," Charlie piped up.

After shooting her brother a look meant to silence him, Amy returned to asking about Nettie. "I understand the man Nettie has recently met is highly intelligent, in fact brilliant?"

"That's where similarities between us end," Charlie said loudly crunching on a stalk of celery. Then, grabbing a fistful of olives, he started juggling them in the air, making wisecracks as he tossed them. "Whoops!" He shouted as he missed catching one and it plopped into the wineglass of a pompous, elegantly gowned matron beside him. Charlie nonchalantly gulped down her wine and fished out the olive.

Amy was furious and signaled the footman to replace her guest's glass of wine while she spat at her brother, "I'll take care of you later."

Charlie met his sister's anger with a grin. He had managed to break through her infuriating pretentiousness, which he detested.

Mae quickly turned to the guest on her right, asking, "Have you seen the buffalo?"

"Yes, just this morning. They are certainly huge fellows. Have you seen them?"

Mae shook her head. "No, and I'm not anxious to."

After taking another gulp of wine, Charlie informed the dinner guests, "I'm going to give this party a bang-up surprise to celebrate. It will knock you all cock-eyed."

The guests questioningly looked at each other without comment.

Just then, a footman whispered in Amy's ear. She jumped up and raced to the hall. They heard her screech, "Not here!"

"Orders from the boss, ma'am," a workman told her. Then, with the help of another workman, he hoisted a huge buffalo head from the taxidermist up on the wall.

Amy was in tears. "That ugly thing will ruin the decor!"

The men ignored her and went on nailing up the mammoth head. Amy, sobbing, fled up the stairs.

With no hostess, all formality disappeared. The guests kept the footmen busy filling wineglasses. Maybelle signaled Mae to meet her in the hall, then invited her to join her and Bob for a walk. But Mae shook her head. "I'm taking no chances of meeting a monster like this one in the hall. I think I'll go and see Amy's little boy."

"Oh, you mustn't see him!" Maybelle blurted.

"For heaven's sake, why not?" Asked Mae, looking very puzzled.

"B...because Amy forbids it."

"What's wrong?"

"Amy doesn't want anyone to know."

"What?"

"It's a very well-guarded secret."

"Quit stalling and tell me what's wrong."

"The boy is a mongoloid, so ugly it's repulsive."

Mae was stunned. So that was the reason she had heard nothing about him. Turning to Maybelle, she urged, "Go for your walk. I'm tired and am going to bed early."

Under a million twinkling stars, Maybelle and Bob strolled hand in hand when Bob asked, "What has become of my little miracle hunter? I haven't heard you mention miracles for a very long time."

Maybelle laughed. "Because I've found the most wonderful miracle of all."

"Tell me who he is and I'll kill him." Bob started taking off his jacket as if getting ready.

Maybelle giggled. "It's you, silly."

Bob shrugged back into his jacket. "Well, it's a relief to know that I'm the only one."

"Who said you were the only one?" Maybelle eyed him saucily.

"Don't play games with me," Bob warned.

"When I fell in love with you, it surpassed all miracles."

"It will take a miracle to get us through this big bash Amy has planned."

"Don't let your knees buckle now, not after all the hard work you've done to build this show place of show places."

For the next two days everyone was rushing around decorating the vast ballroom, reception room, and foyer. An arbor was built and festooned with what Mae thought must be tons of white silk roses and lilies imported from France. Fir branches sprayed with silver were woven between the stairway latticework. Gasoliers sagged under the weight of yards and yards of draped white-satin ribbon, caught up with white, waxed fruit.

Mae, stepping back to view their work, said to Maybelle, "It's like a fairy land, and you'll be Cinderella."

Maybelle gave a snort. "If my fairy godmother doesn't get over her tantrum, my coach will turn into a pumpkin, the horses into mice, and the clock will strike twelve before I'm married."

"It's as bad as that?" Mae asked in alarm.

Maybelle nodded. "Worse. I feel like taking that darn buffalo head down myself."

Mae tried to be reassuring. "Don't worry. Your Prince Charming built the castle and will fix everything."

Doc and Nancy arrived. Nancy refused to be overwhelmed by all the luxury and told the girls, "I feel like I've had all this opulence before and feel entirely at home in it. Isn't that ridiculous, when all I've ever had were simple things?"

"No, Mama," Mae assured her, "you've got luxury in your blood. You've inherited it from your ancestor who fled France."

"Maybe so," Nancy sighed. "Anyway I'm going to enjoy it while I'm here."

The morning of the wedding, Mae went early to Maybelle's room to find her sitting up in bed, frowning. "You're supposed to be broadly smiling on your wedding day," Mae admonished her.

"Well, I'm not." Maybelle flung the covers aside.

"I assure you, your fairy godmother is in the best of spirits. The buffalo head has been removed for the occasion."

"It's not that."

"The prince has sent his love, so what could be wrong?"

"Charlie. He's been too mysterious to be safe. He's up to something and you heard what he said at dinner about a bang-up surprise. I'm afraid it could be something that will spoil my wedding."

Mae brushed this aside. "I think you're getting wedding jitters."

"No I'm not. Whenever Charlie sneaks around like he has been, something upsetting always happens."

"Nothing but wonderful things are going to happen and, to make sure, I'll do some sleuthing around. I'll have the maid bring your breakfast so you can rest until it's time to get dressed."

Mae left to look for Charlie and found her brother innocently drinking coffee and munching on a Swedish crescent roll. "Charlie, you are worrying your sister. What are you up to?"

"What am I up to?" Charlie cupped his chin in his hand. "Let's see. I'm going to help the groom saddle Kaaran so he won't kick the guy's head off. Then I'm going to climb the ladder and tie wedding bells above the altar, then I'm going to roll out the red carpet, then I'm going to..."

"That's enough. I don't want your whole life's history. But Charlie, promise me you're not going to do anything to upset the wedding."

"Me, me? Upset the wedding?" Charlie looked shocked. "What do you think I am a...a..."

"A very unpredictable brother." Mae patted his shoulder. With that she returned to Maybelle and told her, "You have nothing to worry about. He promised to be good."

"I still don't trust him."

Mae peeked between the curtains while a maid was helping Maybelle dress, telling her sister, "The driveway is filling with carriages. So many guests! Oh, there's Judge Frankland and his whole family."

"Do you see Abigale?"

"Not yet. She probably will come with the Millers."

Maybelle gave a little laugh. "This is one Andrus wedding Mrs. Aims will miss."

"I would never rule out Mrs. Aims. Did you know Papa lets her use a wheelchair now?"

Maybelle spoke to the maid. "Hilda, I don't believe I'll need that shorter petticoat."

"But Ma'am, it will make the wedding dress more bouffant."

Mae continued looking out the window. "Oh, Reverend Snider and family are just coming up the steps. And there is Neville looking very dapper with a redhead on his arm."

"Mae, didn't you know he married while you were visiting Anna?"

"No, I did not. The poem you wrote and sent him must have done the trick."

Maybelle, letting the maid put on her white satin slippers, anxiously asked, "You're not feeling any pangs of jealousy?"

Mae snorted, "Why should I? Tom is far the better man."

Maybelle let the maid sweep up her hair in combs to accommodate a tiara of orange blossoms which would hold the heirloom veil.

Mae suddenly gasped, "Oh no, I can't believe it!"

Maybelle rushed to Mae's side and they both stood looking in amazement as Old Cryder wheeled Mrs. Aims up the sidewalk with two footmen helping to get the wheelchair up the steps.

Maybelle gave a mock sigh. "What a relief. Now my wedding will be safe from the devil with Mrs. Aims on guard."

A footman came and spoke with the maid, who turned to speak to Maybelle. "Ma'am, the bridal bouquet is missing."

"I'll find it," Mae promised, fleeing down the stairs.

Mae paused on the stair landing, looking down on the foyer at the receiving line near the door. Her father looked so distinguished and handsome in his black tux and her mother elegantly charming in a Worth's original of chartreuse green, draped in shimmering silver, with a corsage of tiny pink sweetheart roses and violets. Mae felt her bosom swelling with pride that this handsome couple were her parents. Standing closest to the door, Amy profusely greeting each guest. Mae recognized her gown as the exact copy of one of Lillian Russell's. Although the style was outdated, Amy had insisted on wearing it. It did rivet discerning eyes on the exquisite broderie anglaise with its shocking décolleté.

Remembering the lost corsage, Mae sped on down the hall, bumping into Bob in his white tux, looking more handsome than she had ever seen him. He seemed distraught. "No one knows where my boutonniere is and my best man seems to have disappeared."

"So has the bride's bouquet," Mae said. "And I saw Charlie just a few minutes ago."

Bob was extremely nervous. "If Charlie doesn't show up, I'll skin him alive. I've got to see Maybelle."

"You can't. She's dressed and it's bad luck for the groom to see his bride in her bridal dress before the wedding."

Bob's fist hit his forehead in agitation. "God, I wish I had kidnapped your sister and eloped."

Mae tried to soothe him. "Fannie regrets she was married by a justice of the peace and wishes she had had a wedding she could fondly remember. This wedding will give my little sister wonderful memories. Don't forget she is still very young and it's like being in a fairy story to her." Suddenly, Mae slapped her head. "Oh, ye gods, the bride's bouquet!" She headed for the kitchen where chefs and maids were scurrying to finish the last details.

The kitchen staff joined Mae in a search of the flowers. Closets and cupboards were banged open and shut. Four iceboxes held no flowers. Mae was desperate when a footman came into the kitchen, surprised at all the fuss for he had put them down in the cool basement.

Grabbing the bouquet, Mae dashed back up the stairs just as the first notes of the Mendelssohn's "Wedding March" were being played by a twelve-piece orchestra. Maybelle calmly took the huge bouquet of pink rosebuds and white lilies, dripping with tiny nosegays tied to white satin streamers. For a moment she stood, hesitating at the top of the stairs. The guests murmured their admiration. Doc, standing at the foot of the stairs, looked up, proudly smiling at his daughter. Slowly she descended. As she placed her hand on her father's arm, out bounced Teddy, dressed in a white satin coverlet, wearing a sprig of orange blossoms tied on top of his head and carrying in his teeth a white satin pillow with the wedding ring tied on. The guests smiled on seeing the little dog docilely trotting in front of the bride. Six bridesmaids attired in chartreuse green gowns attended the bride.

Mae rushed down the aisle to be seated in the front row. Bob stood alone near the minister. Mae cast anxious glances around. There was no sign of Charlie. As the bride on her father's arm neared the arbor, Charlie leaped to Bob's side, slicking down his tussled hair and straightening his tie.

The tension was not broken until Charlie chased Teddy to retrieve the ring. At last the groom kissed his bride and everyone formed in line for the traditional kissing of the blushing bride.

Charlie disappeared, saying he was going to bring the bridal carriage around, as the bride and groom were to take a train for New York soon after the refreshments were served.

The ballroom was sweltering, so it was decided to have the refreshments outside on the lawn. Since it was getting dark, lanterns were lit and fragile French chairs were brought from the ballroom to cluster around dozens of card tables, set with white tablecloths and centerpieces with glowing candles.

A larger center table held the six-tiered wedding cake, festooned with white sugar roses and topped by a Dresden bride and groom. It was rumored there were diamond rings, jeweled brooches, and garnet earrings baked in the cake. When Bob and Maybelle took the sterling silver cake knife to cut the cake, the guests grew excited with expectancy. The orchestra struck up a lively tune and just as the knife cut into the cake, a rocket of dazzling beauty lit the sky, followed by a burst of amethyst purple stars. Each firework was launched with a sizzling crackling sound. The guests looked in awe at the beautiful display of lights. Up shot a streak of fire descending in a shower of colored sparks accompanied by a loud sizzling sound.

Suddenly the sound grew into a rumbling roar, sounding like a crash of splintering wood. A large dark tide of moving shaggy beasts headed directly for the refreshment tables. Charlie had forgotten the buffalo pen was between the house and his fireworks scaffolding. He grabbed a lantern and frantically waved it, trying to turn the tide of the stampede, but the fiery red sparks in the sky were more formidable to the terrified animals than the feeble light of Charlie's lantern, and they never swerved from their flight to escape. Guests were climbing up poles and crawling under tables. The wedding party was in shambles. Bob grabbed Maybelle into his arms and flung her into the waiting carriage; leaping in after her, he took the buggy whip to the team. The buffalo swerved around the corner of the house and Maybelle and Bob disappeared in a sea of humping buffalo.

# Chapter 23

# Fulfilled Destiny

Back home, Mae would have suffered an unbearable letdown had it not been for Tom. It weighed heavily on her that she was the only one remaining at home, and she missed her sisters terribly. Tom had made a point of being with her as much as his work would allow. The first evening he came, she told him about the buffalo breaking up the wedding party and they both laughed hysterically.

Tom asked, "And what happened to the bride and groom?"

Mae wiped the tears from her cheeks, still laughing. "Oh, the buffalo finally outran their horse and when the herd had passed, they reined their team around and headed for the railroad station. They boarded the train, just as the conductor was calling 'All aboard.'"

Tom asked, surprised, "In their wedding clothes?"

Mae nodded. "Their suitcases bounced off during the stampede, so Maybelle had to wear her wedding gown all the way to New York and, of course, Bob had to wear his white tuxedo. Luckily, they had a private compartment all the way."

Tom grinned. "I can imagine how surprised the hotel clerk must have been when they signed the register in all their wedding finery."

"Oh, it turned out wonderful. The manager insisted the newlyweds be the hotel's guests for a sumptuous dinner. He even sent a large vase of flowers to their room and a basket of fresh fruit and a bottle of wine."

"They have given up the homestead?"

"Oh no! On their return, they are going to spend a couple of weeks seeing that the cabin is completed."

"Why don't I take a day off and we go out and check on the place? You can write them all about it."

"Oh, Tom, what a splendid idea! How soon?"

"How about tomorrow morning? I'll rent a horse and buggy from the livery stables."

"Why don't we take our buggy and old Molly? I'm sure Papa won't mind. He said just the other day Molly wasn't getting enough exercise as he's been too busy in the office to go anywhere."

"If you're sure it's all right with your father, I'll get Molly from the stables and pick you up about ten."

"I'll be ready."

It was a perfect day for a trip to the country. A light layer of clouds kept the bright sun from causing a scorching-hot day. As they left town, a light sprinkle settled the dust. They passed farmers working in the fields. Mae breathed deeply of the freshly new-mown hay. She loved the fragrance, saying to Tom, "I've always wanted to sleep all night on top of a haystack."

Tom smiled. "It would certainly give one a good view of the stars."

"I think sometime I'll ask old Cryder if I can park on one of his haystacks for the night."

"Which reminds me. Have you heard the latest?"

"About what?"

"Don't tell me you don't know of the newest sizzling romance in town."

"Sorry, I'm ignorant of any such thing."

"Prepare yourself for a shocker,"

Mae grabbed the edge of the seat. "Okay, I'm ready for the shock."

"Old Cryder is courting Mrs. Aims."

Mae gasped. "I don't believe it."

"Saw it with my own eyes. I went over to her house to take back a saw we had borrowed, and Cryder was kneeling by her wheelchair declaring his love. He was mad at the interruption and barked, 'Can't a fellow go courtin' without some one bustin' in?'"

Mae was speechless. "I saw him wheeling her around town, but I thought he was just helping to get her out in the fresh air."

Tom said, "Cryder told me later 'By God, I've found someone who needs me and I'm goin' to treat her right.'"

"But I don't understand. She's been sending him to hell for years because of his swearing."

"Maybe she's reforming him."

"Now *I* believe in miracles. Oh look, Cryder is painting his farmhouse."

Tom shook his head, laughing. "That's a sure sign of love."

Mae plucked his sleeve. "We turn off here."

It had been a warm spring, giving the grouse eggs weather for a good hatching and trees seemed thick with brownish-gray birds. The road was lined with thick bushes red with berries, which reminded Tom of a grizzly he had once seen near the Arctic Circle. The bear had been lying flat on its back in the middle of the trail, scooping berries with his paw onto his chest, then using the other paw to push the berries into his mouth. "That old guy was enjoying such a good meal, we didn't want to disturb him, so we detoured."

Mae was fascinated with his stories of the North. They came to the homestead before she realized it. Tom lifted her down and they walked over to the half-finished cabin. Mae touched a peeled log with her foot. "I wonder if they will ever finish the cabin."

"They will. Because they'll need this place to refresh themselves."

"There are usually deer and elk, but there's nothing now," Mae said, gazing around.

Tom had been looking closely at the ground. "They've been here. See their tracks? Elk and what looks like a bear." Tom knelt, taking a closer look and nodding his head. "Bear with young."

They leisurely walked down a trail to the pool. The pool was as still as a mirror—not a ripple. A stillness pervaded over the water, as if danger lurked.

"Tom, I believe old Curl's pets are scared of you, being a guide to hunters and fishermen," Mae commented.

"They are perfectly safe. My thoughts are not on fish today."

Just as he said that, the darkness of the water parted and a shiny nose surfaced, then splashed back into the depths.

"I wonder why they are so shy today?" Mae said, rippling the water with a finger.

Tom pointed to some bushes where two beady eyes shown between branches. "There's your answer."

"What is it?" Mae asked, turning to look.

"A wild cat, probably been pestering them."

"I guess we won't be able to see the trout today. I'm hungry, let's go back to the buggy and get the lunch. By the stream would be nice place to eat."

As they sat eating ham sandwiches and hardboiled eggs, Mae kept pointing out the beauty of the place. Finally, Tom said, "Yes, it's a nice place, but in my opinion it can't compare to Canada's far North. There is real freedom to enjoy the enormous herds of caribou, unhindered by fences, which migrate for hundreds of miles. It's a thrilling sight. Then there's the white Dall sheep living among mountain-top glaciers, and the silver-tip grizzlies make a picture in the fall when the leaves have turned crimson. And the moose are the largest of their kind on the continent. The Indians up there live on moose. Nothing can taste better than moose ribs roasted over a campfire."

"Do you live in an igloo?" Mae asked seriously.

Tom laughed. "No, I live in a fairly large log cabin situated on the banks of Talatin Lake. One can almost fish from the doorstep for whitefish and pike. I'm usually too busy in the summer to fish, so I net them under the ice in winter."

Mae leaned back against a large rock. "It must be a wonderful place to live."

"It is, the best place in the world. Mae, I'm asking you to share it with me. I want you to marry me."

Mae sat straight up. She had half expected this, but she was caught by surprise. She had been hoping before he asked that some arrangement could be made so her parents wouldn't be left alone.

"I...I don't know what to say. Papa and Mama only have me now. I just can't leave them all alone. Oh, I forgot to tell you, Charlie phoned to say he received a wire from Bob and Maybelle threatening to get even with him for breaking up their wedding party."

"Mae, I'm waiting for an answer."

"Must it be now?"

Tom rose to his feet reaching out a hand to help her up. "Come let's go back."

"But we just got here."

"Your refusal to give me an answer must mean you're turning me down. If I get back now, there will still be enough time for me to finish putting in the windows. I'm leaving for Canada at the end of the week."

Little was said driving back. Tom looked stoically straight ahead. Mae felt so torn up inside she wanted to cry. To think of saying good-bye to the only man she ever truly loved was unbearable, but the idea of leaving her parents almost broke her heart. How would her mother ever manage without her when she was so busy just helping with her husband's patients? Nettie, who was supposed to be his nurse, had certainly let him down and her mother was trying so hard to fill the place Nettie had promised to fill.

Reaching the Andrus home, Mae thanked him for a pleasant day and rushed into the house with tears burning her eyes. She tried to dash upstairs without being seen, but her mother stopped her.

" Mae, there's a package for you from New York," she called.

Mae slowly came back down and took the package her mother handed her. She said, "It has to be from Maybelle. She's the only one I know who is in New York." It was a large suit box, evidently wrapped by some store clerk, for Maybelle would never wrap a package so meticulously perfect. Tearing off the wrapping revealed a white beribboned box. She looked inquiringly at her mother. "This box looks expensive. I wonder what Sis could be sending?"

"I would guess nothing practical."

Lifting the lid off the box, Mae said, "Oh dear, oh dear." Nestled under thin white tissue paper was something soft and sheer. With tender care, Mae lifted out a gown of exquisite beauty. She gasped, "I...it looks like a wedding gown." From the folds of tissue she found a note from Maybelle,

Dear Mae:
    If you haven't already said "yes," you'd better. This dress is meant to be worn at a wedding. Name the first girl after me.
    Your loving sister, Maybelle

Nancy looked at her daughter with concern. "Yes, I told her you were hanging back because of your papa and me. My dear, your father and I got along very nicely before you children came along and we can do so again."

Mae hugged her mother. "Oh Mama, do you really and truly mean it?"

"Of course I do. Now you better tell your young man you have a wedding dress that needs to be worn."

Mae gave her mother a kiss. "You're such a dear, Mama. I love you heaps. Now I better give Tom his answer."

Mae was running down the street towards the Nelson's new house when she saw a familiar figure coming fast towards her, holding out his arms. Mae flew into them and he whirled her around happily, laughing, "By your eyes, I know my answer. After I smashed my thumb a couple of times and broke a window, I knew I couldn't leave without you. I was coming to plead my cause again."

"Oh, Tom, I've loved you so much all the time."

The next day, another package, but smaller, came with foreign stamps. Nancy, handing it to Mae, said, "I think it's from France."

Mae, taking the package, noticed the return address. "It's from Nettie. Has she eloped?"

"No, I just think she is visiting his parents."

"Then it's pretty serious." Mae carefully unwrapped something with veils, pink ostrich plumes, and roses. Taking it out, she exclaimed, "It's a dream of a hat and from Paris too. Oh how wonderful!" Nancy handed her a note she plucked from the box. Mae asked her mother to read it as she put the hat on.

Dear Sis:

I just couldn't resist. It looks just right for you to wear on your honeymoon. Mama told me all about Tom. He must be a wonderful guy to have won your heart. I've just said "yes," and we'll be married here at his parents' home before returning to finish our education. Then we'll come to Dayton for a visit. See you then.

Love, Nettie

That evening Mae put the confection on to show Tom. "How do you think your Yukon moose will like it?"

Tom grabbed her and, after kissing her, said, "They will love everything about you."

Nancy, with the help of Abigale, planned a lovely but simple wedding.

Mae drifted down the old winding stairs with her misty white veil floating behind her, just as she had dreamed it would. Her dear papa stood at the foot of the stairs to escort her into the parlor where Judge Frankland, now the governor of Washington, waited by the old Victorian marble table, holding the large, worn, black Holy Bible, ready to marry them. Pausing on the stair landing, Mae smiled when she saw her mother had decorated the parlor with her choice dazzling white peonies. Looking through the archway, she saw the few dear close friends she had invited. Her eyes smarted; she had known them since childhood and memories flooded back. Dear Mrs. Miller with her passion for peaches; Reverend Snider and his sincerity in trying to save his little flock from hell.

Yes, she had invited Neville and his wife because he had fed Teddy so much ice cream. She had made sure Mrs. Aims wouldn't crash another wedding, so she had been invited, and her face was beaming as she looked at Cryder by her side.

Nancy, having put the finishing touches on the luncheon table, sat down with satisfaction and looked at the tall man who would soon be her son-in-law. Moral integrity showed through every pore of his face. She felt pleased he would be a member of the family.

Doc, standing at the foot of the stairs, held out his arm, and his daughter, with a radiant smile, slipped her arm through his.

Nancy had once declared to Abigale "This is one wedding I'm not going to cry at," but she couldn't help but sneak her handkerchief to the corner of her eye. She took a deep sigh when it was over and went up to kiss the bride and groom after Mrs. Aims had kissed them and told them very severely, "Your marriage is for eternity, so be careful and watch your step."

In the center of the refreshment table was the sparklingest, whitest, tiered wedding cake with white sugar doves winging their way around each tier.

After the guests had gone and Tom had left to see to some unfinished business, Doc found Mae alone in his study adding Tom's and her names to the old Bible's registry of marriages. He was fearful maybe the wedding wasn't all she had dreamed, and he asked her, "Mae, did it come up to your expectations?"

She gave him a hug. "Of course, Papa, it couldn't have been nicer. The groom had impeccable morals and incorruptible character and the bride was a virgin. Yes, it was a perfect wedding."

A week later, after the newlyweds had left for the North, Abigale came for a visit, thinking her friend might be lonely. "Nancy, whatever are you going to do now that all your fledglings have flown the nest?"

"Why Abigale, I'm going to be busy enlarging my peony beds and making a quilt for each of my children." She sighed. "By then I'll be having grandchildren coming for visits, and," she gave Abigale a fond smile, "inviting my dearest friend over for her favorite dish."

"Oh, delightful." Abigale leaned over, kissing her friend of many years.

Through the weeks, Nancy kept receiving letters coming from North, South, East, and West—letters that told of her children's struggles and enjoyments of life, and after the arrival of their babies, letters of understanding of what their mother went through in raising a family.

There were pleas for advice, which formerly they had shunned.

Doc, along with his friend Professor Hoagland, was still working hard to implement in the American Constitution a freedom of choice, giving Americans their preference between either alternative or orthodox medical treatment.

Amy came for a visit wearing so many jewels that Nancy feared burglars would come and rob them. But she had thoughtfully brought her parents a new Edison phonograph with a morning-glory horn and a case of cylinder records of classical music for her mother, even one with Madam Shumanhike singing, which pleased Nancy immensely as the contralto was her favorite opera star.

Doc preferred old-time fiddling, and Amy had remembered and brought a cylinder of his favorites.

## Chapter 23 - Fulfilled Destiny

It happened a month later. Nancy suddenly sat up in bed, awakened by Teddy's howling. The room was in flames, as was the rest of the house. She shook Doc awake and, grabbing Teddy, they dashed out through flames. So hot was the fire that Doc's robe began to smoke and Nancy's hair was singed. Doc went to look for help while Nancy stood in a daze watching her beautiful Queen Anne home collapse room by room under billowing flames and smoke.

Abigale, having been awakened by the brightness lighting up her bedroom, had slung a robe over her nightgown and came running to grab Nancy in her arms. Abigale tried to comfort her friend; instead, it was Nancy who offered comfort. "Why Abigale, don't take on so. As long as we have our lives, there is a lot of living to do."

A huge burst of bright blue flames called their attention back to the fire. Nancy said, "There goes my walnut bedroom set." Half a wall collapsed, sending up showers of sparks. Half-laughing and half-crying, she choked, "That must have been all my homemade quilts."

Abigale took Nancy by the arm. "This won't do, watching everything you own burn up."

"All the playthings of my dear babies too."

"You're coming home with me."

"Not yet," protested Nancy and she continued to gaze at the blaze.

Several times the firefighters attempted to save what they could, but the flames drove them back. Doc could only stand by helplessly and watch almost a lifetime of work turn into ashes.

It seemed the whole town had come; when they could do nothing to stop the inferno, they offered help in many ways. Some suggested giving a big barn dance to raise funds to help replace some things that were lost. Others thought it better to take up a collection or to have each farmer donate a horse or a hog and auction them off to help.

Abigale finally was able to persuade Nancy to come to her home for a hot cup of tea. As they were sipping the fortifying brew, Nancy said, "Now that the old home is all burned up, it opens the way for wonderful new opportunities."

Abigale set her cup down with a thud. "I can't see anything good coming out of this terrible disaster."

"I've been after Nelson for years to retire."

"What would you do?"

"Nelson has always wanted to grow herbs and do research to find new remedies to combat disease."

"Where could you grow herbs?"

"What better place than Curl's old homestead? Bob and Maybelle will be too busy building mansions to spend much time there. I'm sure Bob will sell us the place. I'll send for Tom to come and finish building the cabin. After that we can hire a man to do the heavy work around the place."

"But it's too far out of town for his patients to come."

"Nelson can retire from his practice. He's been in touch with a young doctor who is looking for just such a practice as Nelson's. Don't you see? We never would have had this wonderful opportunity had it not been for the fire."

Abigale grudgingly agreed but wasn't convinced anything good could come out of this catastrophe. She threw up her hands in despair. "What are you going to do for dishes, bedding, and a thousand other things that went up in flames?"

"My dear, this is a test to prove Nelson's and my faith in our Creator, that He will provide."

Indeed the Creator did amply provide for their needs. Packages came by the drayload from all directions. Nancy was delighted in the replacements so different from her old things. How strange she thought how their children sent things more appropriate for a log cabin. From Arizona Fannie sent several beautiful, bright-colored Navaho rugs, and a set of earthenware dishes with gay designs to replace her collection of Spode. From Idaho, Anna sent Pendleton blankets. Abigale, being there at the time, exclaimed, "Just the thing for a cabin." An immense box came from Canada with a merry note from Mae saying Tom had shot it himself and had it made up just for them. It took both of the women to lift out a very large grizzly bear rug. Nancy looked at it, uncertain as to whether she might have preferred an Oriental rug. When Doc saw it, he was delighted and thought it would be just right for what was going to be the study. Teddy had his own idea about it, grabbing it by the ear and shaking it until Doc stopped him.

Maybelle and Bob sent armloads of linens from New York, assuring them they were welcome to live at the homestead as long as the young couple could visit whenever their nerves couldn't take the strain of civilization.

From Kansas City, Nettie sent stainless steel cutlery to take the place of their ornate Grand Baroque sterling silver, which took so much time to polish. Nancy was pleased over its simple design.

Amy telegraphed them that a freight train was bringing them furniture. When it came they were still living in the hotel until the cabin could be completed, so they had to put a pine wood dining and bedroom set in storage.

Tom and Mae came back from Canada at Bob's request, and other carpenters were hired to finish the cabin as soon as possible.

Abigale had told her, "You better build a little cabin for me, so I can visit you often and not be in the way."

"My dear, I've already thought of it, and Tom has promised to build it not to far away from us."

They waited four months for the cabins to be completed. Old Cryder, with a couple of other men, helped them move the things from storage out to the homestead. The young doctor had come to take over Nelson's practice, so Doc was free to drive out to the homestead each day to happily putter around fixing things. Nancy preferred to wait at least until the roof was shingled.

Mae was at that stage of being in the family way to not be of very much help, but just to have her there was a great comfort to her mother. She stayed with her husband in a tent on the homestead so Tom could live on the job.

Sadie hung around most of the time, seeming happy to have people for companionship again. At times, though, she was a nuisance, having a dislike for Teddy, who had to keep out of her way, as deer were known to be efficient in winning a fight with their feet when they attacked dogs.

Brownie, the little black-tail deer, only came in the early morning and seemed to like Teddy, for they spent hours playing with each other.

Every day, Doc brought ground hamburger for Curl's pets; Mae declared it was making the trout to fat too occupy the small pool. If anyone wanted to arouse Doc's temper, they had only to suggest how good they would be in the frying pan.

One day Nancy was over visiting Abigale when she told her friend, "You know, I have a strange feeling something I don't know about is going on."

"Whatever could it be?" Abigale asked.

"I don't know, but anyway it won't be another wedding."

"Don't be too sure," Abigale said with a quick glance at her friend.

"Just what does that mean?" Nancy sharply looked at her.

"Cryder came the other day, hinting that if you let him and Mrs. Aims be married out at the homestead, he would rebuild your rotten old fence."

Nancy started laughing. "Of all things! Well, out there it wouldn't be so hard. We could give them a picnic afterwards. Is that the cause of my strange feelings?"

Abigale only gave her friend a sly look.

A couple of weeks later Abigale planned to go to the homestead and begged Nancy to go with her. "It's such a lovely, lovely day and it mustn't be wasted. You haven't been out there for weeks. Come with me. We can have dinner there. Tom told me they were going to have grouse."

Nancy was uncertain. "I've planned to finish this quilt for Mae today."

"Oh come. I'll help you finish it tomorrow."

"Well, all right. I guess I can spare one day," Nancy relented and went for her coat.

Abigale had made arrangements to use Molly. The day was so nice Nancy was glad that her friend had insisted on getting her out of the hotel. When they came to the turn-off to go to the homestead, Nancy, looking down, remarked, "There are so many wheel tracks."

Abigale shrugged her shoulders. "Probably the workmen getting supplies."

Everything smelled so fresh and fragrant after the night's light rainfall. They were amazed at how much wildlife was around. When they came to the old place, Nancy exclaimed, "There are so many carriages."

"Probably curious visitors from town to check on what's going on," Abigale said climbing down.

They were stepping onto the porch when they heard laughter. Someone threw the door open, and as they entered, many voices yelled, "SURPRISE!!"

Nancy was stunned. Abigale put her arm around her friend. "All your children have come for a family reunion and to help you get settled, to baptize the new house." Nancy was overwhelmed; every one of her children had come. They gathered around her, hugging and kissing. They had brought even more things. Nancy couldn't believe even Anna and Fannie had come from so far away.

Charlie had masterminded the whole thing and just about browbeat any of his sisters who hesitated. Over and over he insisted, "Time to have a bang-up family reunion and help our folks get settled."

Nettie had come the farthest and brought her husband, Pierre. Charlie sized him up before shaking hands. "My sympathy to you, old fellow, for looking like me. You even have the wart on your cheek. You're one guy who can sympathize with my cowlick. Your hair sticks up at the wrong place just like mine. Be sure you keep on good behavior. I don't want any of your misdeeds blamed on me."

"I assure you, if I should make the wrong step, I'll take the rap."

The children hadn't come to loaf around, but to get their parents settled. The girls' husbands dug a pool much larger for old Curl's pets; they spaded a large area for Doc's herb garden and built a small shed for his drying racks. They built a greenhouse for living in the country, knowing they had to be more independent of the stores. They laid stones for paths while the girls arranged furniture, put up curtains and had fun unpacking the many things they had sent. Amy had wanted to bring one of her maids to help, but Charlie set his foot down.

"Nope, this is going to be just for family," he had insisted.

One evening they were all standing by the river watching some of their children play in the water when there was a large splash, throwing water over everyone. Charlie sat waist deep in the water, sputtering, "Why in hell did you push me in like that?"

Maybelle was laughing. "That, my dear brother, pays you back for wrecking my wedding party."

Charlie sloshed out, muttering, "Give me credit for doing one thing right. This is one whale of a reunion."

There were a few things Nancy wanted in town. Charlie and Pierre volunteered to make the trip to pick up the few things she wanted. They had become fast friends, which delighted Nettie immensely. As they were leaving, Nancy called to them, "Don't forget to pick up my jewel box at Abigale's."

"No problem," Charlie reassured his mother.

In town they had a great time confusing the people of Dayton. Making the rounds of stores, the clerks stared at them in amazement. They did a double take, as to which was which. Half the time they were calling Pierre "Charlie" and the other half asking, "You Charlie or the other guy?"

There was trouble at the General Delivery store when Charlie wanted to charge his order. Old Hans balked. "No, I ain't doin' no chargin' I might be chargin' to the other guy and not get paid." After a long argument during which Charlie produced evidence he was Charlie, the old man made a sign saying "I am Charlie" and stuck it on him, muttering, "You keep it on so you don't mix people up."

Back at the homestead, they were unloading the buggy when Nancy ran out asking for her jewel box. Charlie started rummaging through the boxes. "Abigale gave it to me, so it's got to be here some place," Charlie said with certainty.

"Oh, I hope you didn't lose it," Nancy said.

"Nope, here it is," Charlie said, handing it to her.

Taking the sterling silver jewel box, it slipped out of her hand and when it hit the ground the lid flew opened and the jewels were flung into the tall grass. "Oh good heavens!" Nancy cried.

Charlie yelled for help. "Come on out, all you lugs, and join the treasure hunt."

Maybelle, Nettie, and Anna came running and everyone dropped to their knees searching while Nancy kept naming the contents of her jewel box. "I simply can't lose my diamond ear rings your father gave me on our wedding day. Try and find my ruby ring which once belonged to my mother."

One by one, diamonds, rubies, pearl necklaces, and bracelets were recovered. Maybelle gave a yell. "Mama, I found your brooch," she said and handed it to Nancy, who said with disgust, "It's no good, it's broken and I can't ever wear it. It's time I threw it away."

She drew back her hand to throw, when Pierre yelled, "Mon dieu, don't!"

Everyone stared at him in amazement over his outburst. Slowly, Pierre took from his vest pocket a shiny object and laid it in Nancy's hand beside her broken brooch. Everyone gasped. The two pieces fit together perfectly. They looked at each other in shock. Nettie broke the stunned silence. "You never once even hinted you had it."

"I thought you might think it foolish for me to be carrying a piece of broken jewelry."

There was a hubbub of reaction as Pierre stood smiling. "I've carried this piece of jewelry for most of my life, it seems, because Grandmama vowed someday I would find the other half."

Nettie clasped her husband's arm. "Just think, after all these years."

Pierre smiled lovingly down at his wife. "Oui, mot de tenighe."

"What in hell does that mean?" Charlie demanded.

"It means we now have the answer to the riddle of Mama's brooch," Nettie answered.

"Grace a Dieu," Pierre spoke with reverence.

"Hey Sis, you've married your cousin which is against the law."

Pierre laughed, "Cousins so remote, it is not to be mentioned."

Nancy, still holding the broken pieces of the brooch, started to laugh. "Do we draw straws to see which one gets to wear it when it is repaired?"

"Flip a coin," Charlie grinned.

Pierre solemnly spoke. "Madam, it is yours, as is an estate outside of Paris waiting for you to claim it."

Nancy shook her head. "No, I will never leave old Curl's homestead. Never!"

Maybelle shocked everyone by asking, "Did he kill someone and have to escape to Canada?"

Pierre shook his head, "Our ancestor was what you call a grand seignior. Being so close to the king, he was slated for the guillotine."

Nettie put her arm around her mother, "Mama you always said blood tells and you've always had such an aristocratic air about you and..."

Nancy shook her head. "I'm just a pioneer and proud of it."

There was little sleep among them that night for there was so much to question Pierre about.

For the remainder of the few nights left, they gathered around the campfire singing songs and telling stories of their wild childhood escapades. The last night of their stay was special. Each of them expressed their gratitude to their parents for the love and hundreds of little things that had made their childhood so memorable.

Bob made a ceremony of giving the deed of ownership of Curl's old homestead to his father- and mother-in-law with the stipulation that he and Maybelle could visit when outside pressures became unbearable.

Amy asked her mother to make a speech. Nancy shook her head. "I'm not a speech maker, but I think I've done a good job in life. There is no greater thing a woman can do than to raise a family a nation can be proud of."

Amy turned to her father. "Papa, please, before we part, give us some good advice."

Doc smiled on his children, "Well, my dears, always go forward. Life brings many difficulties and disappointments that will cross your path, but you will bear them. There will be no problems so great you cannot solve them, no load so heavy you cannot carry it. Face them all with a resolute heart and a determined spirit and each day thank your Creator for giving you the priceless privilege of living free."

# Bibliography

*The Divided Union*  Peter Bally

*Civil War*  Bruce Cattoni

*Green Leaves of Barley*  Dr. Mary Swope

*Healing Herbs*  Michael Castleman

*Cosmic Forces*  Colonel James Churchward

*Back to Eden*  Jethro Kloss

*Wild Flower Guide*  Helen A. White

*Brave Warriors*  Caxton Press

# Order Form

| QTY. | Title | Price | Can. Price | Total |
|---|---|---|---|---|
| | Why Wait for Heaven - Dolores Cline Brown | $19.95 | $26.95 CN | |
| | Shipping and Handling Add $3.50 for orders in the US/Add $7.50 for Global Priority | | | |
| | Sales tax (WA state residents only, add 8.6%) | | | |
| | Total enclosed | | | |

**Telephone Orders:**
Call 1-800-461-1931
Have your VISA or MasterCard ready.

**INTL. Telephone Orders:**
Toll free 1-877-250-5500
Have your credit card ready.

**Fax Orders:**
425-398-1380
Fill out this order form and fax.

**Postal Orders:**
Hara Publishing
P.O. Box 19732
Seattle, WA 98109

**E-mail Orders:**
harapub@foxinternet.net

**Method of Payment:**

☐ Check or Money Order

☐ VISA

☐ MasterCard

Expiration Date: _____
Card #: _____
Signature: _____

Name_____
Address_____
City_____ State____ Zip_____
Phone ( )_____ Fax ( )_____

Quantity discounts are available.
Call 425-398-3679 for more information.
**Thank you for your order!**

# Why Wait For Heaven